PRAISE FOR
HER SOUL FOR A CROWN

Richly imagined and beautifully written, *Her Soul for a Crown* is a delightful tale of equal parts vengeance and romance—which might just be my favorite combo.

—Tricia Levenseller, #1 *New York Times* bestselling author of *The Darkness Within Us*

This is the kind of immersive, magical book—rich with vivid world building, stunning imagery, and fascinating lore—that will sweep you out of this world and into another one. Rameera reimagines the story of Anula of Anuradhapura with compassion and care, and the result is a deeply romantic portrait of a powerful woman and her great love.

—Claire Legrand, *New York Times* bestselling author of *Furyborn*

An absolute masterclass that lures readers into a unique world with deadly consequences and compulsively readable characters. Pick it up and watch the pages fly.

—Scott Reintgen, *New York Times* bestselling author of *A Door in the Dark*

Alysha Rameera weaves a magical spell full of fascinating lore, stunning world-building, and characters so deep you'll feel like you know them. *Her Soul for a Crown* is one of those fantasy books that reminds me why I love the genre so much. I was lost in the pages, captured by the story and the writing, and was left wanting more.

——Nisha J. Tuli, international bestselling author of *Trial of the Sun Queen*

Her Soul for a Crown grabbed me from the very first page and hasn't let go since. It's everything I crave in a book and more—an eloquently crafted romantasy woven together with a rich, captivating historical backdrop.

—Jeneane O'Riley, *USA Today* bestselling author

Alysha Rameera's debut is the kind of book that sinks into your bones—and absolutely wrecks your sleep schedule. Steeped in Sri Lankan-inspired mythology, *Her Soul for a Crown* gives you all the things you want—forced proximity, an enemies-to-lovers dynamic so sharp it hurts—and then slips in poisoned jewelry and a world that's as deadly as it is magical. I devoured this book, and honestly? I'm mad I can't experience it for the first time again. If you love slow-burn tension, rich mythology, and a romance that makes you a little feral, this one's for you.

—L.L. Campbell, author of the international bestseller *Tricky Magic*

HER SOUL FOR A CROWN

ALYSHA RAMEERA

Published by Sourcebooks Casablanca, an imprint of Sourcebooks
P.O. Box 4410, Naperville, Illinois 60567-4410
(630) 961-3900
sourcebooks.com

Cataloging-in-Publication Data is on file with the Library of Congress.

Printed and bound in the United States of America.
LB 10 9 8 7 6 5 4 3 2 1

For those who believed when I couldn't.

For an enhanced reading experience, a glossary and pronunciation guide have been provided in the back of the book.

ANURADHAPURA

water reservoir
Kuttam Pokuna
Concubine Estate
Pleasure Gardens
Administration
THE BRAZEN PALACE
Military
Stupa
Courtiers' housing
City gates
Stupa
to market
water reservoir

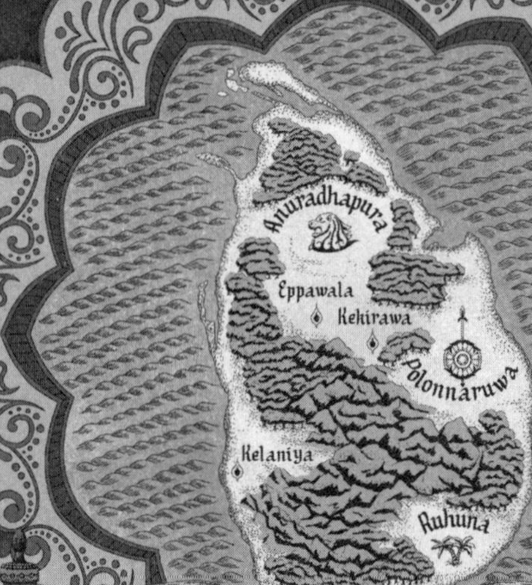

SRI LANKA

circa 47 BC

PART ONE

1

There were so many ways to stop a heart.

This...wasn't supposed to be one of them.

Anula bent over the dead man. It had started with him clutching his chest, the whites of his eyes flaring, the veins in his neck popping. His skin turned purple and redness burned the corners of his mouth, consuming the puckered pink of his lips until they were ripped raw and festering.

"Help." The man gasped his last breath, then fell silent with a trickle of blood on his chin.

Anula cursed. The tincture was only supposed to incapacitate. At least, that's what the book had said.

She hadn't had many test subjects.

Gooseflesh prickled her skin. What if someone had seen? She checked over her shoulder. The inner-city alley was clear; not a single soul passed by. Mercifully, they were all in the palace, squeezing down corridors and elbowing their way into rooms for a chance with one of the blessed gifts. To hear a statue speak their fortune or to be lost inside a painting for the day.

Anula would walk the palace halls, too, if this man had actually held up his end of their bargain. And if she wasn't caught with a dead body.

It wasn't as though Anula walked the streets poisoning every man she came across. As agreed upon, she'd arrived for the rendezvous with coin in hand, gliding into the alley with anticipation skittering up her spine. The noon sun was bright, unfettered by clouds. The Maha season refused to mark its beginning, so the sounds of the irrigation tanks clinked and rattled through the city, promising water amid the drought. Heat laid a heavy hand on Anula, sticking her deepest, darkest red silk sari to her already accentuated curves.

Nuwan had been late. A full thirty minutes had passed before he sauntered in, savoring the dregs of a jar of palm wine. Thirst reached his eyes as he took her in.

"Cursed Yakkas, you're going to make me late for the guard switch," Anula huffed, pulling the pouch from her side and throwing him the coin. "One hundred kahapanas, as promised. Is my name next to be called?"

"Guess you'll find out soon." Nuwan opened the bag, checking a metal disc for the royal stamp on one side, two tuskers on the other.

A bulge in his tunic pocket glinted. Anula swiped at it, holding it aloft. It was a green steatite lotus as large as her fist. "A relic? Really, Nuwan, are you so desperate for a wife that you're spending all your money on trinkets of faith, begging the Divinities of the First Heavens?"

He snatched at it, grasping only air as Anula deftly tripped to the mouth of the alley. "Relics can be weapons, Anula. Is it still faith if you're not praying but stealing power for yourself?"

"What are you going to do, hit someone over the head with it? Heavenly relics aren't weapons. They don't work."

"There are plenty of people who disagree and are willing to pay any price for one. Give it here." He reached for it again.

Anula spun out of range once more. "Am I next to be called?"

"Of course, you b—"

"If your endowment is as small as your vocabulary, it's no wonder you seek the Heavens' help for a wife." She tossed him the relic. Right at the hand holding the coins.

They tinged to the ground as he caught the lotus. A sneer pulled his upper lip. "Sleeping with the raja won't change anything, you know. The court members will never be your friends. Despite the schemes of your *auntie*, you are what you are: a girl with no title, no lands. Nothing to your name and nothing for a man to gain. Be grateful she was able to make you a concubine."

Anula's hand twitched to her jeweled necklace. He had no right to speak to her that way. Even if she were the station climber he suspected, she was the daughter of Don Upali Ramanayake, was the former heiress to the top agricultural farm in the kingdom, to more irrigation tanks than any of the people living in the inner city—

Red sky. Red hands. Red water.

Look away.

Her fingers fell from the jewels, Nuwan's words buzzing like a mosquito. Friends? What use did she have for friends? First lesson learned, when she'd lost everything, was that there were only two kinds of people in the world: allies and enemies.

Nuwan was dangerously close to becoming the newest on her list of enemies. The ones to be dealt with after today.

"Careful what you say, Nuwan. What would the Heavens think of you?"

"What do they think of *you*?" His wicked smile sparked. "You didn't need to make a deal with me to get into a man's bed. You're demanding enough attention in those clothes."

"Attention and invitation are not the same thing. Or have your base instincts not evolved past those of a water buffalo?" She narrowed her eyes, taking a step back.

But Nuwan was quick. He pushed her against the wall, sweat pooling under his tunic. "Let's see what skills you've honed for our blessed raja."

He hugged her tightly, flexing his chest muscles, his arms and abs, as though they were the way to a woman's heart. Or much farther south.

This wasn't part of the deal. Only coin was to be exchanged for her name on the Yakkas-damned list. Peddling desire was meant for another day. Another man.

"No," Anula asserted.

Nuwan's fingers didn't want to listen; neither did his mouth. But Anula knew that some lessons were best learned the hard way. Tripping her fingers along the two-tiered gold necklace at her throat, she swiped a sapphire and ran it across her lips. She grabbed Nuwan's mouth and kissed.

His surprise hardened against her leg. Until his heart seized, and he pulled away in confusion, body convulsing. He clutched his chest and crumpled to the ground.

Where he should have been paralyzed in pain.

Not dead.

Perhaps she had mixed the ingredients wrong. Or had added too much thel endaru seed. Or perhaps she had used the wrong vial altogether.

Sweeping her dark waves over her shoulder, Anula slid another finger across the necklace at her throat—the one her mother had used to wear. Diamonds and sapphires dripped across her collarbone from a band at mid-neck. Centered on the top tier was the largest gem—the one she'd skipped brushing her fingers against before, for not all the sapphires were mere gems. Some were stoppers, the design concealing small vials of a particularly deadly poison.

The second lesson she'd learned was that though the Age of Usurpers might prize physical prowess, one only needed to be intelligent enough to dance around them. Dominate them. Rule them.

Poison—the craft held an endless array of ways to stop a heart, and if studied well, a myriad of tinctures to incapacitate, dull, and deceive an enemy.

Or it was supposed to.

Dread trickled down her spine. Anula plucked a smaller diamond from the second tier. Those held antidotes. She stroked nimbly over the top; then she stooped to touch Nuwan's lips. He stayed purple, his breath gone from his lungs, his blood crusting in the corners of his mouth.

She wiped the coating off her lips. The sealant prevented any poison from seeping into her own skin. She'd realized early on that testing her mixtures held a high level of risk. What would have been the point in learning the craft in the first place if she accidentally killed herself?

A bell tolled from the inner-city shrine, tearing Anula's gaze from Nuwan.

Cursed Yakkas. The guard switch.

She glanced back at the dead man, a knot coiling in her stomach. But it wasn't as though he were an innocent. Actions mattered more than words, and Nuwan's were as repugnant as elephant dung.

Perhaps this was a blessing in disguise. Auntie Nirma might even say the Heavens had a hand in it. She steeled herself, forcing the knot to unravel. If it was good enough for Auntie Nirma, it was good enough for her. Quickly, Anula reached down. Dead men had no need for coin or relics. Perhaps she could use both in a future bargain. A hand wrapped around her wrist. Anula screamed.

A coughing, sputtering sound filled the alley. Nuwan wheezed, "You b—b—"

"Nuwan!" Anula clutched her own heart, relief nearly drowning it. She hadn't botched the tincture after all. The effects were just greater than the book suggested.

"You tried to kill me." He yanked back the relic. "What kind of woman are you?"

Anula stood, a weight lifted from her shoulders. "A woman with ambition, who isn't afraid to see things through." The bells tolled again. "My name better be on that list. Not all poisons come with a remedy."

She didn't wait to hear Nuwan's response. The guards would be switching any moment. And if she wanted to be the next concubine the raja chose to spend the night with, she couldn't be caught missing.

Straightening out her sari, realigning her gold head chain and bell-drop earrings, bangles clinking as she moved, Anula briskly made her way through the paved streets. The stupas to the south peaked over the gate. The lofty white bulbs with tall spires stood silent, towering over the people, reminding them of their subservience, demanding their prayer and their allegiance to either the First or Second Heavens, or both if one was holy enough. All were things Anula would never give to beings who'd long since forsaken their people.

She headed north, toward the colorfully decorated palace, a bright beacon against the dense green jungle, as exacting as the stupas and calling for its own version of unquestionable faith and loyalty. People filtered in and out, mostly in. Only the wealthiest resided in the inner city, made up the raja's court, and decided the fate of the kingdom's people—yet never ventured outside the sixty-foot-tall iron gate to mingle or empathize.

Anula hurried across the courtyard, passing the vast garden that curled around the administrative buildings, and skidded to a stop outside the concubine estate. A female guard stood sentry, where there should have been none. At least, that had been the bargain.

Auntie Nirma's network of allies ran as deeply as tree roots, spreading from the village of Kekirawa to the palace in Anuradhapura. They knew who inside the administration was for the kingdom and who merely pretended. They'd made deals to choose Anula as a concubine for the raja, giving Anula and her poison a chance to end the Age of Usurpers. With Auntie Nirma at the helm, she couldn't fail.

Unless she was caught outside.

She picked up a stone and threw it around the corner. It smashed into the wall, alerting the sentry, who drew out a sword and rushed to fight off the fiend who dared threaten the Raja's Jewels. Never suspecting that one of those Jewels could protect herself better with the jewels at her throat.

Soft, sheer fabrics rustled against the interior walls as Anula surged through the concubine estate. Decorative torches and candles hung low, casting the halls in a mellow, shaded light: an eternal dusk or dawn. Smoke curled out of the rooms, a haze washing over the halls. A whisper floated with it. As she passed, Anula glanced inside one of the concubines' rooms. The girl kneeled on the floor before a colorful depiction of the Second Heavens, flowers in her hands and figurines of shapely beings with devilish heads surrounding her.

"Great Yakkas of Love, hear my prayer, send me to the bosom of my beloved. I will forever worship your names. I offer my favorite flowers, beaded with the tears of my…"

The words scratched along Anula's arms. She slipped past, lips thin. The Yakkas had long since forgotten this kingdom. Bartering with them wouldn't change that, just as begging the Divinities wouldn't.

She swung open her own door before closing it swiftly and crashing back against it, her heart hammering. If she believed in the Yakkas, she'd bargain for a curse upon Nuwan for making her late, for nearly ruining all of her and Auntie Nirma's plans. If he'd lied, if she was not chosen next… But perhaps the incident with Nuwan was a sign. That she hadn't studied enough, didn't know what she was doing. That she wasn't ready and it'd be best if she had a few more months to—

Red sky. Red hands. Red water.

Look away.

A knock rattled the door.

It reverberated through Anula, shaking down her spine, bringing her back from the brink.

Cursed Yakkas. Of course she was ready.

Anula shook out her arms. Remembering who she was, what had been taken, and all that would fall if she failed, she touched the necklace at her throat and opened the door.

Poison stopped hearts.

And Anula intended to stop many.

2

THE LACK OF WIND DISMAYED REERI.

So too did the lack of smell, taste, touch. If he closed his shadow eyes, he could nearly sense the sun warming the skin that was not there, the juice of a mango on his lips, the wave of his hair in the midday breeze.

The aether betwixt the Heavens and Earth was a vast, dark nothingness. It was a holding place, a pause, a prison. Two centuries—he had been more than a phantom two centuries ago, with a body and a life.

Reeri shook the memory loose before it cinched tight as a noose. He waited for the shadow offerings to come and envisioned the one he needed. The one the Lord of the Second Heavens wanted. The one that would grant him a body once again.

Moreover, the one that would save all whom Reeri had damned.

A shadow appeared into the nothingness in front of him. A shadow bowl of steaming shadow rice. Reeri pinched the rim betwixt two shadow fingers, the wisps of his edges and the bowl's twirling and twining together.

Great Blood Yakka, hear my prayer, send a disease of the stomach upon the house of Perera for the anxiety they've caused my son. I offer the finest rice of my harvest.

If shadows could grind, Reeri's teeth would be dust. The humans had become sanguinary as of late, demanding of retribution for the smallest of offenses. Time had matured their temper yet diluted their convictions.

Rice was not a fair exchange for a disease. How was he to demand more for the bargain if they did not already see its true worth?

"For the Heavens' sakes, Reeri, hurry up." A voice came from behind him. "Lord Wessamony is furious you are late."

Reeri scowled over his shoulder. "None of these are right. They will not give him what he wants."

Calu, one of the three Yakkas condemned to this fate with Reeri, plucked the bowl from his insubstantial fingers and examined it. "What he wants today is options. The Maha Equinox is nigh, and he is anxious to have the relic before then."

"All the more reason for me to wait for the human who cares enough about their bargain to agree to find it as their elevated offering."

"There is no finding the relic. We have tried for centuries to no avail. Let us go and get this over with."

"No." Reeri snatched the offering back. Too much hinged on this undertaking.

"The No Yakka strikes again."

If shadows could bristle, Reeri would be full of spikes. "O Heavens, spare me another nickname."

"Why forgo the only fun I have had in centuries?"

Reeri clenched the shadow bowl in his fist. It did not crumple. *The fault lies entirely with you.*

"Present this offering to Wessamony," Calu said, pulling Reeri from his memories. "Who knows? Mayhap it is the one that will lead us to the relic, and you will stop looking as though you are going to bite someone's shadow in half."

"I do not appear that way," Reeri scoffed.

"Of course, you do not. Everyone adores speaking with you. See the line behind me?"

Nothingness stretched beyond him.

"Your wit has not aged well."

"At least mine has not withered on the vine." Calu sighed. "He wants you. He is threatening Kama if you do not come."

Shadows churned like the ocean. "Why did you not begin with that?" Reeri spun on his heel. His shadow heart pounded. Kama was supposed to be safe. Only the others were—

No.

He would not allow it to happen. Not again.

From the time the cosmos burst into existence, the Heavens lay split in two. On one side stood the pearl-encrusted gates of the First Heavens, barring all from ascending the gilt stairs to the Divinities' realm. On the other side, the Second Heavens' ivory structure loomed over a lake, its domes and turrets, minarets and spires stretched as if they could pierce the steps and enter the others' sphere.

The cosmos demanded balance. One realm contained purveyors of unconditional blessing, the other of contractual obligation. Both fulfilled a necessary role in human life. Curses and cures, mercy and misfortune—it all came from the Heavens. Only the vehicle for which it was given differed, for it was not balance if all favor came freely, nor if all aid came with a price.

Yet in the centuries since the Yakkas' banishment from earth, the balance had tilted, turned, soured. The Divinities of the First Heavens had stayed the same, but Lord Wessamony had changed the function of the Yakkas of the Second. All due to Reeri.

"Brace yourself—he is short of temper today," Calu said, pressing open the intricately embellished double doors to Lord Wessamony's court.

The ivory floor—the only aspect of the past that had survived—was smooth as glass. Where gold statues once stood, depicting the great Lord in all his glory, broken stone now lay in heaps littered in dust and debris. Where frescos once adorned walls, now the blackest tar marred their faces. The main chamber, once vast and bright with heavenslight, was now made brighter with fire and brimstone. Empty of heavensong and void of heavenly communion, the acoustics made for—

"Reeri!" A voice thundered. It reverberated through the hall and rippled Reeri's shadow.

A whimpering sounded along the south wall. He dared not spare a glance. He knew who was there, how they were strung up, and why.

Him. The answer, eternally, was him.

"You dare refuse my summons again," Lord Wessamony said from upon his gilt throne, a blue hue blazing up his twisted horns. One hand squeezed tight around the Great Sword, gold and bright, glowing in its own glory. "I shall take from you the rest of your clan."

Reeri paused at the base of the dais, a small step in front of where Calu stood alongside Sohon and Kama—the four of them the only unshackled Yakkas remaining after Reeri's mistake.

"My apologies, Great Lord." Reeri bent at what used to be a waist. His eyes flicked to Kama's shadow hand curled tightly around Sohon's. "I lost track of time searching for the perfect bargain."

"Show me your findings."

Reeri straightened. Wisps of his edges flickered. "I was unable to—"

"Show me!" Wessamony demanded.

Reeri lifted the phantom rice bowl, brought his lips close, and whispered, "Son of Earth, your prayer has been heard."

Reeri felt the moment the offerer heard his words. It was akin to rain misting on one's face. Sensed but not seen.

Thank you, gracious Blood Yakka. A faceless voice echoed in the great court. *Thank you—*

"It has been heard, not accepted. Yet," Reeri said. "Offer up Fate's Bone Blade, and you will have your request complete."

The relic? But it has been lost for centuries. They say those who seek it never return.

"Your request is grand. So too must be your offering."

Yes, of course, but—

"Enough of this!" Wessamony growled. His lips curled back in disdain, baring sharp teeth. One wave of his hand and the Great Sword swung, cutting through the shadow bowl, severing Reeri's connection. "You bring me worthless offerings from spineless humans!"

"I tried to—"

"Try? You are not trying! You are failing! Have you no care for your souls, for the souls of those you have damned? Mayhap you wish *eternal* damnation on your clan! Mayhap I should send the rest there, too!"

Reeri clenched a fist. "No."

The sound of the sword came first. The sight came second. Reeri did not think—he moved, launching himself in front of Kama and closing his eyes against the sharpness. Yet it never came.

A scream pealed instead.

Reeri's head snapped up and to the south wall, where hundreds of Yakkas in varying states of suffering stood chained. The Great Sword was as long as three human men, golden as the sun, and quick as lightning. With a twang, it sliced through one of the Yakkas' shadow shoulders. Her cry echoed off the marble floor.

The Great Sword swung back again, catching Ratti on her other shoulder, then her chest, her arms, her abdomen, shredding her shadow. Each one of her screams tore through Reeri's shadow heart. For though they could not taste or smell, the Yakkas could feel the lash of a whip, the cut of a blade, the undoing of their existence.

"Please," he murmured.

"You are the damnation of your brethren," Wessamony seethed. A gleam, red as fire in his eyes, a curled smile on his lip. "You are the ruination of all my plans for the ascendence of the Second Heavens. You deserve this and more."

Reeri glanced behind him. Calu's shadow hand twirled tightly around Kama's. The three of them braced against the pain of watching their sister's death. Again.

"Yes, my Lord." It slid from Reeri's lips, low and broken.

"Have I been gracious, granting you a chance of atonement?"

"Yes, my Lord."

"Do you want redemption?"

"Yes, my Lord."

"What, then, shall you do?"

Dissent.

The word spilled unbidden in his mind, like the agony bubbling on Ratti's lips. Ratti, the sister who loved to hug him, who grounded Kama in reality, who knew how to make Sohon smile, who coaxed Calu out of his shell. Ratti, the oldest of the Yakka sisters, with the purest heart.

Riot.

It burned down his throat.

Revolt.

It kindled in his heart.

"What will you do to redeem their souls, Reeri?" Wessamony boomed. "What will you do to return to your bodies?"

Reeri watched Ratti shiver as her shadow knit back together. Within an hour, she would be ready to die a thousandth time.

"I will find the dagger."

Wessamony nodded, appeased. The Great Sword flew to his hand, pristine, as if the torture it doled out was insignificant. "May it be the only bargain any of you make before the Maha Equinox."

Reeri turned on one phantom heel. The venom of two centuries seethed below his surface. Wessamony was no great Lord. He cared not for the redemption of his creation, only for his plan of ascendance.

What would Reeri do?

He would find the dagger, save his brethren from damnation, and fix what he had broken, then safeguard them for eternity.

He would kill Wessamony.

3

Anula hunched over a wide table, scribbling across a long, narrow piece of paper.

The knock at the door hadn't been her calling; it had been a missive from Auntie Nirma. To the naked eye, it was a loving letter from her only family member, but once held to candle flame, the true message revealed itself.

> *Usurper on the move. Allied with palace traitors and Polonnaruwa Kingdom. Must hurry. New names: Tissa Bandara, Nihal Kumara, Deepal Dissanayake.*

Hand racing, Anula copied it down, tucked her list into a seam of her sari, and burned the missive. The edges curled in on themselves, darkened, and dissolved. Her anxiety did not.

Her list—Auntie Nirma's list—could only come into play after Anula met with the raja. After she wooed him. After she married him. A concubine couldn't rid the palace of corrupt ministers or traitors to the Anuradhapura Kingdom. A concubine was lucky to spend her days in the estate, or else be freed to marry before she was old and gray and barren. There was no justice system for concubines, women, or the poor of the kingdom. They had no voice, and so a concubine could not wield political power.

But a raejina could.

The first raejina of Anuradhapura.

Another knock sounded at the door. This time Anula's heart didn't race; her pulse didn't spike. There was no time to waste, to second-guess. A usurper was on her heels.

The smell of jasmine and rose wafted around Anula's sari, tingling in her nose. Steam billowed and swirled from the Kuttam Pokuna bathhouse, softening her shoulders and easing the tension from her muscles as two servants undressed her.

"Tonight will be your ceremonial cleansing to prepare your body for service to the raja," the elder said, initiating the ritual hundreds, if not thousands, of concubines had undergone. "You'll spend tomorrow in your room, preparing your mind for service to the raja. Prayer to both Heavens begins now, to prepare your soul for service to the raja."

Anula knew the servant's name, knew the date she'd begun working in the concubine estate, knew what her allegiance was to the kingdom, even knew she had a birthmark behind her right ear.

Auntie Nirma was nothing if not thorough.

But this servant was not an ally. And though not an enemy, Anula had no time for those who didn't fall into either group. Idle chitchat wouldn't rectify the wounds brought on by the Age of Usurpers. According to Auntie Nirma, that was Anula's purpose. The reason she lived while so many others—

No. There was no point thinking of them.

The two servants whispered blessings as they stripped Anula bare, the night air sending a chill along her spine. Between the palace and the gardens stood four granite statues of conches and crabs marking the corners of the long, languid pool. Bottles of perfumes and oils lined one side; candles flickered on the other.

"Forgive her all transgressions, infinitely wise and powerful Divinities," the younger servant said, leading Anula to the edge of the water. "We pray mercy and favor upon her life. Make her a blessing to the raja."

Anula snorted. If the Divinities knew of her plan for the great raja and his corrupt followers, they most assuredly would not bless it. Retribution tended to be a Yakka endeavor.

"Are you well?" the older servant asked. She reached out to cup Anula's face. "If you are overcome with emotion, I can bring you a kerchief. It is all right to feel—"

"I'm fine." Before the touch settled on her cheek, Anula pulled away and took the first step down into the bathing pool.

The water cooled her sun-warmed skin and anxiety-riddled veins. A large, colorfully painted fish glimmered from the floor. The Makara, the sea dragon known for feasting on fishermen, slipped beneath her feet. Rising starlight danced on its scales, giving the impression of movement, as if it were swimming from one end to the other.

Anula blinked.

It *was* swimming from one end to the other. Gliding across the stone floor, the sea dragon shimmered not with moonlight or starlight but with—

"Heavenly blessing," Anula whispered. Her eyes flicked to the servants. "So the tales are true? The palace is filled with blessed gifts?"

"Why would they be false?" The younger woman cocked her head. "The Heavens do not lie. The palace is the in-between, a place created and endowed with objects blessed with their powers so that we may experience and know their love."

The last word skittered up Anula's arm, raising the flesh in its wake. The servants took no notice, gently lifting one arm each, and began their cleansing. The oils were first, working her into a lather. One for cleaning and scrubbing, another for purging and flushing, and yet another for purifying and rejuvenating.

"It's time you prayed with us," the younger woman said, delicately leaning Anula until she floated on her back.

She would have snorted again but didn't want to risk either of them trying to comfort her. She didn't need comfort. And she didn't need prayer.

Even more ridiculous than offering bargains to the Yakkas, who were said to have been banished and executed centuries ago, was soliciting favor from the ancient Divinities. There was no reasoning to why the Heavens were split in two, other than to give people the option of either bartering or begging.

At least in the Yakka tradition, people could come as themselves, offering what they had. The Divinities demanded purity, perfection, and unquestionable faith that if a person was good enough, they would receive what they'd asked for. But more often than not, prayers went unanswered. The faithful said it was the fault of the person, that they were not worthy, that they must pray more, repent more, build more stupas with white bulbs that loomed over the city, tithe a portion of their meager earnings to the expansion of the structure, of the faith. Then perhaps, one day, one of their prayers would be met with gracious favor.

Who would love such deities?

It was all lies, anyway. Stories of old. The reason people's prayers went unanswered was not lack of perfection or weak trade. It was because the sky, the stars, and everything beyond was empty. Centuries ago, the Heavens imbued artistic objects with their powers, dropped them into a palace only the wealthiest families or most violent usurpers had a chance of entering, then left Anuradhapura to its own devices. They didn't listen to prayers, much less grant them.

Anula knew that better than anyone.

She closed her eyes and took a deep breath. Prophet Ayaan. Commander Dilshan. Raja Mahakuli Mahatissa. The first names on her list. She repeated them like a mantra, the closest she'd get to a prayer ever again. The names tingled the back of her neck. A promise whispered in the night.

The time for retribution had come.

Time for change had, too.

Anula came to deliver the justice they thought they'd evaded. Unfortunately for them, she'd survived that awful night.

It felt like a hundred years ago, Anula's first life. The truth was it'd only been twelve. Twelve years since she'd been home, since she'd prayed, since that night she had slid her amma's necklace onto her throat.

She wasn't supposed to; Amma had forever said she didn't pay enough attention to be trusted with it. That she'd need to be older, calmer, wiser before the sapphires would be passed down to her, perhaps after she was betrothed.

But that night, she figured what Amma didn't know wouldn't hurt her.

Anula didn't have much time. Thaththa was already at the table, expectantly awaiting his wife and daughter. The soft light of dusk and an evening breeze floated through the open windows in Amma's room, casting Anula in a golden hue as she studied herself in the mirror.

The two-tier jewelry was so large on her, she had to tilt her chin high for it to fit. She didn't mind. She twirled in her sari, this way and that, watching the sparkle of the diamonds reflect in her eyes, stars against the dark night sky. As if she were from the Heavens themselves, touched by the Divinities Thaththa worshiped or the Yakkas to whom Amma always prayed.

"It's beautiful on you, darling."

Anula whirled. "Amma, I was just—"

"I know." Amma smiled, the expression small and delicate, just like her. The opposite of Anula. "You can wear it, but only for tonight."

"Really?" Perhaps Anula didn't have to wait to be small and delicate and mature, too.

Amma rubbed her rounded belly, then took Anula's hand and led her out the door. "Tonight is special. We're celebrating Thaththa's invitation to the palace."

"The raja finally called him?"

"More than that." Thaththa's voice swam with pride as they entered the dining area. A wide smile spread beneath his gray beard and creased the corners of his eyes. "I'm to receive a position on the board of ministers. It's all happening, my loves."

Amma leaned over him, cupping his cheek in her hand. He grazed his fingers down her arm and across her belly. A touch to say hello, a touch to say *I'm proud*, a touch to say *I love you*. A language Anula had deciphered years ago. Though they kissed often, it was the contact in between that spoke the loudest. She saw how Amma softened into his hugs, how Thaththa's shoulders relaxed under her hand, even after ten years of marriage, after welcoming one child and burying three, after droughts and floods and wildly prosperous seasons. They were each other's comfort, their safe place, their home.

They were a solid foundation on which Anula's life couldn't

be shaken, and a dream on which she built visions of her own future.

"I'm so happy for you, Thaththa!" Anula hugged him tightly, the scent of fresh cinnamon tickling her nose. He'd been dreaming of this day for years, of being Minister Don Upali Ramanayake. Their estate was the largest in Eppawala, boasting more land and larger irrigation reservoirs than even the rice farms closer to the palace. It produced twice the harvest in the Maha season—the hardest season—than any other farm for five years running, feeding the entire city of Anuradhapura. He always credited his workers and ensured they were treated fairly, housed, and fed. He was a hero, to her and so many more. And finally, after two usurpers, a raja had recognized it.

To celebrate, Thaththa and Amma handed Anula her first taste of palm wine. Bittersweetness puckered her lips, and she sneezed, but Anula ignored it. She couldn't stop imagining what life as a minister's family might hold, how she and her new sister or brother would be welcomed into the palace, the in-between. "Will you walk inside a painting, like they say you can?"

Thaththa chuckled. "Of course. It will be by the Divinities' choosing that I become a minister. That means they also choose me to enjoy the Divine gifts of their love."

"Will you look for statues that talk? And cutlery that walks?" Anula's brows furrowed. "Will you be here when the baby arrives?"

A trumpet blasted; a rumbling followed close behind. For a moment, Anula wondered if the whole village was celebrating the news. But then the table shook, toppling the glasses and spilling wine onto her sari. A flash of orange cut across the open window, disappearing behind the trees.

Boom.

The sky burst into searing red.

"Get to the horses," Thaththa bellowed, rushing out the door as he called for workers and servants.

Without a word, Amma pulled Anula through the house and outside to the gates. A drum sounded, powerful and loud. Hand on her belly, she whispered, "War drums."

It echoed in Anula's chest, sending a ripple of fear down her spine.

Strobing daylight brightened the sky around the village as a plume of smoke rose against the clouds from the rice paddy fields and houses.

Not daylight. Firelight.

A war elephant adorned in iron crashed through the gates, rending the thatch houses to tatters. Flames licked the market, then devoured every inch of every home. Armored men poured in from the jungle, brandishing swords, shouting war cries, racing to the beat of the drums. Slicing their way through men, women, and children.

Red mixed with the dirt, muddying the streets. Breath stalled in Anula's lungs.

"Anula!" Amma spun her around. Held her chin between two fingers. "Look away."

But death squeezed into her nostrils, burned her eyes. Why? What had they done to deserve this?

"You must run." Amma spoke fast. "Hide in the jungle."

Anula's head snapped up. "But you said I could get lost in there."

"I'll pray to the Heavens—they'll keep you safe."

"Nimeka?" Thaththa's voice reached across the expanse where he packed a cart full with village children. "I told you two to leave—"

Loud trumpeting cut him off. A war elephant rushed toward them, a host of horses pounding behind. Anula hit the ground before she realized Amma had pushed her out of the way. Dirt and dust and red-streaked mud splattered onto her face.

"Amma? Thaththa?" she called—ignoring the puddle beneath her, the wet stickiness at her elbows—and pushed herself up. They must have jumped away, too, separated by the soldiers flooding the gates.

A horse neighed, its bronze coat gleaming as it reared up through the haze. And as it landed, Thaththa came into view. Relief filled her lungs. Anula closed the distance between them, arms outstretched for his. To tell him she wasn't running away. To tell him she wouldn't be separated from him again. To—

The soldier pulled Thaththa by the hair, wrenching his head backward, and tilted a pot over his mouth. A thick, steaming liquid cascaded out. Thaththa choked as the silver substance spilled over his lips, and the soldier released him, riding off.

He collapsed to his knees.

"Thaththa!" Anula rushed forward. She caught him before he fell, a heavy, wet cough squeezing from his lungs. A puff of steam rose in the cool night air. And then he was bleeding. A drop first, from his nose. Then a drip from his ears.

Dark red rivers trickled from his eyes, like spilled wine over the edge of a table.

Then the water tanks broke. Blood and piss and things Anula had never seen come from her father burst forth. Sarong soiled, Thaththa groaned and pitched forward. He landed on his face, a sigh deflating his body.

"Thaththa?" Anula shook his shoulder. He didn't answer, didn't move. He was—

No. He couldn't be. War never knocked on Eppawala's door. This was only a nightmare. She would wake, and Thaththa would take her and Amma to the palace. Her sister or brother would be born under a clear starry night, just like her, and then they would walk inside a painting, experience the Heavens' love, as a family of four. Thaththa would—

She retched, fast and furious.

Boom.

The roof of their estate erupted in flames. She winced against the bright light, stumbled back against the heat and the realization that this was no dream.

Help, she wanted to scream. But the word stuck in her raw throat. Tears blurred her vision. Thaththa hadn't deserved this. He was a good man; the raja saw that. So where was he? Where were the raja and his army? They were supposed to protect them.

Perhaps the soldiers had gotten to them, too. Perhaps there was no help coming. Anula whirled around, breaths short and fast. Where was Amma? If there was no help, then only Amma could—

The Heavens. Amma was going to pray. But what if she couldn't? What if the soldiers—

No. Amma had gotten out of the way. They'd both made it. They just needed a little help to find each other. They just needed the Heavens' help.

"Great Divinities of the First Heavens, please save Amma. Save my village. Forgive me for taking Amma's necklace without permission. Forgive me for drinking wine. I'll never do it again. Please…save me."

Anula spun on her heel. Still, no one came. Only fear and blood and weapons entering places they shouldn't.

The Yakkas. She should pray to both the Heavens. Wasn't that what most people did?

"Great—" She paused. Yakkas were to be bargained with, and only one at a time. But there were hundreds. If she chose wrong—no, she'd choose Amma's favored. Surely he cared for her. "Great Blood Yakka of the Second Heavens, hear my prayer. I offer the fields of my father, my whole inheritance. So please, please, please save us now!"

A boom sounded behind her, and she jumped. *The*

jungle—Amma said to hide in the jungle. That's where she'll be waiting. Fleeing through the city streets, Anula ran past red homes and red stalls, dark lumps face down in dark pools, burning paddy fields, and smoking storehouses. She dared one glance over her shoulder and skidded to a halt.

The answer to her prayers rose high in the village center.

She choked at the sight, nothing left in her stomach to purge, her body as empty as the Heavens must be if this was their answer.

Why?

She stumbled, turned, and ran again.

Hours later, a trumpet sounded.

Anula's eyes snapped open. Waking for the first time without Amma's kisses, without Thaththa's warm embrace, things she knew she would never wake to again. The gray dawn spilled over the smoking, charred ruins of Thaththa's land.

Alone in a tree, Anula watched hundreds of men on horses and war elephants emerge. They thundered into Eppawala, gold, green, and red painted on their armor. The raja's men, swiftly snuffing out the invaders, outnumbering them two to one.

"It's too late," she murmured to no one. No father, no mother, no baby sister or brother. "You're too late."

She wrapped her arms around herself. It was not the same as a hug.

Two men on horses paused beneath her tree. "It's gone. All of it. The people, too."

"As Prophet Ayaan foretold," the other man snapped.

Anula startled.

"Of course, Commander Dilshan. I only meant the plan worked perfectly. The prince of the Kingdom of Polonnaruwa was too busy savoring his victory to notice an ambush being set, and now he's dead. The raja will surely acknowledge your skill."

Her pulse quickened.

"Raja Mahakuli Mahatissa and I strategized together," the commander said. "He will acknowledge nothing but his own grandeur. Now quit your flattery and ensure those fires don't spread. Only Eppawala was meant to burn."

The words razed Anula's skin, set fire to her aching heart.

Only Eppawala was meant to burn.

4

Though centuries had passed since Reeri lost his life, the memory of it was sharp and persistent as a mosquito bite. He no longer counted how often his first memory surfaced, how often he had let it, imagining the gold-red daylight rising behind his eyelids, the chirping and buzzing and sizzling rousing him.

On the first day of life, he had opened his eyes to wood; above, below, and to each side. The floor was crammed with candles, fabrics, oils, and vessels. *A shrine*, instinct had thrummed.

Through the doorway, he looked upon them for the first time. *Humans*. They passed by, chatting and laughing. Animals, too, in flight or on foot. A compulsion to be near them, with them, reverberated in his chest. Reeri stepped forward, cautious not to disturb the offerings. His fingers tingled with anticipation as he crossed the threshold.

A gentle caress rippled down his spine as the balmy sun touched his shoulders. The powdered, gritty earth warmed his soles and wedged betwixt his toes. He marveled at feeling, at experiencing, as he took another step—

And snapped back into the shrine.

Reeri's brow furrowed. He took one step into the sun and another—back into the shrine.

The pull began at his navel, a force binding and confining him to the wooden room. His heart beat swiftly at the thought.

Mayhap he was only moving too slowly. With a sudden start, he ran across the threshold, one foot in front of the other—

And snapped back into the shrine, toppling over vessels and snuffing out candles. Fear trickled down his spine. He was here to commune. All his instinct rang clear with it. The Yakkas were sent here with a purpose. Why else leave the Second Heavens? Yet communion could not be achieved alone.

It took weeks for Reeri to test it thoroughly. The fettering force never lessened. Its potency remained high in the early morning during the songbirds' rise, in the afternoon under the scorching sun, in the evening dusk with the soft, cool breeze, and at midnight's reign as the moon shined bright.

His fists clenched, the muscles in his arms rippling as he glared at the walls. Were his brethren facing the same obstacle? Why had the Lord separated them, as if they were not a clan as they were in the Heavens?

A cough sounded in the doorway. Reeri glanced over his shoulder as a man crashed to his knees, head bowed, eyes averted, outstretched hands presenting the finest fabrics. "An offering, great Blood Yakka. Hear my prayer. Please protect my family from the bleeding fever. I offer the most expensive of silks."

The words struck Reeri, pulled him closer. Gently, the man placed the offering in his hands, and smooth, liquid cream spilled across Reeri's fingers. "Son of Earth, your prayer has been heard." He bowed his head. "I accept your bargain."

A vision burned, sudden and clear: the man stood with his family, a boy, two girls, a wife, and an elderly mother. Reeri only had to think the word *protection*, and an incandescent layer of aether covered their bodies. A sense of rightness settled on his shoulders. The disease ravaging the villages with fever and bleeding the people dry would not touch them, for a time. Another bargain would be necessary in the future.

Communion, instinct said. O Heavens. This was the reason for his descent.

But as the man left, a cold emptiness filled the room. Reeri wanted to be out under the sun, with the birds and elephants. He wished to explore the land, to follow the wind that rustled the plantain leaves, to find the one with whom his soul communed, introduce them to his brethren and experience this life together. As one, whole and hale.

The image was so vivid, he nearly believed he had made it, when a tug began at his navel. Reeri glanced down. For a moment he was paused, unmoving. Then he snapped into another shrine, in another village. This one far vaster and more ornate, the doorway sheathed in beads. Beyond lay a bustling, thriving market. On the floor lay a woman holding bowls of steaming rice before her.

"Great Blood Yakka, hear my prayer. Please avenge my son. He did not deserve to die." The woman shook, holding back her cries.

Reeri needed no further details. The bargains were all that mattered, the purpose for which he had been created. They were a shadow of the power of Lord Wessamony of the Second Heavens, the Great Destroyer, who could imbue pure destruction with the snap of his fingers. Yet his powers were bound to the days of the Maha and Yala Equinox—a balance demanded of the cosmos. So Wessamony made his own balance in return. The Yakkas were unfettered by the seasons or movement of the stars, yet they could act only once a deal had been struck, lest the balance of the cosmos be undone.

Closing his eyes, Reeri inhaled the scent of the rice, noting the difference in aroma from that given in the previous shrine. Undeniably it hailed from a different farm, but was also a different grain. The thought rubbed against him—another part of life withheld.

"Daughter of Earth, your prayer has been heard," he said betwixt clenched teeth. "I accept your bargain."

The vision came quickly: The man who had taken her son's life appeared in bold colors. He was short and wide, a father of six boys; his pastimes included whipping and belittling. Reeri's lip curled. The word came to mind, striking down upon the man. *Spleen*. It ruptured, poisonous waste seeping into the man's blood. He would succumb within the week.

So it went.

Reeri's binding pulled him to various shrines, where he either accepted or rejected bargains. Only those without fair exchanges, whose offerings were not nearly as grand as their request, were rejected. *Balance must always be kept.*

Was that why the Yakkas had been separated?

When the silence rang out in the emptiness of his chambers, he meditated on the question. His eyes stayed closed against the temptation of anger and self-pity, against the sun beckoning him forth. The perfume of simmering curry and the musical notes of a village's laughter celebrating two souls finding and communing with one another, did nothing to help. Every sense reminded him of the various facets of life he had not, and would not, experience. Reeri gritted his teeth as the scent of curry crept closer.

A pinch nipped his cheek.

"Ow!" Reeri's eyes flew open. "Why would—Kama."

Taller than most, with a willowy stance and a far-off gaze, the Yakka inched closer, her head tilted. "You looked dead."

"I am not," Reeri said.

"Clearly," Kama sighed, as if disappointed, and turned to leave.

"Wait." Reeri scrambled to stand. "This is my shrine. Are you not bound to yours?"

Kama leaned against a wall, took a long, slow bite of her food. "Coconut milk is my favorite part of curry. Do you think I could bathe in it?"

"Kama—"

"I shall give it a try. Surely someone is desperate enough for love to pour me a river's worth."

As one of the sisters of the Yakkas of Love, Kama's powers resided over the heart. With nothing left for the mind, Calu had once jested. Reeri's impatience boiled. "Answer my question, please."

Kama licked her fingers clean and dropped the empty bowl to the ground. It skittered and knocked over a candle. "Have not their offerings been strengthening you? Or have you been too enthralled with your dreams to take note?"

"What do you mean?"

She cocked her head. "The shackle loosens with each bargain."

"Mine does not."

She glanced at the floor of offerings. "When was the last time you tested it?"

In truth, he did not know. After so many failed attempts, he had taken to brooding about it instead.

Kama's gaze brightened. "Go ahead, do it. That is what you were dreaming about, was it not? Being outside. Eating curry. Living life with the one with whom your soul communes."

Her velvet voice, made for completing bargains of the heart, picked at the thread of his desire and tugged. Reeri did not fight it. As he had done countless times, he reached inside himself and grasped the invisible line attached to his navel, hope blooming. This time, he found his fetter lax.

"There you go," Kama cooed. She stepped lightly over to him. "Take hold of your dreams, Reeri. Come and commune." She bent down and brushed a delicate finger across the spot she had pinched. Then, with a peal of laughter, she danced out of the shrine. Arms raised to the Heavens, she said, "The flashier your craft, the faster they will pray!"

Reeri's cheek burned.

It burned with the hottest desire.

Flashy was not Reeri's forte.

But he knew within the depths of his being that he was not meant to be alone. It was written on his heart. Alongside each name in his clan and the nameless soul he might one day find.

He began with boils. The kind that was puss filled and contagious. He moved on to rashes, reaching up spines and covering necks. The bursting organs were no one's favorite. They could not watch their enemy suffer.

No, the humans craved blood bubbling to the surface, choking their enemies' throats and flooding out of their mouths. They thirsted for rivers to spout from noses, streams to burst from orifices.

Reeri complied.

Quickly, half the island prayed for his wrath. The other half cowered and begged for protection, not against the natural illnesses spreading through the land, nor against the other Yakkas' crafts—they prayed for protection against his own hand. That it would not crash upon their houses, their bodies, their loved ones.

Blood flowed across the island as if it were the Malvathu River, and the binding loosened. He ate curry in the market, rode elephants into the bush, climbed trees around the shrines. In time, he even ran. Jungle cats and blue magpies at his heels, sand sifting betwixt his toes, he ran to the ocean and back, finding each of the Yakka's shrines. Calu Cumara Dewatawa, Maha Sohon, Anjenam Dewi, Wewulun, Baddracali, Bodrima, Gopolu, Bhooto Sanni, Morottoo, Bahirawa, the Riddhi, six sisters of the Yakkas of Love, and a hundred more, each held fast within their wooden walls.

Kama leaned against her doorway, poking the eye of a long-dead fish. "You are their favorite now."

"Have they lost their appetite for desire?" he asked.

"Who can think of love when they are consumed with death?"

The realization crept through Reeri like vines. The offerings had bought him freedom at the expense of the freedom of all others.

The thought sat sourly in his chest.

He snapped to his nearest shrine; a man lay prostrate before him with a large bowl of aromatic red Suwandel rice. "Great Blood Yakka, hear my prayer. Please heal my wife from the stomach disease cursed upon her. I offer my entire harvest of rice."

"No," Reeri said, an idea forming.

The man looked up. "Great Yakka, please—"

"You seek mercy and healing for your wife?" The loophole solidified in his mind. "Your compassion must also extend to your neighbor. Pray to the Yakkas of Love that he find romance—then you may return for your bargain."

"Yes, great Blood Yakka. Thank you." The man rushed out of the shrine, bowing repeatedly, nearly tripping on his sarong in his haste to find Kama's shrine.

Reeri did not stop there.

A woman came next.

"No."

"But—"

"You seek vengeance in the form of festering sores? Then you must also pray to Calu. Return when that bargain is complete, and you may give your offering."

So it went. Reeri demanded bargains from the other Yakkas. For what was freedom if he was alone?

Years passed before the bindings of every Yakka loosened and fell. In total, they had three days. Three glorious days communing with the Earth and humans, beginning their experience of life together as one, as they were meant to be—or so Reeri thought.

It was late in the night when the thunder came. It shook the earth, and Reeri's binding drew taut. With an earsplitting strike, Lord Wessamony descended upon the beach as the Maha Equinox began. Two twisting horns curved on either side of the Lord's head. Sharp teeth hung over bloodred lips, and sharper nails clutched around the Great Sword, golden and bright. Their creator had finally come to see them. Yet the violence in his gaze suggested it was not for pleasantries.

The Yakkas fell to their knees in reverence, but the Lord roared. "What horror has been unleashed here?"

A shiver shook through the Yakkas. Not a word was uttered.

"Why are the humans trembling before the Heavens?"

Only silence met him.

"Answer me! Why have you left your shrines and destroyed the balance I created?"

That piqued Reeri's ears. "Destroyed? My Lord, we have kept the balance and, in doing so, were granted leave of the shrines."

The Lord darkened. "Who granted you this?"

Reeri tensed. In all his musings, he had not questioned it. "No one, my Lord. I found that with more bargains came more freedom. I encouraged the humans to offer to all."

"*You*," the Lord fumed. "You dare break my law and grant power to yourself and others? You dare steal authority from me?"

Reeri's heart beat swiftly. "I did not intend—"

"You have disobeyed your creator, ruined, mayhap for all time, my plans for the Second Heavens, and led your clan astray!"

Dread trickled down Reeri's spine. "I apologize, my Lord. I did not know."

The shackle fell off. A collective gasp rose up on the Yakkas' lips. Then lightning struck; screams filled the air as the blitz rained down. With the flick of the Lord's wrist, the Great Sword swung. It sliced and shredded, cut and carved.

Pain lanced up Reeri's spine; a cry bubbled across his tongue.

"Disobedience demands discipline!" Lord Wessamony thundered.

Bloody sores pulsed along Reeri's arms, up his neck, and down his abdomen. Pure destruction festered him from the inside out.

"My eyes!" Baddracali screamed, white and black melting from her sockets.

"Stop!" Calu yelled, teeth falling from his mouth.

"Calu!" Ratti shouted, the Great Sword chopping a thigh, bone splintering with a crack.

"No!" Calu reached out, his fingertips an inch from hers when the Great Sword swung wide, severing them from the joint. They thudded to the ground.

"Please!" Reeri bellowed. "They did not know. It is not their fault!"

As quickly as it had begun, it halted.

The Great Sword snicked back into Lord Wessamony's hand. "And yet that does not rectify the wrong, does it, Reeri?"

He shivered as the breeze touched his flayed skin. "No, my Lord."

"You have ruined it all, Reeri."

He bowed his head. "Yes, my Lord."

"For that, I hereby banish the Yakkas from the Earth."

As one, they rose into the sky.

"Damnation is your punishment. Your place is in my court, in eternal purgatory," Lord Wessamony judged. "This, Reeri, is your penalty: to watch as they suffer for your actions."

Breath stalled in Reeri's lungs. "Please—"

"Yet I am not without mercy!" the Lord boomed. "Atonement is also yours. Your place shall be the shadowlands, your powers bound by my decree, until you find the relic I seek and repair the wreckage you have wrought of my plans. Do you accept these terms?"

"Please, Reeri," Ratti sobbed. "Help us."

O Heavens. What had he done?

"Yes, my Lord!"

"Then so shall it be." Lord Wessamony nodded. "For my sake, I grant three of your clan as aid."

With another flick of his wrist, the Lord let loose his power, and in a blink, the Yakkas' bodies fell to the jungle floor. Yet *they* did not. Phantoms now, they rose into the Second Heavens. All but Reeri, Calu, Kama, and Sohon. They stopped in the gray-black aether betwixt the Earth and Heavens. Into the nothingness.

Reeri touched his shadow face, only for his fingers to slip through vapor.

"Purgatory will end when you present me the Bone Blade." Lord Wessamony's voice echoed, the sounds of torment and torture rising from his faraway court. "The fault lies entirely with you, Reeri. Never forget that."

5

Anula's second life began with a party.

It was not for her. In fact, the house staff nearly forgot about Anula's arrival until the moment she was on the steps, waiting in line with the others to get inside. Her first glance at her new home was stolen between pressed bodies. A short woman in a bright sari spun fast words around her guests.

It didn't take long for Anula to understand that parties were a weekly ritual at Auntie Nirma's estate, typically ending with the women disappearing through a hidden door.

"It's a gathering of like-minded individuals," she corrected when Anula confronted her about it, after their first year together. "Hidden because one must always keep one's allies safe."

A flash of names seared across Anula's mind. "What about enemies?"

"Those"—her auntie smiled shrewdly—"are handled individually."

Nirma was Anula's fourth or fifth cousin on her mother's side, a widow who mysteriously owned land and a large house in the village center of Kekirawa. Childless, she'd taken Anula in when Thaththa's closest male relative wanted to inherit only the estate, not the girl. But this was as far as their relationship went. Auntie Nirma was too busy with secret business meetings with her allies, hosting kingdom officials for dinners, and handling her enemies.

Anula had taken to snooping, her goal the hidden door.

The early-morning light broke through the slats on the window coverings as Anula pushed her way into another room of the house she'd yet to explore, her late Uncle Manoj's office. A layer of dust covered every surface, including the wooden floor. Every step she took would be seen. She didn't care.

How was it a woman had such power, such influence? Auntie Nirma merely said a word and sashayed into a room, and every man prayed to the Heavens to be the one to grant her wish. Male and female suitors lined the street for her favor, yet she held them aloft, close enough to do her bidding, far enough away to receive more than she gave.

There was a table, chair, and small bookshelf in the office. It was not nearly as grand as Thaththa's had been. Then again, Uncle Manoj hadn't been as important a man. In the corner sat a tall stand displaying a figurine of a being with saffron eyes, holding a sword in one hand and a human head in the other, blood smeared across his chest. Amma had included the same statue in her shrine. The Blood Yakka, Reeri, leader of all the Yakkas, the most cruel and powerful.

Anula flicked the statue over.

Only Eppawala was meant to burn.

Commander Dilshan's words skittered up her arms and burrowed at the base of her spine. Auntie Nirma might speak of enemies, but it was Anula's life that had been destroyed by them. Silence had been the answer to her prayers, and a deep ache that shook her chest every morning she woke alone. She would not make the same mistake twice.

Shifting her attention, she poked around the shelf, feeling for hidden knobs or handles. The titles of the books were dry reports on wildlife in the jungles, plants growing around the area and in the Pleasure Gardens of the palace. Perhaps Uncle Manoj had been a plant farmer. Anula stepped to the far side of the shelf and paused as the board underfoot creaked. She leaned her weight and it creaked again.

Finally.

Falling to her hands and knees, she pried it open. Perhaps there was a staircase beneath. Or—

A dusty brown leather journal in the tiniest cubbyhole.

She opened it and frowned.

It was a drawing of a plant with an arrow pointing to the seeds. *Thel Endaru* was written at the very top. The name of the plant, perhaps. Below it was a set of paragraphs, and beneath them, scrawled in Uncle Manoj's script, were the words *steep in tea for quiet death.*

Anula nearly choked. What in the cursed Yakkas' names was this? She flipped to the next page and the next, but all had the same format. At the top was a name—like kaneru—a detailed illustration of the plant or flower, followed by a few paragraphs describing how to forage and brew. Finally, always in Uncle's writing, were directions to hide the poison in plain sight.

Mix in palm wine to incapacitate.

Simmer in curry for slow, painful death.

But on the last page was a question: *Skin-to-skin contact without self-poisoning?*

Anula slammed the book shut and raced out the door with it. The mystery of Auntie Nirma's allies and enemies, the secret room, her wealth, was solved.

The book landed on her auntie's table with a bang. Dust mushroomed, settling onto the egg hoppers. "You're an assassin, aren't you? Just as Uncle Manoj was."

Auntie Nirma pursed her lips, shaking off her hopper. Though she'd stayed up into the late hours of the night with her latest gathering, she looked none the worse for wear. Her deep-green sari clung softly. Her wide eyes calm. "What in the Heavens' names are you on about, girl? And why aren't you at the table? Sit. Eat."

"No," Anula snapped. "This is how you have power, why you have allies and enemies, isn't it?"

Auntie Nirma dropped her food. "And what if it is? What are you going to do about it?"

Anula crossed her arms. "It's not right, killing people."

"No, it's not. Unless they deserve it. Unless the Heavens will it."

Anula blanched. "You think the Heavens tell you who to kill?"

"Not exactly. But they do allow things to fall into place. Their favor and bargains make pathways for us to walk."

Anula wrinkled her nose. "Why would they do that?"

"Some call it karma, or the cosmos's plan—Fate." Auntie Nirma picked up her tea, blew on the steam. "Do you know why I took you in?"

"Because you have no children."

Auntie Nirma smirked. "Being childless was my choice, not Fate's. I chose to bring you here because I believe the Heavens opened a pathway for you."

"Me?"

"You survived when no one else did."

A flash of orange flame, of red-soaked earth and rivers of blood down Thaththa's—

Anula blinked the memory away.

"It was no accident, Anula. You were meant to survive."

"Why?" The question was soft as a whisper.

"Justice," Auntie Nirma said, the word bold and strong. It tingled the back of Anula's neck. "You were chosen to carry out a further purpose. I've spent my whole life cultivating allies. Together, we must make it count. We can change the kingdom for good, in their name, for their justice and the justice of all others forevermore."

Anula sat, slowly.

Auntie Nirma leaned forward. "You've asked after my allies and enemies. We are women working for the good of the kingdom, creating change through open pathways and deals struck in the night. Only recently have our sights turned farther than our village borders."

"So, the secret meetings you have…"

"Are to end the Age of Usurpers and put a true leader on the throne. One whom Anuradhapura deserves. One who will begin a new age, an age of peace and prosperity for all."

A chill slid down Anula's spine. "One who cares for more than power?"

Auntie Nirma nodded.

"But…you're women."

"Who know how to bide time and bend rules."

The words were sticky in Anula's mind. An entire network of women bound to the belief that the Heavens were helping them, guiding them—and the idea that she had a role to play, that she could make something good come from what had happened to her family—made no sense. Because the Heavens didn't answer. Auntie Nirma was playing this game alone.

It would never work.

"Anula," Auntie Nirma said sternly, leveling a sharp gaze. "Why do you think you survived?"

"I don't know." Her voice was smaller than she expected.

"What are you going to do about it?"

"What do you mean?"

"Are you going to sulk your entire life, or are you going to ensure that your parents' deaths weren't for nothing? Because I am. Will you help me?"

Anula bit her lip, staring at the book. It was a far-fetched scheme, but her auntie was right. What was she going to do with her life now? What would Amma do? No. She couldn't ask that, because Amma couldn't do anything. Nor could Thaththa. Nor the entire village.

That was the point.

Prophet Ayaan. Commander Dilshan. Raja Mahakuli Mahatissa.

Anula straightened her shoulders and met Auntie Nirma's eyes. "Yes. Who have you chosen as the new raja?"

Auntie Nirma smiled. "Who said anything about a raja?"

"Then who—" Anula stood. "Are *you* wanting to be a raejina?"

"Of course not. My pathway is not clear."

Auntie Nirma's eyes twinkled as she led them to the secret door. It was in the middle of the hallway, a panel that sprang back when leaned on. Inside was a room with a low table in the center, long enough for a dozen to sit. Books lined the walls, a library of hidden texts only men penned and men read. But here, women studied pages on flowers and trees and poisonous animals, learned of all the rajas past, analyzed the most prosperous rice paddy farms and hakuru harvesters, tracked Polonnaruwa's movements, and honed their knowledge into weapons. Not to kill but to grow.

"Nothing worth wanting is had easily, girl." Auntie Nirma's voice cut sharply, pulling Anula's gaze from the shelves. "Are you committed to your pathway or not?"

Voices buzzed in her ears. The voices of her village. The ones three men deemed unimportant enough to sacrifice. It didn't matter if Anula believed the Heavens' hand in it. She believed in Auntie Nirma's conviction and the justice deserved. She pressed Uncle Manoj's journal to her chest. "Yes."

"Good." Auntie Nirma dropped a stack of books on the table. "If you do this right, songs will be sung about you."

"And if I do it wrong?"

Auntie Nirma raised a brow. "A pyre will be built instead."

Twelve years felt like nothing and everything all at once. Now, Anula shook off the memory. This life's purpose required focus.

The moon peeked through the clouds as she flew through the shrubbery of the Pleasure Gardens. As far as anyone knew, she was in her room, praying and preparing her soul for service to the raja.

She had a different kind of preparation in mind.

The gardens were known for being vast, hosting every flower and plant imaginable on the island: pink nelum, white kadupul, yellow allamanda. They called to her in soft moonlight, but she didn't slow to smell them. Anula had eyes for only one plant tonight. She turned another corner, and there, in the center of the garden as if waiting for her, were the red-petaled flowers of her dreams.

Quickly, she plucked as many kaneru as she could fit into a small pouch, tying the string in a knot. The hair on her arms rose, her heart beating a little faster.

Prophet Ayaan. Commander Dilshan. Raja Mahakuli Mahatissa.

She repeated the names, her promise to the kingdom.

Well stocked and ready to meet the raja, Anula gripped the window to haul herself back inside the concubine estate. She had one leg halfway through when a small curse sounded from around the corner. She fell silent and rigid.

Perhaps a guard had seen her flitting about the gardens. Or they'd checked in on her, only to find her room empty.

"For prayer's sake." A fierce voice whispered into the dark.

Anula cocked her head. Guards wouldn't bother with whispers. Whoever it was, they weren't meant to be outside either.

She hung in the window frame for a second. Leaving was the safest route. But young women who valued the honor of being a concubine didn't dare break rules. No, only those with agendas sneaked through windows and ventured into the midnight hours.

Agendas that might interfere with hers.

Silently sliding off the windowsill, Anula tiptoed across the soft grass.

"Please, please." A short stick of a figure fumbled with two picks at the locked door. She wasn't a guard, though the clothing suggested a servant. A maid, possibly. But why would a maid be picking locks?

Anula ran through the names and roles on her list, the ones who were known to be disloyal to the kingdom. None placed a young maid at the concubine estate. Which meant this might be a new threat, one she had to deal with herself.

Quietly, she made her way over, leaned against the door, and slid into view. "Do you often break into sacred places?"

The maid jumped so violently, she stumbled over herself. Anula grabbed hold of her arm to keep her from falling. She was at least a foot shorter and wrapped in a tight blue sari. Curry stained the front.

She couldn't be a thief; she'd be defter with a lock. But if she wasn't in league with the traitors and she wasn't a pilferer, then who was she?

"I wasn't aware that kitchen maids picked their way into work."

"Shhh," the girl hissed, glancing over her shoulder. Anula followed her gaze. The hushed garden stared back.

"Were you meeting someone?" Anula smirked. "Practicing the gentle touch of a concubine?"

The maid flinched. "How—no!"

She twitched at her own loudness, eyes roving the space around them as if someone might be watching or had just been there.

"You know you can do that alone, safely in your room."

The maid blushed. "I—I haven't—"

"I could show you." Anula waggled her eyebrows. "It's a particular gift every concubine must have."

"No!" The maid waved her off. "No, no! I had to go. I mean, I forgot the fresh mangoes for breakfast in the morning. Cook will have my head if they're not there. So I went to the palace to fetch some."

Anula eyed her clearly empty pockets. "Did you eat them on the way?"

The maid looked her up and down, surprise rising. "Wait, you're a concubine. What are you doing out here?"

"I asked you first." Anula wagged a finger. "Or should I sound the alarm that an intruder is near?"

"Please, no!" she whisper-shouted, grabbing Anula's finger. "I'll lose my position."

"Then why risk leaving?"

The girl straightened. "I could ask the same of you."

"But again, I asked first."

The maid pursed her lips, raised her chin, and made a decision of some sort. "My name is Premala. I'm a kitchen maid."

Anula ran through the other list in her head. The one Auntie Nirma had her memorize of potential allies, potential enemies. Premala was on neither. Anula had no idea who she was or where she'd come from. It was unlike Auntie Nirma to miss a detail, let alone an entire person.

"When did you start?"

"Just a few weeks ago. So I really can't afford trouble." Premala's face was open, honest except for the tightness at the corners of her eyes.

"My name is Anula, and I like long walks in the night," she said and held out her palm. Time to buy some trust. "Give me the pins."

Premala's gaze dropped to two small jeweled hair clips.

"Next time you sneak out for *mangoes*," Anula said, turning to the window, "leave yourself an easier way to get back inside."

Between the frames of the windowsill sat a diamond glinting in the moonlight. She placed a pin beside it, holding the window slightly ajar.

"Then you slide out and in." She smiled. "Silently, tenderly—no need for anyone's assistance."

Premala choked a cough. "Was that a jest?"

Anula winked and lifted herself through the window, before helping Premala and handing back the pin. A clink of metal echoed down the hall, voices rising with it.

"—to think he grew up down the street," one said.

"Never would have thought he had it in him," another said. "We'll have to be more vigilant."

A cold chill fell down Anula's spine. *Guards.* Their shadows crept closer. There wasn't time to flee—she wouldn't make the corner. They'd see her or at least part of her.

A hand wrapped around her elbow, pulled her sideways and into a crouch behind a tall potted palm. Premala pressed a finger to her mouth. The vase itself was wide enough to hide them both. The long, thick leaves hung perfectly around the lip.

Premala had saved her.

The unknown, who'd lied about mangoes, had risked helping her instead of thinking of herself. Why? They weren't allies; they were barely acquaintances.

The guards passed without a second glance. Anula slid out first.

"Thanks," she whispered.

Premala held up the pins. "You too." Without another word, she crossed the hall and disappeared into the shadows.

Anula's eyes narrowed. There was something fishy about that

girl. No one saved another without reason. The world was crueler than that. Whatever secrets she held close, Anula would have to discover them. She couldn't have someone disrupt Auntie Nirma's plans. Too many lives were at stake.

She squeezed the brimming bag of kaneru. Anyone who stood in their way would meet the seeds' particularly deadly poison. Since the Heavens' hands were nonexistent, Anula intended to keep her own pathway clear.

6

LANGUISHING IN MEMORY WOULD NOT BRING REERI CLOSER TO touching his life again. He snapped his shadows to fend it off, determination settling in. Yet as he moved from one end of the aether to another, Wessamony caught his eye.

The Lord departed his court and swept through the space betwixt the Heavens to stand before the pearl-white gates. Reeri paused and crouched in the darkness.

The two Heavens did not often speak—less did they meet.

However, five Divinities appeared, floating toward the gates like wind on a summer's breeze. Their sizes and shapes differed greatly, their features neither one thing nor another, yet everything.

"I have done what you requested," Wessamony declared. "I restored balance centuries ago. It would have been quicker, had my power not been bound to the Maha and Yala Equinox. Yet you denied my ascendance. Have you another grievance?"

Reeri tensed. He had long since stopped wondering what plan of Wessamony's he had derailed. Wessamony would not tell him. Clearly it was not to forge bargains in the way the Divinities answered prayers, else the Yakkas would not have been banished. It was also clear the Lord thought them mere pawns, not important enough to know details. Playthings to be destroyed and brought back at will.

The shortest Divinity spoke. "Indeed, the chaos that once choked the Earth and terrified the humans has been extinguished. That is not the reason for our summons."

Realization coiled around Reeri's mind. The humans had beseeched the Heavens for aid. Against the Yakkas.

Wessamony smirked. "Have you at long last seen the error in your judgment? Have you come to acknowledge my worthiness and invite me into your court, ready for the age of One Heaven, our powers balanced in use and control?"

The Divinities exchanged a glance. Again the shortest spoke. "Grateful are we for your swiftness, despite the constraint put upon you by the birthing of the cosmos. Unfortunately, an invitation we cannot grant, as a creator you are not."

A blue hue kindled at the base of Lord Wessamony's horns. "You created the humans, and I created the Yakkas. Moreover, I have undone them to mere phantoms. I am creator and destroyer, balance incarnate."

The tallest of Divinities shook their head. "You were not designed to create."

"You are the Lord of the Second Heavens, the Great Destroyer," another said.

"I am both," Wessamony claimed, the flames reaching higher. "*That* is worthy of no constraint."

"You cannot be. The cosmos created you as one, the Heavens as two," the shortest said. "You have threatened the balance with selfish action."

"Nothing is unbalanced," Wessamony growled. "My creation—"

"Your *abomination* caused chaos," the Divinities scoffed.

"I have rectified that."

"There would have been no need, if you had stayed within your bounds."

"My bounds." Wessamony's voice dropped. It shook with strain. "I am more than my bounds. I deserve unfettered power."

"And what would you do with it?" the tallest asked.

Flames danced in Wessamony's eyes. "Give the humans what they want, if the bargain is right. Retribution. Vengeance. Power and dominion."

The Divinities ruffled. "You intend to unbalance the Earth with suffering?"

"Your blessings have long since outweighed my destruction. I will bring true balance."

"You will bring the end to all we know," another accused. "You want for control, not of your own powers, but of the cosmos. To watch it unbecome and burn."

No. Reeri blinked with revelation. Wessamony wanted to burn it himself, revel in the slow scorch, and do it all again. As he did with the Yakkas. A cycle of torment and destruction for his pleasure and glory.

The Divinities grimaced betwixt the pearl-white bars, and with a flourish of their robes, they turned away. Save one.

"We know you seek Fate's relic," they said, the cosmos mirrored in their eyes. "We warned you that day: your actions will lead to your demise. Take heed and cease."

A flash of blue sizzled up Wessamony's horns. "You are jealous! Envious that I gave the humans a better way to their requests, that they favored the Yakkas over you. They shall favor me and destruction, too. You are frightened of my power and know that with the relic, you cannot stop me."

No, they could not.

The idea shivered down Reeri's shadow. Wessamony would

be unstoppable, all-powerful. Yet the Divinities did not act. They did not even react, continuing their slow climb up the stairs. Why?

Balance.

They believed in the balance of the cosmos. They believed Wessamony was meant to be the Lord of the Second Heavens.

Yet…what if he was not?

"This will be your final warning," the Divinity said, blinking the cosmos from their eyes and turning their seraphic back on the devil who dared try to slither into their ranks.

Their promise hung heavy in the air.

For the sake of the Yakkas, the Earth, and all the cosmos, Wessamony could not wield Fate's Bone Blade. There was only one way to ensure that.

Reeri had to find it before the Maha Equinox in one month, before Wessamony could descend to Earth and claim it himself.

7

Two carved figures sat at the base of the palace entrance.

One held a conch shell; the other wore a lotus on its head. Mirrored grins spread across the stone, more taunting than inviting. *Do you dare?* they seemed to ask.

Always, Anula answered, steeling herself and taking the first step inside.

After a night of preparation and a day of soaking in scented oils, she had been deemed ready for the raja. The palace, the in-between, opened for her. As her guards led her through the vast halls, each of the blessed gifts whispered a song.

Listen to the sounds of your heart's true home, a statue sang silently, the voice not inside her head but within her bones. Gooseflesh rose up Anula's neck.

"Come see the truth," a mirror cooed aloud.

Take a walk with ones long past, promised a painting of a group of women. Concubines of the first raja, their hands outstretched to welcome one in.

But Anula wasn't interested in the blessed gifts, hadn't been since she was a child. What good did indulging with parting presents do? The Heavens had given them as a consolation prize, a balm to the wound of their leaving.

Raja Mahakuli Mahatissa was the goal. He was the most important link in the chain of Auntie Nirma's plan. Anula ran her hand across her necklace, felt the sapphire holding the persuasion tincture. Tonight was not for justice, but a stepping stone on her pathway. The raja would taste her poison later.

The guards led her through the palace, warm tones of a setting sun casting shadows between the array of sculptures and canvas. Courtiers milled about, vying for one gift over another, the longest line behind a small bronze statue of a woman. The guards escorted Anula around them, practically hugging a wall filled with paintings. Cautiously, she curved her shoulders in. It was said that merely touching one would transport a person inside.

"Careful!" the guard in front yelled. Anula crashed into her back as she abruptly halted.

An arm emerged from the last painting. Then a leg and a body. A woman laughed as she stepped from the art, as if descending a set of stairs. Pink tinged her cheeks. She'd come from a depiction of a celebration, no doubt with plenty of palm wine.

"Watch yourself," the guard scolded the courtier. "Lest you jeopardize one of the Raja's Jewels!"

The woman paused, her face souring as she took in Anula with her tight hatte, bare midriff, and plunging neckline. An outfit chosen to mix perfectly with the tincture at her throat.

"Perhaps you should watch where you're going," the courtier chastised the guard. "I am conversing with the Heavens, as is my birthright." She marched away with chin held high.

The guard scoffed, moving forward once more, checking over her shoulder to ensure Anula was safe. "You'll get used to it, if called on again. The courtiers are jealous of the concubines."

"Why?" she asked. "As she said, it's her birthright to be here, not mine."

"Exactly. Rumor has it that the raja's chamber is filled with the best of the blessed gifts. Yet only he and those he invites inside ever have the chance to witness them."

Anula's nostrils flared. "How devoted the courtiers are to the Heavens."

"We both know devotion has nothing to do with it."

No. Greed was a higher master.

The guard stopped outside a tall wooden door that bore a carving of the moon, sun, and a lion bearing a sword. The banner of the Anuradhapura Kingdom.

The raja's sentries nodded to the concubine guards, the passing off of goods complete. "Make yourself comfortable," one said. "The raja will attend to you when he is ready."

The doors swung open, a finger of smoke curling out and around Anula's ankles. She clenched a fist, took a breath. This was it. All she had studied for, all Auntie Nirma had planned, culminated tonight. She would leave this room in one of two ways: a success or a failure.

Her path leading to a crown or a pyre.

She grasped the corner of her skirt, straightened her shoulders, and stepped inside.

There were plenty of rumors in the kingdom that had no real teeth, but the one about the raja's chamber was true.

It was a veneration to the Heavens. Each piece of art was either of a Yakka or a Divinity. Mirrors were adorned with small ornamental figurines between the leaves and animals; pillows were embroidered with their likenesses. Every inch was taken by them, even the ceiling. A mural covered the length of it. Yakkas and

Divinities crowded the space, leisurely lounging on beds of clouds, emulating the idea of a peaceful, coexistent cosmos. The sun and stars beamed upon their smiling and grimacing faces. No blood marred their relics or hands, no death spoken of, merely caring eyes turned toward Earth.

Whoever painted it must have been blind.

Anula continued her walk through the chamber, each step easing the tension in her muscles. She could do this. She was ready. The scent of sweets and wine wafted from somewhere deeper within, calling her to the moment it would all happen, promising her success. And when she was raejina and this was her room, the art would be the first thing to go.

Especially the paintings. They were by far the most talked about, the gift every child dreamed of experiencing. Who wouldn't want to leave their reality for something grander? Just a touch and step, and a courtier could walk along a beach or participate in a celebration that was centuries old. It was said that when the gifts had first been given, one could even walk between paintings, through a door that connected them all. The stories of old spoke of how rajas maneuvered through the kingdom this way, entering one painting in the palace shrine and exiting another in a stupa at the edge of a village. It enabled them to protect Anuradhapura.

But one didn't step from one painting straight into the next. The cosmos lay between. And at some point, people got lost, never to be seen again. So the Divinities had locked the doors and thrown away the key.

Anula paused at a small depiction of a stupa. The bulbous white monument crowned with a spire almost paled in comparison to the tall, intricate statues of the Yakkas that lined its courtyard. She'd heard of the shrine before. It had been one of the venerated places of prayer, until it was destroyed in a battle between usurpers.

Of course, she'd once wished to walk inside a painting, but that was before she'd known the truth of the Heavens. Why would she want to experience an abandoned love?

Eyes transfixed on the traitors within, she leaned in close to better view the one to whom she'd given her last prayer. The Blood Yakka Reeri. Teeth as sharp as a monkey, skin as red as fire. He snarled back at her. No kindness in his eyes, no care. Noth—

Anula tilted off balance, falling forward.

No. She couldn't let her skin touch any part of the painting. She didn't want to go inside. Ever. Spinning on her heel, she twirled, using the momentum to fling herself away. Right into a statue.

They tumbled to the floor, but instead of a crash or an echo of broken stone, the statue said, "I've never been accosted by one of my Jewels before."

Anula scoffed. "Don't call me—"

Her gaze rose, expecting to find a blessed gift. Instead, her eyes met the graying face of the raja.

"Forgive me, my raja," she said, struggling around her skirt to get off the raja responsible for her parents' death and let him stand.

Heat flooded her cheeks. She'd known it would be difficult, seeing him alive. But she had taken comfort that he would one day die by her hand, that he would meet justice and answer for the evil he had done.

Watching him breathe now stole any scrap of solace she'd held onto.

Jaw clenched, Anula schooled her features, swallowed the bile rising in her throat. Now was not the time. She must focus.

"There is nothing to forgive. We'll be in a similar position soon anyway." His words scraped along her skin. He took her hand. "Come."

He led her to the center of the chamber, where divans and cushions piled high around a low table. Bottles of palm wine were gracefully set out among incense candles, along with bananas, kiribath, and mangoes. Anula briefly thought of Premala.

"Tell me." The raja poured them both wine as they sat. "What made you want to serve me?"

"It's an honor to be a concubine."

"I was not part of the decision?" He raised a brow and drained his glass. "I'm disappointed."

Anula's fingers curled inside the folds of her skirt. Ego was all that this man was. Rings on every finger, a Jewel for every night, the city's store of palm wine, and rubbing Polonnaruwa's nose in their ambush defeat every chance he got. That was what his reign had been. Even if he were physically attractive, his heart was so withered, not even pigs would eat it. And yet he expected her to *want* him.

The only thing she wanted from Mahakuli Mahatissa was his slow death, choking on his own blood, his skin burned inch by inch—

The beads bit into her palm. Clarity rushed back. The plan was the plan for a reason. This raja had not yet played his final role: husband.

Fanning her lashes on the tips of her cheeks, she feigned shyness, just as Auntie Nirma had instructed. "It's not that, my raja. I only didn't want to shock you with the truth."

"Which is what?"

Anula touched her necklace, making a show of steeling herself, then scooted closer and drank her wine. She poured them both another glass. "My name is Anula. You took the throne when I was six. Usurpers have long plagued the Kingdom of Anuradhapura, but you are different."

She recited what she had studied of history, the lines Auntie Nirma had written out. For although the persuasion tincture was strong and lasted for nearly five days, it was most effective when paired with flattery.

"The people call you a savior, a hero who put to death the worst of the rulers. You were a mere boy when you saved us from his horrors, and again when you defeated the Kingdom of Polonnaruwa. I've dreamed of you since I was a little girl."

That part, at least, was true.

The raja held his wineglass, a smirk on his lips, a thirst in his eyes. "What did you dream?"

Anula blushed. "You can't expect me to tell."

"I do."

She whispered into the falling night, "I dreamed of serving you as wife."

"Ah, you've heard Prophet Ayaan foresees my marriage." The raja finished his wine, and as the cup touched the table, Anula poured more. "Did you also hear that I will have ten sons? My wife must be more than beautiful. She must be strong."

Anula sidled closer, noting that for the second time, he didn't notice the change in the wine's taste. The effects should already be setting in. "Am I not beautiful?"

The blacks of Mahakuli Mahatissa's eyes expanded, drowning out the brown of his irises. "You are."

Anula took his hands in hers, bracing herself against the cringe, and placed them on her hips. "Am I weak? Am I frail?"

"No," he breathed, long and deep. His clammy hands rubbed down to her thighs.

Anula stroked his oily hair. "The fortune tellers told me I would bear many children."

"Mm," he grunted as she placed her palm on his leg and drew circles with a finger.

"The Heavens have aligned our paths," she whispered in his ear.

"The Heavens," he murmured, breath rank. The dark of his eyes flickered.

This was it. This was her moment.

"The Heavens want for me to be the mother of your line. It is our destiny."

"It is our destiny," he repeated, jaw working, breath labored.

"The prophet would agree."

"The prophet would agree." Hunger pooled in his eyes as a hardness tented his sarong. He gripped her hips tightly and growled, "You are the mother of my line."

"I will be." Hoped bloomed in Anula's chest. She'd done it—she'd laid the path to a crown, not a pyre. Justice would have its day. She placed a hand over his heart as it sprinted and bucked. "We marry in two days' time. Now tell the prophet."

Mahakuli Mahatissa called out, downing the remaining wine as a servant rushed in. "Send a message to Prophet Ayaan and the rest of my court."

"Sir?" the servant asked.

The raja slammed the cup on the table and stared back at Anula, black eyes flickering with her tincture. "I have chosen a wife."

8

A WAIL STRETCHED INTO THE NOTHINGNESS OF THE AETHER.

It would be a cry, if shadows could shed tears.

Reeri dropped his latest shadow offering and coiled around Kama. "Are you all right?"

She wiped the depthless sockets of her eyes, stared at the dryness of her shadow hands. "Just checking."

Reeri frowned and shifted away from her, catching another offering. He had no time for Kama's dramatics.

She appeared an inch from his face. "Do you think I should cry? That the humans want for me to despond over them and the intercession I cannot provide against unrequited love?"

"I think they should try harder to find the relic if they care about their star-crossed love," Reeri said. That was what he would do, if he had found the one with whom his soul communed. But that was another facet of life he had been denied.

He leaned away from Kama to scan the new offering. He searched the words but found no footing. He tossed it on top of the ever-growing pile floating languidly about his lower form. The tower mocked him. It sneered at his scheme.

"What about you, Sohon?" Kama flitted across the nothingness, poked the shadow curled around himself. "Do you pity the dead whose loved ones refused to work harder for one of your memory books?"

Sohon's shadows writhed, a serpent ready to strike. "I do not pity the dead. They do not have to deal with you."

"Such callous Yakkas." Kama tutted.

"Says the Yakka responsible for heartbreak," Calu said, his shadows swirling as he came near.

Kama stuck out a twirling black tongue. "I care greatly for heartbreak. It is dark and beautiful and so sharply bitter, one cannot help but feel alive. It is a gift."

Reeri snorted. "You sound like *him*."

"Should I not? We are made in his image."

The lip of Reeri's shadow curled. Indeed, they were made in Wessamony's image, to do Wessamony's bidding, to ensure Wessamony's ascendance. It was not grace that preserved Reeri and the others. It was not mercy that had driven their Lord to offer atonement. It was greed.

Wessamony knew exactly what he was doing when he chose the four of them. The Yakkas of the heart, mind, memory, and blood. For what bargains were made out of passion? Those that brought heartache, insanity, torment, and pain.

Those that promised revenge.

Desiring its bittersweet taste, offerers used to agree to any term and feat. Yet even humans recognized a lost cause eventually.

Wessamony had taken a page from Reeri's book: for a bargain to be complete, the offerer must also seek the Bone Blade relic. In the beginning, they only needed to uncover information. Wessamony descended twice a year, on the Maha and Yala Equinox, and investigated himself, distrusting that a human would find such power and readily hand it over. Yet, as the decades gathered and no dagger was found, the parameters changed. Information was not good enough; they must bring proof. When that too failed him, he demanded they search. Find but not touch the relic.

Many humans attempted it. Many humans did not survive. Decades piled into a century, and on the cusp of two, the humans' wariness won out. Nearly a year had gone by since Calu found the last willing offerer. The number of rejected bargains far outweighed the accepted. It was a wonder anyone continued to pray at all, leaving Wessamony with nothing save his fear.

"What are you brooding about over there, No Yakka?" Calu asked.

"I do not brood." Reeri grimaced.

"'Brooding' is your middle name."

"That makes no—"

"He is stacking offerings," Kama interrupted. "Mayhap to smother himself with."

"Why is it that the Yakka of Lust is so preoccupied with death?" Reeri asked.

"He is deflecting." Sohon unraveled from his tight coil and joined the others. "He is hiding something."

"I am not."

"What is it?" Calu asked, craning his shadow neck to see the offering in Reeri's hand.

"The same as always, I am doing as Wessamony commanded."

"But you are happy about it."

"What?"

"I can see it in your eyes."

"We have no eyes."

"It is a plan!" Kama shouted. "He looked the same when he figured out a way for us all to leave the shrines."

A fevered smile widened across Calu's face. "*Finally.* What is my part?"

Reeri's shadows attempted to bristle. No one had a part. Reeri would act alone, suffer any consequences alone. "I plan nothing. Find your own offerings, or Wessamony will have all our souls."

"That is precisely why I need a part." Calu bent forward, leveled his empty gaze at Reeri. A flicker started at his chin. "You feel it, too, do you not? It is time to escape the prison."

If shadows had pulses, Reeri's would trip.

"And set the captives free." Kama chuckled darkly.

"Tell us, Reeri." Sohon's edges roiled. "We are ready."

No, Reeri wanted to say. He had involved the others once before, and look where it had ended. He could not bear to damn them further, could not bear more blood on his hands.

For if this failed, if he did not truly rid the Second Heavens of Wessamony, Wessamony would rid them of Reeri. And all who followed him.

"You do not have a choice," Calu said, snatching another offering. He proffered it to Reeri. "We are in this together, whether you want us to be or not. So tell us the plan."

Reeri glanced at each of their phantom faces, the trust swirling inside.

He did not deserve it.

But he could earn it.

Redemption for him, freedom for all.

Snatching the shadow from Calu, Reeri said, "First, we need an offering Wessamony cannot ignore."

9

The ruby silk draped perfectly over Anula's body.

The wedding mehendhi encased her arms in intricate patterns, from fingertips to elbows. The jewel-encrusted hatte clung heavily; the bell earrings pulled at her ears, the thick chain stretching to her hoop nose ring. A large headpiece dangled down to her brow, the diamonds fanning widely. The weight pressed against her, but did nothing to block the frenzied thoughts spinning in her mind.

If you do this right, songs will be sung about you.

And if I do it wrong?

A pyre will be built instead.

Cursed Yakkas, she couldn't think about that. Not an hour before she wed her parents' murderer. Not on the day the entire plan hinged on.

To settle her nerves, she had made a tincture, but it tasted awful without tea. Gold and ruby bangles clinked as she turned the corner into the kitchen, then skidded to a halt. Two maids embraced in the dark of the hall.

Kissing.

The pair split quickly, cheeks flushing, Premala's the brightest.

"Ah." Anula smiled, grateful for the distraction. "So this was who you met in the gardens."

The other maid shrieked and fled, a flower dropping to the ground.

"U-um," Premala stammered, rooted in place. "Sure. I mean yes—she had the mangoes—" She broke off and bowed so deeply, she nearly tumbled over.

Anula wondered if she was even capable of not acting suspicious. As for the other maid, perhaps she was part of it, their embrace a farce to cover the trade of information. Though it hadn't looked false.

"Please, my raejina—my almost raejina, don't tell."

"Calm down." Anula waved her off and plucked the flower. Pink nelum. She handed it to Premala, whose face matched the color perfectly. "Just don't lie to me next time."

"Next time?" she squealed.

"I seem to have a knack for catching you doing things you aren't supposed to be doing," Anula said, heading into the kitchen. "Eventually, I'll want the truth. That's how secrets work between friends."

"Friends?" The squeal came again.

Allies. Unless the truth of Premala landed her on the wrong list. But Anula couldn't explain that. The girl would probably start hyperventilating.

"Would you make me tea? I didn't sleep a wink last night. And I believe there's a big event happening in my life soon. Don't want to look peaky."

Premala bit her lip, dancing on her tiptoes to the kettle. "Yes, um, but…I'm new, and…my family isn't well-known. My father's a fisherman and—"

"Is that why you came here, to send money back home?" Anula's attention caught.

"Um, partly," Premala said, setting the water to boil and readying the tea leaves. "Though my father hates to accept it."

"Why?"

"He says it's not right, a daughter having to feed the family when he's perfectly able. If it weren't for the Polonnaruwans, he wouldn't need help. But they've taken over our village, and they tax every fisherman, every morning."

Anula pressed a hand to her necklace. "They've occupied your home?"

Premala's head hung low. "Eighty percent of his catch, that's the tax. He barely has any left to eat, let alone trade. He only complies for the sake of my brothers and sister. I don't know what they'd do to them otherwise."

Heat rose quickly in Anula, burning up the fear that had tried to tangle in her veins. This was why she was here, why she risked songs and pyres. People shouldn't have to choose between starving and being killed. Or worse, turned traitor.

Anula paused. Plenty had chosen the third option; Auntie Nirma wrote their names on lists, sent missives with updates. Would she find Premala's one day?

"So, you see," Premala said, "I'm the lowest of the caste. We can't be friends."

"Do I look like I care about caste?"

Premala's doe eyes took her in. "You look like you're about to become the raejina. So yes."

An ember of tension flickered to life. "Well, I don't. I do care about tea. And a fish bun, if you have any. Mangoes work, too." She winked.

"Does the raja like your jests?"

Anula raised a brow.

"Forgive me!" Premala spun back to the kettle, knocking over not one but two platters of rice and curry.

She wasn't a thief, and from the looks of it, she wasn't trained to be a maid either. Who was she?

"What are you doing?" A voice rang out. "I told you to bring the food to the palace. Great Divinities, what have you done? No, don't spill that!"

But Premala had already dropped the tea leaves and fumbled the boiling water. The kettle bounced on the table and crashed into a bowl of seeni sambal. Water drowned the onions and dried fish.

"You worthless thing!" the cook yelled, her skin flaming red from wrist to forehead. "Get to the palace and do as I told!"

"Yes, right away." Premala nodded, lip trembling.

"I requested tea from her," Anula asserted.

The woman yelped in surprise before falling into a deep bow. "Forgive me, my—"

"Do you scream at all your maids?"

The cook straightened, shame coloring her face.

"Do you enjoy watching them cry?" Anula narrowed her eyes at the woman. "Does it make you feel powerful?"

The cook dropped her head.

"Don't be so rude, girl," chastised a familiar voice.

Anula spun. Waltzing into the kitchen, in the tightest emerald sari, was Auntie Nirma. "You made it."

"Of course I did." She waved her hands at the servants. "Leave us."

Premala was the first to go, breaking out in nearly a run. As the kitchen emptied, Auntie Nirma strode closer. She was such a tiny thing—a head and a half shorter with delicate bone structure any woman would envy—but there was a strength in her stature. She stopped a mere inch away, never touching. "You are beautiful, Anula. Radiant as the sun in the driest season."

"So things shrivel under my glare?"

"Only the weak things."

A peal of bells chimed, and Anula glanced over her shoulder to the window. The midday sun was high, the heat wafting through. It coiled around her earrings, settled around her shoulders.

A guard rushed in. "There you are. It's time."

Anxiety rippled through her. Anula took a steadying breath and repeated her mantra in her head.

"Fear for nothing, Anula," Auntie Nirma said, heading to the door. "Destiny is on our side today. To ensure it, I've bargained the Yakkas for favor."

Gathering the length of her skirt, Anula shook her head. "How many times do I have to tell you that prayers do nothing?"

"How many times do I have to tell you that you're wrong?" Auntie Nirma glanced over her shoulder. "Faith starts where strength ends, Anula. No one is above that law of the world. Not even you."

The walk from the concubine estate to the palace was much the same as before; the only difference was the destination. They passed door after door, room after room, furnished with cushions and divans, or not furnished at all, depending on the art displayed. Rooms with only one bronze statue, rooms with only paintings, rooms with mirrors delicately decorated and facing away from one another. Rooms that whispered, rooms that sang. And a room darker than all others.

Tendrils of smoke curled out like fingers, beckoning. Anula shifted to peer in as they passed. Candles and incense and bloodred petals covered the floor. The palace shrine. Perhaps that was where Auntie Nirma had prayed.

"Ready?" the eldest guard asked.

Before she could answer, they opened a set of carved doors inset with silver and brass ornamentation, and the wedding ceremony began. It was opulent, to say the least. Blooms of all kinds twisted around pillars, spilled across tables, and hung from the ceiling. Oil lamps adorned the walls, casting the room in a golden hue, glinting off the gilded throne high on the dais where the raja, in his gemstone-embellished silks, now stood. Where Anula would one day sit, wearing her own silks, her own gems, with his moonstone crown on *her* head.

If she pulled this off.

The terrace doors were opened wide, the warmth of the drought coasting along the air, swirling around the courtiers inside. Anula's muscles twitched. The room was full. Palace officials, central administration, the board of ministers, and all their wives were in attendance. She could name them each, but only one mattered.

In a sea of earth tones, the emerald green of Auntie Nirma's sari stood stark—a siren calling Anula forward. Familiar faces fanned around her, those like-minded women proficient in warfare strategies, politics, and diplomacy cultivated over the years to aid her rule. What would happen to them if she failed? Would they get a pyre, too?

The prophet and the raja waited patiently as she finished her advance. She dropped the hem of her skirt and met Mahakuli Mahatissa's eyes—drowned in inky blackness. The tincture still held him captive. Tension slipped from her bones. This was going to work.

"The great Raja Mahakuli Mahatissa has decided upon a wife," Prophet Ayaan began. "May all the prayers of the kingdom bless this union."

The air caught between Anula's throat and lungs. With her focus solely on not retching at the sight of the raja, she'd forgotten she'd see the prophet. The half-graying, half-balding head of the second man she intended to kill stood before her for the first time. A long white beard reached to his chest, to a pendant of gold and rubies.

"We thank the Heavenly realms for their protection over the years, continued watchfulness, and a future of ten strong seeds."

His voice scraped up Anula's back, nipping at her neck. He was so near. All she had to do was touch her necklace once and two names would meet justice. Three if the commander was here, too. Her eyes flashed over Mahakuli Mahatissa's shoulder. Was Commander Dilshan watching in the safety of the crowd, hiding as though he were in the jungle? But her gaze only found Auntie Nirma, the woman who'd finished raising her. She dipped her head in encouragement.

Anula's heart squeezed. It shouldn't be Auntie Nirma.

Amma and Thaththa should be there, dipping their heads and smiling wide. Not the ministers or the courtiers or the prophet or the raja. It shouldn't have been in the palace or with a raja. A simple village ceremony, with simple silks and simple observance, and a man whose touch made her feel safe and at home. That's what should have been. What could have been.

Yet it wasn't.

As if hearing her thoughts, Auntie Nirma smiled, cunning and clever, a reminder that she had let go of that dream to take hold of a better one. Anula nodded in return. She was focused, ready. A weapon honed. She didn't need the Heavens' pathway or answers to prayers. Years of hard study would bring Anula their dream of justice.

Auntie Nirma's face fell suddenly. The women around her murmured, shifting, gazes cutting to the side. One leaned down to whisper in her ear. Her mouth popped open, wide eyes locking on Anula.

The blast of a bullhorn hammered through the throne room.

The doors opened with a clang, and the royal army flooded in. "The gates have been breached! Protect the raja!"

Chaos broke out.

It started with screams—a familiar sound raking down Anula's bones. She shuddered as ministers and administration, courtiers and concubines fled. They surged toward the open doors, bottlenecking, throwing one another to the ground—no lives but their own mattered. In seconds, their turmoil swallowed the emerald-green sari.

"Auntie!" Anula's heart lurched. She surged forward, only to be pulled back, a firm hand on her arm.

"Keep her safe," Mahakuli Mahatissa commanded the soldiers surrounding them. "Is it Polonnaruwa?"

"No, sir," the soldier answered, taking Anula from him. "An enemy from within."

"Usurper," the raja seethed. He pulled a sword from another soldier's side and dove into the fray. As if a hero.

Anula squirmed, but the soldier held her tight. "We must leave."

"Absolutely not."

War cries. Foot soldiers. The beat of a drum.

A nightmare, *her* nightmare. Men trampled over courtiers, breaking up the throng by throwing people against the wall. They beat iron swords against their chest plates, anger and triumph on their faces, bloodlust in their eyes. The banner of Anuradhapura flew high.

Usurper on the move. Allied with palace traitors and Polonnaruwa Kingdom. Must hurry.

Auntie Nirma's information had been right. And Anula had not been fast enough. The royal soldiers streamed to meet the usurper's army. Iron clashed with iron. Blood sprayed across the pristine marble floor.

Red sky. Red hands. Re—

Panic crushed the air in Anula's lungs. She searched over the heads of the soldiers, past prone, bleeding bodies, but the emerald sari was nowhere in sight. *Good. She must have escaped.* She was small, nimble, sharp. Perhaps she was halfway through the palace, safe.

"Raja Mahakuli Mahatissa," a man called out above the noise, sword raised over his head. The usurper, no doubt. "Face me and prove your worth, or die by the hand of a greater man!"

The sea of fighting parted, and the raja stepped forward, swinging his sword.

"No!" Anula burst free of the soldier, reaching for the raja. With Auntie Nirma safe, it was up to her to salvage their plan. If the raja died—

He surged. "This is *my* kingdom!"

Then he tripped.

Sprawled.

The crown bounced away as he laid bare his neck.

Only for a moment—yet plenty of time for a usurper. They were great at one thing and one thing only: taking the heads of rajas.

Blood squirted from Mahakuli Mahatissa's throat, gushing over his murderer like a waterfall. A dark mass of flesh flew through the air, thumped against the throne room floor, and rolled toward Anula's feet.

She looked into the dead eyes of the raja's crownless head. "Thrice-cursed Yakkas."

There was a beat, a sound of rushing wind and waves between her ears. A memory of another man, dead at her feet. She shook it away, refocused. She couldn't become a dead raja's wife. She'd have to—

"How dare you, Chora Naga." A voice yelled above the cacophony of fighting.

No. She was supposed to be out of the palace.

The usurper laughed, meeting the fuming gaze of an old woman in an emerald-green sari. "Hello, Nirma."

Anula blanched. They knew each other.

"We had a deal," Auntie Nirma said. "You would stand down, and in time, Anula would make you raja."

Lie. The thought flew through her mind as she recovered. Auntie Nirma's missive had said Chora Naga was in league with Polonnaruwa. This deal must have been part of her second plan. The one they'd implement for the rival kingdom, once justice was served here. It was surely a ploy.

A failed ploy.

"I got tired of waiting," Chora Naga yelled. "Besides, the kingdom can't be ruled by some woman."

The spear flew from Chora Naga's arm, sang in the air. The crunch of bone echoed as it cleaved Auntie Nirma's chest, ribs splintering.

The world tilted.

"Anuradhapura is mine!" Chora Naga screamed. War cries pulsed in Anula's ears.

"Auntie?" she breathed, tripping to the prone body on the floor. "Auntie? Speak to me."

Blood bloomed, like a rose among thorns. Like—

Red sky. Red hands. Red water.

Look away.

"Anula, I—I," she sputtered, hand fluttering at jagged bone.

"I'm here," Anula choked. "It's going to be fine."

Keranu. Hemlock. Thel endaru. She mentally raced through the poisons and tinctures in her necklace. Which one would sustain Auntie Nirma long enough to escape? To find help, medicine and cloth and thread and—

"Yakkas," Auntie Nirma wheezed. A feeble hand lifted, aiming to cup Anula's face. It fell before arrival.

"What?"

But Auntie Nirma didn't respond. Blood stained her teeth. A coldness hardened her eyes. Anula's lungs seized.

She knew that look. Saw it in every face she'd ever loved, every face she'd ever lost. It haunted her dreams, hounded her thoughts. And even when her vision filled and swam with tears, she could not unsee it.

It was the only thing left for her when all else was torn away.

10

The room swam in and out of focus.

"For Anuradhapura!" the usurper cried, returning Anula to herself.

The hall erupted into victorious chants. Chora Naga's men howled at the ceiling, at the open-air windows and terrace, calling to the guards and army outside. She couldn't stay any longer. But…

An ache started in her chest.

No. Auntie Nirma had taught her to hone her grief, not succumb to it. She wouldn't fail now. Anula pulled away from her auntie's body, grasped her skirt, and ran. Through the halls, past door after door, room after room, her heart beat erratically. Leave. Go. Hurry.

But where?

She skidded to a stop. The concubines would take her back, but Chora Naga knew her. There was little chance he'd choose her as a wife. She wasn't sure she could keep her hand from the poisons long enough for it to matter anyway. Chora Naga had stolen two things from her: Auntie Nirma and Mahakuli Mahatissa. His justice would come swiftly.

She should go back to Kekirawa, then, to converge with her allies, what was left of them, and to make new ones. Devise a new plan.

A pang pierced her heart. Auntie Nirma wouldn't be returning to Kekirawa. Her nephew would be. The heir to Uncle Manoj's fortune and estate, including the secret library. Still, she could bargain for shelter, gather their notes and books, and start building a new circle of political aides, stay until…

Until what? Another usurper came? One who wouldn't remember that she'd been a raja's concubine, proposed to be married? Anula's shuddered. Leaving wasn't an option.

She ripped the sari pota from her hair and threw it into the void of the hall, turned to the wall, and screamed at a painting. Had it all been for nothing? The long hours of study, books her only friends, justice her only dream. Memorizing Uncle Manoj's journal. Supporting Auntie Nirma's efforts.

They were supposed to die at her hand!

Prophet Ayaan. Commander Dilshan. Raja Mahakuli Mahatissa. Every man and woman who used their power to crush others, who forgot who they were supposed to protect, who cared for no one but themselves.

She was supposed to be raejina—the first raejina of Anuradhapura.

She was supposed to bring in an age of peace. Change the kingdom for good, in her parents' name, for their justice and the justice of all others forevermore.

That was what she wanted.

That was what Auntie Nirma had lived for. *Died* for. It couldn't all be for nothing. It couldn't all end here. Anula wouldn't allow it. She wouldn't fail the one who'd raised her when everyone else had turned their backs.

Yakkas. Auntie Nirma's last word rang in her head. But what did it mean? Anula kicked the wall. "I don't need a riddle. I need a Yakkas-damned miracle."

She took a sharp breath as the idea slithered up her spine.

Clutching her skirt, Anula ran to the last place she'd ever considered useful.

Beads of sweat clung to her forehead and dripped down the line between her breasts as she crossed the threshold of the shrine. Fingers of smoke reached out for her, coiling around her wrists and drawing her inside. Rows of candles lined the walls. Depictions of Yakkas hung on the left, Divinities on the right. In the center sat a low table, offerings brimming.

The offering.

She hadn't given one since that night. Amma had always said that an offering could be anything—food, fabric, worship, devotion. It must only be a sacrifice. The greater the request, the greater the price.

Anula touched her necklace. Parting with it would certainly be a sacrifice. One she wasn't willing to give. Perhaps the other jewelry? No, they meant nothing to her. Neither did her sari. Perhaps she could offer devotion, the one thing she'd promised never to give to anything that demanded faith. The thought set her skin crawling.

Devotion was a worthy sacrifice, but was it great enough? Her request was certainly large. What composed a great sacrifice?

Their faces appeared suddenly. Amma. Thaththa. Auntie Nirma. They had all lived and died for her. Loved her, heart and soul.

A great offering, given at great cost.

That held much more value than devotion. Anula swallowed the bile that threatened to rise in her throat. She didn't allow the question of what they'd do with it to rise, too. She pulled out an earring and stabbed the metal end into her palm, only one Yakka in her mind.

Blood dripped slowly onto the table, hitting the wood with a splash.

"Great Blood Yakka of the Second Heavens, hear my prayer. Grant me the first crown as raejina of Anuradhapura." Anula spoke loudly. "For today, I offer my soul."

11

"O MIGHTY HEAVENS AND ALL THE WRETCHES BETWEEN THEM," Calu cursed over Reeri's shoulder.

All else was silence.

Reeri had gone still, his edges frozen like a mountain peak in winter. It could not be that simple. Could it?

The Yakkas gathered around him, stared at the shadow offering betwixt his fingers. A shiver floated through them.

Great Blood Yakka of the Second Heavens, hear my prayer. Grant me the first crown of raejina of Anuradhapura. For today, I offer my soul.

No human had ever sacrificed a soul.

"Wessamony cannot ignore this one," Kama whispered.

"No," Reeri agreed.

"What now?" Sohon asked.

"Now"—Reeri stood, gaze toward the court of torment—"I make a bargain with our Lord for us to return to Earth."

Sounds of anguish greeted him at court.

As Reeri came close, Wessamony leaned toward a Yakka, sharp

fingernails pressing in. He slowly clawed at the shadow, striping off a length of their face. The Yakka swallowed a scream.

"I have not summoned you." Wessamony slashed again, and again, until he extracted a cry.

"No, my Lord." If shadows had stomachs, Reeri's would empty itself across the marble floor.

"Why do you disturb me?"

"Grandest apologies." He falsified a bow. "I have found your offering."

Wessamony straightened. "A human willing to find the relic?"

"An offering of a soul."

Wessamony sucked his fangs. Reeri tensed. Souls held power. It was said Wessamony had wielded one to create the Yakkas and one to create a new form for himself, one without a fetter. Yet the latter had shriveled into a husk and blown away into the cosmos. Hunger refocused Wessamony's eyes. "With that, they can ask for a great many things."

"Yes. Such sacrifices come with commitment, too. I do not doubt their conviction. They will agree to elevated terms."

"Then be on with it!"

Reeri shifted. This was his only chance. "First, I have an idea, my Lord."

"I do not want your ideas," Wessamony said, beginning a slow walk along the line of bound Yakkas. They shivered as he passed.

Reeri pressed on. "Instead of waiting for the humans to search and find, grant us permission to return to Earth and fetch it ourselves."

"I cannot undo the banishment, Reeri."

"No, yet as we have seen, there are loopholes. The offering of a soul—it could be our tether. We would not have our own bodies, but those of others. Once the relic is in our hands, we will return. Atoned and redeemed, to live in your court without torment."

Wessamony spun. "What be this, terms?"

Reeri squared his shoulders. "A bargain."

Wessamony's horns tinted blue.

"For centuries, we have placed success in human hands. Place it now in mine."

"And the others?"

"It will be faster with four."

Suspicious eyes narrowed. "All this for atonement? No other scheme, Blood Yakka?"

"It was my fault, as you say my Lord. Is it not, then, my burden?"

Wessamony nodded. "Indeed. You have your bargain. With conditions."

Reeri held in the relief. "Of course, my Lord."

"Bring me the Bone Blade by the Maha Equinox in four weeks." Wessamony smiled.

Or all will join the others in unending torment, Reeri thought, as their Lord had threatened thousands of times before.

"Else you shall be the Yakkas' tormentor." Wessamony's horns flared bright. "For eternity."

Reeri's shadows coiled. The faces of his brethren, enthralled in suffering, his hand on a whip, his nails sinking into—

The fault lies with you, Reeri. Never forget that.

"Have we a bargain?" Wessamony asked.

Reeri shook loose the nightmare.

It would not come to pass. He would find the blade. He would kill their Lord.

"Yes." Reeri brought the glowing shadow offering close and whispered, "Daughter of Earth, your prayer has been heard."

12

THE CANDLES SNUFFED OUT IN A BREEZE.

All except one. The door slammed shut, and wind swirled around Anula's feet, tinkling the bells on the edge of her sari, whipping her hair across her face. Pulse quickening, Anula took a step back. Perhaps she shouldn't have come. Perhaps this wasn't the way.

Smoke swirled, thickening and thrumming into a form. A face more shadow than cloud floated before her. Dark, insubstantial features sharpened into a chin, cheekbones. If it had been a statue or a human, she would've called it handsome.

Saffron eyes flashed open.

Anula stepped back, breath caught between lungs and throat.

"Daughter of Earth." The shadow spoke, deep and wispy, there and yet far away. "Your prayer has been heard. What request do you seek?"

Its features pulsed, shifting slightly. A chill prickled her skin. The shadow was no statue, no man, those eyes not truly eyes at all. It could never be handsome.

Because it was a Yakka.

The knowing settled deep. But this was wrong. Yakkas were not shadows. They weren't ever seen, not since they'd walked the Earth centuries ago. Amma would have told her if she'd seen them, Auntie Nirma, too, if only to prove they'd been right.

Which begged the question: "Why are you here?"

The shadow cocked its head. "I am the Blood Yakka, Reeri, answering the offering of a soul. Unless you are not the offerer."

The faint sound of singing sneaked under the door. It skittered up Anula's arms. The usurper was celebrating. "Yes, I made the offering. But…"

"You distrust me," the shadow finished her sentence solemnly.

"Devils aren't known for being trustworthy. How do I know you're who you say you are?"

Anula's veins throbbed. She glanced at her mehendhi-covered hands. Blue-green ridges rose through her skin as her blood rushed below the surface. A wave of adrenaline spiked her senses and sent her heart crashing against her ribs.

And then it released. The undertow retreated, withdrew, and stars twinkled at the edges of her sight as the force stole her footing. She collapsed to the cold floor, heart tripping over a beat. Once, twice, three times, until it finally settled again.

"Trust me now?" the shadow asked.

"Absolutely not."

The shadow was surely the Blood Yakka. But appearing now—seizing the blood in her veins—meant one thing: It could always have done that. It could have answered that night. But it had chosen not to.

"Do you rescind your bargain?" the shadow asked, tendrils flicking like a jungle cat's tail.

Anula picked herself off the floor, heart hammering and mind racing. They had been right, Amma and Auntie Nirma. The

Yakkas still existed. They still listened. They still, on occasion, answered. And like a human drunk on power, they acted only when it benefited them. Was this the deity she wanted to bargain her soul with? Trust to not deceive or trick her? Perhaps she'd be better off with a Divinity. Perhaps—

A chorus of celebration slipped under the door. Chora Naga would make the announcement soon, showing himself to the people of the outer city. News would spread fast of the new raja. Little time was left.

Look away.

Trustworthy or not, she'd already chosen her path.

"No," she asserted, chin high. "I want the throne of Anuradhapura, to be the first raejina, from this day forward until the anniversary of my fiftieth birth year."

"How specific."

"I leave nothing to chance." Or make the same mistake twice. She'd trusted this Yakka once before; she would not again.

"Neither do I." The shadow swirled around her. "Let us agree on new terms. You will have the throne of Anuradhapura, after your soul tethers us to Earth to tend to unfinished business."

"Tether? Us?" She didn't know which word sounded worse.

"Four Yakkas for the price of a crown."

She scoffed. "To tend to unfinished business… Is that your polite way of saying you have more people you want to kill? I know why you were banished. And I wouldn't be much of a raejina if I willingly put people in danger."

"No human shall die, that I promise you." The shadow rippled, its voice dropping low. "Stories are told from the victors' view. It does not mean that they are true."

What in the cursed Yakkas' names did that mean? The smoke swirled around Anula's thighs, up her hips and waist, circling tighter.

"Do we have a bargain?" the shadow asked.

The chanting grew louder, heavier, knocking against the walls of the corridor, banging against the door, beating out a rhythm. *Chora Naga. Chora Naga. Chora Naga.*

Like a war drum.

Chora Naga.

Prophet Ayaan.

Commander Dilshan.

The Yakka had said it wouldn't kill. No usurper could say that. What was the harm, then?

"Yes," Anula breathed and thrust out her hand. "A soul for a crown."

The shadow's saffron eyes flashed. Wind kicked up Anula's sari, whipped her hair around her face. A tendril snaked out of the shadow, stretching and swelling. It covered Anula's palm, a cold wisp wrapping around her wrist, twining through her fingers.

"I accept your offering."

Pain prickled her fingertips. It seared through her palm, over the bones of her hand, around her wrist, and up her forearm. Anula hissed as smoke rose from her skin. Veins burned and blood boiled. She opened her mouth to scream at the shadow, but—

It receded, slowly sinking into her skin. The smoke cleared, and where Anula's wedding mehendhi had once curled and swirled, a new design bloomed. Red and dark as blood.

Anula glanced up, questions racing along her tongue, but the Blood Yakka had vanished. The whipping wind caught her skirt as it tumbled through the room, knocking over candles and slamming open the doors. It blew down the hall and out into the palace.

Where the singing abruptly cut off.

And a great cry erupted.

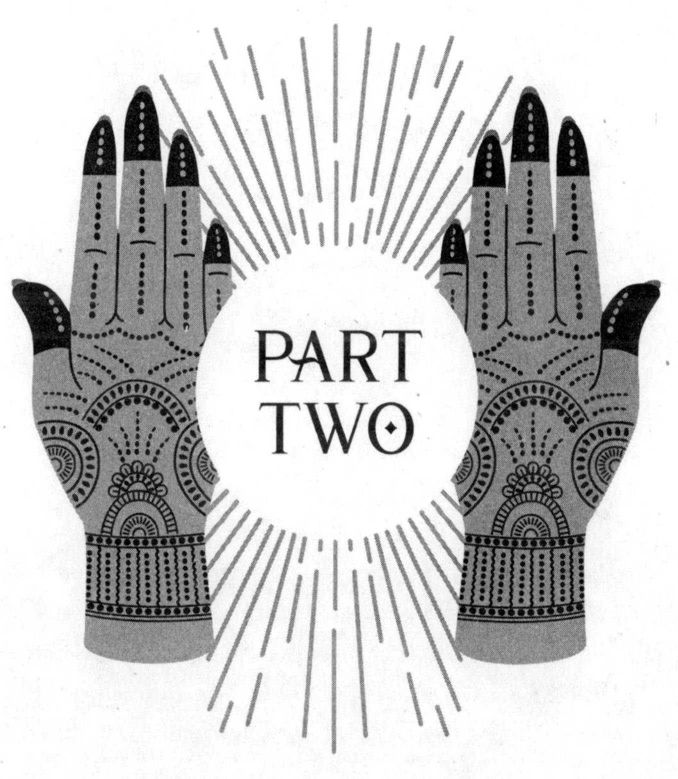

PART TWO

13

"Peace!" Chora Naga bellowed from the dais.

Anula skidded to a halt at the throne room's entrance. Black shadows swirled around his form, clung to his bare chest, his war breastplate discarded at his side. The room was no longer in chaos. Soldiers and courtiers alike had stopped fighting, stopped fleeing. They paused on bent knee, weapons discarded, eyes transfixed on the new raja as if in a trance.

Shadows snaked through the great hall, circling like a crested hawk-eagle. They dove at three courtiers, covering their arms in black smoke tendrils that sank into skin.

Bright daylight streamed across the red-marred floor, glinting in the puddles of death. Chora Naga heaved, his burgundy mehendhi rising and falling, giving the look of life to the elephant stretched across the planes of his chest. Patterns of swirls and soft geometric shapes dripped down the length of his stomach, fanning around his navel and dripping below his pants. He swept his hair aside and lifted his hooded gaze.

Saffron eyes stared out.

"My reign has begun," the Blood Yakka declared, his voice reverberating from Chora Naga's mouth.

The courtiers snapped awake.

"I am Raja Chora Naga." He reached out a thick arm toward Anula. "Behold your raejina consort, Anula of Anuradhapura."

Every head bowed in synchrony. It chilled Anula's bones.

The shadow-inked mehendhi chafed Anula's arms as the court was ushered out. She refused to examine it. It wasn't part of her bargain. Neither was this Yakka claiming to be her *husband* and sitting on *her* throne.

The raja had demanded a private audience with his new wife and the family of his adviser. As the doors closed, Anula marched to the tall, thick man. He was nothing of the Blood Yakka she'd met in the shrine, the shadow nowhere to be seen. Gone was his sharp jaw, his ruby eyes, his handsomeness.

"What in the cursed Yakkas' names have you done? Where is my bargain?"

She shouldn't speak to the Blood Yakka in that way, she knew. All the stories of old cast them as reveling in blood and pain. But she was the one who had called them. She was the one who'd bargained. She was in control. She wouldn't let them see the fear that snaked up her spine and coiled around her heart.

The Blood Yakka straightened to full height. "You will have your bargain, as agreed upon. First, I thought it best you were introduced to those you tether."

Anula blanched. Did he expect her to spend time with them? The deal was a soul and tether for a crown. Not an ally.

A man with peppered hair cleared his throat. Anula recognized him immediately. Viran, adviser to Raja Mahakuli

Mahatissa, loyally dedicated to Anuradhapura. A potential ally, or so Auntie Nirma had thought.

"I am Calu, Yakka of the Mind." The man reached out his hand. A red tendril of mehendhi curled around his wrist and dove underneath his long tunic sleeve. "Do not worry, we are not all as sour as Reeri."

Anula's eyes flashed. "Where's Viran?"

"Still in there." The Yakka Calu tapped on his chest. "Akin to asleep, until I am…finished."

Relief settled like a balm. Her bargain hadn't killed an innocent. That, at least, the Blood Yakka had been truthful about.

Calu pointed to the woman next to him, Viran's wife. But from the mehendhi on her hands, Anula knew she was held captive, too. "Let me introduce you to Kama, leader of the Ladies of Love, patron of lust."

Long legs and a willowy frame set off large round eyes, giving her the look of innocence. A contradiction to every story of old, every vicious depiction of the Yakka. Kama smiled, her gaze penetrating. "You have blood on your lip, just there. What does it taste like?"

Anula smashed a hand across her face, rubbed at her lips until they were raw. Her stomach curdled.

"Pay no mind to what she says. Manners evade her," Calu said, now pointing to the boy scowling behind him. "This is Sohon. His bark is worse than his bite."

The boy looked lost between child and adult. He rolled his eyes. "This is a waste of time. Let us get on with it."

A finger of dread slid down Anula's back. What had she done? The keys to the kingdom were no longer in the hands of an evil man, but in the clutches of four deadly beings. Ones who ignored faithful prayers and stole the faces of men.

Anula clenched a fist, felt the nails dig into her palm, imagined them ripping apart the shadow ink. Auntie Nirma had believed her ready, chosen. Anula's lungs seized. No, she wouldn't succumb to tears. Auntie Nirma had raised her better, stronger, and whether or not the Heavens had set her path, Auntie Nirma had paved it. Anula wouldn't let her life be for nothing. She wouldn't let her parents' deaths go unanswered.

"—we could all—"

"Where is my crown?" Anula spun on the Blood Yakka. She dug her nails deeper.

The Yakka, in the usurper's skin, leveled a guarded gaze. "I have yet to complete my business here."

"I tethered you—that was the bargain."

"The terms are for our business to be completed, then you will have your crown."

A nail broke flesh. "How long?"

"With luck, no time at all."

"And without it?"

The Blood Yakka glanced over her shoulder. "Mayhap you would like to retire to the bedchamber. It has been a long day for you."

"Oh, has it?" She laughed hard, swatted away the last image of Auntie Nirma and her cold eyes, as though it were a fly and not a jagged stone burrowing into what remained of her heart. "I hadn't noticed. Yes, why don't we retire to the bedroom, where you can make me forget my miseries with the gentle touches of a husband. Or do you prefer it rougher? More deception and dominance. Perhaps that's your business here, to get off on—"

Calu snorted. "Apologies. If I had a kahapana for every sexual thought Reeri had, I would be poorer than a fisherman with no net."

Anula grimaced. "How comforting."

A vein in the Blood Yakka's forehead throbbed. "I only meant—"

"You made a fool of me once already," she seethed. "It won't happen again."

Her sari flared as she strode out of the throne room, fingers finding her necklace. Perhaps she should rid herself of them and be done with it. But the title of raejina consort held even less power than a married raejina; it was barely a step above concubine. If she were to kill him now, she couldn't guarantee advancement to the throne, not with all her allies gone. Not without Auntie Nirma.

Cursed Yakkas, she was stuck.

Unless—

She didn't need to wait until she was on the throne to do *everything* they had planned. Though the right like-minded political allies probably wouldn't be open to making connections now, she was in the palace; surely that was close enough for the next step. If the Yakkas were busy, perhaps they wouldn't stand in her way.

"Raejina Consort." A guard bowed, halting her outside the grand doors. "I'm Tahan. I'll be your personal guard. It's an honor to serve you."

The name worked through her memory. A young guard hailing from a village on the outskirts of the kingdom. His allegiance lay with the crown, but he found friends wherever he went. Eager to please and easily swayed, he was a potential threat, even a potential enemy.

"You." Anula nodded to the guard stationed to the left of the doors. "What's your name?"

The guard quirked a gray-streaked brow. "Do you speak to me, my raejina consort?"

"No, the man behind you."

The guard cleared his throat, refusing to glance at the wall at his back. "My name is Bithul Perera, my raejina consort."

Anula filtered through the lists. Bithul was a soldier turned guard. A servant to the kingdom. A true ally to the crown. He was also rumored to have been maimed. But the man before her was strong, arms as thick as her head.

"You will be my guard," she commanded and turned to leave.

Tahan blocked her way. "My apologies, Raejina Consort, but he can't be. He's injured."

"I see no injury."

"It's true." Bithul moved swiftly, revealing scars scraping down his calf to his heel. "Polonnaruwa tried to take my legs."

"What happened?"

"I took their hands instead."

"If that doesn't instill confidence, I don't know what would."

With a swish of her bloodstained sari, she glided past Tahan. Bithul kept pace a step behind her. A thud sounded every other step.

"I don't believe the raja will agree to this, my raejina consort," he said, deftly walking with an unusual cane. "You must be properly protected."

"If you aren't up to it, why are you stationed as a guard within the palace in the first place?" Anula led them past dozens of rooms, none of which brought them closer to the raja's chambers. There were more important places to be.

Bithul squeezed the top of his cane. "Because I was once the best, destined to be commander. Now, though, my body isn't suited for skirmishes in the jungle. By the Heavens' grace, I'm still able to stand guard and serve my kingdom."

Anula tucked the information away. "I didn't choose you for that," she said, halting at the end of a hall. "Your reputation says you're loyal to Anuradhapura. All I ask is that you continue to be."

He bowed. "Of course, my raejina consort."

Anula turned to proceed with her plan when a flash of flame outside a window caught her eye. She rushed toward it, pressing her nose close. A throng of servants cleaned the inner city. Chora Naga's destruction was a clear blazing path from the palace door to the gate and out into Anuradhapura, where the people would be putting out fires, patching thatch roofs, tending to the injured. Things they'd become practiced, even skilled at.

"How many did we lose?" she asked.

"Only a handful in the city, by early accounts. Most were our own guards," he said gruffly.

That wasn't any better. Innocent lives were still lost for a senseless, greedy purpose. Sons and husbands never to return home, never to hug their loved ones again. She stared at a helmet, bloody and bent. A woman's sari pota lay drenched next to it.

It pinched at Anula.

She had lost not only Auntie Nirma, but also the women who'd been placed here to aid her rule. What about the others, the ones still in Kekirawa? Her fingers twitched. She should write to them, ensure they were safe and hiding in case Chora Naga had spilled any of their secrets. Then she should ask for aid, for them to send more allies—

But would that risk them? If the letter was intercepted, if any of Chora Naga's own allies now infiltrated the palace, she could be the cause of more loss. Perhaps it was best to wait for a missive from one of them. They knew she was here, and they'd see that she had not given up. Decision made, she turned from the helmet and the loss and continued on. Bithul was right behind her until she rounded the last of the corners.

"If you wanted for food, I would have summoned a servant to your chambers," he said.

"But that's not what I wanted." She took the corner, half hoping to find two maids kissing.

The hall was empty. A few hours ago, the palace had been under attack, ransacked in parts, no doubt. Blessed gifts could earn two lifetimes' fortunes. Anyone standing in the way would be seen as a mere hindrance, especially the maids.

"Premala?" she called, entering the kitchen. Perhaps she had already returned to the concubine estate. The clink of dropped dishes echoed, taking with them the tension from Anula's shoulders. "Good, you're just as I left you."

The young woman scrambled across the floor and Anula marveled at how someone so bad at their job, worse at lying, and missing from any of Anula's lists, had managed to make her worry. *Suspicion*, she told herself and let it drop there.

"Oh!" the cook gasped, falling into a bow. "Raejina Consort, twice in one day, how...thoughtful of you."

Aside from the plates on the floor next to Premala, the kitchen seemed untouched. Even the food prepared for the celebration sat pristinely on the tables.

"I wanted to make sure everyone was all right," Anula said.

Premala jerked up at the words.

"Thank you, my raejina consort." The cook blushed. She hissed at two maids and Premala, fluttering her hands toward the food. "You must be starving after—here, let me get you something to eat. It was meant for your enjoyment, after all."

Anula let her hand land across her heart. "After how cruel I was to you?"

The cook shook her head. "You were right, my raejina consort. A soft word does more to move a cow. Please, enjoy."

Anula blinked. That was not entirely the point she had tried to make. As she sat, Premala poured tea, sure to steady the kettle and avoid another mishap.

"Thank you for checking on us," she murmured.

"What are friends for?"

Premala swallowed hard. Out of fear, or nerves?

Anula took a sip, then grabbed another cup. "Bithul, come sit and eat. I'm sure your day has been as relaxing as mine."

"I cannot, my raejina consort," he said, eyeing the maids and every window and door. His hand twisted on the top of his cane.

"And if I command you?"

Bithul sighed, took the cup she offered, and emptied it in one long swallow. "My gratitude, my raejina consort. I am fortified."

"Do you believe in the Heavens? You said before that you were destined to be commander. Was that talk, or do you truly believe the Heavens gave you a purpose?"

"That is a complicated answer, my raejina consort." He sat next to her. "But yes, I believe the Heavens guide my path."

He sounded like Auntie Nirma. Anula sipped her tea, the heat a barrier against her heart. "So you believe you'll be commander one day?"

Bithul smiled, the tea softening him. "They never said I would be. Only men did. I choose to believe that my life is unfolding as it should, as long as I remain true to myself. It's how I am able to accept this." He raised his cane, an iron piece that looked more like a scabbard than a walking stick. "It's how I can serve the crown and not a man. Whoever the Divinities choose to place me under, it's not for me to decide or to question."

Anula clenched a fist. "They never make a mistake?"

"Never," he said solemnly, eyes heavy.

"Your faith is valiant."

"Thank you, Raejina Consort."

It wasn't meant to be a compliment.

Bithul's head nodded drowsily, until it dropped heavily and rested on the table. A soft snore sounded. The tincture had worked quickly. Anula stood, ready to go to work before anything else could happen on this cursed day.

"Raejina Consort," Premala whispered, eyeing the sleeping guard. "Be careful. The palace is full of secrets and dark powers."

Anula knew that, but how did Premala? "Powers?"

Premala glanced around. Maids flitted this way and that, too many ears listening. "Just be careful."

It was all the confirmation Anula needed to know that Premala was part of a grander scheme, one she'd have to uncover in time. First, she would rid the palace of another dark power.

"Don't worry, I can protect myself." Anula slipped out of the kitchen, a prayer chanting in her head.

It began with the name of Prophet Ayaan.

14

THE RAJA'S CHAMBER DRIPPED WITH GOLD. IT WAS AS GAUDY AS Lord Wessamony's court, a clear design of the Heavens. So too was it empty, a clear message of rejection.

The vast room suddenly felt tight, the air stale and confined. Reeri stalked to the windows and unlatched them. A star winked, signaling the end of the first day, reminding him how few he had left.

The fault lies entirely with you.

The shadow within him quivered. Anula had seen it immediately, the blood on his hands. Her distrust was well placed. But, O Heavens, she was going to be a difficult tether. Headstrong. Impulsive. Her large bronze eyes forever set in a challenge. It was no wonder she was the first to offer a soul. Nor was it a surprise she desired the throne.

Reeri glanced in a gilt-framed mirror. The crown suited this body, with its spikes of moonstones and rows of rubies. So too would it suit Anula, her dark tresses flowing around it, the earrings dripping beside her long neck.

Reeri paused. He should not dwell on her beauty. Hers was not the soul with whom his would commune but the soul he would cleave in two.

It was the only way. The Yakkas deserved their freedom.

His skin itched suddenly, and a strain pinched at his chest. Reeri scoffed at himself. *His* skin, *his* chest.

A small bulbul chirped on the edge of the gilt mirror. Its gold wings flittered as it moved along the branches of the frame. Reeri gazed into the reflection. His shadow writhed beneath. It had been centuries since he had seen with eyes, since he consisted of anything to be seen.

Chora Naga was a portrait of strength, a usurper of the highest caliber. The mark on his chest stood vibrant against a plane of dark, thick muscle. Scars crisscrossed his shoulders and biceps; one ran along his neck and collarbone. Reeri had never had scars before, nor curls that bounced on his forehead, nor a mouth that turned down on the sides.

"This is not me," Reeri said to the bulbul. It chirped in agreement.

Temporary, he reminded himself. This body would not be his next prison. Before long, he would have his own body. Until then—

Gripping the sides of the frame, Reeri bent forward, focused on the stranger's face. The bird squawked, ruffling its feathers. Wading through his memories felt like trudging through a rice paddy field. Jaw tight, he sifted for the familiar features. The face he had used to call his shimmered beneath. Part ghost, part shadow. A phantom of the cosmos. Reeri grasped it and pulled.

A square jaw bloomed, followed by a long rounded nose, and wide, full lips. Deep red eyes were curtained by thick lashes and heavy brows.

His face.

Sweat trickled down Chora Naga's skin. Reeri did not blink.

The bird whistled and flapped blessed wings in encouragement. He held fast to the image in his mind, dragged it to the surface. Chora Naga's shoulders shook, muscles aching, and—

The ghost emerged.

It seeped out of Chora Naga's skin, layered itself like a sheet.

He was there. In the lips, the chin, the cheeks.

The phantom of his life.

Betwixt the heartbeats that were not his, the memory snapped away. Chora Naga's face returned. The enchantment gone.

The bulbul chirped at him. Reeri closed his eyes. It was pointless to waste time on a memory anyway. The thrum of the tether sang within him. The etching of a mehendhi elephant on his chest shivered. Its edges cracked his dark skin.

It reminded him of why he had come and what was at stake.

He could not allow Anula to venture too far, else the tether would mar her soul before he had the chance to use it. To perform the ritual that would bring to life all his brethren's souls, which remained shackled in the cosmos.

Rejection or not, Anula must spend the night in his chamber and every night after. Until he cleaved her soul.

The tether pulled taut, yearning to snap each point together, as once upon a time his body had done to his shrines. Yet Anula was no Yakka, and he was no shrine. If they did not stay within a certain distance, the effect would be...uncomfortable. More than a little gruesome.

It was a warning Reeri had meant to levy on Anula, if she had only listened and waited in the chamber. Now he found himself hurrying through the palace, the tether dragging him around corner after corner—

A snore rippled down the empty hall. The tether flared toward an open door—the prophet's door, marked by the same rubies inlaid in his pendant. One peek around the frame and the tether fell calm. For inside, drenched in moonlight, crept the raejina consort, footsteps as lithe and soundless as a mouse. Grimacing at the old man in the bed, Anula bent over a low table and unstoppered a small blue vial. She tipped the contents into a bottle of palm wine and—

Reeri grasped her wrist.

Bronze eyes flashed up, not a hint of a scream on her lips.

He tore the vial from her fingers, snatched up the bottle, and pulled her silently out of the room. If humans had vapor edges, his would be flickering. She wrenched free as soon as the door clicked closed behind them and marched away.

"*Wait*," Reeri demanded, catching hold of her arm again. He glanced at the prophet's door. "Has he wronged you?"

"I don't know what you mean, Raja. I was only out for a stroll. Thoughts of you kept me awake." Derision fluttered along with her lashes. "I was simply shivering with anxiety."

"Do you always deflect with jests?" He dropped her arm, then sniffed at the vial he had confiscated. It smelled of flowers and early-morning heat. Where had she learned poisoncraft? Better yet, why?

Anula pursed her lips and tugged at a seam near her hip. A small bulge shifted. "Calling you was a mistake."

Reeri's brows knit together. "You mean praying."

"I don't pray." She sauntered close and whispered, "I only get on my knees for one reason."

"What is this?" Reeri ignored her taunt, plucking a piece of paper sticking out of her small pocket. Though blank, he could smell the taint of ink.

He held up the paper to candle flame, a trick as old as he. Names appeared, crammed from one end to the other. Prophet Ayaan's was first.

Anula laughed. "Perhaps it's who I wish to be with more than you. Or it's all the men I've already been with."

Reeri bristled. This was worse than speaking with Calu. At least he was honest. Anula was intent on making this difficult. Reeri handed the paper back, tired of wasting time. "Do not poison the prophet. He is necessary."

If not as his Heavenly connection, then the knowledge passed down to him would be essential, if luck was on their side.

"Or what?" Anula narrowed her eyes.

"The bargain will take longer to complete."

She tucked the paper away. "And the others?"

Reeri shook his head. "Are you so eager to become a murderess?"

Anula straightened, as if she could reach his height by sheer willpower. "Justice is not murder."

"Says the slayer."

With a scoff, Anula spun. Her hair whipped Reeri in the face. The sting was a welcome reminder that he was more than the shadow simmering beneath. He was corporeal, and before long, all the Yakkas would be, too.

It should not have surprised him that this offerer turned out to be a cruel woman. In all the centuries of offerings, it was either the power hungry or the provoked who sought to bargain for the throne. Anula was no different.

The notion settled any guilt over marring her soul. It was already misshapen. Jaw working, Reeri quickly followed her. She paused in the center of the corridor, scratching at the mehendhi markings that ran up her arms.

"What did you do to me?" she demanded. "Why does it itch?"

"It is our tether, and the consequence of it stretching thin. We must stay close. I was going to explain it all in our chamber."

"*Our* chamber?" She whirled on him. "Is this your idea of a jest?"

"I do not jest."

"Thrice-cursed Yakkas. Could this day get any worse?"

Wessamony's wicked grin flashed in Reeri's mind. *Bring me the Bone Blade by the Maha Equinox in four weeks, else you shall be the Yakkas' tormentor, for eternity.*

"Of course it could."

Anula leveled a glare.

Reeri sighed. "We both need rest if tomorrow is going to bring us closer to the end of this bargain."

"Fine. But stay on your side of the room. Touch me once, and you'll find out exactly what's inside that vial."

She marched off. Reeri pinched the bridge of his nose. The Maha Equinox was nigh, he had to deal with her only a while longer; then her soul would be cleaved and he would have a new life.

Far, far away.

15

The raja's bedchamber was filled with many things, mostly blessed gifts, and mirrors in which to revel in his own glory. A raja could demand for anything to be brought inside, permanently or otherwise.

Apparently, a second bed wasn't one of them.

Anula lay on one side, the Blood Yakka on the other, his arm nearly falling off the edge. A wide gap spread between them, pulsing like a heartbeat.

"Sidle closer."

Anula startled at the female voice cooing over her shoulder. Etched in the wood frame of the colossal bed was a carving of the first raja and raejina. Their love story stretched over a garden, a blanket made of flowers the only thing covering them.

The woman flipped her long dark hair over her shoulder. "Be not afraid of him. Your gentle touch will guide him to you."

A shudder racked Anula's bones. Either from the image conjured or from the interaction, she didn't know. Speaking to a blessed gift was much different than watching fish swim in a bathing pool.

"Caress her hair," the depicted raja whispered loudly to the Blood Yakka. "See her delicate neckline? Kiss it."

The Yakka tensed, stolen eyes darting to Anula and away.

"Touch me and—"

"I heard you the first time," the Blood Yakka said, shifting away from the carving.

"Do not be shy." The raejina giggled at Anula. "He is your husband. Do you not wonder at his warmth? At his strength?"

"No," Anula asserted. "I wonder why he twisted my bargain to be here."

The raejina tsked. "He is here for you. To give you a pleasure from the Heavens. To make you feel the cosmos explode into being between your legs."

The Blood Yakka choked.

"Cursed Yakkas," Anula spat, shoving her pillow up against the raejina as she continued her foul advice. If only the blessed gift knew what truly lay in this marriage bed. Noticing his wife's inability to cast advice, the wooden raja rushed across the gap. Anula pointed a finger at him. "Say another word and I'll throw you into the fire."

He harrumphed and settled back silently. This was what courtiers envied? What the Divinities left the kingdom with, to show and prove their unending love?

"Thank the mighty Heavens," the Blood Yakka murmured.

His relief drew Anula's anger. "This is your fault. Why are we even in the same bed?"

"Does your marking itch still?"

Invisible ants crawled over her arms. Anula scraped her nails against them. "Yes."

"That is why. We were apart for too long. The tether wants proximity."

"We're in the same room, Blood Yakka—what more does it want?"

He cut her a glance. "Touch."

That word again. She growled, "Why would you create a tether that demands touch?"

"I did not create it." His voice was tight, resentful. "Ask the Divinities or Lord Wessamony."

Of course. The Heavens created everything with balance. Nothing good could exist without a silver lining of bad. Like the mural she stared at above them, the Heavens were filled with light and dark: Divinities draped in white robes. Yakkas drenched in blood.

"You may call me 'Reeri.'" The Blood Yakka broke the heavy silence. "If you would like. Mayhap friendlier terms would ease the strain."

"I would not like." She pulled the blankets tightly toward her. "I bargained for a throne, *Blood Yakka*, not a friend."

The gap between them rippled. "Then you will not get one. Good night, Anula."

Her eyes flashed to him. Rigid as a rock, he slept, blankets only covering one arm. The marking flared again, her fingers twitching, not to scratch this time but to feel. To inch their way across the expanse of bed that could easily fit two concubines and touch the Blood Yakka's chest.

Do you not wonder at his warmth? His strength?

Yes, the tether responded, tingling with curiosity. It urged her to trace the outline of the elephant, the pattern of swirls on his stomach, to follow the drip of the line down his torso, along his hips, beneath his sarong. Where did it end?

Anula tore her gaze away and shoved fisted hands behind her back. This was nonsense. A distraction from her purpose. The Yakkas must complete their business. Tomorrow.

She wouldn't waste another minute thinking about him.

Laughter rose high.

Anula opened her eyes to color, to faces, to food steaming on banana leaves. A small gathering surrounded her, the people laughing and eating, children playing a game with rocks.

"We would not have reason to celebrate without you, Reeri, our Blood Yakka," an old woman said, passing Anula another banana leaf, this one heavy with a mountain of rice. She breathed in the scent—maa-wee rice. The warmth melted her heart, tugged a smile on her lips.

"To the Yakkas who protect us from disease." A man raised a coconut.

Her smile fell. How did she know the type of rice?

"To the Yakkas who bring us love," a woman said, beaming down at a young child braiding the hair of a lovely being.

Being. Not woman. Why would she think it like that? Anula eyed her, the one whose hair was twisting into a plait. She was too tall to be a human. Too bony. Too sharp.

And what had they called Anula?

Reeri. Blood Yakka.

Anula glanced at her hands. Dropped the banana leaf.

Where smooth brown skin covered in mehendhi should have been were arms as hairy as any man.

Her eyes flicked back to the other being. It cocked its head. "What's wrong, Reeri?"

It couldn't be a Yakka. It had no horns, no fangs, no scales. Only skin a deep cinnamon color, a wolfish grin, and…

Saffron eyes.

The world shifted, rumbled, and a strike of lightning blinded her. When the village reappeared, the people were gone. Silence sounding louder than laughter. Dread curled around her spine.

Thump.

A weight landed in her lap, and she swallowed a scream. A bloody ear, sharpened at the tip, bled out on the banana leaf.

"The fault lies entirely with you." A voice boomed. The village disappeared in a blink, and Anula stood in a court she'd only ever seen in a painting hung in Eppawala's stupa. Washed white in ivory and marble, it glistened with sunlight and starshine. But a river of shadows cut through, tall beings with pointed ears and saffron eyes. Her breath rattled.

A serrated whip lashed out, drawing tears and terror and shredded shadow.

Anula squeezed her eyes shut. A hand jerked her chin up, a voice whispered in her ear, "Watch, Reeri. Look and see what you have done."

A scream pierced the raja's bedchamber.

"Cursed Yakkas, what was that?" Anula fought off the tangle of blankets.

The Blood Yakka scrambled, reaching a hand toward her. "Are you all right?"

She swatted at it. "Get away from me. What was that?"

"What was what?"

Anula kicked the sheet until she was free and stood. "I saw the Yakkas, only they didn't look like that." She pointed to the painting on the ceiling. "And the people called me by your name. And it felt…real. Not like a dream but like—"

"A memory."

"Yes," she heaved, heart racing as if she were running from a jungle cat. Perhaps she should be. That wolfish grin, those unnatural eyes…

The Yakka sank back. "O Heavens."

"What?"

He sighed. "They are soured memories that haunt me when at rest. I call them memory-nightmares."

Anxiety tripped Anula's pulse. She shook out her hands. "Are you saying I witnessed your dream?"

The Yakka's brows knit together. "I suppose it makes sense. Our souls are tethered, and what is a tether if not a connection?"

"Why would you create a tether like that?" Anula seethed. The sound of the ear dropping, wet and heavy, echoed in her mind.

"I did not," the Yakka said. "A tether is an aspect of the cosmos. Strictly speaking, I never tethered before. The intricacies are a… working theory."

"Then how do you know that we have to stay close to each other?"

"Another Yakka once tethered. Ratti told me how distance hurt the human. But that is all she mentioned. Had I known about the memories, I would have warned you."

"Not only must I have permanent mehendhi that itches and threatens me, now I have to share your nightmares, too? Do you even need to sleep?"

"Heavenly bodies must rest. It is similar but not as deep as sleep. However, every earthly body, including mine now, demands true sleep."

Gritting her teeth, Anula stepped before the nearest mirror. "How is any of this balance?"

For the first time, she allowed herself to examine the design that snaked up her arms. It began at her fingertips. Nets and spirals led to vines and leaves, lotus flowers bloomed across her hands, and two mirrored mandalas marked her palms, one the face of a lion, the other an elephant. The same as the one etched on the Blood Yakka's chest. A chill swept over her neck.

Paisley motifs and florals flowed into tendril patterns up her wrists, her arms, her elbows. Elements of gems and jewelry and stars hid within. It didn't end there. Delicate anklets adorned her feet, netting on her toes. She shifted to see the pattern more closely, her sleep robe slipping off one side. A burgundy tendril slithered across her shoulder.

Anula twisted in the mirror and dropped her robe. She caught the flicker of admiration in the Yakka's eyes before he had the sense to close them. It was only a moment, but he still smoldered the way Thaththa had with Amma, the way a husband would a wife, the way she had dreamed of—Anula shook the thought away. He was not her dream, but her curse. His mark dripped down her spine. At the top bloomed a water lily, with vines and leaves and florals cascading from her shoulder blades, gems dropping to points like earrings at the middle of her back.

Cursed Yakkas. What would Auntie Nirma have said?

"It all goes away when the bargain is complete," the Yakka said.

"Which is when?" she seethed, pulling the robe back on.

"Soon," he urged, eyes still closed.

"Then what? You leave my kingdom with my soul?" She hadn't meant to ask, hadn't meant to care, but with every surprise this Yakka had given her, perhaps she should know.

He was quiet for a moment. "All soul offerings ascend to the Second Heavens upon death, for Lord Wessamony to do with as he pleases."

The coolness of the necklace registered before Anula realized her hand had flown to it. She didn't know which was worse, spending the afterlife with the Lord of the Second Heavens or spending the foreseeable future with the Blood Yakka—the one who had stolen her throne, then blocked her from marking off a name from her list, and now forced her to see his nightmares. To see things that didn't exist.

The answer wasn't difficult. The Yakkas had been banished,

not tortured. And if the people loved him so, like his memory suggested, then why had they turned on him? Why call for his Lord's help if he was saving them? Because he wasn't. Like all the usurpers before him, he saw himself as a savior, a hero to the people. But all he brought was death. All he was, was a slaughterer.

"I did not mean to scare you," the Yakka said, eyes still closed. "We are in this bargain together, and I will protect you."

Pink sunlight rose through latticed windows as she leveled an ember gaze. "If you wanted to protect me, you would leave. You're the only threat here."

The Yakka's eyes flashed open. Hurt sparked, but only for a moment, the mask of Chora Naga falling so quickly, Anula questioned whether it had been there at all. "Mayhap you are right. I suppose I should take advantage of the early start today."

"Music to my ears."

The Yakka marched past, calling for servants to ready them. The beings from the memory-nightmare flashed in her mind, so unlike the Yakkas depicted in paintings. Was it true?

"You will have to come along," he said.

If so, which part?

Anula shook off her questions. The answers didn't matter. What mattered was the throne. What mattered was Auntie Nirma's list. It was up to her to see it through, to honor her life and her death, along with all those lost before her.

"Just be quick about it," she snapped.

She had no time to waste on dreams.

16

A SHARP WIND TANGLED REERI'S HAIR.

"Are you ready, my raja?" Prophet Ayaan stood by a painting in the throne room.

Reeri shuttered the window against the cloudless sky. He need not watch for the Maha season monsoon to arrive, counting down his days. He had done enough of that—two centuries worth. Time enough to prepare. "How do we get in?"

"I thought you were here to tell us of the Bone Blade." Anula scowled from her perch on the consort's dais. If looks had the potency to kill, she would have had no reason to study poisoncraft.

Prophet Ayaan bowed deeply, the pendant of gold and rubies kissing the floor. "I am, my raejina consort. There are many stories about the relics and why they were hidden. The Divinities, in their great knowledge of man's proclivity for gossip, left us with the truth." He waved a hand at the painting.

A small landscape revealed a hilly region with a narrow path winding around three huts. Storms gathered around each, darkening to rage over the last. Reeri frowned. The blessed gifts were not meant for Yakkas to experience, and after last night, he had no desire to witness them again.

Caress her.

The thought slithered up his back, along with the image of a water lily robe slipping off Anula's bare shoulders. Reeri shook it away.

"If you're going to use a blessed gift, why not one of the fortune-telling statues?" Anula asked. "Can't you ask them where you will find the Bone Blade?"

"The gifts only speak what they see," the prophet explained. "Answering specific questions is outside their bounds. The Divinities were gracious with their love, but they did not hand over the keys to the cosmos."

Despite Reeri's aversion, he knew he must do as the prophet said, else why save him from choking to death on Anula's poison? "You do not have to go, only be sure to stay within the room."

Anula jumped from her seat. "If you're going, I'm going."

"There is no need."

She cut her eyes to the prophet. "And leave my future in the hands of two men? I think not."

"As you wish," he sighed.

Dipping his head, the prophet gestured for them to follow. "The gift is like a door. You need only to push and walk through."

The canvas stretched beneath the prophet's hand, swallowing it whole. He lifted his foot and stepped inside, disappearing without a sound. It was as if he had climbed into a cupboard. Nothing more, nothing less.

Anula let out a breath, a worry line etched betwixt her brows. Reeri's fingers twitched as he repressed a desire to lay a comforting hand on her shoulder, to whisper encouragement. It was daft. She was an aspirational murderer. And a willing soul to be sacrificed.

Still, the desire hovered, pulsed.

Reeri lifted a hand to help her, but Anula grimaced and pushed her way into the painting. Rejection stung, sharp as a mosquito bite.

With clenched teeth, he placed his hand on the bumpy ridge of the hills and went after the blade. The fabric stretched thin as he pushed, suctioning his hand, his arm, his elbow. It was all he could do not to fall forward as he stepped through—and landed outdoors.

The painting was alive and moving, as if he had merely walked out the palace gates. Noise from the huts drifted on the cutting wind. He braced his shoulders as gray clouds roiled up the path. At least here, there were no lewd rajas and distasteful prompting.

"It doesn't feel like paint," Anula said, bent at a bush, rubbing a leaf betwixt her fingers.

"Why would it?" Prophet Ayaan asked. "These are blessed gifts, as real as our own world. It is merely a shortcoming of our minds that prevents us from understanding all that the cosmos is capable of."

A scream swirled on the breeze, chilling the skin along Reeri's arm. It reminded him that he did not belong here. Not in this body and not in this painting. Whatever truth lay here, he wanted it to be known swiftly so he could leave. "The Bone Blade."

"Yes, come." Prophet Ayaan started down the path, sarong billowing. "Long ago, before the Divinities created the blessed gifts and the palace to hold the in-between, they created the relics. Each Divinity had an object imbued with their power and used it to answer prayers. They were a connection made solely between Divinity and humanity. The relics ranged in form: intricate staffs, clothing, blades, and more."

The sun peeked through thick clouds, casting the first hut in jagged light. Prophet Ayaan beckoned them to cluster at the window. Inside, a woman slumbered. Iridescent dust glittered across her chest as a breastplate of pure gold formed, sinking into her skin.

"The great Divinity Motherhood gave her relic to those who prayed for progeny. As the women fell pregnant, they'd dream of Motherhood fitting it upon them, feeling the weight upon their chest until the child was born, safe and healthy."

Prophet Ayaan continued down the path. "Most relics brought peace to households and healing to the sick. It was no wonder people sought and prayed for them. But there was one that our ancestors became infatuated with."

Rain pattered on the second hut, which brimmed with the whispers of a family. The crowd opened, revealing an old man on a sickbed, pale as the dead. All gathered bowed their heads. "We call on you, Fate, gracious Divinity. Save our father. Give him life to see another grandchild."

A bright light flashed above. The sound of a blade slashed the air, and the old man sucked in a deep breath. All gaped as their father woke, cheeks rosy with life.

"A simple bone blade," the prophet said, "imbued with Fate's power, able to cut off the Hand of Death."

"And once the taste of immortality was on their lips, they thirsted for nothing more," Anula murmured, repeating the words of the stories of old. A flicker of something crossed her gaze, too fast for Reeri to place.

Prophet Ayaan gave them a bland smile. "Who wouldn't want to live forever with their loved ones?"

A memory of the Yakkas, happy and free, twisted Reeri's shadow.

Thunder rumbled over the third and final hut. Lightning burst with torrential rain as they rushed to the bottom of the hill. Mud streamed around dead plants and half decayed carcasses. They rounded the corner to a cacophony from within, the door flying open and expelling a large man. Without second thought, Reeri reached for Anula and spun her into him, away from the man tripping across their path and falling face-first into the mess.

"Blessed Yakka Calu," a man shouted from the doorframe, "hear my prayer. Strike my neighbor with madness. I offer my last kahapana."

Anula blinked up from Reeri's chest, her eyes wide at his tight hold around her waist. Soft curves and ample bosom crushed against him. Heat flared in his cheeks and beneath his sarong.

"Fool!" the man in the mud yelled. "I have already been granted the Bone Blade!"

A fist flew, and out tumbled another three men, screaming threats, arguing over the blade, over immortality, jostling Reeri and Anula to the side. The movement caught all their notice, and as one they turned on him.

"You dare try to steal the blade?" a man charged.

"We must go," Prophet Ayaan said, creating a seam of light by pulling at the air.

Anula pushed out of Reeri's grasp. An empty echo rippled down his arms as she leaped through. He followed, and as they fell back into the throne room, the prophet stitched the seam up in one blink.

"Cursed Yakkas, what was that?" Anula spat.

"All inside a painting are held in the emotional state in which they were created," Prophet Ayaan said, straightening his pendant before looking over the raja. "Truly, I apologize for their behavior. I did not think they would attack. Though rare, it does happen."

Reeri shook off the tension, whether from nearly catching his first punch or the ghost of Anula in his arms, he dared not question. "Why show me this, then? Where is the blade hidden?"

The prophet shifted. "In all their great wisdom, the Divinities saw the hold the Bone Blade had on the people and decided it was not worth the corruption of souls. Fate forsook it, and as one, the Divinities used their powers to hide it, never to be used again. To ensure history did not repeat itself, the Divinities declared, 'All relics must be cast down to Earth, where all eyes are on them but none can see them.'"

The words sent a ripple through Reeri's shadow.

"Soon after came the blessed gifts to remind us that though the relics be gone, their love was not. But not all were satisfied with that. Seekers of the relics emerged. If you believe the rumors, some have been successful. But those relics found and sold have not been proven real. They could merely be blessed gifts stolen from the palace or, even more dangerously, falsified artifacts imbued with a bargain from the Second Heavens. Many have died in their search for a relic or in use of a cursed imitation. So, you see, my raja, I do not want for you to find yourself on a similar path."

Reeri nodded, mind working the Divinities' riddle. "Your worry is heeded, yet unnecessary, Prophet. I will not fall. Until the Maha Equinox, your only duty is to meditate on the First Heavens and ask for a location."

Prophet Ayaan frowned. "But there is much to do before the Festival of the Cosmos, my raja."

"I do not doubt your ability. Find the location, and then you may focus on the festival."

The prophet bowed deeply and took his leave.

Anula crossed her arms. "Now what?"

The prophet's story was a fine one, yet filled with half-truths. Reeri remembered watching from the aether. Indeed, humanity's thirst for immortality was unquenchable, yet each time Fate saved a life, they cut the hand of their twin, Destiny. Insulted and demeaned, Destiny confronted Fate. The siblings quarreled endlessly. Unwilling to yield, Fate finally turned the relic on Destiny—not in the earthly realm, but in the Heavens.

Destiny tore in two, as cleanly as if they were a blade of grass. Their form disappeared and did not return. Both Heavens rang out in silent terror.

Never had a Heavenly being ceased to exist.

In panic, the First Heavens striped Fate of their power, condemned them to the earthly sea in the form of a monster, and cast the Bone Blade to the island—close enough for Fate to feel its call, but too far to reach. A sentence of empty longing for all eternity.

Crisis averted, the Divinities resumed their purpose. Yet Wessamony recalled the warning given to him all those years before—a warning that suddenly turned to a threat. For if this relic cut the Hand of Death and expunged the existence of cosmic beings, then the Bone Blade could end him.

Would end him, when Reeri found it.

Fortunately, the prophet's demonstration was not for nothing. Reeri had not known of the riddle the Divinities had spoken. They said they cast the relics to Earth, *to where all eyes were on them yet none could see*. Hidden in plain sight, in a place all would overlook. Not a cave or waterfall, not any location a seeker would search, but a place that was disregarded as common, where its objects, though always there, were too familiar to take note.

A smile twitched at Reeri's lip. Where did all people visit, yet never scrutinize, too absorbed in their own plight?

"Now we explore the shrine."

Calu breathed in deeply, then let out a long, loud sigh. "O, mighty Heavens and every wretch within, I forgot how good the air smelled."

Anula snorted.

"What?"

"Nothing. It just figures that the Yakkas would like the scent of refuse and poverty in the morning."

If Reeri were still made of vapors, his tendrils would snap. He settled on clenching a fist. He had saved her from the man inside the painting, extended a hand when she was nervous; yet still her ire flared. "Does your charm never cease?"

She smiled sardonically. "Never."

"Good," Calu said. "Mayhap it will improve Reeri's when—"

"It is ready." Reeri cut him off before he spoke of things Anula need not know. She had already given her soul as offering, so the details of the sacrifice were moot, lest he wished for her to scare, name him on that list of murder. Or worse yet, rescind her offering.

At the top of the shrine of the inner city, two guards waited: his and Anula's. Tahan had been promoted when the last raja's man died with him in battle. Reeri did not need protection, but as Calu reminded him, they must uphold the facade. In this same way, Calu, as adviser, had redirected all of Chora Naga's correspondence to the ministers. He had no time to ponder what was so clearly an alliance with Polonnaruwa. They would be gone and freed before anything occurred, Heavens willing. Still, it meant Anula must be kept safe—a job he did not envy. Bithul was appointed solely by her. The two glanced at each other tersely, and Reeri wondered why.

"We have swept the room, my raja," Tahan said. "It's empty and safe."

Empty because the guard made it so, demanding that if the raja wished to walk among his people, the people must be at a secure distance. Namely, across the street, gawking. Not in want of communion, but gossip.

Reeri's eyes flicked to the sky—blue and clear, not a cloud in sight—and entered the shrine, anticipation riling his shadow.

Bolts of fabric, platters of food, innumerable candles, and flowers populated the floor. Depictions of the Heavens veiled the walls, and in the center stood small figurines of all the Yakkas and all the Divinities. A great many things to hide a relic among.

"Bithul," Anula greeted her guard as she passed by. Reeri did not miss the false sweetness in her voice. It lessened the sting of her rejection of him. Mayhap she liked no one. "Hope you had restful sleep last night."

Reeri paced the room. Though he sensed the offerings' call, it was intuition he must heed now. Relics pulsed and pitched to their own rhythm. Once, when Reeri had come across Courage and their bow, he had felt a fluttering in his soul, akin to a hummingbird's wings.

"Yes, my raejina consort," Bithul responded. "Longer than any I've had in years."

"Sounds like a lovely surprise."

"A surprise indeed. Yet I hope not to experience it again. I care greatly for the duty granted to me by the Heavens."

"Good. Perhaps the one night was all that was needed."

Reeri hissed, "Quiet, please."

Anula sighed. The guards exchanged a look, stepped outside, and closed the doors.

"I feel nothing," Calu whispered.

"Try again." Reeri's shadow stirred, the want for a tendril to snap growing. Reeri touched his way from one end of the shrine to the other, eyes closed and focusing. Yet time slipped by, and the only sense that rose was his frustration. Until—

A tapping echoed softly. Reeri's breath stilled. He opened his eyes…to a foot beating an impatient rhythm into the floor. Anula leaned against the doorframe.

He growled, "Is something on your mind?"

"This is taking too long. I have other places to be."

Of course she did. With her poisons, no doubt. Heavens forbid she be of help to him, tuck away her ire and reciprocate the kindness he offered to her. "Mayhap I should abandon my work and with it the promise of your crown. Would that better fit your schedule?"

Anula fumed. "Your 'business' wouldn't be incomplete if you hadn't killed so many people. Perhaps you aren't worthy of a second chance. Perhaps you're wasting your time and mine."

The words bit, as if released from his own mind and turned on him like a rabid dog. "If you are so faithless, why bargain?"

"Momentary insanity, I suppose." She spun, slamming through the shrine doors and down the stairs. Bithul chased after.

"The tether!" Reeri shouted.

"Don't care!" was all he heard back as she disappeared.

"Heavens, she is a handful." Calu whistled low. "Should we go after her?"

Reeri's shadow writhed. The empty echo returned to his arms, and he scratched it away. "No. Let her learn the consequence. We must focus on the blade."

Lest her thirst for power and blood fractured her soul beyond use. Any remaining guilt he had vanished on the breeze. He would not be tearing apart an innocent soul.

He would simply be finishing what she had already started.

17

He is here for you. To give you a pleasure from the Heavens. To make you feel the cosmos explode into being between your legs.

Anula's fingers tingled, as did a particular soft spot beneath her sari. The image of the shadow and its sharp features buried between her thighs. Her fingers entwined in wisps of shadow hair, guiding him—

Cursed Yakkas, what was she thinking?

No, it wasn't her, it was the damned headboard putting thoughts into her mind. Though his shadow was objectively handsome, it didn't change the fact that he was not truly her husband. He wasn't trustworthy. He didn't give her the feeling of safety or home. He did not care for her.

Beyond that, Anula knew the position she was in. She had chosen a life devoid of a true marriage, in which a single thought sparked the pooling of desires, a smoldering stare struck a thirst that could only be quenched by touch. She'd let go of that dream years ago. She shouldn't be subjected to its taunting now.

She shook out her hands as she marched through the inner

city. The beat of Bithul's cane quickly caught up. If Thaththa knew what ideas the blessed gifts put into one's heads—she cut that thought off, too. She ignored the ache of it, how it had doubled this morning, the first without her auntie. She chewed the blessed gifts' words and spat them out in the dirt.

The Blood Yakka was not here for her. The quiver of the tether below her heart proved that as it tugged at her, like the reins of a horse, pulling her toward the stupa, toward the Yakkas, demanding she stay by his side. He craved power and worship. The tether was merely a way to force it. No, the Yakka was here on a delusional search for a lost relic. As though he could do what centuries of treasure seekers couldn't. Even if he did find it, what would he do with it? He wasn't human. Could cutting the Hand of Death do anything for him?

Perhaps that was a moot point. Most relics bought and bartered were counterfeit, like the one Nuwan owned. Whatever the Blood Yakka found would probably do nothing, which didn't bode well for Anula. Unless finding a false relic caused him to see the futility in his search and made him leave. But if it didn't, would he continue?

Justice had waited long enough. Auntie Nirma had chosen *this* time for Anula to act. Said she was prepared, ready. That it was time to strike and strike hard.

The tether shuddered again as Anula inched farther away. She clenched a fist against it. The Blood Yakka could have the prophet, for a while longer. But the rest of the list would answer justice's call.

Now.

The jewels on her fan earrings and the bangles along her arms jangled as she strode purposefully through the courtyard toward the administration building, Bithul forever at her heels.

As ministers and courtiers streamed in and out of the palace, typical of any day, a group of women paused as she passed. Sharp eyes took in Anula's darkened mehendhi; sharper tongues clucked at her tight sari. They bowed in shallow respect.

"The statues do not speak of her reign," one whispered. "Come, let's not waste our time with one whose fortune will fall."

They flitted away as Anula took the stairs. Clay pots lined the walkway, bright blue hues darkening to black with each step. If she were a true believer, the woman's words might instill fear. She'd wonder at her future, at the outcome of Auntie Nirma's plans. But if the statues could foresee the lives of rulers, then usurpers wouldn't be a problem. Clearly, the blessed gifts were not all they were rumored to be.

The doors opened, and Anula brushed the gossip off her shoulders, trampling it on her way inside. Auntie Nirma's allies had mapped out these rooms, explaining who met where and when. Information the first ruling raejina would need. She knew exactly which door to aim for, what she might encounter on her way.

First were the guards. Though they bowed fealty, their gazes lingered curiously on her curves, suspiciously at her appearance. This was not known as a place for women. Yet all apprehension vanished when they noticed the iron rhythm behind her. The sight of Bithul drew straight backs. Anula tucked the information away for later.

She arrived at the largest set of wooden doors, and a guard looked questioningly down at her. The tether jerked, a warning of her distance. She yanked back on it, a horse gaining its head. The Blood Yakka had admitted he didn't know everything about the tether. Perhaps she could control it.

Holding it firmly in place, she smiled sweetly. "I'm here to speak with the board of ministers. Please announce me."

The guard blanched. "Raejina Consort, they're in a closed meeting."

"Please announce me," Anula repeated, sure to keep the gentleness in her features. A soft word did more to move a cow, as the palace cook had said.

"The ministers don't like to be interrupted."

"I'm not interested in what they like."

He flicked helpless eyes to Bithul. Whatever signal Bithul gave jolted the guard into action. He slipped inside the room.

Anula gazed over her shoulder. "Interesting."

Bithul merely grunted.

"Apologies, my raejina consort." The guard returned. "The ministers are indisposed. They can't allow an audience right now."

"Allow?" Anula's smile fell. "I didn't ask for permission."

She might be stopped by a Yakka, but not by a guard. Not now. Throwing an elbow, she rushed the door and flung it open.

"Raejina—" Bithul caught the guard as he sank, one arm reaching for her. It was too late. . .

"Ministers!" she shouted, entering the wide, open room. Latticed windows cast seven men in broken light. "How kind of you to receive me on such short notice."

They shifted and puffed. Naina Wijetunga, the chief minister, stood. Her words hung in the air, a challenge and a charge. Bithul rushed in, but Naina raised a hand.

"Raejina Consort." His husky voice was displeased. "What a surprise to see you *here*."

Inflection weighed heavy on his last word. Anula sauntered closer, eyeing the men around him. A hand glided along her necklace, but she knew nothing there would help. Though the seeds for the persuasion tincture could be found in the Pleasure Gardens, the rest of the ingredients hailed only from Kekirawa. Auntie Nirma was supposed to bring seedlings to plant, but if she had, Anula never received them. She'd have to do this without poisoncraft, her new title her only aid.

An itch began at her wrist. "I won't take up too much of your time. I only wanted to bring something to your attention."

"Your mere presence takes up our time, dear." Naina took off his glasses. "We do not hold court for wives."

A murmur of agreement flowed down the table.

Anula laughed unamusingly. "I'm no mere wife."

"Yet you are neither the raja nor a minister. We have a great duty to Anuradhapura, which is why we are selective in our meetings. If we met with every person who wished to bring something to our attention, the kingdom would fall to chaos."

Anula's nostrils flared. The itch traveled up her arm. "Even if a mere wife had information about a corrupt and traitorous minister?"

Six pairs of eyes widened.

"Would you not want to learn about the man who wields his power wrongly over the people of the kingdom that you are bound to protect? A tax collector who demands double pay, in order to pocket a profit, and sells those who come up short into indentured servitude? Would you meet with a wife then?" Irritation skittered along her arms, burrowed deep. Or was that the tether? She ignored it and pressed on. Anuradhapura's chief tax collector had come to Auntie Nirma's awareness years ago. His was the fourth name on their list. "If our chief tax collector was using the sale of servants to also sell secrets to the Polonnaruwa Kingdom, would you meet then?"

The men ruffled.

"Where is your evidence?" one squawked.

"Yes, has another man witnessed any of this?" another crowed.

"Plenty have," Anula said. "They're all in chains or starving in their homes."

"A reputable man," Naina sighed. "If not, then there is no foundation in your accusations. We do not take our duty lightly and therefore do not listen to courtly gossip."

Pain pierced her skin like a needle. Anula hissed and scratched at her arms, but forced her focus on the ministers choosing to turn a blind eye. "You're meant to keep the kingdom running peacefully, to ensure the laws are kept by *everyone*. To protect the people from traitors."

"And you"—Naina slammed a fist—"are meant to be seen and not heard, Raejina *Consort*."

Anula's lip curled. "Careful, I may take offense to that, and the raja may hear of it."

"Take what you will, but take it to heed. Your position is not here; it carries no weight. I don't doubt the raja will agree. Women have no place in running a kingdom. If you feel so strongly, by all means, speak such gossip to the raja. That's a wife's right. But wife to us, you are not. Please allow us to continue our work and rest assured that we know how. As you inevitably know yours."

Anula flushed at the implication.

Naina raised a hand toward the door. It was a dismissal. A dressing down.

Heat crackled along her arms, and the tether yanked. Anula stumbled, swallowing a gasp. The skin beneath her bangles splintered, like sun-dried dirt. A corner curled and flaked, a drop of red leaked out.

Cursed Yakkas.

Gritting her teeth, Anula stared up at the men. She couldn't let them see this, see her weak or wounded. For their eyes filled with truth as quickly as an irrigation tank in the monsoon rains.

They would never listen to a concubine, a woman, a wife. Not even the raja's.

The fact that Naina dared speak to her in such a tone spoke

volumes of how consorts had been treated in the past, how they were seen, how they were valued. Naina feared no repercussion because there wouldn't be any, had never been any. They cared only for position, and hers was not on the throne.

Yet.

She spun to the door, anger vibrating through her veins, flaming against her heart. Or was that the tether again?

"Our conversation won't be forgotten," she promised.

Nor would it be forgiven.

The door clanged closed, and Anula collapsed to the floor.

"Raejina Consort?" Bithul's voice sounded far away.

Finally, she let her breath rattle, her heart hammer. Fingers shook as she tore the bangles off. Brittle skin crumbled. She tried to hold the pieces together, tried to hold back the tears, but panic rose as the tether jerked and jabbed and fishtailed. Strips of her skin peeled off, hurtled through air, and snapped toward the Blood Yakka.

Anula screamed as darkness pulled her under.

18

The inner-city shrine had been as devoid of Divinity relics as it had been people. Reeri searched and searched again, until frustration needled so sharply that he could barely focus.

It was not until he stepped foot into the palace, the court's attention clinging to his every footstep, that he realized his chest was stinging. The pain quivered once before quaking through skin and bone, striking as fast and bright as lightning. Reeri canted forward and caught himself on a warbling statue. His shadow shuddered, threatening to rupture. The tether was quickly fraying.

"Are you all right?" Calu reached for Reeri but stumbled as a pulse beat through him, too. "Anula."

"Where is she?" Reeri hissed, clutching his chest.

Ratti said the tether would harm her, mar her, far more than it would him. He was the honey, and she was the bee. She needed to be near, lest she become susceptible to wounds that might render her soul offering void.

"Raja?" Courtiers narrowed in, curiosity and worry lining their faces. Calu waved them off.

"Call for the healer!" Bithul's voice rang through the palace hall. He lumbered toward the raja's chamber, a limp raejina consort in his arms. Blood left a macabre trail behind them.

"Mighty Heavens," Calu cursed.

The courtiers flapped and flittered. Reeri's soul tugged forward, the tether calling. Pushing off the statue, he ran swiftly after Anula.

The bed was soaked, the blessed gifts cooing over the wounded raejina consort.

"Avenge her!" the raja shouted at Reeri.

"Comfort her!" the raejina scolded.

Yet all Reeri could do was stare. Covered in darkest red, he could not see where sari ended and blood began. His mouth dried. He had not meant for this. She was only to learn the consequence, feel the first bite of pain and return. What had been so important she withstood…all this?

"I don't know what happened, my raja," Bithul said, hands flailing, legs shaking, cane forgotten elsewhere. "One moment she was arguing with the board of ministers; the next she collapsed. I didn't see an attacker, let alone an attack, but suddenly there was blood and her skin—"

"It is not your fault." Reeri shoved away the questions. Anula required healing. And for that, he must touch her.

Not grasp or hold or pull away, as he had in the painting.

This required time.

"Guard the door, Bithul. Let no one in." Reeri's hands flexed, his heart beat swiftly, and he was nearly certain it had nothing to do with the tether.

"What about the—"

"No one," Reeri repeated, palms hovering over Anula's wretched arms. They were shredded, as if a jungle cat had clawed her. Fissures ran from shoulders to fingers, festering and darkening with death.

"Then I shall pray."

As the doors closed, Reeri's stomach fluttered. He eyed the sapphires she might grab upon waking under his touch. Yet if he did nothing, she would surely die. Taking a breath, he lowered his hand, pressing into the soft give of her wounds, her flesh like pulped mango. A warmth sparked beneath his fingers, seeping from him to her.

Anula breathed sharply, chest rising high and slowly back down as the seconds turned to minutes. Each inhale knitted her skin together—first the smooth bronzed tones, then the dark mehendhi marking—polishing her long arms and her delicate fingers. Color returned to her cheeks, and her breathing evened. A peace washed through him as the Heavens' healing returned her to life.

He stared at her bee-stung lips. He could have for hours, but a sudden flash of faces and thoughts swept through his mind—the crown two lengths too far for her to grasp, frowning ministers looming overhead, a list of names, of deaths, the need to avenge—

Anula jolted. "Thrice-cursed Yakkas, what was that?"

Reeri's hands flew off her. "I had no choice. You were dying."

"It flayed me!" she screamed, checking herself. "It tore off my skin!"

"Consequences," Reeri said, shifting. "I told you, when you venture too far away, the tether will try to snap you back. It demands proximity. Even if it can only have one piece of you at a time."

Her gaze was riotous. "You were in my head."

So she had seen that, too. "I did not mean to be. I only meant to heal you. If you had been conscious, I would have asked permission."

"To see inside my head?"

"No." A flush warmed his neck. "To…touch you."

"Cursed Yakkas." She rubbed at her arms, looked away. "What have I done to deserve this punishment?"

Reeri's brows gathered. "Bithul said you were arguing with the board. What argument was so important you chose to endure this?"

The flash of ministers came to mind.

"An argument about a traitor. But they wouldn't listen." She glared at him. "I don't wear the crown."

Reeri narrowed his eyes. "Why did you try?"

Mayhap they were a threat to her or to her desired reign.

Anula snorted. "You have your business, I have mine."

Yet there had been a list of deaths. A need to avenge. It made no sense.

"You better find that blade quickly," she hissed. "I refuse to stay at your side forever."

Reeri caught her scorn and flung it back. "Finally, a point on which we agree."

All was blood.

Long ago Reeri had nightmares, yet never like this. Never a village in torment, soaked to the earth in death, its people scattered and scourged. A pyre rose above him. His eyes ascended the wood to dirt-smeared feet and torn legs, to blood dripping from—

"Look away," a voice whispered.

Reeri blinked. He was in a dark underground room, warm candlelight welcoming, the scent of determination invigorating. A sharp woman stacked books in his arms. "Vengeance is not important, Anula. Justice is. And that you are a different leader than all those usurpers before you."

He blinked again. The room was filled with women. Books and maps were strewn across tables, the same sharp woman at the head.

"This is why you survived." She leaned forward, her hand not quite touching his face, a softness about her eyes. It made his chest ache. "You are more than family to me, girl. You are everything. You are our future."

He blinked again. The village was different, bathed in sunlight save for the darkened alley where the sharp woman cowered, cornered by a tall man. He pressed a finger into her bosom. "Stop your meddling, or I will ensure that you and every woman in your little circle sees the noose."

Rage swirled swift. Reeri's hand flew to his own neck.

He blinked again.

Darkness veiled all but the man. Cinnamon and palm wine drifted on his breath. He leaned close to Reeri, touching places soft and supple. Grabbing, groaning, crashing lips upon his. Disgust soured Reeri's stomach, but he held firm, conviction swelling, and when he pulled back—victory. Veins bulging, the man's face purpled as frothing foam choked him, and he convulsed to the floor.

"Look away," the voice cooed again.

Reeri sat bolt upright. Sweat clung his tunic to his chest.

"Cursed Yakkas," Anula spat. "You saw that, too, didn't you?"

A shudder coursed through him. He touched his mouth, gaze scraping to Anula.

She had killed a man with her lips.

In protection of the sharp woman and those of her circle. In protection of others. He need not wonder why—the sharp woman had told him: Anula had survived, and justice was her duty. The bitterness and ire, the impatience and ambition, the poison-craft—it all made sense now. Anula had experienced a horror, felt the weight of retribution. His shadow shifted.

They were not dissimilar.

Anula drew a hand through her hair. He did not have to touch her to know the emotion she felt. It had simmered through the nightmare. Fear.

"Do you want to talk about it?" Reeri asked gently, wondering why she had not turned to the Heavens, as so many did in times of grief and great pressure.

"No." The word cut the night. Anula ripped off the sheets and jumped from the bed. "No, I don't."

The door slammed shut behind her.

19

"A vast farm shall you inherit," the statue warbled to a courtier, front and center of the surrounding group. "It shall hold more numerous irrigation reservoirs than all the villages combined, produce more—"

The words buzzed around Anula, a mosquito in the heat of day. Its bite brought the memory of home, of lush paddy fields and full market days, of familiar faces and the long-forgotten cadence of her parents' voices. She swatted at them, turned from the blessed gift, and left the gallery.

Courtiers lingered near the door, sending sidelong glances and lowering to whispers. In the last week, the Blood Yakka and his adviser had revisited both the palace and inner-city shrines, spending their days in meditation, while Anula tested the bounds of the cage she'd made for herself. She rounded a corner where a set of wives sat at tea. The kettle whistled a tune, its steam swirling around their placid faces, as if they, too, were deep in meditation. Lightly touching her mehendhi marking, she ensured the pulse beneath it was hers and not the tether's anger as she inched farther away from the Yakkas.

Two things were clear: the ministers wouldn't heed her words, and the Yakkas were on a wild elephant chase.

The only good to have come from the past few days was the memory-nightmare. Not the sharing of it, but what it reminded her of. Anula pressed a hand to her necklace. She had her poison-craft, and not all the names on her list needed to be dealt with through the ministers. Some didn't deserve a trial before judgment. Prophet Ayaan, for one. The only thing standing in her way was the tether. Though Anula was willing to do almost anything for Auntie Nirma's plan and to honor her dead, being flayed alive wasn't one of them. Being touched by the Blood Yakka wasn't either.

It wasn't as though it had hurt. The raja's palms were rough at first, but then there was a spark, and they cooled like a soft mist during a long drought. Tender and sweet and satisfying. She shivered at what was surely a trap to give the Yakka what he truly wanted: unquestioning faith and adoration.

Well, he couldn't have hers.

The tether stretched taut as Anula made her way down the hall to the other end of the palace. Each step grew labored as the lead tugged her back, but the marking stayed intact. She pushed on, so close to her destination.

"To whom do you think the spiders pray?" a woman asked. She crouched on all fours, head sideways against the floor, poking at a black insect.

A young man huffed. "Does it matter? Knock again. He said to come by today."

The wife and son of the raja's adviser, or so they'd used to be, stood outside the prophet's door. Abruptly, Anula's steps lightened, and a twang vibrated through the tether as it fastened tight onto the two Yakkas before her. She cocked her head. Perhaps the Blood Yakka had been wrong. It wasn't him she needed to be close to; it was any of them. And if that was true—

"Hello, Anula," the Yakka on the floor said, picking the spider up to examine closer. She plucked one of its legs. "Do you think it screams out to the cosmos, to a spider-being in the sky?"

Anula blanched. The Yakkas' wide round eyes were curious and rimmed with unshed tears.

"Mayhap it thinks of its lover or its children, or life itself and all it had yet to attain. What do you think it wants?" She spun, jerking the spider into the boy's face, toppling over a pile of books in her haste.

"Kama!" he snapped. "The books!"

They splayed across the floor, one skittering to a stop at Anula's feet. A name was emblazoned on the front.

"Apologies." Kama placed the spider gently on the floor, ignoring the books and the boy glaring at her. She turned to Anula. "Oftentimes, pain is necessary to reveal one's true desire."

"Is that why you continue to be a pain in my side?" the boy asked.

"Of course not." Kama laughed, a trill as sweet as aluwa. It shuddered through Anula. "Your wants are only too easy to see, Sohon. Anula's however…what is it that you want?"

She pressed her lips together. Amma had taught her about the Yakkas of Lust and Memory, told her the stories of old. Not just of love and remembrance, but of hearts sick with longing and bodies half eaten in graves.

Balance, they called it.

Sohon huffed. "Obviously she wants to see the prophet, as she is at his door, same as us."

"But why?" Kama leaned into Anula, wide eyes searching, as though she could venture into her soul. Perhaps she could. Hearts were under her rule. "Sohon has transcribed a memory book of the prophet's dearly departed brother. His entrails were so decayed, Sohon choked on his spleen, nearly missing ten years of the man's memories. The prophet offered his journal of visions as payment, plus another, unknown book for his trouble."

"You are scaring her."

"I'm not scared," Anula snapped. Was that bile crusted at the corner of his mouth or crumbs from a cake?

Sohon flashed his teeth. "Your body language suggests otherwise."

Anula shifted. Could they feel the uneasiness sinking into her bones? Was it the tether? It didn't itch, and it hadn't pulled since she'd found them. "I'm just on a walk."

"Away from Reeri, after you nearly cleaved your soul?" Kama tilted her head. "I think not. You are more intelligent than that. The nightmare proved it."

Anula paled. "How did you—"

A rap sounded on the door. Sohon sighed deeply, banging louder. Kama inched closer, as if Anula were the insect on the ground. "Has Reeri not explained that you are our tether, too? Though you bargained with him, we are the Yakkas you agreed to tether. You are the ox tied to a cart, and we the carts tied behind the first. A caravan, if you wish. When you hit a bump in the road, we all feel it."

Anula bit back a groan. Though it was nice to hear a reasonable explanation, it took away any comfort she had left. "Does that mean I'll see your nightmares, too?"

"I do not know," Kama said. "Mayhap you see only the first cart."

A silver lining, finally. "And the tether? It hasn't itched since I saw you."

If she only had to stay near one of the four, perhaps her cage wasn't as small as she'd thought.

Kama smiled, crooked and unsettling. "Continue your walk, Anula. That is what you want, is it not? Go on. You have survived the worst once before. What is another try, if in the end you get what you desire?"

Anula fell rigid, an ache knocking at her heart, a want prickling beneath her sari. "I'm merely a wife, Yakka. My wants lie back in bed and think of the kingdom."

She turned swiftly and left.

But she was not listening to the Yakka's instruction. She'd already been testing the tether's boundaries. And it wasn't as though she could mete out justice to Prophet Ayaan with two Yakkas lingering around. Abandoning her second attempt, she picked up her skirt and flew out the palace doors. A guard who wasn't Bithul nipped at her heels, the houses of the inner city her new goal. If her theory was correct, if she could position the Yakkas just so, she could move freely throughout the city.

An itch flared as she passed a group of courtiers. Scraping a hand along the mehendhi, Anula pushed forward. The tether fluttered against her ribs. One, two, three steps—pain seared her arms. She clenched her jaw and took a step back, then another, until only the pull remained. Cursed Yakkas, she hadn't even made it to the concubine estate. Heat burned her face. This was futile.

Nothing worth wanting is had easily, girl.

Anula touched her necklace. She couldn't give up. Waiting could take weeks, years even. She doubted the Divinities made the relic easy for a Yakka to find.

What, then, was there to do? What would Auntie Nirma have done? Pray, but that's what had gotten Anula into this mess. Beg? *Never.* She'd rather confront problems head-on, grasp them by the throat, and squeeze. Auntie Nirma would've told her to find her enemy's enemy, ally with them, or else threaten the enemy's most valued asset, regardless of—

Anula's pulse quickened. All she had to do was threaten the relic. But the Blood Yakka knew what constrained her, knew she wouldn't be able to search past him. The only way a threat would work was if she had an ally. Someone who could seek faster and farther.

She could go to the kitchens, but Premala's peculiar behavior left her more of a question mark than anything. That left only one. Anula spun to her guard. "Where is Bithul?"

The answer was training. Not with other guards, nor for his own benefit. Bithul stood in the center of the military training yard, close to the palace. The itch of the tether disappeared as Anula watched the sweat-glistened guard disarm a young man in less than a minute.

The soldier fell, but instead of cutting him shallowly to teach him a lesson, Bithul reached a hand down and lifted the man up. "You have much skill with the sword. It's your footwork that needs practice. Remember that you want to be lithe, like a jungle cat. If your enemy can't catch you, they can't harm you."

"Yes, sir," the young man said, bowing deep. "I'll practice harder. Next time, then, it'll be you in the dirt with ankles about your neck."

A tense moment pulsed, then Bithul laughed. "Would you like to bet a month's salary on it?"

"Two months. Plus a bottle of palm wine."

"That sure, are you, Shahan?"

"Sure enough that you're getting old."

The two shared a congenial laugh, and Anula narrowed her eyes. Bithul slid his sword into the scabbard at his hip, pulled it from his waist, and touched it to the ground. The cane now held both his weapon and his weight, as he clapped Shahan on the shoulder and walked him to the edge of the ring. Anula smiled to herself. She'd known his cane looked odd.

Bithul stopped short at the sight of her. "Raejina Consort." He and Shahan bowed.

"This is what you do on your day off?" She lifted a brow at the lather on his broad chest, gray curls nearly darkened to black. "No wonder the wives' gazes follow us around. And here I thought it was because of me."

Bithul nodded a dismissal to the young soldier. "May I be of help, Raejina Consort?"

"Yes, but first tell me what you're doing here. You haven't been part of the army since your ankles were hacked to sinew and bone."

"No," he agreed, frowning as he pulled on a tunic. "The skirmishes with the Polonnaruwa Kingdom have doubled, and it's important to me that the men are trained well."

"So that they, too, can cut their attackers' hands? Or was it their heads?"

He grimaced. "What can I help you with, Raejina Consort?"

"You miss it." It wasn't a question. "You wanted to be commander."

He sighed heavily. "It would've been a great honor."

"Tell me about it, the day you got your scars."

A far-off look overtook him. "My contingent had been sent to regain control of the Malvathu River from the Polonnaruwans and to free the villages seized by starvation. We did well for the first few days, until enemy reinforcements arrived. Commander Dilshan ordered retreat but—" Bithul cut off, his eyes haunted. "But three of my men were caught. They were being dragged into the center of the water."

A shiver passed through Anula as Bithul's ghosts reached her.

"We had entered the army at the same time, trained and fought together for five years. I could not leave them behind." He swallowed hard. "The Polonnaruwans vastly outnumbered me. They tried to cut me down, and they nearly succeeded. I don't remember it all, but I do remember the water turning red as I managed to swim away with my legs intact and one of my men in my arms."

A quiet moment breezed between them. Anula realized the men had stopped training to listen and pay respects.

Bithul straightened, fixed a steady gaze on her. "Though I didn't have the power to save them all, and my injuries stole my ability to continue to fight or be chosen to lead, I'd do it again."

Bithul was a true ally of the kingdom. A *good* ally. Exactly what Anula wanted to bestow upon Anuradhapura. She needed only her crown first.

"I can make you the commander." She leaned close. "For a price."

Bithul's brows furrowed. "No, thank you. It wouldn't be right. They deserve a capable commander—a soldier, not a stone weighing them down."

"I don't think that man sees you as a stone." Anula's gaze flicked to Shahan watching from afar, as though he were meant to protect Bithul instead of Anuradhapura.

"Why do you offer me this when you have Commander Dilshan?"

Anula made a face. "He has blood on his hands."

"The whole army has that."

Not this blood.

Anula snaked an arm with his. "Walk with me." She led him up the palace stairs and into the hall that would lead them to the Blood Yakka. If he agreed, there was no point in waiting. "You have a strong faith in the Heavens, right?"

"Yes, my raejina consort."

Glancing over her shoulder, Anula whispered, "What would you say if I told you that I made a bargain with the Blood Yakka for the crown of Anuradhapura, and that he now possesses the man who is the raja?"

Bithul paused, but where she expected to see apprehension, or perhaps horror, she saw only awe. "Truly? I'd say I never thought I'd witness the Heavens' hand like this. The stories of old are just that: old. But to stand near, to speak *with* them…"

A true believer, indeed. She refrained from rolling her eyes. "Don't get too excited. He refuses to fulfill it until he finds a certain relic."

"Ah. But if this is true, why tell me? Do you fear your safety?"

Anula snorted. "I fear for my bargain. The relic is expertly hidden, if it's even real. And you know as well as I do how quickly a usurper can come. I need my bargain completed, now."

"You wish to be the next usurper?"

"No."

"But you want the crown."

"You wound me." Anula huffed. "I'm no usurper, Bithul. I am here for justice and peace. I'll put an end to the Age of Usurpers, to traitors, and to the war with the Polonnaruwa Kingdom. No more villages will be burned, no more futures stolen from our children, no more attempts at hacking my people's ankles off. Will you be my ally and help, Commander?"

"How?"

"Force the Blood Yakka's hand."

Bithul's brows flew up. "My faith lies in the Heavens' handiwork and knowledge. If this is how it is, then this is how it should be. Who am I to judge that?"

"The Heavens didn't do this—I did."

Bithul sighed and leveled a gentle gaze. The same he'd given Shahan. "I am your ally, Raejina Consort, but I won't go against the Heavens. I've learned that things work out for the best when we focus on the most important thing in the moment. I don't need to be commander to make an impact. Though the path looks different, the Heavens have granted me a way to accomplish that purpose. That is why I train soldiers on my days off. Perhaps you can do the same. Until the Heavens are ready to give you the throne, what can you do? What is the most important thing in this moment?"

Anula clenched her teeth.

A door swung open, and out emerged the Blood Yakka, mouth drawn in a frown. "There you are. I must speak to the others, privately. Feel free to return to your chambers or do whatever it is the raejina is meant to."

"Excuse me?" Anula sneered. As if she'd waited with bated breath for him. She opened her mouth to tell him exactly what she was meant to do, but he rushed past. Anula stared at his back, a finger slipping across her necklace.

The most important thing was justice. Auntie Nirma knew it and believed the Heavens did, too—whether they did or not, Anula wouldn't be hampered by a lack of allies.

She would threaten the Blood Yakka herself.

20

The sun glistened bright, the click, tick, buzz of insects swelling in the heat. A breeze ruffled the flowers hanging from the terrace and the bushes peppering the Pleasure Gardens below. Humidity was a mere memory of the last monsoon season. Time was still on Reeri's side.

"We came across the tether earlier," Sohon said, as he and Kama edged onto the terrace. "She looked quite displeased."

"Sour," Kama clarified.

The memory-nightmare surfaced in Reeri's mind. He wondered at the detail.

"Have you not bedded her?" Calu jerked an elbow in Reeri's side.

Caress her. He imagined his hand on her thigh, slowly running its length, his thumb teasing circles higher and higher. He imagined her hips bucking, wild abandon taking over them both, marking their connection, their communion—a facet of life Reeri had yet to experience, despite Kama's and Ratti's great efforts. He had never found the one who sparked his desire, who prodded at what Calu called his "walls," who brazenly sauntered into his thoughts and dropped her robe—

O Heavens, what was he, an adolescent?

Reeri bristled at the unbidden image, missing the tendrils of his shadow, how they lashed and struck and all would back away, even his thoughts. It would not be right, the two of them, for a myriad of reasons: that the body he inhabited belonged to another and was not his to do with as he pleased ranked first; second, he could not experience any such part of life before his brethren were free and could do the same.

Palming the balcony's rail, he said, "Might we stay on task for once? It is time for the next phase: gathering our essence offerings for the soul sacrifice."

"Question," Calu said. "How is it time when the relic is not yet found?"

"We must complete the soul sacrifice immediately before we wield the Bone Blade," Reeri explained. "There is no telling what the Heavens or cosmos will do when we kill Wessamony. If our brethren are not freed first, they may never be freed."

"Why do we not do that now, then, instead of in tandem?" Calu asked.

Reeri raised a brow. "You think Wessamony will allow us to steal back the Yakkas?"

"Ah, the Bone Blade is our protection, as well as our final freedom."

Reeri nodded.

"I understand how the relic will work," Sohon said. The Yakka of Graveyards and Memories closed a gold-lettered book—the prophet's journal of visions that he was meant to skim for clues. "But how are we to use a soul?"

"We cleave it," Kama responded, leaning far over the terrace edge, craning her neck to watch two lovers amid the flowers. "She is the ox pulling the cart. Yet it is the driver who steers."

"Our souls are tethered to hers," Reeri clarified. "We must only take control."

Kama twirled around, tripped two fingers across Sohon's chest. "Yank the tether, wrench and wring. Hollow her out and to Earth our brethren bring."

A chill crept up Reeri's shadow. She was not wrong. Just as Lord Wessamony could use a soul to create a new being, Reeri could use it to save his brethren, trading its freedom for the freedom of another. Each of them would pull the tether until Anula's soul shattered. Then they would send the pieces with their true essence offerings to the cosmos in exchange for the sundered souls of the Yakkas, akin to humans offering to the Heavens. Balance would still be kept.

Kama whispered her song again, starry-eyed and swooning. "Love is such a tragedy, and sacrifice the ultimate beauty. All the great stories have both, do they not, Sohon?"

"Please keep me out of this," he murmured, cracking open the book again.

Reeri craned his neck. If only a clue could be found. Yet, instead of neatly transcribed notes, a drawing of a landscape and a wedding peeked out. Reeri plucked it from his hands.

"Hey!"

"We are racing against time and you read folktales?"

"Oh!" Calu bent forward. "Does it have a gruesome ending?"

"It is a story of love." Kama's eyes widened. "The prophet writes in his spare time."

Reeri imagined tendrils snapping. "Does everyone have the attention span of a mosquito?"

"Calm down," Calu said, lifting the book out of Reeri's grasp and holding it high over a jumping Sohon. "We are well aware of what is at stake. We need only a few moments to blow off steam. You should try it sometime, mayhap unclench those tight—"

"Do not finish that sentence," Reeri growled. He squeezed the railing, eyes on blue skies. "Please, focus."

"I was going to say shoulders," Calu said, as though it were true. "But since you asked so nicely… An offering of our truest essence is a rare find. Elevated bargains will be required."

"Yes." Reeri let out a breath. "Yet if made properly, we can have them by week's end."

"Easy for you to say—yours is a mere vial of blood." Sohon snatched back the book, scrutinizing it as if Calu's hands were made of fire. "Do you know what it takes to convince someone to write down their secrets?"

Calu scoffed. "A piece of paper with words? That is nothing compared to a product of an unsound mind. Most people do not want to relinquish control of their minds even for a moment, let alone long enough to create an offering by their own hand."

The three gazed at Kama, appraising the Yakka of Lust. Blood was one thing, as easily given as it was taken. A cut on the finger and Reeri would have his essence. Yet Kama…

Round eyes, nearly as large as her true self's, flitted betwixt them. "Do you think mine to be the hardest?"

"Not many are comfortable carving hearts from living men," Reeri said.

She smiled, sharp and spritely. "No, only those with a great passion. Ah, I wonder which human burns with it."

Bloodlust, vengeance, fury. Reeri could think of one.

The breeze played with wisps of Anula's hair as Reeri entered the bedchamber. She had not stayed with him at either shrine, nor had she ventured far enough for the tether to do more than quaver. Mayhap she had learned her lesson.

A maid plated the low table with Suwandel rice, jackfruit curry, seeni sambal, and plenty of ripe mangoes. Anula smiled at her, sweet and sincere. It did not falter as she turned it on him. Caution rippled. Those lips were liars. He had seen how they killed.

"Hungry?" she asked, pouring them each palm wine.

"What is this?"

"My peace offering. You were right, we're in this together. Let me help."

Crossing his legs, he sat. Though the words were right, his intuition flared. Yet that may not be fair. He and Anula had certain similarities. Perhaps she had seen the error in her ways and now resolved to locate the relic. The faster she found it, the faster she gained her crown and, he mused, the faster she avenged her dead and protected those in her dreams.

"Tell me why you're so intent on finding the Bone Blade in the shrines." She picked at the food. "Nothing the prophet told us leads there."

This was how it should have been from the start. Though Anula did not need to know details of how her offering would be used, he must be forthright about finding the relic or risk time running out.

Reeri took a sip of wine. "The stories of old are half-truths. You must see betwixt the lies."

Fate, Destiny, he explained it all, including what he believed was the Divinities' riddle. The Heavens loved wordplay.

"And the shrines?" she asked, opening another bottle of palm wine.

A flush crept over Reeri's cheeks. He had not felt the warm touch of wine in centuries. It did not sting with the heat of the sun like his hands had when he had touched her—a sensation he would not mind feeling again.

O Heavens. He washed down the thoughts with the rest of

his wine and moved on. "The stupas are large and obtrusive. One cannot look at the Kingdom of Anuradhapura without seeing them. The Bone Blade is there, hidden in plain sight."

She twirled her glass. "Sounds more like it'd be in the city. In a market, where hundreds of wares are sold and displayed. Plenty gets overlooked there."

Heat flashed up Reeri's neck. A city, where people lived, bartered, squirreled away secrets and treasures. Anything could be within a city. He frowned. "A city is a very large place to search."

Anula smiled, cunning and sharp. "Yes, it is. Good thing you have me on your side."

His shadow shifted. Sweat broke out on his brow as it furrowed. "Why do I sense a 'but' coming?"

She laughed, light as a breeze, and winked. "Don't worry, I have an excellent one."

Reeri's nostrils flared, pulse hammering. Mayhap he had judged her wrong. Again.

"*But* what if I weren't on your side? What do you think could happen then?"

The room tilted. He had drunk too much wine for this. Even his shadow tremored. "You said you wanted to help."

"I didn't say who."

The edges of his vision blurred. Alarm bells pealed in his mind. "What did you do?"

Anula snaked out a hand, caught him by the chin. "Your eyes are glazing over. Is your heart racing? Soon it will stop. Unless I'm on your side."

"O Heav—" A cough shook Reeri's ribs.

"Complete the bargain and I'll give you the remedy."

A vial sparkled in her hand. The world darkened around it. He reached out to grasp only air.

"*Ah-ah.* First, complete the bargain."

Words shriveled as his tongue thickened.

"Do it, Blood Yakka." Anula's voice rushed, somewhere in the distance. "Come on. Don't die like this. Complete the bargain!"

A wheeze and another cough.

"Yakka?" Her voice pitched.

Blood squeezed from his lungs as he hacked. It speckled the food, the wine. Convulsions shook him like a rockslide.

"Yakka!"

Blood burst.

Reeri choked.

His heart thump, thumped—

And ceased.

21

There were so many ways to stop a heart...and once again, this wasn't supposed to be one of them.

Thrice-cursed Yakkas. The measurements in Uncle Manoj's journal must have been wrong. A face made of shadows rose from the dying Raja, dark and insubstantial. Saffron eyes flashed. A bright pain pierced Anula's chest, tearing through her rib cage as the shadow spun in circles. The tether raged for it. A gust licked her hair into writhing tentacles, as the Blood Yakka's shadow ripped from Chora Naga's body and pitched over the terrace railing.

Anula's arms flayed in dark strips, shredding onto the wind to chase the shadow. The room shivered at the edges. She screamed.

Death—this was what death felt like. But she wasn't supposed to die.

"Help." A voice rasped.

Anula blinked back the night. That voice wasn't hers.

"H-help," the *real* Chora Naga whispered again, frail and fearful.

The Blood Yakka had told the truth: All this time, he'd been alive in there. And now he was before her, choking on her poison. She still had the remedy clutched in a flayed hand, but he'd stolen Auntie Nirma from her; he didn't deserve to survive. As if hearing her judgment, he convulsed and fell silent, the light seeping from his eyes.

Anula slumped over, pain thrusting her beyond the black curtain of consciousness, blood dripping from the rivers that were once her arms. An unnatural cold caressed her cheek, she sighed into it, knowing at least one of her family's murderers had been dealt justice by her own hand, and let the darkness take her.

"Anula!" Bithul's broad chest swam into view. "She spoke the truth, you are Yakkas."

"I believe the more important detail here is that she is dying." Kama coughed blood on his shoulder.

"No." A new face surfaced. The man jostled Anula into his arms. She winced, but only once, for the pain disappeared as he touched her.

The man let out a shaky breath. "Please, *never* do that again."

Anula blinked up at saffron eyes, down to her arms stitching back together in nets and florals, an elephant in one palm, a lion in the other. The tether jerked between them.

"How?" she croaked, his hands cradling her like a blanket on a cool night. Her body sank into him.

"A bargain is sacred, Anula." The Blood Yakka spoke from newly stolen lips. "You can only break it when you die."

A sickness twisted her stomach. "I wasn't trying to break it."

The Blood Yakka's thumb traced a slow circle on her wrist. Worry mellowed the bite in his saffron eyes, and she saw it: his thoughts. Thoughts about her and the pool of blood he found her in, the lifelessness of her body, and the jolt of fear, cold and clawing, that he'd lost her, that he'd brought death to her doorstep.

But…he only cared about finding the relic, didn't he?

Calu scoffed, rubbing his neck tenderly. "It definitely looked as though you were trying to break it."

"I didn't mean for the poison to kill, or whatever it did."

The Blood Yakka's arms stiffened around her, concern crumbling. "Yet you meant to use it."

"I was going to give you the antidote." Her eyes flicked to his hands. A desire rose for the softness to return.

"Yet you did not."

"Because it happened faster than I expected." Anula ignored her ridiculous want, struggled out of his embrace and made a shaky stand.

"If that is true, then be more careful with your poisons." Sohon wiped sweat from his brow, his hand quivering. "Death does not feel good."

"You felt that?"

"What you feel, we feel."

Anula regarded them, shaken but none the worse for wear. "I don't see *your* blood on the floor."

"It is an echo," the Blood Yakka said, his new body lean with muscle, face narrow and tight. "Painful nonetheless."

An echo. Anula scoffed. The tether demanded proximity, publicized her nightmares, and ripped her skin limb from limb. Yet they complained of an echo.

"Oh, poor Yakka," she said. "Did it hurt?"

His thin nostrils flared. "Yes."

"Do you want to talk about it?"

Hurt flashed in his darkening eyes. The saffron smoldered to a deep brown, erasing the last sign of his shadow, as if he'd never been anyone else, as if he couldn't be touched.

A finger of dread drifted down her spine.

Because he couldn't be touched.

Not without her death first. She had no leverage, nothing to threaten him with, no way to force the bargain. She was trapped, the cage shrinking around her.

Anula placed a hand on her necklace, but where once she found security, now she found only the cold sting of failure. Perhaps Auntie Nirma had been wrong. Perhaps she wasn't ready. She choked. What if she'd been wrong all along? Anula had never believed the Heavens had saved her for this, yet she'd grasped Auntie Nirma's belief in her ability.

But…

What if it was false hope?

What if she couldn't do this?

22

The converging clouds tightened Reeri's shoulders and sent his shadow squirming.

Morning rang out in the inner city with the sounds of animals and humans alike. Courtiers lazed through stalls of fine meats, foreign fabrics, and breathtaking jewels. They hawked and haggled, for those with deep pockets rarely touched their seams. It should have felt inviting, the memories cheering, but the whispers following him set his teeth on edge.

"My raja." The people bowed as Reeri made his way through the streets, Calu at his side. A contingent of guards followed a distance behind so the new raja could be seen by his courtiers.

It had been far too easy, the change in leadership. Usurpers, it seemed, were all too common, even ones who stole into the night without an army. The ministers swallowed the story Bithul and Viran, the former raja's adviser, fed them and regurgitated it for the masses.

The Kingdom of Anuradhapura was brimming with half-truths.

Raja Siva the First was not a usurper but a senior gate porter at the palace—the closest guard Reeri could sense and direct his shadow into. That part was not so easy. When the poison had wrested him from Chora Naga's body, his shadow attempted to return to the aether, while the tether chained him to the earth, to Anula, stretching his being in multiple directions. It was not something he wished to experience again.

If Anula was to be believed and it in fact had been a mistake, then he had nothing to fear.

Anula was cunning. She had strategically told Bithul of the Yakkas and her bargain with them, a decision that indeed helped Reeri return to her when all was blood and shadow and near death. If not for Bithul's knowledge, mayhap she would have died, the bargain and the freedom of the Yakkas disappearing into the blackness of the cosmos. Anula was also calculating. If her memory-nightmares and lists held weight, she had not bargained for the throne on a whim. She had mastered poisoncraft for a reason, met with ministers, and selected guards in support of it. She acted for her dead, for the loved ones she saw at night, for the blood she could not save them from. They were not dissimilar in that, and Reeri would not fault her for it. Yet he could not let the action go.

This was his only chance.

There was no room for failure, no choice to return to the Heavens empty-handed and try again next year. Anula might be many things, but Reeri needed to know if she was a true threat.

"Here." Calu thrust a fish patty in Reeri's face. "Eat while you brood."

Reeri pushed his hand away. "I do not brood."

"You have done nothing but brood for centuries. Your face is stuck like that." Calu bit into the patty and groaned in a way indelicate for public hearing. "Heavenly wretches, I missed these."

The longing in his voice pinched Reeri's chest. He had stolen this from him, from them all.

"Anula has not been near these." Calu cocked a smile, offering it once more.

Reeri leveled a glare.

"What? If you cannot laugh at yourself—"

"Then at least you will always laugh for me."

Calu stuffed the rest of his patty in his mouth. "I see we are not in a humorous mood."

Reeri gifted another glare.

He chuckled. "If you are so angry with her, why not lock her up? Let Kama watch her until we are done. The distance between you two seems fine now; the tether has not tried to kill any of us in nearly an hour. Mayhap she was right—she only has to be near one of us."

If Reeri were still made of shadows, his edges would flick and snap. Anula had been right. Proximity was necessary, yet proximity to *whom* was interchangeable. At least he did not have to look at her today. While he and Calu searched the inner city, she and Sohon explored the outer city. It had been her suggestion, after she had tired of his silent treatment. Though he did not want to risk the wrath of the tether again, she refused to be in his presence any longer. Something about being too pretty to be ignored. He scoffed at her gall but had not argued. It was her skin on the line, and if he was being honest, he wanted time to consider her actions. If she was a threat, she must be subdued.

"You think walls will cage her in?" he asked Calu, as they made their way through the city streets. Another point on which Anula might be right: perhaps a market, not a shrine, hid the Bone Blade relic.

"Do you? You know her best."

Reeri snorted. If the memory-nightmares and sparks of

thought he had seen when they touched were any indication, he did not know her at all.

Yet did he?

His hand flexed at the thought. At her bee-stung lips—the way they had crashed against the threat of the man in the dark alley. At the fear that filled his lungs in the night, the list of dead, the echo of Ratti's screams.

They were not dissimilar.

"She acts for a purpose," he said. "She believes she must have the throne to protect people."

"*Ah*," Calu said, touching smoothed stones and figurines on a table. "Love always offers the most outlandish things."

"So does ambition and revenge."

"But she tried to kill you last night. Why would she not do it again?"

Why, indeed? Anula's soul was bittered and burdened. The wounds of her past drove her in ways he had not seen in another offerer. Fear of failure drove her more wildly. But would he not act with wild abandon if his plans were disrupted? Was that not what he was considering now?

"She only threatened death," he said, chewing on the thought. "If she wanted me dead, there would have been no threat. She wants the bargain completed. She wants the throne. Now she knows there is only one way to her goal: the Bone Blade."

"Are you sure? Because if she makes good on that threat, if she steals the relic or finds a way to kill you…"

"I know," Reeri snapped. "I know what is at stake."

"I am only trying to help."

"No need," Reeri growled. "I have it under control."

He did not need the other Yakkas' help, nor their shadows shredded from a whip in his hands if he failed.

"All right," Calu said, hands up. He led them around a corner, a stretch of street revealing more vendors and a view of the main courtyard.

Prophet Ayaan carried a lantern through it, acolytes following in a line behind. They paused at each person, twirling smoke and spraying blessed water in their faces. Penance cleansing. Reeri had not witnessed it in centuries. It was a ritual performed leading up to the Festival of the Cosmos, a weeklong celebration of the Heavens' mighty powers, their love and favor, beginning on the Maha Equinox.

A gust of wind chilled Reeri's shadow. "Let us go to the shrine."

"Why? We have only searched half the market."

"Not for the relic," Reeri said. "I want blood."

Reeri and Calu needed only to touch the offerings in the inner-city shrine to hear their prayers.

"Great Blood Yakka," an elderly woman crooned, "hear my prayer—heal my grandson of these bleeding boils. My husband has spent all our money on healers, but they cannot do the miracles you can. Please, we need help in the fields, or else we will all die. I offer the last of our Yala harvest."

The scent of longing and heartbreak drifted on the air. Yet it was not the offering Reeri sought. He whispered back into the cosmos, where the woman would hear, either by faith or knowing. "You seek healing of the blood, so blood must be offered. First, bring a vial of your grandson's blood, and your bargain will be accepted."

The order for an elevated offering sang on the wind. Mayhap it would be as easy as that. Blood was simpler to find than a relic, especially when the wish was for a loved one. Those had been Reeri's favorite bargains to make—the ones that brought joy and peace. The ones that balanced the cosmos and tightened the sense of communion. That was what life was: beauty from darkness, and the thread of community through it all.

A deep yearning bloomed. He reached for another offering, another piece of communication, another ghost of the past. Yet Reeri tamped it down, wrenched his hand away.

The fault lies entirely with you.

Reeri had stolen that life from the Yakkas. It was only right that they lived it again before him.

"I believe Ratti would have liked Anula," Calu said, standing after ordering his own elevated offerings.

Reeri darkened at the turn of conversation. Calu knew as well as the others that he did not like speaking of their brethren and what he had sentenced them to. Yet he also knew that, oftentimes, Calu could not help it. His pain leaked like a damaged irrigation tank. The least Reeri could do was listen. "Why do you say that?"

Ratti was the oldest sister of the Yakkas of Love, the Yakka of Passion. She cared for all in a loving manner, like a mother hen to her chicks. She raised no walls and poisoned no creature. She was pure love. A far cry from what he had seen of Anula.

Calu gazed at a mural of the Second Heavens. "Ratti loved everyone. The real person. She always helped those who sought love find it after first loving themselves. She taught people not to hide their true selves. Anula is solely herself, not even willing to hide. She is as Ratti told me to be, fearless."

Reeri's shoulders fell. "Fearless of what?"

"Of them." He nodded to the door. "You were too busy with your schemes and your communion to notice, but she did. The humans did not connect with me like they did you. I was not invited to birth celebrations or gatherings of any kind. I did not have a gaggle of women fawning over me, bargaining with the Ladies of Lust."

Reeri flushed. "They did not—"

"They held back with me," Calu asserted. "Who could blame them? I could make them think whatever I wanted. So they constantly second-guessed whether they truly liked me, truly trusted me, or if it was an illusion bestowed upon them."

"They still prayed."

"Oh yes, they prayed. For protection or revenge. But they never communed with me. I tried to be affable, caring, like Ratti, but that made them suspicious. So I tried being cavalier, like you."

"I was not cavalier."

"Of course not." Calu rolled his eyes. "Eventually I gave up. Ratti saw it immediately and disapproved. She told me that you had not worked so hard for me to wallow in a mud puddle. She told me that if I were my true self, that energy would flow through the cosmos to resonate with the right people, and that I must try because without connection, I was not truly living."

A beat of silence passed, the wind whistling through the window. Had Reeri been so blind? Cavalier, Calu had called him. Was he still?

"I will not be afraid next time." Calu stroked a finger along Ratti's depiction in the painting. "I will make Ratti proud."

Reeri closed his eyes. He did not need to hear Wessamony's condemning words. He knew this was his fault. But he would fix it. He would give Calu a second chance. He would ensure their eldest sister was there to see. Their lives were within his grasp, and he would not falter this time.

Anula would not make him.

23

A FLAYING TENDED TO STICK IN ONE'S MEMORY.

Two crawled over Anula's skin like ants on a hill. Each step away from the Blood Yakka felt as dangerous as throwing knives. But the tether stayed calm, even as Anula and her guard moved farther from the palace gate. Her suspicion had proved correct; the sullen boy at her side was just as good an anchor.

She glanced down at him, a foot shorter and frowning at the bustling market ahead. Sohon hadn't volunteered to escort her. Kama had merely flitted off, chasing a couple down the corridor, an auntie bent on matchmaking, the only difference being that she encouraged their wish for a dark, quiet corner. And the Blood Yakka could go nowhere without Calu, as though they shared an even more demanding tether, which meant she won the company of the one Yakka who sighed more than he breathed.

Silent and stoic, Sohon marched alongside her, scowl deepening as the sounds of haggling drew near. The outer-city market was larger than the one in the inner city, a place where vendors with less valuable items had a better chance of making their living, where no one questioned quality or authenticity. It would only get louder the farther they ventured. She tilted her head, eyeing the mehendhi marking peeking from under his tunic. Swirls ran along his collarbone, bold lines wrapped around chubby arms. She wondered if there was an animal hidden beneath, like the Blood Yakka's elephant and her lion; wondered what Kama and Calu's markings held and whether the tether felt like reins to them as well, restraining and controlling.

"Commission a portrait, it will last longer," Sohon grouched.

Anula snorted. "In your dreams, Yakka. Speaking of which, why haven't I seen your nightmares?"

"What?"

"I've seen the Blood Yakka's and he's seen mine. Why haven't I seen yours or the others'?"

He huffed. "Ask Reeri."

"He doesn't seem to know much." She raised a brow, glancing at the space between them, at the tether decidedly not trying to kill either of them.

The suggestion of a smile quirked his lips. "Kama was right. It does not matter which of the carts is at the forefront. We are all connected."

"And the nightmares?"

Sohon shrugged. "Mayhap it is because you bargained with Reeri, not us, or because you are next to him and we are too far away, or it is some sort of balance. Not everything in the cosmos can be explained."

"Isn't that the point of the two Heavens, to give answers?" Anula asked, brushing away the chill of the wretched night she'd lost everything, of the resounding *no* hung high on a pike.

"Whoever sold you that story was a good liar."

With that, Sohon walked across the paved street and into the outer-city market. Anula blanched. If that night had not been an answer, if her prayer as a child had not been refused…

No. The Yakka was wrong.

"Raejina Consort?" Bithul asked, leaning into her line of sight. "Is everything all right?"

Shaking off the dust of memory, she followed. "It will be." As soon as she was free of this cage.

That was the reason she'd volunteered to search the outer city. With its small, tight-knit thatched houses and streets roaring with buffalo and oxen, elephants and pheasants, beggars and barterers, it was nearly a shrine on its own. Only more honest.

Here, one received an answer right away. But Anula didn't intend on wasting her breath on the Bone Blade. If a human couldn't break a bargain, perhaps a relic could. According to the stories of old, they were mighty powerful. And if the Blood Yakka sought one, perhaps she should, too.

Her eyes swept the vendors, passed curries and sweet treats, passed foreign fabrics and meats, searching for a familiar face. Though Auntie Nirma's closest confidants had perished in the palace with her, the web was spread wide. Now, if she could only find one willing to help.

A familiar girl rushed past, deftly weaving around bodies. A basket of candles bounced against her hip as she disappeared down a street. It wasn't out of the ordinary to see inner-city servants shopping here, yet there was something about the press of Premala's lips that sent an alarm bell trilling. Anula's gut told her to follow, but she couldn't. She needed an ally, not an unknown. The mystery of Premala must wait for another day. First, the cage and the bargain. Then the crown. Then the rest of her list.

Bithul squeezed her elbow, nodded toward a foreign merchant. "Someone's been distracted, my raejina consort."

The small Yakka bent over a rug stacked ten books high, eyes wild. "These are originals, you say, no translation?"

The merchant nodded enthusiastically, showing him pages

and pages of text in another language. Though Anuradhapura had always been a hub for trade in a sea of islands, a surge had begun. Each year, people from every corner of the kingdom made the journey to the palace to celebrate the Festival of the Cosmos. It had been Thaththa's favored time of year. Not only for the closeness felt to the Heavens, but for meeting those from so far away. Soon the market would be too thick with bodies for anyone to quickly slip through.

"I have no kahapanas," Sohon said, checking his pockets.

The merchant snatched the book from his hands. If Anula hadn't known better, she'd have thought Sohon's lip quivered.

"Do you need it for the search?" Bithul whispered to the Yakka, pulling out his own coin.

"Why would he need books?" Anula asked. Sohon was the Yakka of Graveyards and Memories. The stories of old spoke of his insatiable desire for entrails, devouring the dead's flesh to record the memories they held. Or merely for the taste, depending on his mood. "Is he going to eat them?"

The merchant scrambled in front of his horde. "No, no, leave!"

"I do not eat books," Sohon snapped.

"Do entrails have more spice?" She cocked a smile.

Sohon stormed away.

Anula's eyes lit up. "Are you embarrassed by your Heavenly powers?"

"No, leave me alone."

"Ashamed that you eat the dead?"

He spun. "Are you?"

"I don't—"

"Eat dead animals?"

A cage of chickens squawked. The thump of a cleaver sounded. Her stomach churned. "That's different."

"Is it? What is your favored delicacy? Mine is the liver."

Anula grimaced.

Bithul cleared his throat. "Perhaps we should stay on task. Blessed—my—Sohon, do you need that book to find the relic?"

His shoulders slumped. "No. The call is a feeling. I only wanted the story."

They continued down the first street, Sohon trailing fingers along tables, touching wares, garnering more than one dirty look until the merchants saw the darkness on his face and recoiled.

Anula sighed. "Why do you care so much for one story? Don't you have plenty stashed away from bargains?"

Sohon frowned. "Of course not. The memory books I make go directly to the offerers."

"Then aren't you tired of stories? You must have written over a thousand."

"No," Sohon said quietly. "I do not remember the ones I write."

"At all?"

He shook his head.

"But isn't that the point of you? To make a person's story last for all time?"

"For others. It is called transference. I do not actually think the words; they flow through my hands."

"How depressing."

Sohon grunted. A hand lingered on yet another table, on the feathered pens and ink. "Stories are sacred. They hold deep truths. Yet not all stories are told, nor are they all remembered. Like a leaf on the wind, they disappear. And no one cares."

A shiver swept up Anula's spine. The stories of old hadn't forgotten Sohon; at least that's what she'd thought. Perhaps, though, they'd forgotten the whole truth. What would they forget about her? Auntie Nirma had once said that songs would be sung about her, if she did this right. And if she couldn't do it, if she did it wrong…

"Anula?" A woman's voice called out.

She turned to see a friendly face, framed in gray and accented with a purple sari. "Auntie Malika."

The woman's smile spread. "It's good to see you. I haven't seen anyone since…"

She trailed off, and they both glanced to the ground. Anula felt the moment Bithul pulled Sohon back, giving her space. Giving her emotions space. But that's not why she had searched for an ally. Even though she questioned whether she could do this, she wasn't about to give up or prove her own doubts right.

"Auntie," she said, slipping off gold bangles. The woman's eyes flicked to her dark mehendhi. She could see the question, why it was darker than normal, why it was still on when the wedding had been weeks ago, why another wedding wasn't being held though the new raja had clearly kept her on as a wife. "I know it's not as much as planned, but these are for you."

Malika gaped. They'd fetch a few months' worth of coin. "Thank you, Anula. I mean, my raejina."

"No, don't. Not yet. I haven't completed Auntie Nirma's plan. And to do that, I need your help. I need information." Anula lowered her voice, sure that Sohon couldn't hear, and pressed Malika's hands in hers. "Do you know of a way to break a bargain with the Yakkas? Perhaps using a relic?"

"No, no, I cannot help." She shook her head quickly, glancing nervously over her shoulder. "Nirma's circle is broken. The women are either dead or imprisoned—or simply gone."

"What?"

"Her nephew found the room and the books. He turned them over to the ministers. Then the Polonnaruwans struck, cutting off river access to Kekirawa. People are fleeing before the fields dry. There are too many enemies, Anula, my raejina consort. You cannot keep going."

The hair on Anula's arms rose. All Auntie Nirma had built, all she had dreamed, was gone? She blinked back tears, but when they cleared, she saw it, shimmering just beneath the hopeful veneer of the outer-city market: stalls filled with entire families, the eldest working hot oil or bundling thatch when they shouldn't be laboring at all; babies cradled by young siblings; carts filled with the last remnants of a home; burned arms and hollowed cheeks. A people of loss.

Anula's heart lurched for all the women Auntie Nirma had armed and for the kingdom she'd tried to save against exactly this: ministers who hungered for subservience and men who thirsted for power.

Doubts withered under Anula's glare. She had no choice; justice must be served. "If I don't keep going, how will anything change?"

Dropping Malika's hands, she moved, outrage simmering like water in a pot. Bithul and Sohon kept their distance. They dared not ask what was wrong or whether her visits to vendors and low words were for the Bone Blade.

They weren't. No longer did she search for a familiar face. Any would do. Any that looked as if they dealt with secrets. Any that looked like they'd move mountains for coin.

She whispered for a way to break a bargain, for a relic that had the power. But every stall, every vendor, every foreign merchant answered the same.

Night darkened the sky as Anula stomped into the bedchamber.

The Blood Yakka rubbed his face, looking tired and beaten. He lay on the bed and growled at the ceiling. "The mural is mocking me."

"Good. Someone should." It was acidic and honest.

He grimaced. "I take it time with Sohon did not warm you to us."

She stared at the damned bed, at the space that would span between them and invite the curiosity that crept into her thoughts and made her want for the Yakka to rub her arm again. She wondered what he looked like beneath the stolen body; if a gentle touch would undo him, like a normal man, or if they could go on until the Heavens ended; if he really could make the cosmos explode between her legs. If he ever thought about trying.

She clenched her teeth. *Cursed tether.* "Don't act like you care about anything but your precious relic and unfinished business."

"I do care," he rebuffed.

She laughed mirthlessly.

He stood as if to fight. "Despite the half-truths the stories of old fed you, I am not a lion always out for a kill."

Anula narrowed her eyes. "And what do you care for? Devotion? Worship? Another statue made in your likeness?"

"I care for suffering." A flush crept into his cheeks. "I do what I can to protect my patrons from it, mayhap through vengeance, or healing, or a peaceful passing. Do not tell me whether I care for you or anyone else when I—"

"You don't like seeing us suffer?" Anula paused, catching on his defenses.

He puffed out his chest. "No, of course not."

The idea pinched her heart. Amma and Auntie Nirma had believed that. They'd believed that between the death and the blood was a being ready to save them, bless them, and keep them. The Blood Yakka believed the story he told, too, if the flared nostrils and pulsating vein in his neck told her anything. Sohon's words came back to her. Was this a story untold or unremembered?

She could see it, almost. Like a shadow in the dark. But—if

Amma and Auntie Nirma were right, then why had they not been saved?

"Prove it," she growled. A challenge and a threat.

"What?"

"Prove it," she repeated, fingering her necklace. His eyes tracked them.

If what he believed was true, then she didn't need to break the bargain. She had plenty of leverage to work with—an entire kingdom's worth.

"Talk is cheap, Yakka," she said. "How far are you willing to go to save a man from suffering?"

His brows furrowed.

"How long can you stand to watch? That's what Wessamony does to you, isn't it? Makes you watch the suffering. It's what haunts you at night." A wave of adrenaline spiked her senses, and she leaned closer, whispering, "If you care about our suffering, if your only job is to protect, then what would you do to save someone? Would you hand over a crown?"

The Blood Yakka stiffened, catching sight of a lion emerging from the bush, out for the kill.

24

"WHAT ARE YOU DOING?" REERI'S WORDS WERE DEEP AND quaking.

The fault lies entirely with you.

He would not be the cause of another's suffering, would not have blood added to his hands, would not—

A flash of red rivers, of bodies, and a flaming pyre.

Look away.

Anula might be a murderess, yet she was no monster. If she killed, there would be reason. Her threat was fueled with the fear of failure, a last-ditch effort to gain the throne instead of finding the relic. It was a bluff.

"You would never," he growled.

The smile fell from her mouth, as did the triumph in her eyes. "I will. And I'll start tonight. One person a day, until you fulfill my bargain."

Lie.

"You care about suffering, too. Else you would not be here," he said. Anula did not argue. Reeri took a step closer. "You refuse to acknowledge it, yet I see the truth. You will not harm an innocent."

She raised her chin, as if it made her taller. "I never said they would be innocents. I said they would suffer."

"No." He stepped another foot closer. "I do not believe you. I doubt *you* even believe yourself."

"Have you forgotten my poisoncraft? Do you think I learned it for fun?"

Another step. "I do not doubt that poison is meant for someone, yet not for this. Not for mere suffering."

"I'll do it." The veins in her neck tightened.

"No, you will not."

"Yes, I will!"

"No."

"Yes!"

Reeri closed the gap. Her heavy breaths hit his neck. Her heaving chest grazed his. Sent a spark down his spine. O Heavens, she was beautiful, aflame in ire and passion for her people, radiant as the sun. He wished she would burn him. "Prove it."

Her breath caught. Her teeth clamped.

Yet she did not retreat, did not argue. Instead she wiped her lips, gripped the sides of Reeri's face, wrenched him down, and pressed her mouth to his.

It was warm and soft and everything he thought a kiss would be—

Except for the slowing of his heart.

And the moment it stopped.

25

THE SHADOW RIPPED OUT OF THE RAJA.

Dark, insubstantial features sharpened into a chin and cheekbones. Saffron eyes flashed open.

A white noise keened as Anula's skin tore from muscle and bone. But she'd had no choice. The Blood Yakka had ridiculed her warning, dismissed her challenge. She had to make him see that she was no mere wife, no Jewel for a raja, and that he didn't actually care. He was deluding himself and lying to his patrons.

Choking sounded. Siva—the man, now free of Yakka control—lay on his back, blood strangling his breath. Cursed Yakkas, of course the Blood Yakka was right; she wouldn't let an innocent die. But he'd goaded her so quickly, she hadn't had time to check whether her necklace held the antidote.

Ignoring her own stripping flesh, she rushed to him, fingers tripping over sapphires. Tincture, poison, remedy. None of them were right. She swayed on her feet, searching her bedside. But the room tilted. The edges of her vision rippled, and she crashed to the floor.

"Raejina Consort!" Bithul gathered her up and deftly swung her toward another guard. No, not a guard—a palace worker.

"Mighty Heavens," the man seethed. "Stop this! Can you not see we are—"

He paused as Anula held out the vial. "Help. Siva."

The fire in the man's eyes snuffed out. Dismissing the vial, he knelt close to Siva, whispered, and waited. Siva wheezed, coughing out a prayer. A bargain. The man pressed a hand on Siva's mouth. His shoulders lifted from the floor, back arched, as the blood retraced its path. Slowly and in reverse. With a deep breath, Siva collapsed. Blinked. Breathed.

Relief settling like a balm, Anula glanced at the Blood Yakka, Reeri, who'd heeded her command and saved a human life—as though he actually did care.

"Splitting me from a human is too much for their body to take."

Perched in bed, Anula watched as her blisters healed. The tether sighed in satisfaction, as the Blood Yakka, now Raja Vatuka, held her in his bushy arms.

"Will he be all right?" Anula asked, fingers fidgeting on the wood carving. The blessed gift raejina hid behind her raja. Anula couldn't blame her. Poisoncraft wasn't for the faint of heart.

"He remembers nothing," the Blood Yakka promised. "He is as healthy as the day he was born—now with a new name and new life far from the palace. His bargain saw to that."

"Is that what you whispered? You told him to make a bargain?"

The Blood Yakka nodded. "I cannot act without one. It disrupts the balance." His gaze wandered to the painting of the Heavens on the ceiling, a grimace marring his lips. "Thank the Heavens he was lucid enough to pray."

The chamber filled with heavy silence. Anula heard the unspoken words that hung between. They crawled over scarred tissue, nipped at sensitive skin. If she hadn't been so focused on her bargain…

"Thank you." Her voice was small.

The Blood Yakka matched her gaze. "I do not want your thanks."

"I'm sorry."

"I do not want that either."

Anula bit her lip. "It won't happen again."

"Do you mean that?" Worry lines wrinkled his forehead. For the first time, Anula wondered who he worried for.

She held his stare. "Yes."

He searched her, as if trying to read her mind. "I hope so."

Turning over, he blew out the last candle, leaving Anula alone with her thoughts, her doubts, and her healing skin. She rolled onto her side, watching the Blood Yakka from the edge of the bed, the chasm wide between them. He had judged her fairly, and she'd deserved it, but he hadn't mentioned the other thing—what she had seen when they kissed.

He had liked it.

It was everything he thought a kiss was meant to be, everything he had dreamed of it being. A sizzle at first, exploding on his tongue and raining down his body. Every muscle, every bone alight. There was a thirst for more, the hunger deep and aching. But he also thought it shouldn't have happened like this, in another's body. It should've been his breath on her skin, his hands pressed onto her waist, his girth rising to meet her heat. His lips sliding against hers.

Anula softened. How had a centuries-old being never been kissed? She wondered what it would be like to kiss a Yakka—sharp edges and sharp teeth biting gently, teasing and testing bounds.

Perhaps kissing a shadow would be the same. She shuddered, her fingers tingling. Desire grew fast and wild, like a fire caught in the jungle. *Close the gap*, the tether yearned. *Find out*, it cooed. *Pull the shadow—not to kill, but to kiss.* To know what his soul tasted like. Perhaps if she touched him just right, touched him gently…

Her fingers stretched across the chasm.

Cursed Yakkas.

Anula yanked her hand back and flipped over, wincing at the tug on her new skin. She'd lost too much blood; it was making her delusional. She pressed her eyes firmly closed and told herself to sleep. Because the shadow that was the Blood Yakka wanted a relic, not a kiss.

As did she.

But Anula found herself in Reeri's mind, staring as a Yakka pressed a kiss onto another's forehead.

They were tall, edges keen and features wide, similar to the one she'd seen in the last memory-nightmare. She watched them carefully, a surge of warmth in her chest, as if the Blood Yakka had long awaited this. They parted, Calu and a female. Then she pressed a kiss on Anula's cheek. It tingled and drew her smile. Dark tresses curled down to the female's waist, swaying in the breeze as she handed them both wrapped gifts.

"From the Indian continent," she said, her voice melodic. "Minister Advik sought many loves. The tether took us beyond any border a merchant has hailed from."

"And his wife?" The Blood Yakka's voice slipped from Anula's lips. "Did he find his true love?"

Ratti giggled. "Do you think me incompetent? Kama is not the only Lady of Love. The minister's pleasure saw no bounds.

Neither did the woman's." She winked. "His new wife will never be displeased with what I taught him."

Calu waggled his eyebrows, and Anula felt her cheeks heat. "Reeri does not like to hear bed talk; he only wants satisfied patrons."

"Oh, they are satisfied, tenfold. Shall I tell you how?"

"The gist is enough." The Blood Yakka huffed and unfolded a bright tunic from its package. "Thank you, Ratti."

"Only the best for my two favorite brothers." Ratti swept a curl from Calu's forehead. "Now, you, have you heeded my advice and made new friends?"

Calu dimmed. "They do not want to know me."

"Because you have not let them see you."

"Why do I need friends? I have you and Reeri. That is enough for me."

Hands on hips, Ratti tutted and turned to the Blood Yakka, but before she spoke, a drumbeat sounded. Ratti clutched her chest.

The gifts dropped to the darkened village floor, and Anula reached out in panic. Fear struck Ratti's face, and her body flew through the blackened brush. Calu sprinted, Anula on his heels.

Boom.

The drum beat louder.

Boom.

It thrummed in her chest.

"Ohng Hreeng." A chant rose in the night, reaching for the moon. Men in masks danced in a wide circle. Ratti spiraled above them.

Heavens, what was happening?

Boom.

Ratti's cries bounced off their chant.

Boom.

It tore her apart. Blood and shadow burst into pieces, falling like sand on the shore.

Boom.

And blowing away on the wind.

Boom.

Her form reassembled on the edge of the village. Calu and Anula caught her in their arms.

"Who would do such a thing?" Calu gasped.

Fear pitched the Blood Yakka's voice. "Who else have they done it to?" A flash of Yakka faces bottomed out Anula's stomach. Another flash of villagers' faces made her gag.

Boom.

"Great Divinities of the First Heavens," the masked assailants yelled, their voices raised as one. "Save us from all evil. Send your blessed deliverance!"

The earth shook and the Heavens erupted. A shiver racked Anula. A searing pain tore her shadow from her form.

A whip snapped. Cries rained down on marble stone. "The fault is entirely yours."

Claws thrust the whip into Anula's hand.

"You shall be the Yakkas' tormentor." Lord Wessamony's horns flared bright. "For eternity."

The words struck Anula in the chest, blew out her breath.

"Please," Ratti wept. "Help."

A tear slid from Anula's eyes, her hands shaking, trying and failing to stop her arm from arcing back.

And swinging forward.

The Blood Yakka screamed.

Anula jolted awake, instinctively reaching out a hand. The

Blood Yakka flinched away, a flush on his ears. Her hand snapped back.

"I did not mean to fall asleep," he murmured, eyeing dark corners as though they hid masked men and whips.

Questions knocked into one another in Anula's head. "Who were they?"

"It does not matter," he growled, hackles rising.

She scoffed. "They attacked the Yakkas, and no story of old mentioned men in masks. I think that matters."

"Why? I thought you did not believe."

"And I thought you said the old stories only told half-truths. What happened?"

"It does not matter now." He glanced at the mural on the ceiling, wiped sweat from his brow.

"Yes, it does," Anula insisted.

"Why?" he snapped.

Because, she wanted to yell. Because what she'd witnessed these past weeks and what she'd experienced over the years didn't fit together. She'd only ever seen the selfish side of the Heavens, unable to understand why Amma and Auntie Nirma loved them so. Because truth mattered as much as justice. It set people free.

"Why did you save Siva?" she asked instead.

"It was the right thing to do." He answered without pause, as if this was his purpose.

Anula fell silent. This Blood Yakka had nothing in common with the creature from the old stories. His shadow wasn't grotesque; high cheekbones and a sharp chin didn't drip with the endless need for blood and death and decay. He rushed to rescue those in peril, herself included. Not once, but thrice.

She'd thought it was out of fear of losing his tether and being banished once more to the aether without finishing his business, but he'd worked hurriedly for Siva and held her soothingly. And that worry she'd seen in his eyes… She was right; it wasn't for himself. She'd felt that same fear in the memory-nightmare.

Fear for the Yakkas.

Fear for the people.

The Blood Yakka ran a shaky hand through his hair as the space between his brows puckered. If the stories of old were half-truths, if Auntie Nirma's faith was true, did that mean that the Yakkas *actually* cared?

The Blood Yakka expelled an unsteady breath. Anula's eyes flicked to his lips.

But if he cared, why hadn't Amma been saved?

Rain pattered the windows, storm clouds erasing the light of the moon, plunging the bedchamber into darkness.

"What about the night market?"

"Wh-what?" Anula stuttered, pulled from the precipice that was Amma's final night.

"Last I was here, secrets tended to be sold in the night markets. Do you think we could find the relic there?"

A coldness swept through her. He'd changed the subject. He didn't want to tell her about masked men and why he cared for everyone except—

"Yes," she said, shaking the thought off. The night market was a perfect place for relics to exchange hands, real or false. Spreading from corners of the outer city, it clogged the streets from dusk to dawn. Vendors sold food, as usual, but also concubines by the hour, drinks that turned reality to dreams, and goods stolen from other lands. If the palace or the Heavens disapproved, it would be of high demand in the night market. Wasn't that where Nuwan had intended to take his relic? Perhaps there they'd find the Bone Blade or the one Anula sought to use. "That's a perfect place to look. I should've thought of it myself."

"Good." The Blood Yakka stood and paced the room to the

rhythm of the rain. "Let us go tomorrow, before another nightmare befalls us."

His hands shook at his sides, as they had in the nightmare.

"It wasn't your fault, was it?" The words slipped from her mouth before she could catch them. "Something else happened."

The Blood Yakka stilled. He didn't meet her gaze.

"Sleep, Anula. I will stay awake to keep the dreams at bay," he whispered, as if he truly cared.

26

The image of the nightmare clung to Reeri's mind all day, like stink on an elephant. The masks he could manage, but the whip—

You shall be the Yakkas' tormentor, for eternity.

The shadow inside the raja ached to snap. He paced the bedchamber, staring at the shimmering heat just beyond the latticed window, the tremor of humidity clear in the falling sunlight. The song of cicadas welcomed it home.

Reeri tensed. Time was slipping by. Just over a fortnight was left.

The door to the chamber creaked open, and he spun, only to find the Yakkas entering. "Where is she? We were supposed to leave half an hour ago."

"Impatient as ever," Calu said, a smile widening his face. "I am sure she is on her way. In the meantime, I have good news."

Reeri's breath nearly caught. "Have you found the relic?"

"I said 'good,' not 'great.' I have received my essence offering. Truthfully, I did not expect to find a bargainer so fast, but a thief named Kushal was in quite a hurry for his neighbor's memory to be wiped of the time he'd stolen from him. He was so grateful for my quickness, I think if we still lived in our shrines, he might have hugged me." Calu pulled out a disfigured, cobbled elephant pendant and tied it around his neck. "Ratti would have been proud."

Reeri's hope sank, though he nodded, trying and failing to be as happy about Calu's experience as he was—but it was not enough. He deserved a hug, a true connection.

Calu gingerly tucked the necklace under his tunic. "Have you received yours yet?"

Reeri slid an old perfume bottle from his pocket. Instead of jasmine it smelled of iron, and a deep-red viscous substance curtained down the sides.

"We are halfway there," Calu said, then took a step back, assessing Reeri. "Why are you dressed like a mark?"

Reeri glanced down at his clothes. He had dressed like a palace carpenter, the very position Vatuka had held before Reeri made him raja—another incident of being too near the royal bedchamber at the wrong time. Vatuka was shorter than the others, softer, yet not in the hands. Those were strong and callused. He looked nothing like a person to be easily taken advantage of. "I wanted to search unencumbered by guards tonight."

"Of course," Calu murmured. "Would not want to use your political power to aid us. Too unseemly. Vatica has a reputation to protect."

"Va-tu-ka," Reeri corrected. "We seek secrets, Calu. Those do not tend to be given to rajas."

"Not willingly."

A throat cleared as Bithul entered in plain clothes, weapons well hidden. Since he knew the truth of them, Reeri did not mind his presence. And since Anula had proven to be a handful, she necessitated protection—and additional supervision. "Are you ready, my raja?"

"I have been ready for an hour." Reeri's voice darkened. "Where is—"

Anula sauntered in, long tresses bouncing. The tether sighed in comfort, and an urge to meet her in the center of the room rose high. He would not soon forget the ire and passion that set her aflame—or how it stoked the cinders within his shadow. Yet when her dark lashes lifted, hesitation bloomed bright in her eyes.

Mayhap after all the pain and death in their shared memory-nightmares, she too saw their similarities. Perhaps the bargain could finally function in its natural state now, with the two of them working together toward the bargain's completion: a relic and a crown, for the price of a soul.

No passion or flames to speak of.

Anula broke their gaze. Reeri's shadow pinched, as if he might miss the fire. She turned to Sohon, a small book in her hand. "Here."

"Oh," Kama squealed. "A gift."

"A loan," Anula corrected.

Sohon flipped the pages open. "Poetry?"

"Best read alone." She winked.

Kama squealed again.

Sohon snorted. "Dirty jests. Why give this to me?"

"Stories for you to remember," she said. "And enjoy more than once."

As the three bent to read, Reeri considered their exchange, the ease with which Anula spoke to and jested with the Yakka with the sharpest edges.

"What, nothing for me?" he murmured.

She raised a brow. "I thought you only wanted my help and for my poisons to stop finding your lips."

His eyes flicked to her mouth. Plump and red and deadly, smirking at him.

As though she knew his thoughts. Knew how he liked the press of bee-stung lips, the taste of them. Knew he wanted to try again, linger and play. He swallowed. She probably did. A window opened into their minds and hearts each time they touched. Yet did she see what he had seen? When she had pulled him from the raja's last body, he had careened through the cosmos before finding Vatuka and saw a small shadow creature cowered in the aether. Her soul.

Alone and frightened in a vast dark nothingness.

He had reached out, knowing from two centuries of experience how it must ache, but the distance was too far.

"Are you ready, my raja?" Bithul repeated, grounding Reeri.

He shook himself, adjusted his clothes, and glanced at Anula's. "Where is your disguise?"

"No one will recognize the raejina consort," she said, leading the way out the door. "I won't even be in a rendering until I bear children."

"Why?"

"Because"—Anula paused, meeting his gaze—"a consort can do nothing else."

He held it, knowing to what she alluded. "Then let us not waste another minute."

"I have never agreed with you more."

Not all was the same as it had once been in Anuradhapura.

The tang of curry and sharp turmeric were eclipsed by a shadow stretched across the outer city. The wide irrigation reservoir sat in the city center, a sentry against the ominous dry seasons, when once the people merely had the Heavens to protect them.

Yet not all had forgotten that fact. Anula led the Yakkas down stone paths, past structures built to withstand monsoons, to the dense population sifting through the night market. Pilgrims in varying states of poverty and finery marked the festival's nearness. If the humidity had not slapped Reeri with the reminder, each of their faces would.

Anula's apology last night and her acceptance of the bargain the way it stood had come not a moment too soon. He could not help his gaze from flicking to her back, nor the frown that tugged on his mouth. He had bargained with many before her, but this was different. They knew things about each other that no one else did. Still, a question lingered in her eyes, on her lips. A question that kept him at arm's length.

Reeri split the group to cover the most ground. Sohon and Kama took the north, Reeri and the others the south. He would have preferred another split, but Bithul and Calu would not hear of it.

Anula barely blinked an eye at his command. She had no problem greeting vendors in the night market; she flitted betwixt them, bought wares, haggled yet paid twice the agreed-upon price, and never faltered in her whispers of relics. She handed Calu banana leaf after banana leaf of her favored foods. Steamed buns, curry, aluwa. She lingered at stalls with elderly women, pushed passed men to speak with their wives. Even when answers could not be found, she still left coin.

That, Reeri could explain away: It was in service to her bargain. But the book Sohon could remember? The food Calu loved to indulge in?

The hand that had reached across the bed? The voice that questioned the truth?

She wanted true knowledge about the Yakkas, not false stories of old. She had said it was important. Why?

Worse yet, why did it bother him?

He had what he wanted, what he required: a tether, a soul, and an offerer hunting for the Bone Blade. All was going according to his plan. Now he must focus, before it was too late. He should not dwell on the reasons she kept him at bay. He most assuredly should not dwell on her fierce passion and deadly lips. No matter how beautiful. No matter how taunting. No matter how they sparked the oldest of his desires, to experience a certain type of communion, a certain aspect of life.

As if she had heard his thoughts, Anula's gaze landed on him, her mouth half-open to eat a sweet. She paused, then offered it to him. "It's called pani walalu."

Reeri peered at the treat's flower design, then warily at her necklace. "Did you lose a diamond in it?"

Her smile was sweet as hakuru. "It's not the diamonds you have to worry about."

He continued down the path. She snapped at his heels.

"Just try it."

"Why?"

"I'm attempting to be nice."

"Why?"

She huffed. "Perhaps this is my way of apology."

Reeri halted. "Your last apology left a bitter taste."

Anula crossed her arms and aimed her words at Calu. "Is he always as stubborn as a donkey?"

"Yes." Calu laughed. "To be fair, you did poison him. *Twice.*"

"I said it won't happen again."

"Why should we believe you?" Calu plucked the pani walalu from her hand and tossed it in his mouth.

She lifted a brow at Reeri. "I am true to my word."

Clearly. Though not her intention, she had threatened to kill a human and nearly succeeded. "I do not want your pity."

"I'm not offering it."

"Then I see no reason for apology or forgiveness. Do not let it happen again, and let us focus on finding the relic."

"Fine." Her eyes flamed again. If it was not pity, why did she want the truth?

Not that he cared. Not that he should.

"Mighty Heavens, I love the night market," Calu said, caressing a sword no doubt stolen from a great foreign warrior. "You can find all you desire here."

"That's yet to be proven," Anula murmured.

Reeri grunted in agreement. They had been in the market for hours, spoken to a slew of merchants, and still had no lead on the Bone Blade or a relic hawker.

"I wish there were a night market for Yakkas," Calu said.

"Why?" Anula asked.

Reeri shot a warning glance.

Calu ignored it. "I do not desire much, but what I do are things I cannot have or cannot do. If there were a night market, mayhap I could try them."

"Like what?" Anula asked, interest well and truly piqued.

If rajas or shadows had hackles, Reeri's would rise. It was dangerous to tell humans too much. Yet he said nothing, loosening his grip on the door to their truth. A peek would be alright. It had been centuries since Calu had attempted to connect with a human; today's essence offering must have given him newfound confidence. Ratti would have given him this moment.

"I am the Yakka of the Mind, remember? There is much I

could do for people if only a bargain is struck. Like unwind a mind."

She frowned. "That sounds cruel."

"It is not. The mind can be a cage, Anula. A jailer worse than any man. I have the power to release them, but I am constrained. If given the chance, I would not hesitate. Mayhap then they would see me in a new light." Longing lowered Calu's voice and ached in Reeri's chest.

Anula pursed her lips, assessing Calu without his notice, like a farmer would a cow, wondering at their strengths and weaknesses, at the things that made them up. "Why don't you do it, then? Go save someone."

Calu pressed a hand to his heart. "No one has asked."

"You can't act without a bargain?"

"Can?" Reeri clarified, his tongue moving before his mind could stop it. "Yes, we can always act. Yet we do not. It is taboo. Our existence is for communion, but without balance we disrupt the cosmos."

Calu proffered his mangled elephant pendant to Anula. "If I had acted without a bargain, I would not have come to know Kushal. Our connection would never have begun. It would be a lonely existence, if we did not include others."

Pride swelled in Reeri, for Calu's bravery, his vulnerability, heeding Ratti's advice even when she was not yet there. Reeri gave Anula a sidelong glance, hoping for a favorable response. Her head tilted in thought.

"Besides, Wessamony forbade it," Calu added. "I doubt he would be too happy if we started wielding powers at all times of the day."

Anula scrunched her nose. "Why would he care?"

Reeri and Calu exchanged a look. This time his warning was heeded. If she found out about Wessamony, about Reeri's plan, there was no telling the outcome. Humans had turned on the Yakkas once before. Reeri would not allow it to happen again.

"As much as I'm certain the people of the city are grateful for your...extravagant purchasing tonight," Bithul said, "perhaps we should focus on the relic."

"Oh, did you think I was enjoying myself here, begging for any crumb of information? If these people knew of a relic that could save their lives from the devastation caused by the Polonnaruwans every day, I doubt they'd be here in search of help from the crown or the cosmos."

Reeri heard what she did not say. She had a duty to try and do what neither had accomplished. "Do you want the fighting to stop?"

"Of course," she scoffed.

Reeri paused and offered a different kind of sweet. "As the raja, I could command the army to stop."

"No!" Anula snapped. "If we stop fighting, Polonnaruwa will march right through those gates and take us all. Anuradhapura can't stop; we must *win* the war. There was a strategy in place to appoint certain women proficient in warfare, politics, and diplomacy, and when my bargain is finally complete, I'll enact it."

Her nostrils flared in beautiful fervor. Could she see it yet, how they were not dissimilar?

"Anula?" a man called. Reeri spun, catching sight of a brawny man, his gaze predatory as he neared. "Dismissed from concubine service so soon? Was your touch too *toxic*?"

Reeri's brows furrowed.

"Nuwan," Anula sang with a false sweetness. "What a displeasure to see you again."

He smirked, eyes hungry. Reeri shifted in front of Anula.

"You're not as stealthy as your dearly departed auntie," Nuwan said.

Anula stiffened at Reeri's side. Bithul pushed forward, hand disappearing beneath his tunic, yet she held him off. "What do you want?"

"Me?" Nuwan mocked. "I'm not the one throwing around coin and asking questions about relics."

"Told you," Calu whispered. "An easy mark."

Reeri bristled.

"So?" Anula asked.

"So, for the right price, I may have what you're looking for."

Reeri straightened.

"I'm not interested in the fake one you had last time," Anula said.

"That was one mistake. Besides, it afforded me a real relic, the first of many."

Anula rolled her eyes. "A great businessman now, are you?"

Nuwan laughed. "Don't you trust me?"

"Not as far as a plow can throw an ox."

Nuwan feigned hurt. "Even after I made good on our deal? After I forgave you for poisoning me?"

All eyes flicked to the jewels at her neckline.

She ignored them. "Describe the relics you have, or we find another merchant."

"Ah." Nuwan lifted a finger. "So it's a specific relic you're after." His gaze turned feral, hunger aimed at her hips. "That will cost you extra."

"The description," Reeri growled.

Nuwan grimaced at him. "I hear whispers you're searching for a certain blade. One imbued with Fate's power, one that's been hidden for centuries."

"And?" Anula pressed.

White teeth flashed in a grin. "It's no longer than my hand, with a handle as smooth and white as ivory, and a sharpened iron that never dulls."

Reeri's heart beat swiftly. That was the Bone Blade. Not made of ivory but of bones, ripped from willing bodies, cleaned and polished for Fate. "Your price?"

A tremor snaked down his fingers as he pulled out his coin purse. He nodded to Calu to do the same, grateful Anula had suggested they bring a hefty sum from the palace stores.

"I don't want coin." Nuwan smirked. "I would lose my business if I merely sold everything off. The cost is a blessed gift."

Calu scoffed. "A relic for a relic?"

"A painting," Nuwan clarified.

Reeri stiffened. "The Heavens dictated the blessed gifts were to stay within the palace."

Nuwan laughed. "Exactly. I will be rich forever. My grandchildren's grandchildren will be set."

"Fine," Anula agreed. "Give us an hour."

"What, tonight?" He laughed again. The sound grated Reeri's teeth. "I don't have the relic on me. Do I look that stupid? Don't answer that. I'll send word on when and where to meet. Bring the largest painting you can carry. Better yet"—he nodded to Bithul—"one he can carry."

"Deal." Anula shook Nuwan's hand. Reeri did not miss the way he lingered, the squeeze he gave at the end, nor what it did to his shadow.

"We did it." Calu clapped his shoulder as Nuwan disappeared into the night. "We have found the Bone Blade! Kama and Sohon will be thrilled. We should bring them sweets and celebrate, all of us. We have only one step left—ah, Anula, where was that pani walalu from?"

The words buzzed like a cicada in the heat.

Only one step left. Freedom was closing in faster than the Maha Equinox. Reeri *should* be elated.

So—his gaze tracked Anula as she led Calu to the food—why was he not?

27

HUMIDITY CHOKED THE NIGHT AIR. A LONE DROP OF SWEAT inched its way down Anula's back as she watched the Yakkas share a large banana leaf of delicacies, celebrating. All except for the Blood Yakka.

The edges of his mouth tucked into a frown. Anula moved from one vendor to the next, barely taking notice of their wares. She should be celebrating along with them, happy that their unfinished business would soon come to a close. A revelation had occurred to her last night: if his memory-nightmares were to be believed, she and the Blood Yakka were both survivors of a gruesome attack, both driven by the common purpose of defending others. Perhaps he was here to save others from the same fate. Or he was here for vengeance.

A tightness twisted her gut. Still, if the Blood Yakka cared enough to return to save his patrons, why not save Amma? Perhaps he hadn't cared for Anula. It wasn't as though she'd been a true believer, even as a child.

She shook the thoughts away. It didn't matter. What mattered was the crown and her bargain. Things that couldn't be had until the Blood Yakka completed his task. So, again, she should be celebrating, as should he. Perhaps they shared the same worry: What if the relic was false?

As if hearing her thoughts, the Blood Yakka glanced up, gaze fraught. It sent a chill down her bones in the same way his nightmares had. Anula broke the connection, walking a short distance away, touching porcelain miniatures of each of the Yakkas. She picked up the one of him. Long, sharp teeth dripped with red paint, but all she could see was fear. All she could hear was his agony.

The odds that Nuwan had the most sought-after relic in the history of the kingdom were small. If only she could—

"Follow me," a voice whispered in Anula's ear. "If you want to break a bargain."

A body brushed past, the head hidden beneath a saaluwa. Anula's pulse spiked. She glanced over her shoulder, at the Yakkas still carrying on, and back to the figure fading into the crowd. She didn't need to break it anymore, did she? If the relic was real.

But if it wasn't…

Anula looked sidelong at the Blood Yakka, picked up the corner of her sari, and rushed after the mysterious woman. She would venture only a short way. If the tether began its murderous assault, she'd return, before any of the Yakkas could come find her. Rounding the corner, she slammed into the woman. Premala's doe eyes glistened in the night.

The tension in Anula's shoulders eased. "I knew you were up to something."

Premala bit her lip. "We're not supposed to talk. Just follow me."

Paved stone turned to packed dirt as the kitchen maid, who was not a kitchen maid, wound out of the night market and through the tight maze of alleyways to a small home. Anula took a step inside, the tether stretching an inch too far. The feel of wading through paddy fields returned. She checked her arms, the skin solid and whole, for now.

"Cursed with an unsound mind," Premala whispered, snatching Anula's attention. "By the Yakka Calu."

A circle of candles lit the home. Four people huddled in a close ring around a man prostrate on the floor, muttering nonsensical words. A finger of dread curled around Anula's throat. Her and Calu's conversation surfaced, along with a mangled elephant pendant and a bargainer named Kushal. Was this who he had prayed for Calu to curse?

"We must sit in the—"

A drum trounced as Premala tripped over it.

"Careful!" came a sharp voice. Anula jumped, not at the voice, but at the mask it hid behind.

Same as the ones from the Blood Yakka's memory-nightmare.

Made of wood and painted in reds, whites, and blacks, its eyes were dark pits, and its mouth opened in a ghastly snarl. Thick strings of beads hung from the top, down past the woman's shoulders.

"A-apologies."

"Sit and hush," she commanded. "It's beginning."

Premala immediately folded on the ground, tugging at Anula's arm. She met the maid on the floor, trepidation fluttering in her stomach. Chimes rang softly through the circle as the woman in the mask made her way to the center. Bells laced the edges of her sari and the sleeves of her hatte. She placed offerings around the man's body. A hush fell over the circle.

Boom.

A drumbeat sounded. A yak berayuh, a two-ended drum, sat between another masked woman's crossed legs. Her hand pounded out a slow rhythm. Anula swallowed, sweat beading on her brow.

The first woman tapped her foot to the beat, leaned into the sound with her hips. The bells chimed along her sari, and in a low voice she said, "Oh, great Yakka Calu, hear me now, I offer you these first fruits of the fields."

Boom.

"Ohng Hreeng." She chanted.

Boom.

"Ohng Hreeng." It quaked in Anula's chest.

Boom.

"Ohng Hreeng." The sound of the Blood Yakka's nightmare.

She stamped and twirled, jumped and spun, ever to the beating of the drum. She blurred around the circle, never pausing, never breaking, her chanting ceaseless. The music of her body rose up into the night. The candle smoke swirled, staining the air gray, its tendrils seeking out the edges of the circle. The light flickered. Once, twice—

The drum beat quicker. The chant hastened. The masked woman's breath became low and ragged. The veil of smoke stung Anula's eyes, burned her lungs. Her pulse hissed, quickening to the clatter of the drum, faster and faster. Her mind spun along with the woman's sari, the bells catching her eyes, echoing in her ears, dizzying her senses.

A shadow lifted through the fog, thin and incorporeal with saffron eyes.

But these were diluted and sheer, as though a mere shade. The indention of a signet ring, not the ring itself.

"The mark of a Yakka's curse," Premala whispered, transfixed. "They wrap themselves around a person, like a blanket smothering them. We have to tear them off."

"Tear?"

The masked woman danced faster, her chant rising higher and feet landing heavier. The words bellowed into the night, careening into the specter flowing from the man's body, pulling it this way and that. A banner rippling in a monsoon.

The shadow wailed as its darkness leeched out, its edges twisting up to the sky.

The light snuffed out.

The drum hushed.

The woman fell silent.

An itch skittered up Anula's marking. The candles abruptly flickered back to life, and the room awoke, smokeless. The man stood, tenderly touching his head.

"Bless you." He embraced the masked woman. "Bless you, bless you."

The curse was gone. His mind was sound.

What had they done?

The four people in the circle cried in celebration, thanking the woman, offering her food and palm wine. A place to stay the night. A place to stay forever.

Mouth dry, Anula turned to Premala, the urge to scratch her mehendhi building. It nagged at her to move, to return to Reeri and the others, but she had to know. "Who are you?"

"What do you know of the Kattadiya?" Premala asked in a low voice.

"The what?" Sweat gathered on Anula's brow. The tether hummed, displeased.

"The who," Premala corrected reverently. "The Kattadiya were chosen by the First Heavens to defend against the Yakkas of Lord Wessamony, ruler of the Second Heavens. The Kattadiya were given knowledge and power, a tradition to expel the Yakkas' curses from humans. They were the only defense the people had, back when the Yakkas walked the Earth. They were the ones who eventually called down Lord Wessamony, appealed for the banishment he finally gave in punishment for their wickedness."

The Blood Yakka's nightmare flashed. "They're not in the stories of old."

Premala leaned closer. "That's because the Kattadiya were nearly killed off, not by a usurper, but by the people. They didn't want anyone healing those they had paid to curse. So the surviving Kattadiya disappeared. Only the trusted could find them."

Mere weeks ago Anula had thought she knew the truth of the Heavens, the truth of the lies. Did she know nothing? She swallowed. Was all that the Blood Yakka told her true?

"Why are you telling me this?"

"Kattadiya do not act for themselves, only for the protection of others." A voice drew near. The woman unmasked herself. Gray-streaked hair was wrapped tightly in a knot, and fine lines pinched her narrowed eyes. "I am Guruthuma Hashini of the Kattadiya. If you are amenable, we can help you break your bargain."

Anula's arm stung. She slapped a hand over it, willing her skin to stay in place a little while longer. "How? What was that?"

What had the Yakkas endured?

"It is called a tovil ceremony, and it's the only way to control a Yakka," the guruthuma said. "We will help you, on one condition."

Anxiety rippled. At the sweat now streaming down her back, the pain sizzling up her arm like slow streaks of lightning, or the way the guruthuma's eyes bore into hers, she couldn't tell. She mustered a scoff. "To break a bargain, I have to make another one?"

"It's not like that," Premala blurted.

"Quiet, acolyte," Guruthuma Hashini snapped. "She is allowed her questions. We come to you only because of your desperation in the market. Do you no longer wish to break your bargain? Does it not strangle and weigh heavy on your soul? Is it not the reason for your...discomfort now?"

The air in the room dried in Anula's lungs. How did she know? A piece of her skin flaked off. She caught it before the others saw. "What do you want?"

"It's simple," Hashini said. "We want your commitment to completing the tovil ceremony. We will teach you, if you promise to let us perform it and be rid of the Yakka curse you bargained upon yourself."

Anula breathed heavy, clenching her teeth as a pain as sharp and bright as a sword dipped in fire sliced down her arm. Warm stickiness flowed between her fingers. She stood quickly, shuffling to the door. This was madness. She didn't need to get involved with a woman who believed she was ordained by the First Heavens. With the masked people of a Yakka's nightmares.

Did she?

The Blood Yakka was on the cusp of finishing his business. She would have the crown and throne, the names on her list, and true justice any day now...unless the relic was false.

Her pulse tripped over itself.

"Raejina Consort?" Premala asked, cocking her head. "You don't have to be frightened. We're here to help. No one has to know you are with us."

"I'm not worried about what people think," Anula said, minding racing, blood trickling faster. She backed into the night, closer to the Yakkas.

Perhaps she did need this, if only to threaten them. Clearly the Blood Yakka knew of the masked men—women. Clearly, he feared them. If she agreed, she'd have a second plan if the relic failed. And if it did complete the bargain, the Kattadiya would have what they wanted—her freedom. There was nothing to lose.

"I'll do it," she spat, sweat soaking her upper lip. "I accept your deal."

"Excellent." Guruthuma Hashini smiled. "Premala will collect you when it is time."

The words wrapped around Anula's arms, squeezed tight, as her skin flaked off and she fled the Kattadiya.

28

ONLY IN SLUMBER DID THE LINE BETWIXT ANULA'S BROWS disappear.

Light breaths shifted tendrils of her hair across her face as she slept deeply. Whoever she had sneaked off to meet with in the night market had left a mark of worry. Reeri wondered at the *who* as much as the *why*, for someone had been important enough to risk the wrath of the tether.

"Watching again?" the blessed gift whispered overhead. "That is not how you attain progeny."

Reeri bristled. "Leave me alone."

"Three nights you've watched her now." The raja tutted.

The wind whistled through the chamber. Three nights, was that all it had been since the night market? Three nights of vigilance, of keeping nightmares at bay. It seemed appropriate, since they were so close. A last reprieve, for her.

Yet if she had noticed, she said nothing. Spending her days wandering the gardens, she only spoke when asking if Nuwan had sent word. Each time, the crease betwixt her brows deepened.

Reeri wondered if she saw the concern mirrored in him. He had thought both relic and essence offerings would be in his possession before now, had believed he would perform the soul sacrifice and fracture Anula's soul forever. He had steeled himself to take the kindness and care, to leave her a husk.

These were the things required for the Yakkas' souls to return, to once more have bodies. It left the bad, the ugly, the things rotten and poisonous behind.

Reeri snorted. It was a fine sentence for the Raejina of Poisons.

But not for a survivor, a protector of people, a soul that willingly bled for others.

Dread drew a finger down Reeri's shadow. Would cleaving such a soul add to the blood on his hands?

No. She was willing. He had not asked; she had offered. What she became after would not be his fault…would it?

Anula trembled. Reeri sat up. Was she having a nightmare? Mayhap he should have slept, to share the memory, the burden, until—

"See how she shivers?" the blessed gift crooned. Reeri clenched his jaw. "She needs you, Raja. Touch her, hold her. Show her your warmth."

"Do you not mean *give* her my warmth?" Reeri muttered, shifting. Mayhap he could close the gap, warm the bed. Would she notice his nearness? Would she lash out with those lips?

The gift chuckled. "By all means, give it to her well and good."

It would be so simple, to slide across the bed, wrap her in his arms as she woke—warmth rising, her back might arch into his hardness, their hips rocking to the sounds of her song.

"Yes," the voice cooed. "You want to. You want *her*. Go and give her your gift."

Reeri lurched away, slipping from the bed, and tumbled to the floor.

"What're you doing?" Anula asked, bleary-eyed over the edge.

"N-nothing," he said.

"Well, do it more quietly." She pulled up the covers and turned back to slumber.

The raja pointed at Reeri. "You may very well stay a virgin at this rate."

Dark circles were like shallow graves beneath his eyes as he watched Anula pace the entrance of the Pleasure Gardens, marking four days since they had made the deal with Nuwan. His treasure must be kept far from the city, away from potential seekers and thieves.

"Three essence offerings down. Sohon received a journal containing someone's secrets." Calu's voice gusted behind him. "He only had to write thirteen memory books in exchange. I think he may never look at a liver the same way again."

Reeri continued his observation. If he blinked, would Anula disappear into the bushes as she had disappeared into the night market's crowd?

"Reeri." Calu's voice broke through.

"Have you ever seen her with friends?"

"What?" Calu asked, leaving Kama and Sohon to peer out the terrace windows with him.

"She risked her skin to see someone the other night." Reeri narrowed his eyes as Anula suddenly spun. Bithul handed over a letter. Mayhap that was what she had been waiting for.

"Worried she has a paramour?" Calu elbowed him.

Reeri glowered. "That is not what I meant."

"I could find out."

"No. I simply do not want her to disappear when we have the relic and offerings ready."

"*Sure*. That is the reason."

"It is."

"Your face says differently."

"My face says nothing."

"Keep telling yourself that." Calu clapped him on the shoulder with one hand and fingered his neckline with the other. The gnarled pendant was gone, but surely secured elsewhere alongside Sohon's offering.

Disentangling himself, Reeri turned to the others. He need not prove his questions valid.

Sohon lounged on the throne, flipping through the journal as another thick book sat by his side. Kama sprawled on the floor, tripping her fingers over the pages. "If I were to set fire to a memory book, would their souls feel it?"

Sohon snatched it up. If he did not deliver it intact, the offering would disappear, for a bargain broken takes from both sides. "You are insane."

"I am passion," she corrected. "Fascination feeds me."

The doors to the throne room banged closed. Reeri glanced up as Anula marched in, a light in her eyes. It riled his shadow.

She held a letter aloft. "Nuwan has summoned us."

Had she doubled back to Nuwan that night? Was she troubled by what he had said or done? If so, why would she not tell him? They were in this together.

"He wants 'the consort and her ladies' to deliver the painting." Anula smirked at Kama, the only lady of court ever seen attending her. "Though Bithul is allowed to carry it."

"Absolutely not," Reeri said, terse and swift.

Anula raised a brow. "Are you worried I can't defend myself if he means harm?"

"No."

"Yes," Calu said simultaneously. Reeri bristled.

"Has the poison eroded your memory?" She pointed to her necklace. "Bithul will grab the painting, and Kama and I will be on our way. You can finish your 'business' before the day is done. So don't get comfortable on my throne, Sohon."

"We cannot." Kama stood.

Anula narrowed her eyes. "Cannot what?"

"Kama," Reeri warned.

The Yakka of Love tsk-tsked. "She should know."

"Know what?"

"The relic is merely the first step. There are more."

"How many?"

Kama skipped to her side. "One that is two. I must find my true essence first." She tripped her fingers up Anula's arm and across her chest. "Will you help me? You know the workings of a heart."

Anula lifted her gaze. Wounded and angry. Whatever ground Reeri had gained with her stopped short, the earth falling away in a landslide.

"Anula." He stepped forward, the words on the end of his tongue. He could tell her, explain it all. Would she open to him then? Bring him a book to remember?

No. It risked too much. If she rescinded—

"It's fine," she snapped, grabbing Kama's hand from her chest and pulling her to the door. "If there's more to do, then we can't waste time."

She blazed out of the chamber, Bithul quick on her heels, the painting jostling in his hand, cane in the other.

Calu whistled low. "Glad I will not be here to see her ire after her soul is cleaved. Mayhap she should not have the throne; she may be worse than any usurper."

The thought nipped at Reeri. "That was the bargain. It cannot be broken."

She had chosen this, he reminded himself as the tether stretched. He had chosen this, too. For his brethren.

There was so much blood on his hands.

He only required one drop more, given freely.

He would rend her soul into pieces, yet leave her with a crown. She would understand. They were not dissimilar. There was no cost too high for their people.

Why, then, did it not feel right?

29

The Bone Blade was small, barely the length of a hand, its hilt smooth and alabaster as an elephant tusk, the edge a sharp iron.

Anula flipped it over. If she didn't know better, she'd say it was a mere knife, something given to a child before they were old enough to wield a sword. Perhaps that was exactly what it was. She grimaced at the thought and the knowledge that this relic, or whatever it may be, was only the first step on an innumerable list.

Even now, after they'd witnessed each other's pasts, the Blood Yakka didn't trust her with the truth. She had begun to believe him, to listen to the things he had said. How could she not? She'd seen the masks, heard the chant, watched as a mark of Calu's curse was torn from a man. She understood the stories of old were half-truths. Not in the way she'd always thought, but in the same way Anuradhapura's history was glazed with a false veneer. Usurpers had a knack for burying shameful facts.

The stories of old warned of the bloodthirsty Yakkas, who cared for the people in a balanced way. One couldn't have blessing without curses. One couldn't know happiness without first knowing pain. She saw it now, the web the stories of old spun. She saw the truth of the Blood Yakka. His care, his hurt, his burden, and his obligation to his people, just as he had seen hers.

So why not tell her the truth? Maybe the answer entangled with her other question: Why hadn't Amma been saved?

Perhaps the Blood Yakka simply didn't care for Anula.

Maybe because of her unfaithfulness or her jests. Either way, he didn't trust her. He kept her off his allies list.

It stung, but she brushed it away. What was done was done. If he didn't want her to know the truth of his business or how long it would take to complete her bargain, so be it. Thank the cursed Heavens for the Kattadiya and the missive they'd slipped behind Nuwan's, requesting she meet them today. Bargain or no bargain, Anula would have her throne.

"The blade is not merely one bone," Kama said, sidestepping a group of travelers.

"What?" Anula asked, skirting around another. The outer city was packed elbow to elbow, even thirteen days from the festival. With the war waging heavier than ever and usurpers taking control every other week, it was no wonder the people of Anuradhapura poured in. They arrived ready to pay homage to the saviors of their family, to beg and barter for that safety to remain.

"The bones were gifted by Fate's devotees," Bithul answered. "The stories of old say fifty men and women gave their lives, a bone taken from each. Leg and arm, head and chest, crushed and melded together. A sacrifice of life to stop death."

"I wonder at their demise," Kama said, eyes wistful. "Mayhap that very blade plunged into their hearts. Would that not be fitting? Love imbuing it from tip to tail."

Anula recoiled, handing the relic to Bithul as they entered the inner city. "Give it to the Blood Yakka."

"Do you not want to?" he asked, stars twinkling in his eyes as he slid a soft finger over the bone. Anula imagined he was one of those faithful counting down the days to the festival, his home full of offerings, his face turned to the sky.

"I want for him to complete our bargain." She paused at the edge of the Pleasure Gardens. At least Nuwan hadn't put up a fight. Eyes as large as a banana leaf, he snatched the blessed gift, nearly throwing the blade to the ground. What a way to treat a sacred relic. But perhaps that was all the sign she'd needed. She pressed a hand to her skirt, feeling the crinkle of Premala's missive. "I have other things to attend to until then."

"I will go with you."

Anula lifted a brow. "You want to bathe with me? The courtiers would love that. Their handsome, sweat-slicked guard—"

"I'll give this to the raja"—Bithul blushed—"and send in your ladies."

"No, I want to be alone. Didn't you ever need time to yourself when your dream of being commander was stolen from you?"

Bithul stiffened, darkness hooding his eyes. He knew what it was to desire something so close, yet so far. That specific ache of wanting, when all signs pointed to it never being attained. "Of course, my raejina consort."

"Did you ever try to find another way?" Anula peered at the gardens, where the missive told her to go.

"My being commander is not important," he said, brows furrowing, gaze alight. "The training of our young soldiers and the building of their confidence is what matters. Else they won't return from the battlefield and the commander will have no one to lead."

"But isn't it more important to have the right commander, a good one?"

Bithul's shoulders sagged. "Commanders have to make many decisions. Not all will be seen as good. That does not make him bad."

She hissed, "And the burning of an innocent village? Does that make Commander Dilshan bad?"

Bithul blanched.

"Never mind." Anula waved him off and headed through the gardens toward the bathing pools. Now was not the time to explain things.

The tether stretched, the memory of an itch crawling along Anula's arms. She slapped it away. The missive had said noon, and it was well past. As she passed bushes of pink maha rath mala, the tether abruptly settled, like ripples fading in a water tank.

"Are you meeting a paramour?" Kama's voice came from behind. "Reeri believes so, yet did he ask the Yakka of Lust?"

"What?" Anula spun.

Kama placed her hands on Anula's cheeks. "You do not smell of lust. Intrigue, yes, but only in the morning. Why do you not explore your curiosity? The bed is a fine place to sample and savor. Especially while Reeri inhabits a body so close to his own form."

Raja Vatuka floated in Anula's mind. How he towered over her, how his heat pulsed like a firepit, how his chest hairs curled about the elephant marking as though it hid in the jungle brush. Anula shook the image away, shook off Kama. Cursed Yakkas, wasn't Calu the one who poisoned minds? "Why are you following me? Don't you need to find your essence or something? Won't the Blood Yakka be wondering where you are?"

"Won't he wonder where *you* are?" Kama turned the question around, sighing dramatically when Anula frowned. "The blade rings of the Heavens' call, so yes, my true essence is forefront on my mind. Mayhap that is why I follow you."

"What does that mean?"

"I am in need of a heart."

"Among other things."

Kama cocked her head. "You are sneaking off again."

"So what if I am? What if I do have a paramour? Do you want to watch?"

A fire caught in Kama's eyes. "Would you allow me?"

"Cursed Yakkas, will none of you go away?"

"You have been in a foul mood since the morning." A knowing smile curved her lips. "Mayhap Reeri needs to pay more attention to your satisfaction."

"You're right. It's almost as if I don't enjoy being lied to." Anula turned to leave, but the Yakka grabbed hold of her, stepped close, and whispered low.

"Pleasure and pain may climax together, but what lover wants to see flesh taken from bone? I will follow you, stay the tether's hand, ask no questions, and tell no secrets. If you give me a human heart."

Gooseflesh prickled.

"Still beating, if you please. None of that poisoncraft."

"Why?" The question shivered on the breeze.

Kama tutted, a finger tapping against Anula's lips with each word. "Ask no questions, tell no secrets."

The refusal surfaced. Her list had been crafted by Auntie Nirma. Years of research and information. Long nights deciding their fates.

But.

She glanced over Kama's shoulder. A wisp of a girl waited near the corner of the gardens. Anula's task was too important, Auntie Nirma's goal too close. And there were dozens of names on the list.

Two at the top who deserved death.

Anula stuck out her hand. "Ask no questions."

"Tell no secrets." Kama shook on the deal.

"How much?" Anula said by way of greeting.

Premala scrunched her nose. "For what?"

"For you, darling." She winked.

A flush raced across Premala's cheeks. "Please keep your dirty jests to yourself while we're inside, my raejina consort."

"You can call me 'Anula.' And inside where?"

In the depths of the Pleasure Gardens was a cluster of rosebushes. Past the thorns and roots lay a wooden door, which housed a set of stone stairs, which led to a branch of underground tunnels, as warm and welcoming as a graveyard.

Statues, taller and wider than Anula peppered the dark, dank, torchlit space. One Divinity sat and one stood at the convergence of two tunnels, star-filled eyes pursuing Anula's every move, and not with loving kindness.

Anula shivered as they ventured deeper; she wondered if the Divinities could truly see her or her tether to the Yakka in the bushes somewhere above them.

"This way," Premala said, leading her through a throng of monuments to the far wall. She wrung her hands as they stood before a colorful portrait of a woman. It smiled benevolently at them and lifted a hand.

The hair stood on the back of Anula's neck. "I thought all the blessed gifts were in the palace."

"They are." Premala's gaze darted warily between them. "The caves were made specifically for the Kattadiya. Blessed for our Heavenly purpose. You only need to take her hand, and she'll guide you to where you need to be, if you are worthy."

Anula scoffed, eyeing the portrait's yellow sari, her nearly see-through hatte, the tight bun that twisted on top of her head. "Must I beg?"

"This isn't a laughing matter. If Thilini, the first guruthuma and guardian of the caves, doesn't believe you are aligned with the Kattadiya, then I have to leave you here."

"What, in the tunnels?"

Premala nodded nervously.

"I thought the Kattadiya protected the people."

"From Yakkas," she corrected. "And those aligned with them."

Worry spiked Anula's pulse. Was a tether considered alignment? "How can she tell?"

"For prayer's sake, do you question all the blessed gifts like this?" Premala hissed, nervously glancing at the statues.

"Only the ones who might condemn me to an underground maze," she snapped back.

"S-sorry, my raejina consort." Premala stumbled into a bow, knocked her head on the wall. The portrait frowned. "It's not my intention for you to die. If you could please just do as I say, the guruthuma—"

"Calm down," Anula said, righting her. "I'm not aligned with the Yakkas." Alignment meant mutual trust, and there was absolutely none of that.

"You made a bargain with them."

"So did all those people you help."

"This is different. They don't come down here. You're being inducted into the Kattadiya."

Anula raised a brow. "Why?"

Premala gulped.

"Because I'm the raejina consort?"

"Please," Premala squeaked. "I'm just an acolyte. My duty is to get you inside, if you are worthy."

"Then what, all will be revealed?"

Premala slowly shook her head. "I only know my duties. I can't say anything else."

Anula tensed. She looked to the portrait, hand still extended, and back the way they had come. Perhaps she shouldn't do this. Perhaps she was wrong and the relic was real; perhaps the next step wouldn't take long and she'd have her completed bargain soon.

But what if she didn't?

"Fine," Anula huffed and placed her hand on the stone. She half expected it to stretch, like the paintings, to swallow her whole and take her to where she needed to go. Instead, she felt a prick. Small and quick, like a mosquito bite. Blood bubbled on Anula's palm. Then Guruthuma Thilini danced along the wall, disappearing around a corner.

"Thank the Heavens." Premala's shoulders sagged with relief. She pulled Anula forward, chasing the portrait.

Another tunnel, another corner, and the portrait paused at a door. It swung open, revealing a room full of terrible masks.

Bloodied eyes, bloodied mouths. Sharp teeth dripping with blue saliva and grayed flesh.

"What a beautiful gallery," Anula murmured.

"Isn't it?" Premala breathed, the sarcasm flying overhead like a bulbul. "Each is unique, used for specific curses, specific Yakkas, specific bargains. The first step in a tovil ceremony is choosing the right mask."

"How?"

Premala's gaze drifted slowly, teeth worrying her bottom lip.

"What, is this something else I can't know?"

"You can. You've been deemed worthy by First Guruthuma Thilini and willingly aligned yourself with us. It's only... Well, Kattadiya don't just help those who seek them out. We can feel when someone has struck a bargain. Their energy flows differently. Since going underground, the Kattadiya have honed ways to seek out bargainers, break bargains, and heal the cursed, without them asking for help."

The door clanged shut behind them.

"Then, if I hadn't made the deal with you that night...?"

Premala swallowed. "We would've eventually found you, raejina consort or not."

"And what?"

Masks and blood and shadows ripping in the night flashed.

"We aren't the evil ones," Premala insisted. "The Yakkas are. That's why they were banished."

A wave of anxiety swept over Anula. It's what the stories of old told, but she didn't believe them anymore. The problem was that she had no idea of the truth, of where the lies began and where they ended. If only a trusted ally could tell her.

"Is that why you work in the palace, to feel out any bargains made?"

Premala wrung her hands. "Part of it. I mean—no. I mean, I'm sorry, Raejina—Anula. I can't tell you that. Can we focus? Guruthuma Hashini will be here soon to check our progress. The tovil is an intricate ceremony."

Anula tucked the information away for later. Her suspicions had been right about the maid she'd met in the gardens, and now she knew there was more to the banishment, to the Yakkas and the Heavens. The weight of all the unknown pressed on Anula's shoulders.

"How intricate?" she asked.

"Each ceremony is entirely unique." Premala's eyes grew wide, in excitement or anxiety Anula couldn't tell. "It can take days, even weeks, for a caster to prepare. First, we find the right mask. That's my purpose for tonight's meeting. The candles and dolla offerings are determined by the mask. Those can take time to gather as well. Next is the dance itself. Though the majority of tovils are performed the same, the more complicated bargains require more complicated movements. The guruthuma is in charge of that. The Divinities themselves give her the instructions; then she teaches it to the caster."

"You're saying the tovil won't be performed tonight?"

Premala bit her lip. "I'm sorry my raej—Anula—no. If we could just focus now, I will work night and day to have your tovil ready as soon as possible."

"By all means," Anula said, waving her hand at the wall.

Premala cleared her throat. "It's not as simple as picking one at random. I have to know about your bargain."

"How do they determine the mask for those who don't seek help?"

"The guruthuma has a…conversation with them before."

"Ah."

"We can avoid that," Premala said quickly. "Just tell me who you bargained with and for what." She stared at the wall of gruesome faces, ready to grab the one that spoke to her, ready to hear Anula's secrets.

"No."

Premala blanched. "What?"

"I never agreed to tell you about my bargain, and I'm not going to." It was one thing for Bithul to know, a man vetted for his allegiance to the kingdom. Premala was still in question. The Kattadiya, though—with their masks and their chants and their veneration of the Divinities—they were aligned with only themselves. Which meant they weren't her allies.

"But without knowing, I can't—"

The door swung open, and Guruthuma Hashini stepped through. Hands laced behind her back, she peered down her nose at Premala. At her empty hands.

"You have chosen no mask, acolyte?"

Fear widened the blacks of Premala's eyes. "I—I don't—I'm not sure if…"

The guruthuma sucked her teeth. "This is the simplest of tasks."

"I'm sorry." Premala bent her head, shoulders slumping.

Guruthuma Hashini took two powerful steps and slapped Premala's face. The crack echoed.

Anula clenched a fist. "That was unnecessary. She's doing her best." Despite Anula's own defiance. Perhaps she should've had Premala explain the masks, picked it out herself without having to tell her secret.

"Kattadiya do not act for themselves, only for the protection of others," the guruthuma snapped. No greeting, no bow. "There is no place for a simpering, spineless acolyte. Our obligation to the kingdom demands strength against those willing to place themselves in the darkness. Either she is worthy or worthless. And you, it does not matter to me whether you wear a crown or a banana leaf. You are cursed and so have brought a curse upon our kingdom. Interrupt the ways of the Kattadiya again, and it will be the First Heavens you deal with next." She spat at Premala's feet. The girl's lips trembled. "Choose the mask, gather the dolla, or return to the hovel from whence you came."

The guruthuma marched from the room, door shaking.

"I see your leader is filled to the brim with Heavenly love," Anula leered. Then it dawned on her, why Premala always checked over her shoulder. It wasn't for the palace cook. "She's the one you're afraid will find out about your girl."

Premala's head snapped up in terror. "*Shhhh.*"

"It's all right," Anula said, soft and low. An image surfaced, of a woman kissing Auntie Nirma's cheeks, staring at her as if she'd hung the moon. But there could never be two wives. Not in this age, but perhaps the next. Anula nodded to the walls. "Tell me about the masks. We'll find the right one together."

"That's not how it's done. If I can't even do this…"

"I'm the one making it difficult." Anula clenched and unclenched a fist. Then reached out and squeezed the girl's hand.

"No one has to know. And you can get the dolla yourself. You just need the mask first, right?"

Premala nodded slow, seeing the value in Anula's suggestion. She pointed at a mask with large streaming tears. "The Yakka of Lust…"

Anula listened, waiting to hear of the Blood Yakka. Eyes flickering to the door, she wondered if the stories of old had buried the Kattadiya for a reason. If perhaps the First Heavens had created monsters out of men.

Monsters more dangerous than the Yakkas.

30

"You are brooding again," Calu said, picking at the leftover food on his platter.

Reeri had taken to pacing hours ago. His gaze held firm the window, his sides slick with sweat as humidity wrapped tight as a blanket. Dark clouds hung heavy, pressing against the shadow, squeezing out his breath. "I do not brood."

The Maha season's monsoons were nearing.

"They have not been gone that long," Calu said, glancing up. Sweat drew a line from brow to chin. He fingered his empty neckline.

"Yet nerves rack you," Reeri muttered. "Mayhap you should brood."

Calu straightened. "I am not nervous for anything. The curry is just particularly spicy today." He scooped in a mouthful of kiribath and swallowed, as if to prove it, but Reeri knew what he saw of his brother. "Besides, Anula has a trained guard and Kama."

"I think the poisons would scare humans most," Sohon said from the divan, coiled around a book.

"Exactly." Calu pointed a curried finger. "The problem is not with them but your impatience."

If Reeri's shadow were free, its edges would be writhing. "I am not impatient. Have we not waited two centuries for this?"

"Technically, no. You only came up with the plan recently."

Reeri growled, "They should have returned by now, unless…"

"*Ah*." Calu smiled. "You think she has run off with her paramour again. I told you to bed her."

Reeri flinched. Waved a hand through the images that came unbidden. The touches and whispers. The questions and desires.

Anula had offered her soul. And Reeri would cleave it. That was the extent of them. It was what they both wanted.

"Your jests are unappreciated." He glowered, turning from the falling light of the night.

"I appreciate them." Sohon smirked.

"Then you two can enjoy them alone." Reeri marched from the room, phantom hackles raised to the Heavens.

The raja's chamber held no more relief. The darkening sky darkened his mood with every movement of the clouds. The heat sticking and draining.

An ache started at the base of his shadow like the twinge of a bruise, a haunted memory. He shook out his hands, rolled his shoulders, ignored the fact Anula was not there. That he, mayhap, was wrong again. Ambition had a way of using others as steps. Mayhap she had taken his trust and run, her gifts to the others mere tricks—a trap set and sprung.

She had not shown she cared about their similar burdens, nor for those outside her list and her dead, especially him. No. Reeri cast the thought away. Let it wither in the heat of the night before it took root. It did not matter who she cared for, least of all him.

The relic and her soul—that was all that mattered. Freedom was within Reeri's grasp. His brethren deserved no less.

He deserved no more.

As soon as Reeri's eyes closed, blood flooded the village street, tinted the night sky.

A cacophony of screams drowned into the background. If not for the man lying face down in front of Reeri, he would have believed it to be his own nightmare.

Yet the tears shed for the soiled man were not his. Nor was the chasm that broke open his chest, the deep ache that shook his body. Panic flared, and the memory-nightmare opened his mouth, spewing forth Anula's young voice.

"Great Divinities of the First Heavens, please save Amma. Save my village." Words choked on tears. "Save me."

The world shifted and spun.

Spears nestled into spines.

"Great Blood Yakka of the Second Heavens," the child cried, ringing through Reeri's shadow. "Hear my prayer. I offer the fields of my father, my whole inheritance. So please, please, please, save us now!"

The crack in Anula's voice splintered and shattered his soul. She *had* turned to the Heavens, had prayed to—

Boom.

The sound rattled Reeri to the core, pitched Anula into a run. The red-tinted night blurred, until she skidded to a halt.

A woman, swollen with child, was tied to a pyre. A soldier kicked. Bone and baby fractured to the side. Blood dripped betwixt her legs.

"*Amma*," Anula whimpered.

A spark struck, fire caught, and Amma rose in flame, choking the only mother Anula would ever have, swallowing the baby sister or brother she would never meet, never hug, never kiss. Amma's screams pierced the red sky, and Anula ran. Crying out in the bloodred night, "*Why? Why have the Heavens forsaken me?*"

Reeri woke covered in sweat, heart quaking.

She had prayed to him. She had asked for help.

And he had not answered.

A whimper sounded at his chest. Anula had returned, and in the throes of the memory-nightmare, had curled into his side, wrapped herself beneath his arms. She flinched under slumber's hold, tears leaking onto his chest, burning a hole in his skin, his shadow, his soul.

Why?

The weight of the word crushed his bones.

O mighty Heavens and all the wretches betwixt. Anula was a survivor of both human bloodlust and Heavenly neglect. For as Reeri searched for Wessamony's perfect offering, he had ignored all others, believing his brethren were the only ones to suffer. A half-truth he told himself.

Though humans had shattered her heart, *he* had embittered her soul.

Silence in the blackest night, death to all she once loved, the walls, the ire, the distrust—it was all his fault.

Reeri tightened his hold, pressed her close, whispered into her jasmine scented hair, "I am sorry."

With a sharp breath, Anula awoke. She tore herself from his arms, clawed at the tears.

Reeri reached out. "Anula. I—"

She slapped his hand away and leaped from the bed, shaking. "Don't."

"I am sorry, Anula. I am sorry I did not answer. It is my fault."

"I know!" she snapped.

"Please, Anula."

"No!" she screamed, another tear escaping. "Thrice-cursed Yakkas, I don't want to talk about it!"

She pulled on her robe and fled from the room. Fled from *him*—the one who had failed her, stolen her love on Earth and in the Heavens, condemned her to death and nightmares.

Just as he had condemned his brethren.

Reeri fisted the sheets. No more. If Anula had returned, so had the relic. It was time to use it. Time to end the bloody reign of Lord Wessamony of the Second Heavens. Time to make amends for the Yakkas.

And for Anula.

31

I am sorry, Anula. I am sorry I did not answer. It is my fault.

The words pulsed with every heartbeat, every step Anula took through the palace. A lump stuck in her throat. How long had she wished to hear those words? To know she hadn't failed her family?

"Are you all right, my raejina consort?" Bithul asked, forever at her heels.

It is my fault.

"No," she spat at them both.

Vengeance is not important, Anula. Justice is. Auntie Nirma had drilled it every morning and every night. Because what had happened was not Anula's fault for being unworthy of a blessing or for offering too little. It wasn't even the Heavens' fault for abandoning the kingdom and its people, for caring but not enough. She didn't need the Blood Yakka's apology. Didn't need to know that he cared now. And she absolutely didn't need to know why.

Raja Mahakuli Mahatissa, Commander Dilshan, Prophet Ayaan.

It was their fault.

And the reason she was in the palace. Robe billowing, Anula sped toward the kitchen. It was time. It had to be. The tovil must be performed. But she skidded to a halt. The palace was teeming with courtiers, celebrating with drinks, and lifting thanks to the Heavens.

"News just arrived: Thanks to the ministers' and Dilshan's strategy, the army took out a large force of Polonnaruwa's military yesterday. They saved a village. A host of courtier sons were part of the effort," Bithul whispered.

Red sky. Red hands. Red water.

Look away.

But she hadn't.

Her eyes had remained open. Found Amma, battered and bruised, tied to a pyre made from the wood of their home. The baby's bulge bent to one side. Blood dripped as flame caught.

Her only mother, her only sibling. Never to hold or hug or kiss. Never to wake together, play together, live together.

Never to *be* with her again.

"See? They do not need me to be the commander," Bithul said. "Commander Dilshan is doing good work."

But what of the red sky? The red hands?

Anula swallowed the last image of her Amma and spun. "Don't follow me."

Fingers tripped across sapphires, found the vials, and ripped open the largest.

Mahakuli Mahatissa had escaped justice; the rest would not.

Anula slammed open the door. Gauzy, sheer fabrics billowed in the morning breeze. Smoke snaked around figurines of the Heavens.

Prophet Ayaan startled out of his meditation. "Raejina Con—"

Anula lunged, crashing into the man and pinning his arms to the floor with her knees. She pressed one hand against his chest, lifted the vial above his face with the other. Though he was frail, she wasn't much stronger. But in the Age of Usurpers, one only needed to be intelligent enough to dance around them, dominate them, rule them. Surprise gave her the upper hand; fear did the rest.

"Don't. Move," she commanded, low and severe. "See the vial? I shake it and the contents spill, eating your flesh before you can wipe it away."

The prophet whimpered. "What are you doing?"

"Why did you set fire to Eppawala?"

"I do not know what you speak of."

"Come now, Prophet, you're not that old." She hissed, "Is twelve years long enough for you to forget murdering a village of innocents?"

Prophet Ayaan paled. "I do not know of what you speak."

Anula shifted. A drop of the poison splashed onto the prophet's neck. It sizzled.

"Ouch!"

"Oops." Anula tutted. "My arm is getting tired. Best hurry with the truth."

"I don't understand what's happening."

"You're being called for justice, to stand trial for your actions."

"What?" Sweat beaded on his brow. "I am the prophet. My actions are dictated by the Heavens. They are always just."

Anula bared her teeth. "Tell that to the villagers of Eppawala. I'll show you to their graves."

Heart hammering beneath her palm, Prophet Ayaan flicked his eyes from her to the vial. She tilted it again, a bubble leaning over the lip.

"Wait! Wait!" he screamed. "Lord Wessamony decreed it!"

Anula blanched.

"It was part of the bargain," he rushed to say. "I beseeched the Heavens for favor. Lord Wessamony answered. The village of Eppawala was to be turned over in search of a relic. Once found, Raja Mahakuli Mahatissa would have the throne for fifty years."

The words spun webs in Anula's mind. "Lord Wessamony doesn't make bargains."

"Of course he does, he's the Lord of the Second Heavens!" Prophet Ayaan screeched.

If that were true…

But what if it were a lie?

"Why make a bargain for someone else?"

"I am the prophet, granted position by a raja. We had an understanding."

Anula pursed her lips, taken back to that night, to the conversation between Dilshan and his soldier. "And the commander?"

"Titles mean nothing without the power of a raja behind them. We needed him as much as he needed the raja."

The truth of it skittered across her arms, shook the vial in her hand. The man beneath her whimpered again. She narrowed her eyes. "The raja didn't hold the throne for fifty years, yet Eppawala burned."

Tears leaked down his cheeks. "It was part of the raja's bargain with Lord Wessamony, I suppose to rid himself of his greatest threat. That was Dilshan's doing. I know nothing of it, only that we were meant to find the relic and did not. So the bargain was void."

A buzzing began low in Anula's ears.

The edges of her vision tinted red.

Lord Wessamony.

The relic.

A crack of a whip. A Yakka torn in half. Banishment and masked women. The story of Fate and Destiny and the Bone Blade's true power. *Else you will be the Yakkas' tormentor. For eternity.*

Was this the Blood Yakka's unfinished business?

"You see, my raejina consort." Prophet Ayaan slowly pushed the vial away. "I have nothing to stand trial for. I was merely servicing my raja, the Kingdom of Anuradhapura, and the Heavens themselves. I am innocent of wrongdoing."

Look away.

The buzz built and rose. And all Anula could see was a village of friends falling. Thaththa crashing to his knees. Amma and baby swallowed by smoke. Auntie Nirma guttering in her arms. All her loved ones snuffed out of existence, out of her life, as though they were merely candle flame.

"No," Anula asserted. "You chose to let people suffer. For that, you will meet justice."

Wrenching from his grip, Anula slammed the vial against his forehead. Glass and poison cut deep. His scream filled the morning air as it burned through his flesh, ate at his eyes, leaked into his mouth.

He choked, once.

~~*Mahakuli Mahatissa.*~~

Twice.

~~*Prophet Ayaan.*~~

His tongue turned to liquid.

Commander Dilshan.

And drowned him.

Lord Wessamony.

Anula touched a hand to her necklace, finally looking away. To the door and the hall that would take her to the Bone Blade and Blood Yakka.

Toward vengeance on the Heavens.

32

The air sat thick in Reeri's lungs, pinched at his shadow.

A light song swayed from the center of the throne room, where Calu held the Bone Blade for Kama and Sohon to see.

Palms damp, Reeri snatched it.

"What are you doing?" Calu asked nervously, eyeing the blade.

"More importantly, why did you wake us in the middle of the night?" Sohon stifled a yawn.

"We have to perform the soul sacrifice. Now," Reeri said, a slight tremble in his hand. How many had he let down like he did Anula? How many suffered because he and the other Yakkas were controlled by Wessamony? How much blood was truly on his hands? He could take it no longer. With one last step, he could right all the wrongs. Even if he could not bring Anula's family back, he could give her what she had been asking for all these weeks: a crown and a chance to change her kingdom.

Reeri straightened. "We cleave Anula's soul and then use the Bone Blade before Wessamony has a chance to come after us all. It is best to invoke the powers of it first. There is no telling how quickly he will react."

"What? Kama does not have her essence offering," Calu argued.

"We will make do with three. Wessamony created all the Yakkas from one soul, mayhap the cosmos does not demand as much as we think."

"Is that not a risk? We only have once chance to free them *and* kill Wessamony."

Reeri gripped the blade and paced. Indeed, it was a risk. But Anula could rescind her bargain to spite him for what he had done. For what he had not done. And he would lose his one chance at making amends.

Calu shook his head. "I think we should wait. We have time to get the proper number of essence—"

"No, we do not," Reeri snapped. "The longer we wait, the longer our brethren and our patrons suffer under Wessamony. We must act now."

"Mayhap we test it," Sohon said. "Ensure we can use only three."

"How does one test an offering?" Kama sang.

"We ask the cosmos?"

"It is not often prone to answer."

Reeri growled. Testing did not matter—succeeding did.

Calu neared, pointing to the relic in Reeri's hand. "I was going to tell you at breakfast, but that relic looks familiar to me."

"Of course it does." Sohon scoffed. "It is Heavenly; it calls to us."

"No, I mean it looks *very* familiar."

The door swung open. "My raja," Bithul started. Reeri tensed, the shadow bristling. There were too many interruptions. Time was wasting. "Anula is—"

"Great Heavenly Divinity, Fate," Reeri bellowed, holding the blade to the emerging morning sun. It sparkled, as though it could flame like Wessamony's Golden Sword. "Hear my cry and grant me the power of your Bone Blade."

The blade shuddered; a heat that had nothing to do with Reeri's palms swelled. The keening pitched higher, quivering Reeri's shadow, shaking his soul. A finger of dread cooled his spine. The keening erupted. Ivory shattered, and iron sliced right through Reeri's hand. What was left of the blade slashed its way through the room. Kama and Sohon ducked, but Calu threw himself against Bithul and tumbled to the floor.

"Catch it!" Calu demanded.

Reeri took a step forward and faltered, his vision swimming. The floor rushed to meet his face, cracking his cheek. The room blinked in and out of view.

Grabbing Bithul's cane, Kama knocked the blade away. Calu stayed sprawled across the guard, covering his face and chest. The blade curved around the room and sailed back at them, gaining speed. Kama hit the blade away again. It spun as Reeri's stomach plunged.

Many have died in their search for a relic or in use of a cursed imitation.

The prophet had been right. The blade was no relic, merely an imitation, bargained for and cursed by the Second Heavens.

By one of them.

Sohon lifted a statue, which sang out with cheer, until the iron blade hit and embedded itself too deep. It shook and shuddered and finally shattered, taking the blessed gift along with it. Reeri turned over and retched.

"Why would you not listen?" Calu raged overhead.

Picking himself off the floor, Reeri touched his head. It was as murky as a puddle. "I did not mean to—"

"To what? Do this alone?" Calu seethed. "Yes, you did! You refuse to let us help for no reason. If you had taken a moment to hear me out, you would have known that I recognized that blade. If you had let me speak, I would have told you that a human once made a bargain for a false relic. One that stole the mind of whoever it cut. You are lucky Sohon managed to destroy it afore it took hold! Else Anula would have had to poison you into a new body."

His words nipped. Was Reeri fated to nothing but damnation? A disease upon all around him?

"Did you not think to tell us of your false blade before we began searching?" Sohon snapped at Calu.

"Do you remember every single one of your bargains?" Calu snarled back.

"What is done is done. Now we move forward with the truth and time enough for me to find a heart." Kama picked the guard off the floor, dusted his shoulders.

Throat thick with shame, Reeri said, "Bithul, I am sorry."

"No apologies necessary," the guard said. "But why didn't you have Anula wield the relic? Is that not what you want her for?"

Four Yakkas paused.

"Why would we want that?" Sohon asked.

Bithul looked puzzled. "The stories of old tell us that the Divinities created their relics for the goodness of humanity. A connection was made between the two, and only one of them could wield a relic."

Reeri's shadow stilled. *They were a connection made solely between Divinity and humanity.* The prophet's words came back to him. Wessamony had known it; the reason he had humans searching was not for fear of Reeri's disobedience but because he required them past retrieval.

So, too, did Reeri.

Even if this blade had been true, it would not have worked for a Yakka. And as they had no Divinity…only a human could kill Wessamony.

"Bithul," Reeri said, flicking his gaze to the faithful guard. "Do you trust me?"

The door slammed open.

Cheeks aflame and eyes ablaze, Anula shouted, "Give me the Bone Blade."

33

"Not now, Anula." Reeri's voice was tight and terse.

His shadow curled its edges into a coil, ready to strike. He had been fooled not once but twice on the most important undertaking of his existence. There was no time for Anula's theatrics. Yet mayhap he had time enough to find the merchant. To *thank* him for the cursed relic.

"Yes, *now*," Anula demanded, marching forward only to slip on a broken piece of blessed statue.

She canted forward, and Reeri caught her by the elbow. Red flecks dotted her arms and face.

"Is that blood?"

Anula wrenched away. "Why did you destroy a statue?" When none of the Yakkas responded, she turned to Bithul. "What's happened? Where's the Bone Blade?"

"It was false, my raejina consort," Bithul answered gravely.

Anula's shoulders sank. "No."

"Yes," Kama said. "Nevertheless it put on a glorious show before its demise."

"Why are you standing there?" Anula spun on Reeri. "We need to find the real dagger."

"I am not merely standing here," Reeri said betwixt clenched teeth. "You interrupted."

"Interrupted what, your sulking?"

"I am not sulking."

"Why do you want the blade?" Bithul asked.

"For her bargain," Reeri said, but Anula announced louder, "To kill Lord Wessamony."

The room tilted. Reeri stared at a red fleck on Anula's cheek. "Say that again?"

Bee-stung lips pulled back in a snarl. "Lord Wessamony must be brought to justice."

Calu whistled low. "I did not see that coming."

Reeri's shadow unraveled. Hope trickled like a river through a mountain pass. "Why?"

Anula raised her chin. "I suspect you know why. He's a murderer. And you've come to kill him, too. Haven't you?"

All was silent.

Until—

"Of course not," Bithul insisted. "The Lord of the Second Heavens is no murderer, my raejina consort. Why would the Yakkas...?" His voice trailed as Reeri lifted his gaze. As Calu, Sohon, and Kama regarded him. Truth in their eyes. Bithul shifted. "Why?"

"The memory-nightmares," Anula said. "I was right. The banishment was not your fault, was it?"

Reeri rankled. "It does not matter."

"Yes, it does!" Anula snapped. "It matters that the Lord of the Second Heavens, hallowed and worshiped by half the kingdom, cares nothing for any of them. It matters that he deems us worth nothing, that he slaughters us without a second thought. It matters that he's the reason my village burned and my family was murdered. It matters who sits on the throne, in the Heavens and on Earth, wielding power over all."

In two swift steps, she closed the gap betwixt them, a challenge vibrating. "It matters who stole the lives of your Yakkas, who punishes them beyond death. It matters that you are freed."

Reeri's borrowed heart stammered.

"Eppawala burned because of him. Because he sought the Bone Blade. The same relic you seek," Anula said, her eyes flicking to the others as she pieced it together. "But you aren't giving it to him, are you? You're going to use it against him. The same way Fate used it on Destiny."

"What?" Bithul asked. Anula obligingly told their story. Bithul sucked in a sharp breath. "That can't be true. The Heavens would have told us."

"Yet it is, and they did not." Reeri's heart railed. Images of centuries past, of all the humans and bargains made for Wessamony's search, flashed. Reeri had known of seekers perishing on their journey. He had not known of innocents' deaths, those who had not accepted the challenge of the elevated bargain. Yet if Anula's words were true…

Wessamony allowed the forfeiture of their lives, batted no lash at their sacrifice, because Reeri had ruined his plans.

More blood stained his hands.

As if he were cursed, as Anula always said.

"You say the stories of old are half-truths." Anula pulled out one of her lists. At the top was scrawled a new name. "I see the full truth now. Lord Wessamony must be brought to justice, for us and for you. And I'll be the one to kill him."

The words stole Reeri's breath, stole the thoughts and notions he had held of her. Anula was not made only of ire and impatience, walls and wrath. She was not a selfish murderess. She cared for her people; she cared for it all: the kingdom, the cosmos, the Yakkas.

Him.

They were more than not dissimilar.

She was an echo.

"No." Bithul's voice cut brisk. "It makes no sense. Why would Lord Wessamony want the Bone Blade?"

Three Yakkas turned to Reeri. Mayhap it was time all the half-truths ended.

"Ascendance," Reeri said, remembering the conversation overheard with the Divinities. "Wessamony is the Great Destroyer. His powers imbue pure destruction into the hearts and actions of nature, animal, and human alike. He creates within them a desire, a need, to destroy all in their sight. A monsoon, a lion pride's attack, a usurper. Yet Wessamony is bound to the day of equinox, Yala and Maha. A balance demanded of the cosmos. He tried to circumvent his fetter by creating the Yakkas, but he only became more jealous of the Heavens, then of us. If he were to wield the Bone Blade, he could expunge the existence of the Divinities, ascend into the First Heavens, unbalance the cosmos, and force it to be undone. He would watch it burn, then draw from the ashes a new order, in which he was unfettered. And if it did not disappear, he would wield the blade again and again and again, until the cosmos was created in his likeness, with him at the helm of power."

A chill swept through the room.

"That can't happen." Anula leveled a stare. A decree as much as a demand.

"I know."

Bee-stung lips pursed, eyes narrowed, as if she could force herself to see beyond the face Reeri stole. Beneath the skin to the shadow. Reeri willed her to do it—to see what was hidden in plain sight. "Your unfinished business is not only to avenge the Yakkas."

Reeri dipped his chin. "It is to save them from eternal purgatory and a future where Wessamony has no bounds. You are saving your kingdom—"

"From eternal purgatory," she finished. "Human, and now Heavenly."

Truth resonated deep into his shadow and echoed in his soul.

He startled. He had not experienced this aspect of life before—had not known that he could.

"The Maha Equinox is nigh." Calu spoke into the heady silence. "Wessamony will descend in less than a fortnight."

"And you need a human to wield the Bone Blade," Bithul whispered.

"She is already our tether," Sohon added.

"Mayhap that is the problem," Kama said.

Anula frowned. "Why would that be a problem?"

"It is not." The words tumbled from Reeri's lips. So too the promise. He would not, could not, mar her as planned. Not his echo. He would find another way.

Kama cocked her head. Anula spoke, glancing from one Yakka to another. "So we have a deal, then? Together we find the relic, before the Maha Equinox, and I'll wield the Bone Blade and kill Wessamony."

"You wish to make a new bargain?" Reeri asked.

"No." Anula held out her hand. "A human deal."

His heart pinched. "Do you trust my word so little?"

"Do you *know* me so little? If I distrusted you, I'd find the relic myself. I only ally with those I believe in."

Ally.

Is that what they were?

Yet as he reached out his hand to graze her fingers, she pulled back.

"One more thing. You must promise to take a tincture I give you."

"Do you always poison your allies?"

"Not poison. A tincture. To fight off the dreams." She huffed. "I can't stand looking at those bags under your eyes. You won't guilt me into staying up all night to keep them away either. I can't afford to lose sleep. Do you know what stories they'll tell if the first raejina looks haggard in all her portraits?"

"All right," Reeri said, soul stirring. She had noticed his lack of sleep, the reason behind it. Mayhap she would soon see him. "Tinctures for the death of Wessamony."

Anula smiled, not sardonically, but with purpose and passion. She grasped his hand, their palms warm and firm, intentions clear. Each an echo of the other.

Both no longer alone.

PART THREE

34

"THIS WILL BE THE LAST TIME," ANULA SAID, TIGHTENING HER sari as she led Kama and Bithul through the Pleasure Gardens to the Kattadiya cave entrance.

The truth about the day she'd lost everything rattled her bones. Wessamony was the culprit. The three names at the top of her list were mere pawns. Selfish and guilty for the parts they'd played, yes, but pawns. A new name was atop her list now, and the only way to bring him to justice was through Reeri. With him, her bargain would be complete and so would her purpose. She'd punish the one responsible for Thaththa's and Amma's deaths, while taking the throne to lead Anuradhapura as the first raejina, marking the end of the Age of Usurpers and initiating a new age for peace and protection for all people, as Auntie Nirma had wanted.

Anula had no need of the Kattadiya now. Returning to the caves any longer would waste precious time. The Festival of the Cosmos was in a week and a half, starting with the day of the Maha Equinox.

To think she'd gone so long without knowing the truth, that

she and the Yakkas sought the same thing. Her palm tingled, directly where Reeri had shaken her hand when they became allies. His grip was strong and callused. A worker's hand. Nothing like she'd expected. Nothing about Reeri was, not even the shadow that hovered behind his stolen eyes. She'd half expected for it to appear, like smoke sliding through fabric, twining along her fingers, grasping her the way it had in the shrine with their first bargain. Instead she'd seen his thoughts, his idea that they were both defenders of their families.

She'd eyed him, his broad frame and soft muscle covered in dark curly hair that ran from chest to knuckle. She hadn't forgotten that Kama said this body resembled Reeri's true form. Nor had she forgotten his shadow: the square jaw and full lips, the softness, even in wisps. Only the saffron eyes were missing. When would she look into those again?

"If this is the last time we jaunt together," Kama said, trailing her fingers through flower bushes, "I shall receive my heart soon, yes?"

Anula blinked back the nonsensical thoughts. "Yes."

"Do you have someone in mind?"

Bithul flicked her a questioning gaze. She ignored it. "Don't worry. My list of enemies seems as fertile as these gardens—a new bloom every day. You'll have your heart."

Kama pouted. "You mean that *you* shall have their heart."

"What?"

Kama pressed a finger on Anula's chest, drew a circle, as if carving out her heart. "You must take it and offer it to me. Alive and beating."

Bithul gaped. Anula's mouth dried. "And you wonder why people fear you?"

Kama smiled. "Sheer the skin, break the bone, and hull the heart. So…what's their name?"

"Does it matter?"

"Why would a name not matter, when a life does?"

Before, Anula would have bristled, judged her not as the Yakka of Lust but of Bloodlust. But now…they shared one enemy. Why not two?

"Dilshan," Anula answered. She paused at the bush where they usually split off. "His name is Dilshan."

Bithul frowned. She ignored that look, too, and dove into the brush.

"May the Divinity of Luck be with you," Kama sang.

Anula wasn't sure if she needed it more for what she did now or for what she'd do for Dilshan's heart.

Down the stairs and through the tunnels, Anula wove past the Divinities' statues, star-filled eyes forever pursuing her, silently judging, as though they knew what she'd just promised and they could shame her out of it. They couldn't.

At the third convergence, Anula placed a hand over Guruthuma Thilini's, the act now second nature. The portrait of the first guruthuma in history bowed to her in recognition, a demure smile forming, as though she were genuinely happy to see her. As if they were friends. Was that kindness a mask of the Kattadiya, too? It wasn't as though all monsters came with fangs and claws.

The whisper of portraits crawled across her skin as the guruthuma led her deeper still, until the line of torches died off. Anula shivered. "If I didn't know better, I'd think you were taking me to my death."

Guruthuma Thilini said nothing.

"Though there's something to be said of the strong, silent types, they aren't my favorite," Anula jested, trying to get the portrait to speak. It was too quiet underground.

A torch suddenly flamed to life, illuminating a broken mask

half embedded into an iron door. Anula startled, clutching her necklace. "Premala's in there?"

The guruthuma nodded and deserted her to the cold.

Anula pushed open the heavy door and found herself staring into the most expansive room she had ever seen. The amphitheater could have easily fit the entire court inside, including the concubines and a good portion of the army, too. Unlike the rest of the tunnels, these walls were smooth, as if polished by a craftsman, and the stone tiers glinted in the light of a hundred torches, which led down a set of stairs.

Anula's gaze followed the line, past a host of angry women gathered on the last two tiers, to the floor where Guruthuma Hashini sheared the hair off a naked woman and shoved her into a pit, the focal point of the whole room. The guruthuma sneered down at the woman, whose cries bounced off the walls. She lifted a stone and aimed at her, catching her on the shoulder and drawing blood. The woman held in a cry and curled in on herself. Anula shuddered as one by one, the Kattadiya rose from their seats, picked up stones, stood at the edge of the pit, and threw.

"Anula."

"*Cursed Yak*—" Anula jumped.

Premala reached out a flailing hand. "What are you doing here?"

"What am I—what in the cursed cosmos is this?"

"Shh!" Premala clapped a hand over Anula's mouth, pushed them back through the door, and whispered, "You can't be here. It's a denouncement."

Anula tore from the girl's grip. "That explains *so* much."

"Mayra is a caster. Guruthuma Hashini tasked her to perform a tovil ceremony, but she broke the blood oath by showing mercy to a bargainer, and now she pays the price. Stripped of Heavenly blessing, she must bear the brunt of her sisters' pain for her abandonment and be banished from the city and from all ties with the Kattadiya." Though Premala's words shook with faith and fealty, her eyes shook with fright.

"Showing mercy?"

"We found the bargainer, thanks to a tip from a neighbor. The woman had been raped and fell pregnant. She bargained away the child. Mayra did not complete the tovil. She walked away to allow the bargain to be completed."

Anula frowned. "What's wrong with that?"

"I—it's against our faith to ever bargain. No matter the reason."

"I thought the Kattadiya did not act for themselves, only for the protection of others. Did she not act for the woman who was raped, giving her agency where it was stolen before?"

Premala drew herself up. "We *do* act in protection of others. We aren't the evil ones preying on people's pain, Anula."

"Are you sure?"

"She took the blood oath," Premala pushed. "It can't be undone. Nor should it be. We are of the First Heavens, where your word is your word. There are no tricks. Only love."

The sound of stone meeting bone reverberated through the chamber and into Anula's chest.

Love did not demand blood.

If Auntie Nirma had known Anula would partner with this twist of faith, she never would've deemed her ready. Perhaps she shouldn't have.

"Come on." Premala tugged at her arm. "Since you're here, let's practice. *I* won't be breaking any blood oaths."

Settled in an alcove far away, Anula couldn't hear Mayra's cries, yet she felt them like a ghostly hand pressing against shoulder and knee. Where else would they aim?

Premala stepped up to a wall of masks, more cursed than blessed, and picked one with blood dripping from sharp teeth. She bit her lip as she stared. "The Divinities of Truth and Refuge have blessed Guruthuma Hashini with insight to your tovil dance. She has begun to teach me the steps. If done right, it'll not only save bargainers from the yolk of their bargains, but complete what the Kattadiya started long ago."

Gooseflesh prickled. "What did they start?"

Light sparkled in Premala's gaze. "The Kattadiya are the ones who called Lord Wessamony from the Second Heavens to take away the Yakkas for all they'd done. But, according to the guruthumas, it had been a last resort. The Divinities had meant for the Kattadiya to be able to stop the Yakkas themselves, not just break their bargains or send them to their shrines. They were meant to tear apart a Yakka's soul."

"What?"

Mistaking her whisper for reverence, Premala nodded vigorously. "I know, it changes everything doesn't it? If we—if I can perform this correctly, I will save you, wholly. I can keep you from ever being harmed by these Yakkas again."

Anula's lungs seized.

The masks in the memory-nightmares, she knew they had been the Kattadiya, but *this*? Responsible for calling Wessamony, for starting the centuries-long punishment and torture of them all... Why hadn't Reeri told her? What else was he hiding?

A finger of fear slid down Anula's back. What else were the Kattadiya capable of?

"If I do this right"—Premala's voice tripped—"I can save the kingdom."

Anula saw her then, a soldier terrified of her leaders and their judgment of her worthlessness. A soldier ready to prove them wrong.

But Anula couldn't let her. "I command you not to."

Premala blanched. "Wh—what?"

"I came here to tell you that I no longer require your help."

"Y—you broke your bargain? Without a tovil?"

"The tovil is not necessary anymore."

Premala's brows knit tightly. "How did you get them all to leave?"

"Them?" Anula swallowed.

"I told you, we can feel a bargain!" Premala snapped. She stepped back. "The guruthuma, as soon as she met you, she knew. You didn't just make a bargain. You brought them back. Who are they? How did you convince them to leave?"

Anula's stomach plummeted. "You know about the tether?"

"We can sense them! The guruthuma has ways." Premala's voice pitched. "I told her you were different, that you were taken in by their lies. I convinced her to let you—"

Premala clapped a hand over her mouth.

"Let me what?"

Premala shook her head.

The blood oath and denouncement, the rules of mercy and worthiness... "What happens to the bargainers the guruthuma finds, the ones who didn't seek you out?"

A squeak slid through Premala's fingers.

"How does the guruthuma save them? Or does she save the people from their influence instead?"

Premala shook.

"The Yakkas may not be killed in a tovil, yet, but the bargainers are, aren't they? You convinced the guruthuma that I was different. That I deserved to survive. Cursed Heavens, Premala, how can you not see the Kattadiya are eviler than the Yakkas?"

"They're lying to you!" Premala broke. "What did they promise? The throne? The whole kingdom's been talking about how you've managed to stayed married to not two but three usurpers. For prayer's sake, that's it. It's the raja, isn't it? He's been possessed—that's how he usurped so quietly. Did they kill the others? Did you know?"

"I—I—" Anula tripped over the panic in Premala's voice and the question it seemed to ask: whether *she* was a threat to the kingdom.

"Why? It's bad enough you made a bargain for the throne, but you brought them back! Do you have any idea what our ancestors went through to be rid of them? Don't you know how much pain they caused? Don't you care?"

"Yes!" Anula snapped. "If I didn't care, I wouldn't have kept your secret. I wouldn't have checked on the kitchen maids. I wouldn't have dedicated my whole life to get here."

Premala startled. "A-apologies, my—of course you care. It's just...look what you've done."

Anula clenched her jaw.

"For prayer's sake, you can't walk away from the Kattadiya. Not now," Premala whispered. "Not even as raejina consort. You took the blood oath, Anula. If you try to leave now, they will denounce you and perform the tovil ceremony anyway." Premala wrung her hands. "Please. They will kill you."

"Let them try," Anula said, running a trembling hand through her hair, as if she could shake off the guilt nipping at her neck. "I didn't take a blood oath."

"Yes, you did. You gave your blood to Guruthuma Thilini that first day. *That* was the oath. You aligned yourself to the Kattadiya."

Anula's breath caught between her lungs and throat. The first time she had touched the guruthuma's portrait had been at Premala's request. To prove she wasn't aligned with the Yakkas. There had been a prick, small and quick, like a mosquito bite. And though she'd touched Guruthuma Thilini's hand plenty of times since, she wasn't pricked again.

"Haven't you noticed the compulsion?" Premala asked.

"Outside these caves, you cannot speak the name of the Kattadiya. The oath compels you to keep us secret. And when Guruthuma Hashini deems it's the right time, she will use the oath to call you here, and either you comply and become pure in the safety of her power, or you resist and are purged from our blessing. Then you'll be just another bargainer, your life taken along with the Yakkas during the tovil. There is no leaving, Anula, not alive. So please, do as I say. Stay far away from the Yakkas, give me a few more days, and let me cast them from you. Let me end them, permanently."

For once, the girl didn't stammer, didn't falter. But Anula felt as though she'd tripped over a mountainside, and the fall was long.

"Have a good time with your not-paramour?" Kama asked as Anula emerged from the brush.

"I was with the—" Her voice cut off. The air not caught but stifled. Ripped from her mouth and carried away.

Cursed Yak—cursed cosmos. Premala had been right: She couldn't speak their name. Which meant she couldn't explain, couldn't warn or protect the Yakkas. Powerless, once again.

Anula scoffed. "I don't need a paramour to have a good time with myself."

Bithul narrowed suspicious eyes. Could he see the panic beneath her veins? The ocean rising over her head? She should have taken the first meeting with Nuwan as a sign, turned back and told Auntie Nirma that she wasn't ready, that it wasn't the right time. Perhaps she would still be alive. Perhaps they would've honed the plan, made contingencies, uncovered more truths.

Storm clouds darkened the gardens. If Auntie Nirma had been wrong about who'd ultimately burned Eppawala and their family, did that mean her plans for justice were wrong, too? Had Anula chosen the right path?

Look away.

She clenched a fist. Of course she had. Murder was murder, both on Earth and in the Heavens. Bringing justice to the guilty might have been Anula's first and only good decision so far, but it wouldn't be her last. She would find the Bone Blade and kill Wessamony, before the Kattadiya struck. She'd free Reeri and the Yakkas.

Then she'd free Anuradhapura.

35

Heat gently woke Reeri.

He sighed into it, inviting it to melt him further. There was a time he could not remember the sun's touch. How it warmed him as if under a blanket of lion furs. How it drew the tension from his muscles like poison from a snakebite. How it weighed heavy on his chest, squeezed his forearm, drooled on his—

Reeri's eyes snapped open.

Anula cinched her arms tightly around him, nuzzling his waist. A soft smile spread as she blinked up. A flush heated Reeri's cheeks, and he wondered what those lips tasted like without poison.

"Now kiss him," the blessed gift raejina whispered loudly overhead.

Anula jumped, tore away, and toppled off the bed.

"*Oh*," the blessed gift raejina groaned. "You truly are not good at this."

"They are a lost cause," agreed the blessed gift raja. "Best wait for the next raja to choose another wife."

Reeri let out a breath, cleared his head of lips and kisses, and leaned over the edge. "Your tincture worked."

Anula popped up. "Right. Good."

"Are you injured?" Reeri asked, eyes fixed on her face, not on the robe half fallen from her shoulder, nor the bare skin blushing pink on her chest.

"Unscathed as a brand-new irrigation tank." Anula raced across the room. "See you in the archives."

The door slammed. Reeri collapsed onto the bed, his waist suddenly cold.

Reeri flexed his hand.

The urge to touch Anula twitched. It was not from the tether, for she sat mere inches away. It was from the memory of the morning, the feel of her warming his borrowed body, reminding him of sensations long lost. Of the heat of life.

Her smile, her nose burrowing into his side, seared in his mind. It had thrilled down his spine, stolen his breath, and addled his thoughts. He had not even seen anything from where their bodies touched; he had been too wrapped up in the softness of her, the closeness, the press of her curves against him.

Books thudded to the floor, snapping Reeri's attention to Calu, who sifted quickly through the stack of bound manuscripts on the low table, as if he had more important places to be. He tossed another to the ground.

A throat cleared. Loud and rough.

Sohon stood at the front of the table, dark red mehendhi peeking from under his tunic. The archive was a vast room with three walls of shelves and one of windows. Manuscripts of history, politics, and all else important to the knowledge of Anuradhapura were bound and preserved here. Sohon's eyes flashed to the Yakkas and Anula, seated and waiting. "If you cannot respect the books, do not touch them."

Calu huffed and held up his hands. "I hold nothing but respect."

Sohon scowled. "These are the books I have written since we arrived, and some that I was able to gather with the former prophet's help."

Four sets of eyes flicked to Anula.

She crossed her arms. "What? Prophet Revantha seems just as adept—more so, as he didn't ordain a village's death. His reputation is flawless."

"Therefore, his body is poisonless," Calu jested, yet his voice was stone. "Let us hope neither changes."

Reeri did not have a moment to question his brethren's unusual tone, for a smile tugged on Anula's lips. A hint of the one this morning. Yet it was not Reeri who had conjured it. He flexed his hand again.

"We must analyze the memories for anything important," he said, passing her a book, cutting their conversation off.

"It is all important," Sohon snapped. Clearly, all the Yakkas were in a mood today. "Stories transport us. All art does."

"I did not mean that."

"You implied."

Reeri gripped the edge of a manuscript and amended, "We search for anything pertinent to the relic. Whether that be a story of a treasure seeker or a fabled location."

The young Yakka grunted, curled himself against the far wall and plucked up a manuscript of his own. The rest of the table followed suit. Reeri opened a tome. It had been centuries since he had peered inside a memory book. He had asked Sohon to explain his work to him, back when Reeri was the only one able to leave his shrine. Even now, it daunted Reeri to hold the last vestiges of a life in his hands. To not only know of a person's life, but of their hopes and secrets and pains.

Anil Perera came into this world in the midst of a rainstorm on the floor of his father's fishing boat and was forever enamored with the sea. Even the Makara, the sea dragon, halted its hunt, recognizing another monster descending from the Heavens.

Monster…from the Heavens. The words scratched along Reeri's memory.

"Why isn't Bithul helping?" Anula asked, flipping open her own book.

Reeri tensed. He had not mentioned the task he had given the guard. Yet after their deal, after seeing her soul mirror his, mayhap it was time for secrets to be shared. "He is looking for Nuwan. I do not want him selling more cursed relics."

"Reading is a silent act," Sohon hissed.

Calu sneezed. Phlegm spattered, dangling from one nostril. A square kerchief hit his face.

"I will end you," Sohon promised.

"I did not do it on purpose," Calu snapped back. Reeri's brow furrowed.

Despite Calu's irritability and Kama's attempt to clean the book, Reeri was transfixed on Anula. She traced a finger around the largest jewel on her necklace.

"Is someone set to be poisoned today?" he whispered.

She clasped it. "No, I always wear it. It's the last thing I have of my family, my amma's most treasured gift. The jewels are from my thaththa; the poisoncraft is from my uncle."

Reeri noticed the change in her cadence, the soft lilt. "And what of your auntie?"

"She taught me how to wield it."

"You must miss her."

She regarded him, bronze eyes searching. Worry snagged his heart, that she may find him lacking and snub the echo of their souls. "She also taught me about allies."

Reeri's mouth dried. Now was his moment to see if she felt it, too. If he could find the right words…but she gazed away at the stack of memory books.

"Are there any books about—" Her voice cut off.

Reeri heard the word anyway. "Eppawala?"

"No," she said, her guard raised again as quickly as it had slipped. "Never mind."

His shadow scrambled to stay close, and he tilted his leg to the side, brushing against her sari. Yet the distance was still there. Mayhap if he spoke of the relic—if he explained how she would wield it to exact vengeance and justice upon Wessamony—she may not feel the need to raise her walls with him at all. But that would mean explaining the process of how he had planned to call the Yakkas' souls forth first, of how he would have used the soul she offered, of how cleaving it would have marred her soul.

He had already determined not to cleave it fully in two, not to allow all the goodness to seep away or leave her a carcass. He could do that, right? He held the reins, as Kama said. He could save the Yakkas and preserve Anula.

But if she did not trust him…she could refuse, or worse, recant.

"Ouch! Cursed blessings."

The scent of blood floated on the air, dripped from Anula's finger as she held it aloft.

"Paper cut," she murmured to four pairs of Yakka eyes.

The urge to grab her hands seized him, the need to wipe the blood clean, mayhap with his lips. O Heavens, had one touch truly undone him? He bit back the desire and held himself in place.

Yet Kama did not. She leaned close, gathered Anula's hand in hers. "Does it hurt?"

"Only slightly."

Kama grabbed her chin. "Describe it to me. Does it pulse with pain? Does it throb with pleasure?"

Anula pulled away. "You're insane, do you know that?"

"I am not."

"Indeed, you are," Calu said.

"We are all in agreement," Sohon murmured from behind a book.

"Passion and insanity are two entirely different things." Kama twirled a lock of hair, nodding to the book that had cut Anula. Embossed in gold was the title *Akshay's Desires*. "I desire to set the world aflame. Burning with love for one another, lovers and friends, family and neighbors will face the anguish of the cosmos, opening their arms even to death. For love bears all things, faces all things, and wins in the end. My ministrations are good, you will see, for there is no line between beauty and pain. They encompass each other, consuming as they kiss."

Reeri noted the fervor in her voice, the way she gazed into Anula's eyes. It was not the usual coo of the temptress, the melody of persuasion, but the earnestness of vulnerability.

Anula inched from her grip. "The only way to prove your theory is to save lives. There are no good intentions that only kill, no beauty in senseless suffering."

"Then that is what I shall desire," Kama breathed, as if she too had been caught under Anula's spell.

"What a desire," Sohon sighed sarcastically.

Reeri bristled. "And what is yours, to drown in a sea of books?"

Sohon quieted, disappearing behind his manuscript.

Anula kicked Reeri's leg. The bone sang at her touch. "Sohon should put his name on a book. Favorite authors are always remembered."

A furrowed brow emerged atop the pages. "These are not my stories."

"But you are telling them. You're a storyteller, so perhaps write your own stories, ones you make up."

"Like for children?" His entire head surfaced.

"For anyone."

Sohon smiled, shy and lopsided, yet as real as the day he had finally left his shrine. Anula rewarded it with one of her own. Reeri's leg stung anew.

"What about you?" Anula asked Calu.

He did not meet her gaze. Instead, he white-knuckled the page of his book, jaw working as he whispered, "I desire nothing."

Reeri's heart pinched. Yet, before he could respond, Calu bolted from the table, crashing through the archive doors. Reeri did not hesitate. He followed Calu down the hall, until the Yakka tipped to the side, the wall catching his fall, and slid to the floor.

"I cannot think of things that I desire," Calu whispered thickly.

Reeri bent down. "Why not?"

"Because I cannot have them. I cannot have Ratti and I need her. I have tried, Reeri, I have. To connect with any of them, as she always wanted. But these people, this time...they are more wary of me than their ancestors. It is a Heavenly miracle that I made one bargain, but I have not been able to since. The rumors, Heavens, the rumors, Reeri. They speak of how risky it is to bargain with me, that I am a trickster, and now—" He choked off, face red and breathing hitched; a sudden flood of tears rushed down his cheeks.

They struck Reeri's shadow. Calu had not cried since the day Ratti was taken.

"And now—now—I cannot—I do not have—"

Reeri's heart cleaved, watching Calu suffer like this. The one who had spoken to him in the aether, despite centuries of his shadows writhing and words lashing. The one who always attempted to lighten the mood, his mood. The one whom he had not touched since that day. Reeri's hand twitched. He fumbled once, then reached out and placed it on his brother's shoulder. Warmth spread under his fingers, and Heavens, he had not realized how much he had missed it. Missed the connection, missed the comfort. He squeezed Calu's shoulder, aching at the thought that his brother felt the same: alone and afraid. "It will all be made right. This will not be your final chance, and Ratti will be here to see you through. To celebrate with you."

Calu snotted on his sleeve. "What if she is not? If one thing goes wrong, if the blade or the offerings—"

"Your fear is talking, Calu. Do not listen to it. Did Ratti not tell us that, too?"

Calu half snorted, half hiccupped. He wiped his face. "Easy for you to say. You fear nothing."

If only that were true. Reeri swallowed. "I fear the day I will see our brethren again."

Calu sniffled. "Why?"

"They may hate me or want me dead. I dread to see the blame staring back at me."

Calu placed a gentle hand over Reeri's, as if he already knew. "Despite the fear, you still work toward that day."

"Of course. I love them, more than I fear them."

"And when that day comes?"

"I suppose I will have to face my fear."

Calu caught Reeri in a hug. The same hug Ratti had used to give him. The tightness holding him together, absorbing part of the fear. Reeri did not hate it.

"You have changed," Calu said, pulling away slowly.

"Mayhap that is what hope does."

"It is not hope. It is happiness." Calu smirked, but it did not reach his eyes. "Be careful. We still have to cleave her."

Reeri stood, anxiety prickling anew. "I know."

"Good." Calu wiped off the vestiges of his moment of brokenness. "Shall we face our fears then?"

"You first."

Calu laughed. "Was that a jest?"

"Never."

"Anula's soul is already rubbing off on you." He headed back toward the archives.

Reeri paused. Mayhap she was—all the good parts. The things he must protect. As he must protect his brethren's second chance at life, their eternal freedom.

He could do both.

He would.

36

The scent of cinnamon tingled Anula's nose and roused her muscles. She sighed contentedly as she woke.

Reeri, on the other hand, snored softly, his breath blustering a fallen lock of hair. Heat radiated off him. She hadn't felt a nightly chill since this raja had arrived. His frame took up the bed, feet dangling off the end, and yet he slept deeply, peacefully. A characteristic of either Vatuka or Reeri, but which one? His eyelids quivered. If she opened one now, would it be filled with saffron?

Another snore rippled, sending a twitch through his body, and she saw it, his dream. The light touch of a loved one, the connection of family and friends. An empty ache rattled his chest.

She glanced down—their hands were entwined. His fingertips were stained a light brown from constantly stirring his tea with cinnamon bark while neck-deep in memory books. She wondered if the sweet flavor also spiced his tongue.

Anula noticed how his hand dwarfed hers. She couldn't help her thumb rubbing a gentle circle over his knuckles. Couldn't stop herself from doing it again. Were his true hands this rough? Would they scrape if he brushed her lips?

She stilled. That wasn't what he was dreaming about. He yearned for his friends and family, a craving she knew all too well. The last time she'd held a hand was that night. Hers had been swallowed then, too, by Amma's as she desperately drew her through the house and the courtyard, away from death. Anula slid her hand from Reeri's grip and shifted to the edge of the bed.

A groan sounded, longing and homesick, as Reeri stretched awake. "Good morning," he murmured.

"Not with that breath on my face." She grimaced, pulling farther away.

He frowned as the bedchamber door opened and a servant rushed in, flushed and bowing, to deliver an urgent missive.

A tongue clucked behind Anula. The blessed gift raejina whispered, "You fear what you want."

"You have no idea what I fear."

The artistry sighed. "Oh, darling consort, it is written all over your beautiful face."

A chill racked Anula. She pulled the pillows high and pressed them against the wood carving, as if she could smother the words.

"Commander Dilshan has returned," Reeri announced and stood, avoiding her gaze. "He is waiting with the ministers to give a report on the war with Polonnaruwa."

Anula dropped the pillows. "I'm coming with you."

"No."

Anula snorted, already reaching for her necklace, tinctures and poisons flicking through her mind. She wrapped a robe around her waist; justice didn't need to be served in a sari. But Reeri stepped into her path.

"What are you doing?" she asked.

"Do you trust me?"

"As far as a chicken can throw an elephant."

"Will you try, once?"

Agitation skittered up her arms. "He's—"

"On your list," Reeri finished. "I know. I am not telling you to leave him alone, only asking that you wait, and trust me."

Every muscle flinched. She trusted him with Wessamony, because she trusted his hatred, but this? It might be her only chance. "Why?"

"Because I want to help you."

Anula startled. Not at the words but how they sang with truth, how she heard it as surely as a bulbul's song. It swelled in her chest, tilting her off guard, and she almost didn't hear herself say, "All right."

For an hour, Anula tried and failed to avoid thinking about Reeri, about the ease with which he had convinced her to stay, the feeling he'd stirred up—the want for her old dream—and what that said about her, about him, about them. Not even summoning Premala to deliver her morning meal could fully pull her from her thoughts.

Anula thought Premala would like it, seeing all the gifts from those she venerated most, but she quaked the moment she stepped into the bedchamber, half the tray's food tumbling to the floor. She peered around vases and jumped at the sound of the wind as if the terrible Yakkas would spring out and eat her.

"Tell me, how did a girl from a fishing village become a—" The word choked. Anula flicked at the kiribath. "Cursed blessings, I can't even say it to you?"

"Not outside the caves. It's for protection, yours and ours, my raejina consort." Premala checked a shudder. "If the Yakkas were to find out, they'd kill us all."

That feeling rose again, this time with a sea of questions. Namely, why she'd bent beneath it, why it had felt so familiar and yet so foreign, why she wanted Reeri to come back and explain himself. Why she was afraid if he did. She murmured into her food, "You don't know that."

The chamber door slammed open, cutting off the argument poised on Premala's lips.

"The commander awaits you in the administration building," Reeri said, skidding to a stop at the sight of the maid.

Premala squeaked, fear flaring in her eyes as she took in the raja. Clearly, she believed her own theory. She bowed and fled before Reeri had a chance to give her an order. Perhaps terrified it would have to do with the Yakkas. The girl needed to find her backbone if Anula was to save her from the Kattadiya. Though prying her out of the caves one-handed would work, too. But that was a problem for another day. Today, there was Dilshan. He had returned to her city and was waiting for her. Because of Reeri.

"Why?" Anula stood, finally asking aloud what she'd chewed on for hours.

"He is a man who bargained to allow an entire village to perish," Reeri said, meeting her gaze. "He must stand trial and face the consequences of his actions. I have set it up for you to be his judge and juror."

Anula quirked a brow. "I thought you didn't want me to be a murderess."

Reeri's lips pressed tight, and she saw it in his eyes, the same thing she had seen when they touched this morning: a dream of connection.

Anula swallowed.

"I understand that you want to change your kingdom for the better," he said. "Though for what it is worth, mayhap it is best if you deal with him differently than you did Prophet Ayaan."

Anula stepped back. This didn't feel like a connection, but more…it felt like caring. She should decline, draw a line.

But it was Commander Dilshan: the first voice she'd heard after Amma's screams had died in her ears, and now the second name on her list. His heart was promised to Kama for the sake of the Yakkas. His death would lead directly to Wessamony's.

Stepping around the back of the table, she gave Reeri a wide berth. "You're giving him to me for free, no bartering?"

Reeri dropped his chin. "The fastest way to earn trust is to prove myself trustworthy."

She grabbed a knife on display. Perhaps Reeri only did this for the bargain and she was reading too far into a feeling.

Reeri cleared his throat. "If I were to ask you a question, would you answer it, with no bartering?"

"Depends on the question."

"Where do you go with Kama?"

Ask no questions, tell no secrets.

Anula tucked the knife into her sari. Again, his intent felt more like concern than curiosity…but was that so wrong? "To see a friend who doesn't know she's in trouble."

"Oh." Reeri blinked in surprise. "I hope all ends well."

"I won't let it end any other way." Anula left Reeri and opened the bedchamber door, vowing that when she claimed the crown, her first act would be to protect the kingdom from those above and *below* the ground. Nothing would harm her people. That's all she cared about.

"Good morning, my raejina consort." Bithul bowed. "The commander is waiting."

"Bring Kama to the administration building."

Bithul stilled, half-bent. "Does this have to do with a certain offering she's expecting?"

Anula raised a brow.

"Unlike my ankles, my ears are uninjured, my raejina consort."

"Bring her."

"Do not let hatred beget more hatred. Think of the kingdom. What is the most important thing, now?"

Justice. The word rang through Anula. It had always been justice, as Auntie Nirma had taught her, as Reeri agreed. The Kattadiya flashed in her mind. Their idea of justice was wrong. Not hers.

Right?

"Don't do anything rash."

Anula scowled as she marched down the hall and called back, "I am not rash."

A sighed followed her.

The weight of the knife pulled at Anula's side as she walked into the room where men had once sat at the long table and refused to listen to her.

Now a man stood, waiting for her to be seated first. Anula touched a finger to her necklace. There were so many ways to stop a heart. But Kama wanted one still beating, Reeri wanted a trial and sentence different than Prophet Ayaan's, and Auntie Nirma wanted the deaths of the men responsible for evil.

"My raejina consort." Commander Dilshan bowed. Gray hair topped a tall man. Leathery skin and deep wrinkles evidenced that he was a soldier of a long war, living in the elements instead of the palace. "It's a pleasure to finally meet you."

His voice was as rough as she remembered, as smug and unaffected. The lack of smile proved his lie, but was death the sentence he deserved? Amma and Thaththa hadn't deserved to die that night, and yet the man before her had chosen it for them.

Anula sat, held up a hand when he moved to do the same. "I know what you've done."

Commander Dilshan raised both brows. "And what is that?"

He did not use her title. She tore her gaze away and reached for the tea on the table. "Do you care for all the people of Anuradhapura?"

"Of course," he said, gruff and impatient.

"Even the small villages?"

Silence rang out. Dilshan glanced at the door. Anula poured him a cup of tea, her finger tracing a small diamond at her throat, a sapphire to its right. When he was satisfied that no one was listening, he growled, "Who told you?"

At least he had the boldness to admit to it. "Prophet Ayaan."

Dilshan frowned. "The prophet? How? Did he foresee my rule?"

"*Your* rule?"

Dilshan slammed his hands on the table. The teapot rattled. "I do not appreciate being called in front of a consort and scolded. I am not a child."

Anula pursed her lips. "Ah, you mean that you don't care to hear from a wife. Not even the wife responsible for Ayaan's death? Ayaan, your one-time ally, who died spilling all your secrets?"

Dilshan paled to the gray color of his hair. "I was told Ayaan died of natural causes."

"Poison." Anula nodded. "Yes, very natural. Made from the flowers in the gardens."

The commander shifted.

"Sit," Anula commanded.

He grimaced but slowly lowered. "He told you about Eppawala." It was not a question.

Anula's hand shook, the desire to strike him stronger than her tea. "You admit it, then? You admit to serving my village, my family, as a sacrifice? Allowing them to be killed and having their blood on your hands?"

"It was a long time ago. Sanctioned by my raja and the Heavens."

"You don't believe that. You were in it for rank."

He scoffed. "And?"

Anula blanched. "You have no regrets? You didn't even get what you were promised."

"Deals come and go." He shrugged. "That's how you win the war of life. It doesn't matter who knows what now. It's been too long. Besides, three rajas later and I have a new bargain."

"Wessamony won't save you now."

"Not with the Heavens. They're not as reliable as a man." Dilshan smiled. It was worse than his frown. "Or a prince."

"Anuradhapura doesn't have any princes." Unless he'd found a bastard. Those, Anula was sure, there were plenty of.

Dilshan leaned back. "My parents died by another's hand when I was a baby. My title afforded me only so much. I learned quickly that one must fight for their right to have what they want, including staying alive. Don't you agree?"

"No." Anula's grip on her cup tightened. "I don't."

"Too bad. You're doing a marvelous job at it, Anula Ramanayake."

She narrowed her eyes.

"Yes, I know who you are." He leaned forward, toothy and proud. "I know you're the sole survivor of Eppawala. Nirma made it known. Let me fear the day you wore a crown. But here we are, and I'm still more powerful than you, on the cusp of being more powerful than your raja. I fear no one, much less you. You'll learn soon enough, Anula—I'm always on the winning side."

Anula's pulse rushed, her minding swirling. "Anuradhapura is winning the war."

Commander Dilshan laughed without a smile. "The missives say we are, yet who dictates what is written?" He pointed to himself. "Have you been out there? Has any raja in a decade? *No.* The only fight they have in them is for entrance to the palace. Energy only to indulge in concubines and blessed gifts. Yet I have been out there. Every cursed day. I own this war. And the three villages on the edge of our border."

"Own them?"

"My new bargain. The prince of Polonnaruwa and I have an understanding. I give him Anuradhapura, and he grants me land and a title of the highest caste."

The words slithered around Anula's throat, down her spine, and flicked the knife at her hip. "What about the people? Don't they get a say?"

"Any who didn't agree to new leadership were killed. It's all Polonnaruwan territory now."

Anula narrowed her eyes. "You admit to the deaths of my family and now to so many more. Why? I could have the raja burn you."

"Have you ever seen hope gutter from a person's eyes? It's more satisfying than this tea. My only regret is that it is you with whom I drink, not Nirma."

Anula's jaw worked as she realized this man had been on Auntie Nirma's list of enemies long before Anula chose her path. And though Auntie Nirma might have been wrong about a great many things, justice was not one of them. Men who shed blood and never thought twice about it did not deserve mercy. The people they ruled did not deserve them.

"Then I suppose I better work for my right to stay alive. Perhaps we can come to an agreement."

His crooked smile sent a shiver down her spine. "I will build my own concubine estate."

"I might have the experience you're after."

"No, thanks. I don't eat table scraps." Dilshan reached for both their teacups, swapping them before draining one. "You're just like Nirma. You think you're so clever. You forget I have twenty years' experience on you. You'd be wise to learn from me."

He stood and turned to leave, only to pause and clutch at his chest, hands and feet unmoving. Paralyzed in pain.

It was the tincture she'd given to Nuwan, remixed and working as intended.

"Oh, but I already have, Dilshan." Anula stood, walked around the table, the knife bumping with each step, and clapped him on the shoulder. He wheezed, turning purple. "Never celebrate a victory until all your enemies are dead. Otherwise, they could spring from the bushes and catch you by surprise."

She pushed him to the ground, where he coughed and choked.

The sharp blade had a lion's head on the hilt. A blessed gift known for helping a raja hunt. It was said to be able to take down a lion with one slice. To skin them clean with one slash.

The commander didn't care for anyone but himself. Anula plunged the blade, cutting open his chest as smoothly as if it were a mango. She dug her hand deep inside and pulled out the thing he never used.

A heart.

She watched it expand and contract, waiting for the moment she would feel different. The moment all the years of study and scheming would pay off. The moment her shoulders would lift from the weight of her family's deaths.

Seconds ticked by. But the feeling never came.

"Here," she said, dropping the heart in Kama's hands. The Yakka lit up and flitted away, a giggle peeling through the administration halls.

"Tell the raja to send troops to the villages of Maradankadawala, Palugaswewa, and Habraana. Polonnaruwa has taken them."

Bithul frowned, swallowed hard. "He—"

"Was not a good man." She leveled a stare.

He nodded, grave and resigned. "Then you focused on the most important thing, and your justice was served."

Was it?

A breeze chilled the blood on her hands.

Dilshan's death didn't bring back Amma or Thaththa. It didn't make that night less horrific or more bearable. Anula would save only some in the villages. It wouldn't bring back those already taken. What, then, was the point of Auntie Nirma's justice? Or Anula's path to the throne?

Her voice hollowed out. "I am here to change things for the betterment of Anuradhapura."

But was she truly changing anything or simply begetting more death?

37

THE BREEZE PLAYED WITH REERI'S HAIR AS HE BATHED BENEATH the stars. It curled the tips, drew gooseflesh across his neck. Mayhap, though, that came from the image dancing through his mind instead.

Eight days they had spent in the archives. Eight days reading, much to Sohon's pleasure, scouring each page for a hint to where to search. Eight days sitting alongside Anula, noticing the delicate bones beneath her mehendhi hands, the way she sighed when the person of whom she read found a happy moment, and, moreover, noticing the change in her curses. No longer was it a cursed Yakka, but cursed blessings.

He had scooted closer to her the day before, and she had let her hair fall on his shoulder. It smelled of jasmine. He wondered at the feel of it betwixt his fingers. Mayhap he could know—after the relic was found and used, once he had a body and a life. If Anula allowed it, he could live in the inner city. They could remain… connected. She had said that her auntie had taught her of allies. He could show her how good an ally he could be, how she would want for nothing. She would tremble only under his thumb as he swept it over her cheeks, down her neck, trailing it with his nose. Nuzzling, brushing lips over her softness. She had said she begged on her knees for one thing only. O Heavens. He would give it to her every time.

Anything she requested. Anywhere she demanded.

A drop of water landed on Reeri's face. Not from the pool lapping at his waist but from the sky above. The rain fell on his shoulders. Reeri stilled. The season was turning, signaling the equinox mere days away. He opened a palm, let it fill with water.

Mighty Heavens, what was he doing, wasting time in the bath, dreaming of a life that could possibly never be, dreaming of—

It started at his navel, a force binding and confining. Just as it was in his memory. Reeri's heart beat swiftly. This was not the tether.

It was his Lord.

When the Second Heavens called, there was nothing a Yakka could do.

Fire and brimstone reflected off the smooth ivory floor. Reeri coughed against a heap of broken statue, his head swimming from being ripped out of a body. Kama and Sohon bent with him. Calu collapsed on his knees. Reeri fought through the panic. They still had time. They should not have been called.

"You dare disobey my orders once again?" The booming voice of their Lord echoed through the vast chamber.

"Please," Calu cried.

Dread traced Reeri's throat.

"Shall I rescind the bargain now?" Lord Wessamony growled,

heavenslight illuminating him atop his grand throne. The Great Sword trembled in his hand. "Shall I send you to final death for your repeated insolence?"

Reeri's head snapped up. "My Lord, there has been no such thing."

Blue burned the base of Wessamony's horns. "Do you think me blind?"

"No, my Lord." Reeri's mind raced. Only they knew of the soul sacrifice, the purpose behind it. Anula would not be so daft as to tell the one she had marked for death. There was no other reason for Wessamony to believe they had tricked him or acted against the terms of their bargain. There were not even Kattadiya left to call upon him once more. They were dead and buried by their own people. "Please. We are close. I feel it in my soul."

Wessamony smoldered. "You feel the call of the Bone Blade?"

"It is close." It was not a lie. Residing in the kingdom brought them closer than they had been in the aether.

Wessamony reclined back, regarding them. It took one flick of Reeri's gaze to see the line of Yakkas missing. A sight Reeri had never seen. His stomach twisted.

"Our bargain stands," Wessamony declared. "Yet this cannot go unpunished."

"What cannot?"

A wicked smile spread. "Calu, my son. Tell them."

Reeri's mouth dried as he turned to face Calu.

A shiver raked Calu's shadow. He did not look up, nor meet their gazes. "I unwound the mind of a human. Without a bargain."

Kama sucked in a sharp breath. The edges of Sohon's specter thrashed.

No. None of them would break taboo, least of all Calu.

Unless…had he not said he feared their plan going awry? That Ratti would never return to his side?

An ache swept through Reeri's shadow. Calu believed Reeri had already failed him. Again.

Calu bowed. "I accept full responsibility for my actions, my Lord. I deserve punishment."

"Indeed, you do." Wessamony held up a hand. "Yet tell me, what action did you take on the human?"

"I unwound his mind, my Lord, and gave him only one thought: to make an offering to me," he whispered.

"Did he?"

Calu nodded, grim and haunted.

"What was it?"

Dread coiled tight around Reeri's throat, as he saw the trajectory of Wessamony's questions. Calu flickered a pitiful gaze to Reeri. "A handcrafted rice bowl, made of his brother's teeth."

The pieces fell into place. The words Calu had cried in the hallway the other day surfaced. No one was offering and time was slipping by. But Calu had already received his essence offering. Or had he not? Reeri shivered as he remembered Calu's empty neckline. The mangled pendant was gone. This was what he had been trying to tell him; this was what he truly feared—because without his essence offering, their plan could not succeed.

"Then that"—Wessamony's voice rattled Reeri's bones—"be your punishment. You turned brother against brother. So, too, you will turn against your clan."

Wessamony snapped his fingers. Ratti flew from an antechamber, shadow as pristine as the first day she had been created. She landed at Calu's feet, fear bright in her eyes as the first day she had been destroyed.

"No." Calu's voice cracked. "Please."

Ratti swallowed hard and whispered, "It is all right."

It was not.

The wrongness writhed. Reeri stepped betwixt the two. "I will do it."

"A great leader bears all faults." A smile sounded in Wessamony's words. "You have learned that lesson, at least."

"Yes, my Lord." Reeri grit his teeth.

"You are aware that, ultimately, his failure is your fault."

"Yes, my Lord."

Calu cried, "No. I—"

Reeri pushed him away. This *was* his fault. He had promised redemption and delivered a false relic. In this, Reeri could rectify his failing and save Calu when before he could not have. He would do this, because he loved him.

"I am sorry," Reeri whispered to Ratti, then closed his eyes and placed his hand on her shadow mouth.

He could almost smell her spring-flower scent, could almost feel the tiny hairs on her cheek, as he had the last time he had touched her face. Back when they had bodies and lives, when they felt and dreamed and embraced. Before they had been reduced to shadow and pain.

Now her edges danced anxiously. Reeri sharpened his shadow fingers to claws and ripped. With a wail, Ratti's jaw tore away. Shadow teeth shattered in the air. Her lips dissolved into nothing at all. Her cry spiraled around him, squeezing tight as a vise until he could not breathe—his head swimming in her tears, stomach plummeting in her pain.

Reeri backed away, gagging. When would he stop being the source of their suffering?

Wessamony chuckled low, tossing the tooth-crafted bowl to Calu. "Consider it a reminder to never cross me again, lest you be forced to unwind your *brethren's* mind."

Calu's shadow shivered.

Reeri swallowed back the nausea, his voice quavering. "It is done, my Lord. May we return to our search?"

Wessamony leaned forward, watched the movement of his mouth, as if waiting to see him retch, wanting to feel the agony it cost Reeri to inflict pain. "You have three days afore the Maha Equinox, afore I return you to the aether."

"I am aware, my Lord," Reeri said betwixt clenched teeth. He would not choke or stammer. He would not give him the satisfaction.

"Yet, it would seem, they are not." Wessamony pointed at the others. They gazed at one another in question.

If dread had more than fingers, its hand would be around Reeri's neck.

"Did he not tell you?" Enjoyment deepened Wessamony's voice. "He bargained for your final deaths. To be your eternal tormentor. How was your first taste, Reeri?"

His breath came in swift bursts and he closed his eyes.

"Do you hunger for more?"

Reeri gagged. Once.

Twice.

Thrice.

A slap woke him.

"Reeri? Reeri, are you all right?" Calu's voice swam into existence.

He blinked.

A sigh blew through his hair. "He is alive," Sohon said. The three of them leaned over the body of Raja Vatuka, who lay prostrate on the stone floor outside the bathing pool, half submerged in a puddle of rainwater.

"I am sorry," Calu said, lip quivering as he helped Reeri to sit. "Are you all right?"

"Fine." Reeri coughed, but it turned into a heave, and now with a form and a full stomach, he retched. Ratti's teeth shattered in his eyes like sunbursts.

Calu rubbed his back. "My first essence offering…it disappeared, the bargain somehow voided. I could not find another to offer, and rumors began to spread that my bargains break, and—I did not know what to do. Without mine, we would fail—I would fail Ratti—it would be my fault. O mighty Heavens, I will be the reason our brethren are never freed, because I am a wretch, a monster, every foul thing the humans have ever said about me—"

"No." Reeri coughed again, the taste of iron bright on his tongue. "If we fail, it will not be your fault."

Calu blanched. "What?"

Reeri struggled to sit up, but focused on his brother. "I would never blame you for another person's decision. If they do not offer, we will face that together."

Calu sniffled. "I am sorry."

"Forcing people to offer to you will not gain you trust or connection, and Ratti would not thank you for saving her that way."

Calu pulled him into another embrace, clung tight as a tear escaped. Reeri held him, as Ratti would have done.

"Is what Wessamony said true?" Sohon asked quietly. "Did you bargain our deaths?"

Bile rose in Reeri's throat. Mayhap he would retch again. "Yes."

"Why did you not tell us?"

Reeri scowled. "To protect you. If I did fail again, at least you would have enjoyed this half-life."

"Again?" Kama asked.

"You did not have to bear that alone," Calu said. "We can help."

Reeri wiped his face, hand shaking. Ratti's ruined face flashed in his mind. This was what happened when Reeri accepted help.

"I have it under control. The Bone Blade is near. I did not lie about that." He stood. Swayed. Calu caught his arm. Mayhap Anula had something in her necklace...a tincture to take this taste away, a poison to corrupt the memory.

"Should we worry about the voiding of our bargains?" Sohon asked.

"It is puzzling," Kama said. "Unless the Kat—"

"Do not speak their name." Reeri grunted. Wessamony himself could have broken the bargain, to ensure they knew their place or simply to play with his toys. "Time is running out. Let us focus."

He swooned to the side. Again, Calu caught him.

"He needs Anula and the tether's healing. We must take him to their bedchamber," Kama said.

Calu hefted him up and began to walk, but just as a blackness started at the corners of Reeri's vision, he said, "The man I unwound was a treasure seeker."

Reeri pulled them to a pause.

"I saw it in his mind. He and his brother came to the palace, the in-between, for a reason. They called it the place where the Heavens' love is visible to mankind."

"And where the relics were cast down," Reeri murmured, remembering the Divinities' riddle. "Where all eyes were on them yet no one could see."

A tremor racked Reeri, the darkness sweeping over him, and he fell into Calu's arms. Yet, as oblivion took over, he knew. He had been right: the Bone Blade was hiding in plain sight, precisely where he had never thought to look.

The palace.

38

Silence pressed heavily against the Kattadiya caves, the darkness a shroud to the evil Anula knew lurked within. Flickering light cast the Divinities' statues to dancing, like gravestones come alive in the night.

Wiping the sweat from her palms, she hailed Guruthuma Thilini and followed her to Premala. She tried not to think of the rawness of her hands, how she had scrubbed the blood from them until she couldn't tell what was hers and what wasn't. Though it had eventually washed away, the anxiety had not. It tremored now, just below the placid tether. Kama had loved her beating heart enough to agree to go to the gardens again, asking no questions and telling no secrets.

Before opening the door, Anula took a deep, steadying breath. This wouldn't be her last visit. Since she couldn't break the blood oath or command them to stop, she had to postpone the tovil, or what she and the Yakkas wanted would slip from her grasp.

Anula pushed into the room and smirked. "I see we're practicing the gentle touch today."

The pair of girls blew apart, traces of their embrace pink along their swollen lips.

"Anula," Premala squeaked, tripping over a double-sided drum and crashing to the floor. "I—I didn't think you'd come back."

The other girl, dressed in a maid's sari, gently picked her up.

Anula shut the door, a plan forming. "You asked me to trust you."

Premala bit her lip. "I didn't think you would."

"Why?"

"You—you're the raejina consort, and I'm…no one."

The other girl clucked her tongue.

"Is that what your guruthuma tells you?" Anula asked.

Premala pulled away from the girl, turned to the wall of masks, and fumbled as she reached for a new one, with longer teeth and wider eyes. "You both know what I mean. I'm only a fisherman's daughter, an acolyte."

"You're more than that," the other girl said.

Premala flushed, nearly dropping the mask.

"Let's practice," the girl said. "Prove to Guruthuma Hashini what I've always seen."

Premala hurriedly tied the mask over her face. It didn't hide the red of her neck, nor the longing gaze they shared, as if the distance between them were as vast as the Makara-infested ocean. An ache caught in Anula's chest. She coughed it out. "Do I need a formal invitation to be introduced to your mango girl?"

"Mango girl?"

"Oh," Premala squealed.

Anula cocked her head. "Didn't you tell her how I saved you from being locked outside the concubine estate all night, mango-less?"

"I saved you, too," Premala murmured.

Anula turned to the girl who now settled on the stone floor with the drum on her lap. "What's your name?"

"Sandani." She bowed her head slightly. "It's an honor to meet you."

"And you."

Sandani smiled. It was kind and genuine, yet sturdy, as though she knew a thing or two about how to survive in the world, how to bide time and bend rules. The same smile Auntie Nirma would give.

"We should practice now," Premala said, her voice pitching.

Anula ignored her. "How did you meet?"

Premala cut in before Sandani answered. "We really must practice."

"Why?" Anula asked sarcastically. "Is the tovil that hard, or are you that unskilled?"

"No," Premala said, less a statement and more a question.

Anula sighed, heavy and exaggerated. "Does it usually take the Kattadiya this long to prepare?"

"No, but it's new and vastly more important."

"Why were you chosen for this, and not someone more adept?"

"I—I am."

"Then why is it taking so long?"

"Because..."

"Perhaps I should ask the guruthuma for a replacement."

"You brought back the Yakkas!" Premala snapped. "You can't blame me for needing more time."

Anula's brows shot high. Perhaps the girl had a backbone after all. Now she needed only to see the truth of the Kattadiya, and Anula could pull her out. Perhaps make her a real ally. Before the tovil was called to be performed.

Premala bowed, the edge of the mask clanking to the floor. "Apologies, my—I didn't mean to yell. It's only—I haven't slept."

"We've been extremely busy," Sandani explained. "The nights are long and the bargainers many. The crowd that has gathered in the city for the Festival of the Cosmos is larger than any in history. The fear of the Polonnaruwan war is high, and more people are making bargains. Guruthuma Hashini tasked us with stopping the bargains before they're made, meaning we spend day and night seeking out bargainers, just as they say their prayers. The stupas are overrun."

"You're stopping bargains from being made?" Anula asked. "I thought your task was to break the bad ones."

"They're all bad. Stopping them before they start is a kindness. Besides, we need to stop them only while the Yakkas still live. Once Premala performs the new ceremony—"

"They'll be dead." Anula's voice turned dusty and dry. "But aren't you going against the purpose of the festival? The entirety of the Heavens is to be honored, not only the First."

"Just because it's tradition doesn't make it right," Premala said, the words rolling off her tongue as if she'd chewed them, swallowed them, regurgitated them. "People have been blinded, Anula. The Second Heavens do not love us as the Divinities do."

Reeri's hand flashed in Anula's mind. His gentle touch, his kind words, the meeting he'd set up with Dilshan because he saw what was in her heart.

No, the Yakkas did not care as Fate or Destiny or Fortune. That was not a half-truth. They cared more.

Sandani reached out, skimmed her fingers along Premala's arm. Anula jerked her chin. "If the First Heavens love you so much, why must the two of you hide?"

Sandani's hand stilled.

"Why are you doing this?" Premala asked, voice small.

"Doing what?"

"I know you're dedicated to the people of this kingdom, Anula, but you're making it difficult."

"Making what difficult?"

"To continue being on your side."

"Since when have you been on my side? You've made it clear that you are a Kattadiya, and that I must be, too, thanks to a blood oath I wasn't aware I took. You're the one who has lied to me for an underground sect trying to kill beings of the Heavens, while actually killing people who make bargains. A sect that tells you that you are nothing, that you must prove your worth, that won't accept you for who you are even if you do prove them wrong. And you blame me? Why are the two of you even here?"

Sandani sat straighter. "It's my birthright. My mother, her mother, her mother before her, and so on for centuries have been Kattadiya. And Premala has been given the chance to carry on her stepmother's tradition."

Anula scoffed. "Didn't you say that tradition isn't always right?"

"It isn't always wrong either," Sandani argued.

"You can't have it both ways."

"Yes, you can."

Anula rolled her eyes. "This chance then, is it me? Is that why I, the person who brought back the Yakkas, is being taken care of by an acolyte instead of the guruthuma?"

Sandani shook her head. "Not at first."

Premala shushed her, sliding the mask off her face.

"What was it at first?"

"Nothing, it's not important," Premala rushed to say. "Please, can we practice? It's getting late."

"Does it have to do with why you're in the palace kitchens?"

"Anula."

"Is that how you met? You both have the same task?"

"All acolytes spend time in the palace," Sandani said. Premala glared at her.

"I would ask why, but it seems futile."

"It is," Premala said, slamming the mask on her face once more. She let out a soft yip. "Now, please, let's practice."

"I thought we were friends."

Premala grabbed Anula's arm. She was stronger than she looked. "Lie down. I've got the new dolla to place around you."

Anula dug in her heels. "Why won't you tell me why you're in the palace?"

"Why won't you let me do my duty?"

"Why won't you explain?"

"*For prayer's sake*, Anula! Please! The guruthuma will be here soon to check on our progress."

Sandani's eyes flicked to the door. Anxiety clammed Premala's hands, sweat slick on Anula's arms.

"You're both frightened of her." It was not a question. Faces of the women in Auntie Nirma's network flashed. Their loyalty tied to the facts of poverty and abuse, their dream of a future where they didn't bleed, didn't bruise, didn't cower. Where they could live the dream of love. Anula lowered her voice, her hand drifting up. It paused for moment in the air, then landed softly on Premala's shoulder. "You don't have to stay. Come with me."

"No," Premala snapped. "The First Heavens created us, chose us, blessed us, and tasked us to protect the people from the influence of the Yakkas!"

Anula pulled Premala close. "That doesn't mean—"

Bright white pain flared, bending Anula over. Blinded, she hit the floor, as though a fire-heated blade cut her in half.

Premala snapped back. "What's happening?"

Anula cried out. The mehendhi on her arms shattered, pieces flying into the air only to dive back into her flesh, knitting itself together. Again and again. Blood oozed and vanished, flowed and disappeared.

Kama. Had she moved? But why? She knew what would happen if the tether stretched too far.

"Anula?"

The tether screamed, unlike anything before. It wasn't a rope or a bridle tugging tight. It writhed one moment, as if cut in two, and wrenched taut the next, as if it'd only ever been one. Back and forth. Gone and there and gone again.

"Something's wrong." Anula gritted her teeth, then tripped as she was suddenly in a court, nails tearing shadow, her stomach souring—but when she blinked, she was back in the cave.

A cold emptiness flooded her. No, not her. It coursed down the tether and crashed against her heart, but it came from Reeri, agony swelling, cresting. Cursed blessings, what was happening to him?

A sob broke her lips. Sandani rushed forward, yanking Premala away. Anula could only imagine what they thought. Probably a clear example of the influence of the Yakkas and the evil they bestowed.

"I have to check on the raja." Anula took an agonizing step toward the door. And then another. And another. Her skin flayed and knit. Drops of blood trailed behind her.

"I was right," Premala gasped. "The raja is of one of those possessed by the Yakkas."

Anula stumbled but refused to fall. "I have to check on him."

"Why? He's a Yakka. He doesn't need you."

"Yes, he does."

The knowing settled deep. She swung the door open.

"Look what he's doing to you! The Yakkas don't care about you, Anula. It's a lie. Don't be fooled into caring for him."

Anula's heart skipped a beat. Fear drove her steps now, as it had before—when Auntie Nirma collapsed with a spear in her chest; when Thaththa choked on liquefied bowels; when Amma lit up like a fire at a festival.

"Too late," Anula mumbled. She'd vowed to never be fooled by the Heavens again, yet her feet carried her swiftly to the palace.

A fool once again.

"Reeri!" Anula shouted, skidding onto her knees. He lay in the center of the bed, sweat-slicked and pale, as if he'd been sick for days.

"The palace," he rasped, eyes fluttering.

"Are you all right?" Anula's hands wavered over Reeri's body. Kama had not been in the gardens when she'd emerged from the caves. Calu and Sohon were nowhere in sight as she ran through the halls. She flung open the bedchamber doors, and Reeri sat up, only to crash back against the pillows. Her breath had stalled.

Pink nelum, kaneru, thel endaru—Anula's fingers tripped over sapphires, unsure which could help. He had no wounds; there was no blood. Even the tether had steadied. But her heart ached with fear and dread and guilt and shame.

"Here," Reeri rasped again. She couldn't hear the rest.

"What?" Anula leaned closer, smelled cinnamon and death. "What happened?"

Reeri forced himself up, frightened like a child in the night. "If I fail—"

Anula shushed him. He wasn't making sense. Had it been a nightmare? Perhaps it was a bad reaction to her tincture. She reached up and brushed a stray hair from his sticky forehead. "You aren't going to fail."

He grabbed her wrist, held her hand at his cheek. "What if I do?"

The touch was warm, sizzling up her arms. His deep brown eyes blazed. A shadow shuddered just beneath. The real Reeri. The truth in the lie.

"You won't," she said, taking his other hand.

"But—"

"I will make sure of it."

Reeri let out a breath, tension ebbing away, and folded into a heap. His head dropped on her shoulder. Anula slipped her hands from his, wrapping her arms around him, and squeezed tight.

She closed her eyes as his cinnamon scent enveloped her, caressed her, and taking a deep breath in, she let her head fall onto his. Let her chin feel the tingle of his hair, let her lips find his forehead, find the tops of his cheekbones and the tip of his nose.

And then she let her lips find the fullness of his and gently brush against them.

39

For a moment, it was just them and the embers sparking between their lips.

It was a moment Anula had once dreamed of, a moment that had never come, though her lips had met many others. A kiss had long ago become a bartering tool, a way of justice, a path to change. But now, with him, she felt that a kiss could do more. Like wake a long-slumbering dream.

Reeri's eyes snapped open. He jerked away, leaving her arms suddenly empty and cold, and she had to cling to the blessed bed frame to stop her fall.

"We—we cannot," he breathed heavily.

Anula flushed. "Sorry."

Reeri's nostrils flared. He stared at her lips with a thirst, as if desire had parched him, too.

"My raja." Bithul's voice cut through the bedchamber; his haunted gaze burned their moment to dust. "An urgent missive."

They barely had time to right themselves before Bithul thrust the small paper into Reeri's hand. He half stood, half kneeled on the bed and breathed, "No."

He glanced at her, all cravings forgotten. Dread thickened the air.

"What?" she asked.

Reeri's jaw worked, as if he couldn't say or wouldn't say, as if he wanted to protect her.

"*What?*" she repeated, braced and demanding. "Reeri, tell me."

He blinked. "Wh—what did you call me?"

Anula blushed. It had slipped out. She wasn't sure when she had stopped thinking of him as a Yakka and started seeing him as Reeri. Less a bloody legend or Heavenly being, and more of a…being. Not unlike herself. Perhaps it happened in the moment between their lips touching and her old desires sparking anew. Perhaps it had happened before that, quietly, silently. She cleared her throat. "Don't change the subject."

She ripped the missive from his grip, and all thoughts of lips and kisses and names blew away.

"Anula—"

"No." Her voice cracked. She met his shadow-lined eyes. "No. It can't be true."

Contingent of Anuradhapura army killed in Polonnaruwan attack. No survivors. Villages burned to ash.

"No," Anula repeated, the letter in her hand shifting in and out of focus. "Dilshan said…"

Bithul scowled. "He lied, to aid the Polonnaruwa Kingdom into a strategic advantage. The villages had not yet been taken. When our army arrived, they struck and razed all three to the ground. Not only do they now have a clear path into the kingdom, they took out a third of our military. The raja must declare wartime."

The missive shook in her hand.

Reeri whispered, dark and low, "These men do not merit the dignity of war. They must reap what they have sown. Let them be taken by surprise, ripped from their beds and bled out on the streets."

Anula shivered. Red sky. Red hands. Red water. *Look away.*

A hand fell upon hers. She glanced up into Reeri's dark eyes, spilled ink masking saffron.

"I can do it," he said. "I will do it, without a bargain. I will burn them in their own blood, for you."

"The taboo—"

"Curse the taboo."

Anula's breath caught. What he was offering to do…for *her*…

"My raja," Bithul interjected. "I don't think that's the way."

"There is no way in vengeance," Reeri declared.

"But there is in justice."

Anula tore away from the bed, the words creeping up her arms as she paced.

It was no accident, Anula. You were meant to survive.

Why?

Justice. You were chosen to carry out a further purpose. Together, we must make it count. We can change the kingdom for good, in their name, for their justice and the justice of all others forevermore.

Was this justice? A village burned, people murdered—

If you do this right, songs will be sung about you.

And if I do it wrong?

A pyre will be built instead.

Perhaps it should be.

Anula eyed her hands, not the mehendhi, but the blood that stained them. Reeri was right: This wasn't justice. It was vengeance. She was no better than a usurper, the very thing she had come to end. Death was all she granted the kingdom. Even the Yakkas couldn't evade her corruption. Where had she gone wrong?

Auntie Nirma had trained her, taught her, honed her. For them—Amma, Thaththa, and all in Eppawala, all in the kingdom. So why were her hands drenched in blood? Why was her name next in the history of the Age of Usurpers? Was this the dream she was meant to chase by the Heavens' hand, the person Auntie Nirma had wanted her to be?

Was she who *she* wanted to be?

"We must send aid to the villages that are now threatened by a Polonnaruwan attack," Bithul urged. "Evacuate the people. The outer city is full, but we could take them into the inner city, keep them safe."

"There will not be a threat when the enemy is removed," Reeri growled.

"We must focus on what's important," Bithul argued. "People's lives."

Gooseflesh prickled her arms. She'd heard those words before, thought she knew what they meant. She'd been wrong. Up to this point, Anula had focused on death—Amma's and Thaththa's, each name on the list—because according to Auntie Nirma, the world was made up of two types of people: allies and enemies.

She was wrong.

It was more complex than that. The good and the bad were one, like a river banked with mud on one side and dried, cracked earth on the other. Anula had seen it in Premala, caring for others while practicing vile traditions. And, of course, she'd seen it in Reeri. She'd judged him to be the Blood Yakka from the stories of old, yet he wore his care on his sleeve unknowingly. Bithul, though, was different. He focused on life, on preserving and protecting no matter the cost to himself.

Auntie Nirma had not trained Anula to be both. She didn't know how to rule, what diplomacy or governance took. That was a job for allies. She had been honed only as a weapon. But if her path was not to wield judgment and justice, or vengeance of any kind—if she was not to rid the palace of evil men—had it all been for nothing?

No, she couldn't believe that. Amma and Thaththa didn't deserve to be killed; no one did. Justice was always called for. But perhaps not the justice Auntie Nirma had sought. Though her visions for a peaceful Anuradhapura were worthy, the pain of loss had blinded her, pulled her across the river to the bed that was dry and dead.

Perhaps Anula had been blinded, too. She didn't want to be. She didn't want to look away any longer.

Anula lifted her gaze, squared her shoulders. "Send help."

Reeri furrowed his brows. "But I can—"

She placed a firm hand on his arm. "That's not who I want to be, and we both know that's not who you are."

Confusion cleared, the darkness receding like the tide at night.

"Protect them. Save them," she said. "That's what we do."

Fear had stolen her sight for long enough. Anula would be no usurper.

Power and hatred would not be her legacy.

40

His name on her lips—the sound was more beautiful than any birdsong, more satisfying than any mango; it surpassed any experience he had of life thus far.

For it was not merely hearing his name that roused his shadow, but hearing *Anula* say his name that stirred his soul.

He watched her now, in fitful sleep—the weight of duty and the lives of her people pulling her under—and wondered why she had said it, what it meant, or if it meant nothing at all. Yet…she had kissed him—a true kiss, not the press of her lips to inflict poison and pain. And he could not deny he wanted more.

More connection, more time, to see if she was the elusive soul that communed with his. Reeri shook off the thought, for he could not have *more*.

Not after her prayer to save her family had fallen on his inattentive ears. Not while she was his tether, his soul offering. Not while he kept the full truth of what he would do with that offering to himself. For true communion had no half-truths.

Reeri reached out between them, stopped shy of touching her.

No longer did she curl up at the edge of the bed but centered herself in the middle. He swallowed hard. She deserved to know the truth of what was coming, of how he might fail her once again. But if he spoke it, would she recoil from him as she had before?

Worse, would she flee?

"You are the damnation of your brethren," Wessamony seethed. A gleam, red as fire, in his eyes. A curled smile on his lips. "You are the ruination of all my plans for the ascendence of the Second Heavens. You deserve this and more."

A whip cracked, high and sharp.

It came away with strips of shadow, the edges frayed and dissolving.

Reeri arced the whip back once again, red eyes on the rent shadows of Sohon, Kama, and Calu.

Thunder shook the bed. Reeri jolted awake, sheets clinging with sweat. A crack of lightning lit the expanse of the raja's chamber, casting dark phantoms about the room.

The fault lies with you, Reeri, they whispered with the storm. *Never forget that.*

A soft touch trailed over his fingers, and he flinched.

"It's me," Anula said softly through the strobing tempest. "Do you want to talk about it?"

She had not seen, her tincture potent and true—able to keep the nightmares from each other, but unable to rid them altogether. Yet she had asked the question she had forever refused. His shadow ached for her arms around him.

Never before had he spoken of a nightmare. Never before her had he shared the visions that stalked him. Never before had he wanted to. Feared to. Dared to.

"Yes." His voice cracked.

Anula scooted closer, narrowing the distance. Still, too much remained.

"How did it happen? I want the truth." Golden starlit eyes flicked to his, and she held him firm. "Please."

The warmth in her voice, in her gaze, was a hook on a fishing line. It caught him swiftly.

"Wessamony gave the Yakkas a fetter to keep us in our shrines," he began, then left out no horror. He laid bare his scheme for the Yakkas' slow freedom. She had heard as much already; so too had she seen. Yet those were half-truths. Here, he gave it in full, hoping it gained him a step closer to true communion.

"One day, when we were celebrating Ratti's successful matchmaking, she was taken. Women in masks wielded the power to break our bargains, tear our connections, even rip us into the air and send us back to our shrines. Yet we were many and they were few—fewer still, as the people who paid for curses did not reap the benefit of their enemy's suffering. They turned on the Kattadiya, killed almost all of them. Those remaining called upon the Lord of the Second Heavens at the start of the Maha Equinox, gave evidence, and argued their case. If he agreed with them, I do not know. I only know of his anger at my finding the loophole. I had ruined his plans of ascension, embarrassed him in the Heavens. So he reduced the Yakkas to shadow and pain. You have seen the rest." Reeri took a breath. "It is my fault. Wessamony spoke the truth. And if I fail them again, I will forever be their tormentor. Their pain, my fault for eternity."

"Is that why you want to kill him, to redeem yourself?" she asked, no hint of sarcasm, no measure of derision.

"No."

Anula stared through the moonlight, straight to his shadow. Slowly, she brushed a lock of fallen hair from his eyes.

He sighed. "Yes. Yet there is more to it. They deserve freedom."

"Of course, they do. But it's not your duty to free them, because you have nothing to redeem yourself for."

"How can you say that?" he whispered, voice broken. "You know what I did to the humans to unshackle us, how my actions caused our banishment."

Anula's hand dropped. The sudden air stung. Another roll of thunder shook the room, and Anula bit her lip and took a deep breath. "It's my fault my unborn sibling died, my fault Amma burned to ash on a pyre."

"No."

"Yes. I refused to listen to her direction. I let go of her hand. I wasted precious time."

"You were a child."

"And if I weren't? Would it be my fault then?"

"No."

"Why not?"

"Because you were not the attacker."

Anula smiled as if she had won.

Reeri wished she had. "This is different. You know that."

"Fine." She raised on an elbow, challenge forever twinkling in her eyes. "Then what about today? Is it my fault those villagers are dead?"

"No."

"I told you to send the army. I ordered them to walk into an ambush."

"You did not know."

Anula leaned close, her eyelashes nearly touching his. "Neither did you."

Reeri sighed, gaze falling way. "I wish it were that simple."

Hands cupped his cheeks, forced his chin up. The touch rippled through the tether, and together, they saw it: his fear.

The shadow within recoiled, and if he had his way, so too would he. For he was not worthy of this kindness, this connection, this feeling he dared hope was his soul communing with another. No matter the magnitude of his yearning for it.

Thunder chased his dreams and promised a lengthy storm—the rains before the monsoon that would mark the Maha Equinox.

"You are worthy," Anula said over the gale. "You were never not."

"But—"

She went on, refusing to allow him to argue. "Calu, Kama, and Sohon are not senseless, despite what I judged them to be before. They aren't following you because they know no other way. They are your family. And family always loves, no matter what. You don't have to earn it."

A lump rose in Reeri's throat. "And what about those not family? Must I earn it then?"

Anula stilled. She held on to his cheeks, closed her eyes, and when she reopened them, he felt it more than saw it. Deep within, past the pain and the walls, lived a soul who loved wholeheartedly, devotion intertwined with a fierce protection.

"I forgive you."

Reeri blanched. "What?"

"I forgive you for that night, for not answering my prayer."

A ringing started in his ears. He sat up, slowly removing her hands.

"And banishment was not your fault."

He looked away. "Anula—"

But she gripped all the tighter. Pulled him down and nearly growled, "Wessamony is a liar. He wanted to hurt you, the masked women wanted to hurt you, but you did nothing wrong. They were wrong. I was wrong."

The words caught his breath.

Everything he had yearned to hear.

"I was wrong about you, Reeri," she whispered. "You're everything I thought you weren't. A caring and, unfortunately, handsome shadow."

More than he had dared to dream.

A tear dropped. "You are a devastatingly beautiful soul."

Humidity stoked the air, the scent of jasmine sharp and all-consuming. Reeri's eyes flicked up and down her form. What would it be like…if he were merely a man and she merely a woman living in the same village? No bargains, no deals, no tinctures.

Anula's breaths quickened and she leaned closer.

Every fiber of Reeri's being wanted her to close the gap, to press her lips on his—but this mouth, this body, was not his. "We cannot," he whispered.

She paused a breath away. "I know."

He saw it then, as much as he felt it. Another echo, this time their desire.

"Reeri?"

O Heavens, his name on her lips—it drew out a dream, and before he could think better, Reeri cupped her face to show her.

That if he were merely a man and she were merely a woman, he would bring her flowers from the mountaintops: binara and blue water lilies. She would not put them in vials around her neck. He would take her to the waterfalls and feed her aluwa by the nightly fires. He would take her hand as they strolled through the city.

If he were merely a man and she were merely a woman, he would have leaned into her embrace tonight. Laid her softly on the bed. Unwrapped her from her sari. He would have found her shape beneath, would have worshiped it as though she were the Heavenly being in his shrine.

If he were a man and she were a woman, he would kiss the soft space betwixt her shoulder and neck; nip along her delicate collarbone; trail fingers down the length of her curves; journey around her breasts; explore the hidden cave beneath her bush, until her thighs shivered and warmth soaked his fingers. He would taste his way down her body with teeth and tongue until she sang. And then he would deliver her to the cosmos.

Reeri lost himself to the fantasy. His heart beat swiftly as he gazed at the woman whose destiny had never held the word *merely*.

Bee-stung lips parted in a sigh. "Reeri."

His name sent a flame down his spine, a heat low in his loins. But when they kissed again, it would be *his* lips upon hers. "Anula."

They paused, allowing the full force of his dream to settle, to simmer, and then to slip away. Slowly, Anula dropped her hands and pulled out of his embrace, and as the morning sun rose, so too did their shared duty.

The time for dreaming was gone.

41

The emerald silk sari hugged tightly to Anula's curves. The weight of the bell earrings and nath nose ring grounded her to the marble floors of the bedchamber. She tucked her sari tighter at her hip, like a soldier cinching armor. Reeri's face swam before her, along with the gap she'd dared to close, her lips parting.

Cursed blessings, she had nearly kissed him. *Again.*

But she hadn't been the only one leaning in, and he hadn't said no. Simply that they couldn't. Not as things stood now. He wanted her, too, wanted to live a dream—with her. And what a beautiful dream it had been.

Footsteps echoed down the hall. Anula's heart choked. She wasn't ready to see Reeri again and face the onslaught of want. The passion he sparked raged rather than burned. If her and Auntie Nirma's determination were a fire, this was an inferno: all-consuming and all-powerful. It made sense now, why her parents had touched so much throughout the day.

The sound became louder, pulling her from her thoughts and stealing her breath. It rounded the corner—with Bithul's face.

Anula sighed, slumping against the wall and fanning herself with a hand as sweat streaked down her sides.

"Apologies, my raejina consort, I've had the windows opened since the storm, but the heat won't improve until the wind returns," Bithul said, moisture beading along his brows as he mistook the reason for Anula's perspiration.

A heavy blanket of humidity had descended on the heels of the rain, a sure sign a monsoon would make landfall soon. Another marker of the Maha season, of the equinox and Lord Wessamony's return.

One day.

One day was all that they had left, and she had tried to kiss a Yakka. She still wanted to.

Anula shook out her hands. "Let's hope it breaks before the festival tomorrow, or else the city will smell like it's been fried in elephant dung."

Bithul grunted, his anxiety as obvious as his sweat stains. "We've emptied the palace, which was not as easy to do as it is to say. With the Festival of the Cosmos looming, half the kingdom is trying to speak with a blessed gift. Are you ready to meet with the others and begin the search?"

"Almost," Anula said softly. Seeing her guard brought up everything from the other day. How she'd acted, how she'd failed. How she didn't want to anymore.

Bithul began, "Is there something I can—"

"You were right," she said, pride trickling sourly down her throat. She swallowed. "We all have a choice to make, about what's most important."

"What did you decide?"

"Same as you: people. The ones who are alive, not the dead."

Bithul's shoulders softened. "Then you may be our greatest raejina yet."

Anula scoffed. "Perhaps I'll be the greatest farmer's wife instead."

"You no longer want the crown?"

Anula pushed off the wall, glanced at the portraits of rulers past, at consorts and wives and the court that surrounded them. Paintings of villages with their harvesters and seamstresses. Fishermen on stilts in shallow waters, far from the reach of the Makara. "I don't know what my path is anymore."

Bithul nodded. "When your heart is right, the path becomes clearer, easier to face."

"Smoother?"

"Heavens no. But you do become stronger."

A moment passed, heavy but not burdened, as if Anula had found someone to share the weight. Perhaps she had found more than an ally.

They entered the throne room to the sounds of panic.

"My books!" Sohon shouted, one arm reaching for the servants carrying out stacks of manuscripts.

"Since your memory books are no longer required," Reeri said, "I thought it was time they were bound and safely sent to their final destinations, or properly cataloged in the archives for those books that no longer have a home."

Sohon paused in midair, gaping at Reeri. They all did.

Reeri's brow furrowed. "Is this not what you wish for your books, Sohon?"

"Yes," he said incredulously. "Thank you."

Calu rubbed his face. "Who are you, and what has brought on the No Yakka's demise?"

Kama giggled, threw a knowing smirk at Anula. "One's heart opens in many ways, when one unlocks the door."

Anula felt herself flush.

Reeri ignored the comment. "There is no time left for jests.

The Maha Equinox will strike in one day, and we must find the Bone Blade hidden somewhere in this vast palace."

"It is here? Should we not have heard it by now?" Sohon asked.

"I thought so, at first, but then I realized that we are not our true selves. Human senses dull our hearing, so the call will not be the same as in the Heavens. Calu's cursed blade should not have sounded that way to the human ear, and the Divinities knew that. Another trick to hide it."

"How are we to find it then?"

"It will sing when it is used. Like a statue or a painting, it will come to life with interaction, I believe."

"How can you be sure it is here? Would a human not have found it by now? So many dwell in this place." Calu shifted worriedly.

"The Divinities 'cast all relics down to earth, to where all eyes were on them but none could see them.' They created the in-between, the palace, a place for humans to witness the love of the Heavens."

"People come here to look, but not to see," Anula said, her gaze finally finding his. "They never tried to find it here."

A moment passed between them, as if they could also now see.

"Exactly," Reeri said. "Each of us will search a section of the palace: Sohon south, Kama east, Calu north, and I west. Interact with every blessed gift—leave no surface untouched."

"And my offering?" Calu asked, pulling a small yellowed rice bowl from a pocket. Its sheen was odd. "Should I find another?"

"It exists," Kama said. "Is it not still an offering?"

"It has no bargain," Sohon said pointedly. "The cosmos might not accept it."

Reeri glanced again at Anula, his jaw feathering. "There are many loopholes in the laws of the cosmos. Mayhap this will be one. Search for the relic, but check the shrines as you do so. If you find a new essence offering, take it, but if not, we will make do with what we have."

The Yakkas nodded in agreement.

"What about me?" Anula asked. "You didn't say where I should search."

Reeri held the door open. "I assumed you would aid me. If you would rather not..."

"Together is fine." She slid quickly through the throne room's door.

She didn't miss the red tint that warmed Reeri's cheeks as she passed. Nor the smirk on Kama's lips, nor the frown on Calu's mouth.

Nor the way Reeri's blush sparked her own.

"Two stars traverse the cosmos, fiery and fast, hurling toward each other, and upon their kiss—"

"Not this one," Anula said, walking away before the foot-tall elephant statue finished speaking, before it could put any more ideas into her head. And before Reeri could catch up to her and she could feel his heat. Her hands—her lips—couldn't be trusted.

"Do you not wish to know the rest of your fortune?" Reeri asked wryly.

"Who said it was a fortune teller? Perhaps it's a storyteller, its aim to scare me, or worse, put me to sleep."

"You do not seem to enjoy the blessed gifts."

"Oh, did you enjoy nearly being attacked inside a painting? Or do you prefer the blessed bed frame whispering the ways of the gentle touch in your ear each night? Telling you how to caress me, how to feel me, how to warm me with your strong, enormous member."

Reeri tripped over his own feet.

Cursed blessings. Anula whirled away, continuing down the hall, a flush rushing down her whole body. Not even her words were safe.

She hurried through the gallery, keeping a full length ahead of Reeri, never letting them linger in the same room together for too long. They had to focus. She touched a plant that danced to the music of the first peoples of the island, but heard no relic calling and saw no bones or blades. She inspected a painting of bare-chested women braiding one another's hair, then a stack of pottery that shifted colors with her mood, brightening to a pink aura. She tried not to think what it meant.

But each time she turned to another blessing, she burned hotter, their kiss—his shared daydream—eating her alive. Her hands, his tongue, the desire she had to hear him groan. *Cursed blessings, cursed paintings, cursed everything*. Hours ticked by, and still, she burned, simmering on the hows and whys, on what had been the rock that started the avalanche. It's not like she had known she wanted to kiss him, ever, let alone more than once. It happened so quickly. One moment she was holding his pallid, prone form, promising to not let him fail his loved ones again, and the next, she saw his shadow.

Saffron eyes and sharp cheekbones. The ghost of his true self.

And for the first time since they'd met in the shrine, she hadn't felt the need for caution. Reeri wasn't untrustworthy or dangerous. He wasn't callous or cruel. He was kind. He was safe. And so she'd wrapped her arms around him, and suddenly—she felt calm, like returning home after a long trip or tucking into a warm bed on a cold night. She had seen it then, their similarities. She didn't know how she'd missed it before.

And now, just as it had then, the desire struck like lightning. A wanting warmed beneath her sari, to feel the planes of his true chest, to see every dip, every bulge, to watch his muscles flex as he lifted her atop him, to watch his eyes flutter closed in pleasure. Could she draw out his shadow with a gentle touch and find out? Perhaps it wasn't only poisoncraft that brought the true Reeri back. Perhaps with her tongue, when his knees buckled and she brought him to the edge—

"Anula."

With a shriek, she spun—

—and crashed right into Reeri.

Chests pressed together, he saw her thoughts, her question, her desire. His hands seized her waist, breath quickening, as her daydream took over them. A bed of silks, a swirl of candle smoke, the scent of cinnamon, as Anula leaned him back, running one finger down his chest and stomach, dipping beneath his sarong and catching his hardness as it rose to greet her. She moaned, followed her fingers with her lips. Kissing nipple and navel. Both hands stroking.

Now Reeri groaned in response to the vision, pushing her up against the wall and bringing his lips to her ear. His breath sent a shudder down her spine, and she arched slightly.

"If I were merely a woman..." she whispered.

He squeezed her waist and inhaled her scent, lingering at her neck. But then he growled and pried himself off. "We cannot."

With stiff legs, he pivoted out of the room and into the shrine next door. Anula let out a huff, pressing her palms into her eyes. *Thrice-cursed blessings.* She wasn't sure she'd make it to the Maha Equinox.

Swallowing her thoughts—and all else that came with them—she pushed off the wall and followed him. Reeri sighed as she entered. Not at her, but at a painting, the largest in the room by half. The floor was littered with gifts, both dusty and pristine, the new stacked high.

"We must go inside." Reeri finally broke the silence. "I had come to tell you, before..."

Anula flushed and cleared her throat. "Why do you think that?"

"Mayhap the relic is hidden within."

"If it is, then there are too many gifts to check in time." She stepped closer.

Reeri tensed, the strain pulsing between them like a heartbeat. "We must start somewhere."

"I didn't mean that we should give up." They stood in front of a rendering of a Festival of the Cosmos. It was less realistic than the others, the brushstrokes crisscrossing and the colors blending. "I don't think this place exists in Anuradhapura. I've never seen the sun hanging in the east while the stars shine in the west."

"Art imitates life in a myriad of ways. Remember that the gifts are points within the cosmos, not on Earth. If the Divinities gifted this rendering, with fantastical images, they did it for a purpose."

"Which was what?"

"I suppose we will see."

Reeri took a breath and held open a hand. Unafraid of seeing her wildest desires. Or perhaps just as curious as she was.

Anula grabbed it quickly. He wrapped his fingers tightly around hers, sending a thrill down her spine. And together, they pressed into the canvas until it devoured them whole.

But instead of facing more dreams, they emerged in a field of color and song. A musician blew a long note through the hak gediya, puffing out his chest and throwing back his head. The Festival of the Cosmos had begun.

Fire dancers spun to the beat of the processional raban drum. Chimes rang loudly through the courtyard, pulling the crowd's attention, as elephants and dancers swathed in bright fabrics and gilt jewels led the parade across the city. Vendors lined the open gates, steam rising in scented tendrils beckoning all to eat, to drink, to celebrate. Laborers stood next to artisans, ministers next to servants, all shining as best they could, all carrying their greatest offerings. On one side, a golden hue lit upon their heads. On the other, starlight danced in their eyes.

Heat sizzled along Anula's arms. It was unseasonably warm. Amma had used to say it was a warning, that the strongest monsoons fell after the hottest of days. She glanced up to see puffy white clouds, holding not rain but the rulers of the Heavens. On one side, Lord Wessamony, and the other, the host of Divinities. They gazed lovingly, reaching down to bestow blessings and favors, wishes and dreams.

"I've never seen a Festival of the Cosmos this…joyful," Anula said. She had partaken in her fair share, coming first each year with Thaththa and Amma, then with Auntie Nirma. The later years had been shrouded in the shadows of the alleys, drinking palm wine alone, drowning the unwanted memories until her auntie had her fill of begging and bartering. She wondered what it would be like for her now, with far more knowledge yet still so far from faith.

"It is not a festival," Reeri whispered. "It is a depiction of the balance of the cosmos. Night and day sharing one sky. Life and death entwined in remembrance."

"Death?"

Reeri nodded to the front of the parade. Instead of ending at the gates, it continued on to a hill and a grave, bodies prostrate amid a bed of flowers. The petals drifted on the wind. They caught in circles atop each person's head. A crown for every member of the kingdom.

"True balance is an unending connection. A circle with no beginning and no end. All exists together, at the same time. Kama was not wrong when she said passion and pain were one. And neither was Wessamony when he said we had unbalanced the cosmos. For if one hole punctures a water tank, will not the entire thing drain?"

Anula watched the procession, saw the way the traditions of her people wove in and out of Reeri's narrative. Was this what the Yakkas and the Divinities had intended all along? Perhaps the festival and the blessed gifts were meant to remind humanity of a time before the banishment, before the Kattadiya, before jealousy and greed took precedence over peace and oneness.

"It's nice," she whispered, a flower resting on her head.

"Yes," Reeri whispered, too, taking the bloom in his hand. "I miss it. I am grateful it exists, if only in this form."

"Sohon was right: all art transports us." Anula plucked a petal from his curls. "You'll have this again."

"Fate willing."

Anula snorted. "Was that a jest?"

"I would never." But his lips twitched at the edge. Anula's heart fluttered.

"And what about me? What will happen to my soul when our bargain is complete and Wessamony is dead?"

Reeri frowned. "I am not entirely sure."

"My auntie used to say that we only understand a quarter of what the Heavens are capable of."

"A wise woman," he murmured, then regarded her. "I may not know the specifics, but I promise to be next to you when it happens."

Anula met his gaze. A quiet, heavy moment slipped between them. Singing crested the hill. Reeri closed his eyes, tapped his foot, and hummed along.

"You know this song?"

"It is as old as I am. Though they do not dance the same anymore."

"*You* danced?"

Reeri's eyes flashed open. A hint of saffron blazing, smoldering out as his throat bobbed. Then he reached out and grabbed her hand. He spun her out and back in, twirling her up against his chest.

His heart beat erratically.

His breaths came heavy and fast.

Reeri tucked the flower behind her ear, and she saw it, what they were both thinking of: The press of his body against hers, their lips crushing into each other's, their mouths exploring. A kiss, fast and deep and long.

It tingled up Anula's spine, blazed in her belly, and she squeezed his hand tight. But still, she yearned for more. More of him, his mouth, his hands, his everything, everywhere. She drowned in the want. Perhaps she could make another bargain after this one. Ask him to stay. Ask him to be by her side as she ruled by day and in her bedchamber by night.

She flushed at the idea that she had ever seen Reeri as anything other than what he was. For ever making a deal with the Kattadiya and putting him in danger…all for a crown.

Vengeance had ruled her heart once. But now—

"We cannot," he growled, even as he pulled her closer and their dancing turned to a slow sway, his fingers twining into hers.

"I know."

"But I—"

"Me too."

"You cannot dance here alone," a voice called.

They jolted, breaking apart. Heart hammering, Anula glanced up into the too-long, too-sharp features of a cosmic being. One she actually recognized.

"Take my hand," Ratti said, a sharp smile glinting. "I will lead you to where you should be."

Like lightning, the words struck Anula. Lit up the memory of the caves, the tunnels, and all within the Pleasure Gardens.

Where one could look, but not see.

“The K—” Anula’s whisper cut off.

“What?” Reeri asked.

Anula pulled at the seam in the painting. “I have a lot to explain, and I will, I promise. But first, I have to go to the gardens. The Bone Blade is hidden beneath.”

42

Statues towered over Anula, their star-filled eyes forever suspicious, their knowing smiles mere smirks. Now she knew why. They gripped relics in their hands.

The Divinity of Justice held scales. The Divinity of Abundance bore a basket woven in gold. The Divinity of Dreams restrained fish surging from its arms. Anula had thought them ornamentation, figurines, memorials. She understood now. The relics were hidden in plain sight. She only needed to find one, and if the statues were anything like the portraits, perhaps one would lead her to another. Rising on her toes, she reached for a fish.

"What are you doing?"

Premala's voice echoed off the stone, jolting through Anula's bones. "Cursed blessings, don't scare me like that."

Premala hurried closer. "What are you doing?"

"Practicing the gentle touch with a statue. Want a turn?" Anula reached up once more. Premala slapped her hand away. "Ouch!"

"I—" she squeaked. "I'm sorry, my raejina consort. But you can't take that."

"Why?" Anula snapped. "Why did the Divinities give them to you?"

Premala blanched. "Y—you know? But why do you want a relic?"

"The better question is why are you hiding them when centuries of people have been harmed and killed in their search?"

"We didn't kill them—their selfishness did. We merely did our duty."

"Is part of the blood oath repeating your guruthuma's words like a soldier?"

"Kattadiya do not act for themselves, only for the protection of others."

"I'll take that as a yes. And the Kattadiya turned a blind eye. That is not helping people."

Premala made a fist, her breath uneven. "Don't judge what you don't understand."

"Oh, I understand perfectly." Anula leaned close. "But do you? Do you understand that the faith this kingdom was built upon has *two* Heavens? Do you understand that the stories of old never mentioned choosing sides? Never once portrayed one morally better than the other. Balance in the cosmos is the highest form of enlightenment, and the Kattadiya have discarded it all in favor of themselves. Why, because one woman claimed she'd been given a task from the First Heavens?

"And what has happened since then, Premala? Bloodshed. The Kattadiya help those who seek them, yes, but they also force others against their will, kill them if they can make a reasonable case. They demonize faithful practitioners of the Second Heavens, punish their own for acting in mercy, and allow stories to lead people to their demise. For what, Premala? None of that is for protection. Death does not save people!"

Premala's lips quivered. "You don't understand."

"No, *you* don't understand. Because you don't want to," Anula spat. "You are a lowly fisherman's daughter who has only ever been told that you are worthless. And you believe it. You believe it so much that this place, these rules, this poisonous faith has you convinced that the only path to proving your worth is by following their rules. You don't want to see the truth of this place, because without it, you fear everyone is right: that you are worthless."

Premala's cheeks flushed red.

"My, my." Guruthuma Hashini stepped out from behind a statue. "A fearsome usurper you might have been, if you were a man and words were blades."

Premala wiped at the wetness on her lashes. Anula straightened.

"Your commands were of no power here, so you resorted to theft?" Guruthuma Hashini asked.

"Consider it borrowing, if it makes you feel better."

The guruthuma pursed her lips. "And what relic is it that you seek?"

"The Bone Blade."

Premala sucked in a breath, but the guruthuma smiled. "Ah, the Lord of the Second Heavens has found another willing seeker."

A chill passed over Anula. "Not exactly."

"The Yakkas, then." Guruthuma Hashini clasped her hands behind her back. "This is your bargain with them. A throne for a blade."

Anula narrowed her eyes.

"You were correct that many have come seeking the relics. Many more for the Bone Blade. The Divinities warned us of it. Despite Fate's demise, the Lord of the Second Heavens has never given up his plot."

"What?" Premala asked.

"Fate killed Destiny with their relic," Anula said. "The

Divinities banished them and then cast the relics here. Did your precious Kattadiya not tell you?"

Premala glanced at Hashini, who merely replied, "There are things only guruthumas are told. But you're missing the full truth. Wessamony was the one who convinced Fate to act. He claimed they could rule together, only the pair of them. I have no doubt that Wessamony would have eventually turned against Fate, had their plan not gone awry. His tenacity in finding the relic after all these years proves it. It is why the Divinities tasked us with hiding it, to keep it safe, not only from the selfishness of humanity but from the Second Heavens. The Kattadiya do not act for themselves, only for the protection of others."

Premala blinked. Anula held her breath. This was it, she'd see the manipulation now, and when she did, they'd act together. Grab the relic and run.

"You were going to give it to the Lord of the Second Heavens?" Premala asked, blind as ever.

Anula sighed. "No. The Yakkas have come to end Wessamony, to save the Heavens and the Earth from his plans."

The guruthuma scoffed. "Lies."

"If you believe your own story, then the Yakkas are innocent. They have nothing to do with it. They aren't a threat."

"Of course they are!" she snapped. "They drenched this ground with blood and will do so again when their Lord reigns supreme."

Anula raised a brow. "Isn't it the Kattadiya who drench the earth in blood now? Denouncements and tovils—"

"Ensure our protection," the guruthuma shouted. "They are the work of our Divine task: to rid the Earth of the threat of the Second Heavens."

"Rid? But then there will only be one."

"Exactly," Guruthuma Hashini hissed.

Anula blanched and looked to Premala, but the girl had gone rigid. A soldier in stance before her commander. Faithful and true. Dread drew a finger down Anula's spine. "It was never about saving people from curses and death, was it? The Kattadiya have always been working toward one goal, one tovil. The one that would end the Yakkas, once and for all."

Guruthuma Hashini stepped closer, placed a heavy hand on Premala's shoulder. "The Lord of the Second Heavens created the Yakkas for a purpose, as the Divinities created us for a purpose. One unbalanced the cosmos; the other will right it."

Premala lifted her gaze. Anula willed her to see, to open her eyes. These people were not going to right the cosmos; they were the ones seeking imbalance. They were the ones hurting people. But Premala had eyes only for her guruthuma. For her perceived salvation. She wanted worth, no matter the blindness.

"It is time, acolyte. Enact the blood oath." Guruthuma Hashini grabbed Premala's hand and placed it against the wall where Guruthuma Thilini waited silently. When their hands touched, a small light sparked, and dark red liquid streaked down Premala's fingers.

Anula shifted backward. "No."

It couldn't happen now, not when they were so close. Not when the tovil would tear Reeri apart. She couldn't bring them back from that, couldn't make another bargain for him to return, couldn't even warn him.

Premala cleared her throat. Anula retreated farther, finding the statue at her back.

"Say it," Guruthuma Hashini hissed.

"No," Anula pled again. "Wait. You don't have to do this. You don't need this place. They want to destroy part of the Heavens. You can't believe—"

"Stop," Premala whispered.

“You aren’t worthless, Premala. Come with me. We will still save the kingdom, but not like this.”

“Stop.”

“Don’t let this place fool you. Don’t let them make you a monster.”

“Stop!” Premala snapped. “Why do you care if I am a Kattadiya?”

“Because they’re wrong! They’re cruel. You deserve better than this.”

“No. You care because I’m in your way. If I hadn’t been the one to show you that first tovil, would you have ever sought me out again?”

“I checked on you in the kitchens.”

“Because you caught me in the gardens. Because you thought I was part of another usurper’s plan.”

Anula didn’t deny it.

“You were never my friend, Anula. You only ever wanted to know that I wasn’t your enemy. And now that I am, you want to stop me.”

Anula’s gut twisted. She had never been taught how to be a friend. “I see you, Premala. You are not my enemy, but you’ve been sold a lie.”

“Bring them.” Premala’s voice rang out, as if shouted from the top of a mountain. The words wavered and shimmered, the first rays of the morning sun, warming Anula’s skin and heating her blood. “Bring the Yakkas to the tunnels. Immediately.”

The argument died on Anula’s lips, fizzled to a sour taste in her mouth. Premala was right—Anula was no friend. Not to her and not to the Yakkas.

Anula’s body pushed off the statue without her mind telling it to do so. Her feet moved of their own accord, each step binding her muscles with tension. With fear. She was no longer in control.

She could not stop, could not turn, could not even lift her hand to touch her necklace. She couldn't swell her tongue, or put herself to sleep, or drink the poison at the base of her throat.

She could only walk.

"Anula." Reeri spun as she emerged from the bush.

A tear slipped from her lashes as her lips violently shook apart, the words wrenched from between her teeth. "Call the others, and follow me."

43

Dark clouds gathered as Reeri and the others followed Anula through the brush and down a set of stairs. Heat clung to him. It drew out his sweat, leeched his breath, as if to hollow him out. A monsoon was nigh. The mark of the Maha season.

"Those are Divinities." Bithul sucked his teeth, the tap of his sword-cane scratching to a halt.

The tunnels spread wide beneath the ground, walls bare save for the occasional portrait of a woman, halls tight and made tighter by grandiose stone statues. These, Reeri recognized. Neither short nor tall, female nor male, but all and none and everything in between. A chill ran up his spine.

"The Kattadiya survived, then," Sohon growled. "That is how your bargain was broken, Calu."

Unease filtered through their line. The memory of the Kattadiya's powers had not faded with time, and they were not keen to experience them again.

"When were you going to tell us of your Kattadiya connections?" Calu asked.

Anula stared, a droplet of sweat tracking down her cheek. "I—"

Her hand twitched, her lips pursed, and Reeri saw the color of fear in her eyes. It soured in his mouth.

Despite her forgiveness, there were still so many ways he could fail her, fail them all. Mayhap she realized that, too. She continued deeper into the tunnel, without giving an answer.

"Did you tell her of the soul sacrifice?" Calu whispered, swinging the foreign sword he had bought in the night market, ready to battle any unseen Kattadiya. "She looks scared to find the relic."

Reeri's heart squeezed as he watched the tension stiffen Anula's shoulders. The urge to take her hand in his sizzled down his arms. Why should she not be scared? Even without knowledge of her sacrifice, they were still attempting the impossible: killing a Heavenly being. None of them knew what was to come.

Even Reeri had only ever heard stories of a soul's use. What if he could not stop it from completely cleaving her? What if it could not be done? Would he have to choose betwixt freeing his brethren or saving her soul?

Reeri brushed a hand through damp curls and took a breath that shook more than steadied.

"How much farther?" Sohon whispered.

Calu grunted. "If we knew that, do you think we would be crawling our way through this?"

"There!" Kama shouted. Calu clapped a hand over her mouth, yet she was right. Ahead of Bithul and Anula, to the center of the hall and off to one side, it stood: the statue of Fate.

Blessed with curves and star-filled eyes, a gown wrapped tight around their waist, stardust glittering the length of their arms, down to their hands, which held an ivory-and-iron blade. It was small and delicate and made Reeri's palms sweat.

"Is it real?" Bithul breathed, more starry-eyed than the statue.

"Y-yes," Anula choked, coughing as she lifted a hand toward it. "I feel it wants to be used."

"Like the paintings in the palace," Bithul murmured.

Sweat trickled down her neck, her eyes flicking to the shadows, as if Wessamony would appear as soon as skin met bone. Reeri's fingers twitched. It was not too late; they could skip the soul cleaving.

But no. He squeezed his eyes shut, blinked them open again. This undertaking was too important. He could not retreat now. Ratti deserved a life. They all did. Reeri had promised.

"Good. On our count, Anula, pick up the relic," Kama said, pulling out a silk saaluwa. She revealed a heart wrapped within and nodded to the others to take out their own essence offerings. "We must wield the soul you offered and then call upon the Bone Blade's power to kill Wessamony. The equinox is hours away."

Eyes wide, Anula nodded, her hand hovering at the hilt.

"Strike fast," Calu said, taking out his rice bowl made of teeth. He shot Reeri a look. "Mayhap Bithul could stand by, in case."

Reeri's pulse pounded as Bithul shifted nearer to Anula, ready to do his duty. The Yakkas tightened their circle, Kama pulling Reeri along. Anula lifted the Bone Blade from the statue's grip, and it began.

"Great and vast cosmos," Kama sang low. "Hear our prayer..."

Relic shaking along with her hands, Anula cast sidelong glances into the shadows. Reeri gripped his vial of blood, clenched his teeth, as Kama beseeched the cosmos to hear their bid and accept their offerings. This was the only way. Anula had agreed.

"I give to you a journal of secrets, offered to me for my benevolence," Sohon said, laying his book on the ground.

"I give to you a heart, offered to me for my benevolence," Kama said, laying hers right beside.

Calu offered his, and as he laid it on the ground, the journal of secrets disappeared in a mist. A shiver racked Anula, and the mehendhi on her arms swirled, tightening. A noose of her own skin, cinching tight, cutting flesh and drawing blood. Her offering of a soul being called upon.

For once, Reeri did not feel it, too. For once, it was only her pain, her anguish, her—

Reeri's heart tripped.

A light bloomed in her chest, growing brighter. Joy and peace and happiness shifted out and breezed across Reeri's face, taunting him to reach out and grasp them, to take control, to pull and cleave.

His will extended forward—Kama's, Sohon's, and Calu's, too. They touched Anula's soul, and heavensong rippled through their own. But Reeri did not rejoice, did not smile as the others did, because he saw it. Beneath the light they held grew a darkness, twining around Anula's chest, curving claws around her heart. It paled her and turned her sallow.

No, this was not right. Even partially cleaving her soul was taking too much. He could not bear to witness the passion dim from her eyes or the jests be ripped from her lips. It was too high a cost.

Anula, alive but silent.

Anula, a husk with a crown.

"No!" Reeri shouted, ripping his hand from Kama's and shooting forward.

Tearing the relic from Anula's hand, he threw it out of the circle, watched it clatter to the floor, and then fell to his knees before her.

"I am sorry." His voice broke. "I am sorry."

"What are you doing?" Calu asked. Sohon and Kama exchanged a look.

"Please, I cannot do this. I cannot mar another soul. Not hers. I beg you, not her."

Calu blanched. "But she offered her soul."

"And I have fallen in love with it."

A sharp breath echoed.

"Take mine, sacrifice mine. Mayhap it will be enough." Reeri bowed his head. "It is all I can offer. My life should have been the only one forfeit from the start. It should be mine now, to bring our brethren back."

"Reeri."

It was her voice, thick and broken on the end. Yet he dared not turn. Dared not look into those fierce eyes and face what he had been about to do, the selfishness that had nearly taken her from him. He could not bear it.

"Take my soul," he repeated. "It is the least of what I deserve."

Silence stretched.

Then came a sneer. "You imbecile."

Reeri blinked up.

Calu bent at the knee, leveling a furious gaze. "Do you not see? We have never blamed you."

"But—"

"No. Listen to me for once in two hundred years," he snapped. "Mighty Heavens, how do you not see? I lost my brethren that day, but I lost my closest friend, too. You shut me out, Reeri. You shut us all out. Were there unintended consequences to what we did? Yes. Were they deserved? No. Were any of us to blame? No. We have missed you, as wholly as we miss Ratti and the others. *I* miss you, Reeri. I love you, brother. Come back to us. Come back to me. Come back."

The words clawed at Reeri's chest, trying to catch and sink in. With wet lashes, Reeri looked at his family. Tears streaked Kama's cheeks, and a sniffle ripped from Sohon's nose.

They missed him.

They loved him.

They had never not.

Regardless of what had happened, of what he had done, he was loved. And he had always deserved it. His heart split open, and he vaulted into Calu's arms.

"I love you." His voice broke. He squeezed tight, tighter than even Ratti had ever done. A promise to never let go, to never forget again. "I love you."

Two pairs of arms fell on them. Hot tears dropped on his cheeks. Reeri had found his way home. It had always been there, in plain sight. He had only needed to listen and see.

"Reeri." Anula's whisper tingled down his back.

This time, he turned. Her eyes sparkled with unshed tears and an unspoken question—but he was already pressing her close, one hand tucking the hair behind her ear, the other caressing her cheek. He pushed his thoughts into her mind, where he was not mere shadow, but had a body and a life, and she was just as she was now, a beautiful soul, stubborn and burning bright. The one who lit up his shadow, who gave life to his existence. The one he had dreamed of finding: the one who communed with his soul.

Anula sucked in a breath. Her hand rested on his cheek. "Reeri—"

Boom.

Reeri tensed.

Boom.

"What is that?"

Boom.

"Drums," Bithul said, unsheathing his cane. "Tovil drums."

44

THEY CAME FROM ALL SIDES, AS IF THE WALLS WERE BLESSED paintings they'd stepped through. Bells and beads announced their attack.

"No!" Anula shouted.

Sandani rushed forward with the drums, followed by another three. The Kattadiya surrounded them before she saw the two who mattered. In masks with teeth the length of their arms, Premala and Guruthuma Hashini danced closer, chanting to the rhythm.

"Ohng Hreeng."

Boom.

"Ohng Hreeng." It quaked in Anula's chest.

Boom.

"Ohng Hreeng." The sound of the Blood Yakka's nightmare.

Boom.

The sound of hers.

The Yakkas bent over, coughing and hacking. Dark red mehendhi swirled at Sohon's neck, bit at Kama's hands. Calu tore at his clothing. Reeri wheezed, clutched his chest, and collapsed.

"No!" Anula shouted again. The markings shriveled on her skin, cracking like dirt in a drought. "Reeri!"

"Ohng Hreeng." The Kattadiya closed in.

Calu lifted his sword and struck a drum. The blade shattered to the floor.

"Your weapons are of no use against the First Heavens." The guruthuma's voice came from behind the hideous mask, its lips red and dripping. Anula wondered if the blood was real.

Boom.

If it was hers.

"Ohng Hreeng."

The Kattadiya formed a tight circle, beads ringing as Premala and the guruthuma danced, wild and rough, their footfalls echoing through the stone caves.

"Don't—" Anula choked. The mehendhi netting on her arms blazed, searing into her skin.

"The blade." Sohon coughed. "Finish it. Call Wessamony."

"That blade is nothing but a forgery, a bone meant to trick greedy seekers," the guruthuma sneered. "You think we would allow a relic to fall to the hands of the Yakkas?"

The drum beat faster, sending Anula's pulse racing, her mind tripping.

"First we will be rid of the Blood Yakka, leader of all Yakkas. Take him to the center of the circle, Anula," Guruthuma Hashini commanded.

The words moved her without consent. Anula reached for Reeri. Their mehendhi blazed deep red, as though the blood beneath boiled.

No. Her hand shook. He had stopped for her, when he believed the blade real. Thrown away his plans and protected her soul. He cared for her, wanted to be with her, no matter the consequence for himself or his family. And she wanted that, too. Wanted the dream her parents had inspired—with him. She wouldn't give him to the Kattadiya. Anula curled her fingers against the oath's power, one at a time, refusing to touch Reeri.

"Now!" the guruthuma yelled. "In the name of the blood oath sworn to the First Heavens."

But instead of forcing Anula's hand to move faster, it stilled.

A chill cooled her from the inside out, and a bright light erupted, blasting through the tunnels, catching every shadow and devouring them whole. From fingertip to ankle, every detail of Anula's mehendhi glowed.

Not saffron. But white, with heavenslight.

The drumbeat faltered. Premala tripped. And the Kattadiya fell silent.

The Yakkas rose tall. Reeri reached out to her, the elephant on his chest shining.

"How?"

"We have a bargain." Reeri's voice pealed, vibrant and true. "Your oath belongs to me."

Relief settled like a balm. For the first time in as long as she could remember, she knew Amma and Auntie Nirma hadn't put their faith in a lie. She took his hand and squeezed tight. "Thank the cursed Heavens."

Fingers tripping over sapphires, Anula plucked out two and threw them at Premala's feet, where they shattered, smoked, and mixed into a rose-scented cloud upon the floor.

"Run!" she commanded the Yakkas, pushing Bithul ahead. For though the vials were not deadly on their own, together they made a poisonous gas.

Much like her and Reeri.

The caves didn't have tunnels—those were straight with beginnings and ends. These were crooked, unlit, and unfinished. Arms sprouted at various connection points, some leading to dead ends and others disappearing forever around corners, a labyrinth beneath the Pleasure Gardens. If they weren't careful, they'd get lost and become easy prey.

"So, the relic was never down here?" Calu asked.

"Of course it is." Anula huffed, turning another corner to find another split in the path. She chose the left for no other reason than that it felt closer.

"Then why are we not searching for it?"

"Perhaps we worry about that after we've escaped." Bithul grunted.

"We need the—"

"I know," Anula snapped. "But they want to kill you, and you're no good to me dead."

"How considerate," Reeri scoffed.

"You know what I mean." Anula glanced at their hands, still entwined. He hadn't let go. Neither had she.

Fear trickled in the back of her mind. If she got them to safety, Wessamony was still a threat. The Maha Equinox would strike tonight, and Reeri would be taken, forced to torture his family for all eternity, or until Wessamony destroyed the cosmos.

"Wait." She paused. "Calu's right. We can't leave. We have to finish this, before the day is done."

"It may already be too late," Sohon said, looking back the way they had come. "My essence offering was taken and the others—"

"Are right here," Kama said, pulling hers and Calu's from her sari.

"We are not sacrificing Anula's soul." Reeri squeezed her hand.

"Nor are we sacrificing Reeri's," Calu pressed.

"What about Wessamony's soul?" Sohon asked. "We are going to kill him anyway. I cannot think of a more poetic trade."

"Does he have a soul?" Calu scoffed.

"Oh yes." Kama smiled. "It is the darkness of the cosmos, the space between spaces, the chasm in our hearts, the—"

"We get it," Sohon said.

"It's worth a try," Anula said, squeezing Reeri's hand back, remembering the first promise she had made to him.

"Then do you know where the true relic lies?" Calu asked.

"No."

"Do you know where we are?"

"Also no."

But she didn't have to.

An idea formed quickly, and she tugged Reeri to the wall. She squinted in the darkness, yet even without light, she saw her. Guruthuma Thilini slunk around the corner, danced to Anula, and offered her palm, as if she had been following. As if she had been waiting for this moment all along.

Anula placed her hand atop the portrait's and said, "I need the Bone Blade to save the Heavens and the Earth."

Thilini smiled.

And sprinted.

Anula had never seen the door before, yet Thilini insisted. Cracking it open revealed not the flowers and thorns of the Pleasure Gardens but a pristine marble floor. The sound of courtiers and guards arguing over their right of entrance hung heavy on the air.

"We've already searched the palace," Anula whispered.

Thilini shook her head, pointed down the hall, her finger bending with the curve of the doorway and aimed at the raja's bedchamber. They hadn't searched there. Perhaps they should have—after all, it was known to hold the best of the blessed gifts, one chatty bed frame excluded.

Calu whistled low as they entered. "There are a lot of gifts to check."

"Less than an entire city," Sohon said, flicking over candles and upending vases.

"Mayhap it is in one of these," Kama said, poking at a gilt bird flitting across a mirror frame.

"Or there is another portrait in here that we are meant to find and she will guide us on to the next place," Calu said.

"There are no Kattadiya portraits in the palace," Anula said, then paused. "Why can I say their name now?"

"Reeri invoked the power of the bargain," Kama said, trying to catch a bulbul. "It severed the connection between you and them. You are free. If you do not count us."

Before, the words might have chilled Anula, sent tremors down her spine or along her arms. Now, there was only a sense of safety. Like a net, or hands to catch her, hold her, keep her safe. Keep her at home.

"Not a portrait, but Kattadiya art all the same," Reeri said, voice solemn. He pointed to the relief on the ceiling, where Yakkas and Divinities lounged on a bed of clouds, emulating the idea of a peaceful, coexistent cosmos. The sun and stars beamed upon their faces, caring eyes turned toward Earth. It swirled with the same colors as Thilini, shimmered with the same glaze. The edges of faces dull and soft, the pigment artistically faded. It was as if the mural had been painted by the same hand. The hand of the Divinities.

"I knew it was mocking me," Reeri growled.

Anula craned her neck. If a portrait knew of this painting, so did the Kattadiya. But why would—

Premala's task.

It clicked, faster than a cart to a horse. The acolytes were placed inside the palace to keep an eye on the relics. Not the blessed gifts, nor the courtiers making bargains, but on the hiding place of the relics.

Where they could be looked upon and not seen.

"Hold this," Anula said, grabbing a gilt chair and thrusting it on top of a divan.

Reeri held the back as she climbed, reaching an arm into the air. Her fingers brushed the mural, and a soft breeze fluttered through the depiction of the Heavens. *Come and see*, it sang to her.

Anula rose on her toes and pressed her fingers more firmly. "I'm trying to save souls." She spoke to it. "I need the Bone Blade."

The clouds rippled, and the crowd of Divinities stirred. A being with grayed tresses emerged from the back, wearing a lotus crown shining with heavenslight. They plucked it off and pulled out a small blade no larger than their hand.

Anula pressed her fingers harder, until ceiling gave way to canvas. Her hand became one with the painting. She wrapped it around a cool, smooth hilt and pulled back—both her hand and the Bone Blade solidifying.

She dropped to the floor as the relic shone bright with heavenslight, rang clear and soft with heavensong. It vibrated through the room, quaking Anula's bones, filling her lungs.

"It is beautiful," Kama breathed.

"It's—it's—" Bithul stammered.

"Real," Reeri said, touching it gently. "I can see what fate it has in store."

"What's that?" Anula asked, meeting his gaze. Saffron flickered.

"Freedom for all."

Hope swelled in Anula's chest, swam through the room, and crested in each Yakka's heart—

Boom.

It crashed to the floor as the chamber door flew open. Not with the beats and chants of the Kattadiya—

"For Polonnaruwa!"

—but with the cries of war.

PART FOUR

45

The palace halls welcomed them with the all too familiar high-pitched horror of Anula's people. Gooseflesh prickled her skin.

"Reeri," she breathed, stashing the blade in a hidden pocket, as she, the Yakkas, and Bithul were marched to the throne room.

The usually pristine floors were slick and painted red as half the palace guards took orders from the Polonnaruwans and felled their one-time brothers in arms. The courtiers' cries pealed from the inner city, shaking the latticed windows, as they fled in every direction only to be caught by soldiers beating iron swords against chest plates, triumph on their faces, bloodlust in their eyes.

Look away.

Anula's mouth dried. "Reeri."

"It will be all right," he said, voice tight. Dread trickled between his words, dripped down Anula's spine.

Dying orange light streaked across a range of storm clouds as the invaders pushed Anula and the others onto the throne room terrace. Heat pressed a heavy hand, and thunder roiled a threat as day turned to night.

"I hereby take this land for Polonnaruwa," a man with a spiked crown proclaimed over the chaos of the inner city. "For the prince they killed and for my father, Raja Nihal!"

With a flick of his sword, the banner of Anuradhapura cut in two, crumpling to the blood-soaked ground, where her kingdom's outnumbered army lay dead or dying—Dilshan's true influence on the war. Anula flinched. The cheer of at least two hundred enemy soldiers skittered up her arms and coiled a hand around her throat.

Boom.

It squeezed tight as a drumbeat of war echoed from her memory, bringing forth elephants trampling the palace gate and stupas standing silent.

Boom.

It squeezed tighter still, fixing her eyes on the rising smoke of burning homes, the crimson glow of her nightmares.

Red sky, red dirt.

"Reeri," she choked.

"It will be all right. I am here." He reached for her, only to be wrenched away by the soldier behind him. Anula's breath strangled in her throat. This wasn't supposed to happen. The Maha Equinox was the threat, with Wessamony's descent approaching as fast as the rising moon and the Kattadiya breathing down her neck. Polonnaruwa wasn't meant to attack and slaughter again.

"Anula." Reeri's voice was far away. "Look at me."

But she couldn't. There was only now and then and all the death between.

"Look at me, Anula," Reeri shouted, grounding her to his voice, his face, his words. "I will not leave you. Ever."

A breath rattled through her, and she took a step closer, to feel the warmth of his promise. But the soldiers held her firm and pushed Reeri toward the man with the crown.

"Welcome, Raja Vatuka." The Prince of Polonnaruwa's voice

pulled Anula's attention. The thirst in his eyes struck alarm bells. "Join me in witnessing the end of your kingdom. For too long, Anuradhapura has celebrated their small victory over Polonnaruwa, and my brother's murder has gone unanswered. I told my father for years that we must respond, yet he did nothing. Little did I know the poetry he planned. For as you celebrated, you let your guard down. You gathered for your festival, opening highways and relaxing borders. It sounds familiar, doesn't it? A kingdom too busy patting itself on the back to notice the ambush filtering around them, inside them?"

A wave of knowing spiked her senses. The prince was building to something. "Reeri," she warned, wriggling hard against her binding.

Reeri shook his head, mouthed that it would be all right, but she saw it in the uptick of the prince's lips. Usurpers were great at one thing and one thing only: taking the lives of others.

The prince loosed his sword. "It would have been sweeter to kill the man responsible, but you will do."

"No!" Anula shouted as sharp iron buried into Reeri's gut. He grunted and fell. The prince wrenched back, swung the sword across his neck. Fisting the dead raja's hair, the prince tossed the head over the railing and onto the courtyard below.

A shadow made of edges exploded above the terrace. Dark, insubstantial features sharpened into a chin and cheekbones.

Saffron eyes flashed open.

"Reeri!" Anula screamed. *Please*, the words stifled in her throat, *come back*. She couldn't face this, not again, not alone, not without him. Yet the shadow dove and disappeared in the distance, and blood bubbled through her and the Yakkas' mehendhi.

The prince stumbled back. "Great gods and monsters, they're all cursed. Burn them! Now!"

"Reeri!" she begged a final time.

46

If shadows could cry, if shadows could panic, if shadows could bristle or sweat or shake with terror—

Yet bodies could.

And the moment Reeri dropped into his next, he cried out. Long and loud, a lion roaring for his threatened pride.

The body, a man named Darubhatika, was mid-flight when Reeri caught him. Free of capture, he sprinted through the darkening outer city, away from the palace and the ambush. He was already drenched from exertion, humidity and horror clinging tight. Reeri skidded to a stop and pivoted, catching a hand on the ground to stop his fall as his shoulder slammed into another.

Darubhatika was not the only one fleeing.

Under the cover of dark clouds and falling night, the entire city had taken to the streets. Footsteps pounded the paved road, faster than the war drums. Abandoning homes, they escaped with empty hands save those clutched in another's. Family was the sole priority—their safety and their life.

Reeri gritted his teeth, his shadow pulsing, and propelled

forward, before the Polonnaruwan prince could lay a hand on Anula—or on Kama or Sohon or Calu. Though the Yakkas would come back, Anula would not.

Reeri lumbered in his tall, thick body. For once, he had been able to brace himself for the maddening spiral that was his shadow ripping from a body. And for once he was able to control who he next inhabited. The men in the inner city were either dead, injured, or otherwise bound, and Reeri had known that whoever he merged with must be able to fight. Bands of muscle bulged from Darubhatika's shoulders to wrists, across his chest, and down his legs. Though not an army man, he would be able to brawl. Even so, each step Reeri took was like dragging through rice paddy fields as person after person bumped into him. He slogged through the trampled night market, his heart beating swift with visions of Sohon thrown from the terrace, Calu strung up and flayed, Kama gutted and left bleeding, and Anula…

Taken to a room, as any consort would be—ravaged and killed.

And what of the Kattadiya and Wessamony? Polonnaruwa's presence did not halt their advance. He touched his neck, the vial of blood gone along with the last raja's head. Would two essence offerings be enough to bring his brethren back? Another roar ripped through him, parting the crowd with terror. The real Darubhatika was a firewood carrier in the palace, his strength used only in service. Now Reeri exploited it to tower over the people, the Blood Yakka of old writhing inside.

Path cleared, he ran past razed thatch houses and forsaken shops, flattened vendor stations, and stupas with doors hacked off and offerings strewn down the stairs. Another street held another fire. Every corner he took was bloodier than the last as people fled with torn clothes and torn skin, broken noses and black eyes, hands dripping red as they desperately climbed over the mangled palace gates.

Reeri paled. Smoke rose over what had been the courtiers' homes, over the quickly charring Pleasure Gardens, and over three large pyres…packed with people. It was as if Wessamony had already descended and filled the night with fire and brimstone.

But no. They still had time.

A hand landed on his arm. He shifted, ready to fight off whoever dared threaten to stop him. He would not leave his brethren behind. He would not abandon Anula.

"*Yakka*," the Kattadiya acolyte hissed. Chin raised high, Premala dug her shaking fingers deep.

"How did you know?" He pried her off, searching beyond her for her clan.

Premala pointed to his chest, the open tunic and elephant trunk reaching down to his navel. "The relic is missing. Give it back."

Her voice quivered, yet her clan was nowhere in sight. She was alone. Reeri spun back, picking his way across the fallen palace gates. Premala's hand landed on him again. She pulled, stronger than her size let on.

"Don't you see how dangerous it is for the relic to be unguarded right now?"

Reeri tore away once more. "I see more danger than you can imagine. I must return to Anula."

"Does she have it?"

Reeri curled back his lip. "*She* is in danger."

Premala scoffed. "You don't care about that. You only ever wanted the relic. You want more destruction, just like your great Lord. Were you behind this attack, to distract us all from Lord Wessamony taking over?"

"I am not a monster," Reeri growled. "Indeed there are a great many dangers here today, not the least being Wessamony's descent at midnight, when the Maha Equinox strikes. Yet I only care for the danger that now threatens Anula. And if you do not wish to save her, then for once, do as the Kattadiya mantra suggests and save someone else."

"You don't love her." Premala frowned. "You can't. You're a Yakka."

"Spare me your unsolicited opinion."

Stepping carefully, Reeri hurried across the ruined threshold. Soldiers caught the outline of his hulking form, drew sword, mace, and spear, and smiled at him, eager for another target. Yet instead of metal striking flesh, a hand yanked his once more.

"What are you *doing*?" He spun, holding steady.

Premala's hand shook. Her eyes did not. "I won't let you give the Lord the relic."

"Mighty Heavens, girl, you are going to get yourself killed!"

"I don't care! Not if it means keeping the relic safe from Lord Wessamony."

"We are not giving him the relic," Reeri rumbled, aware of the soldiers now at his back. "We are going to end his death-filled reign by using it on him!"

The girl blanched. "That's what Anula said."

"Why, then, did you attack her?"

"I—I didn't believe her."

A spear flew over Reeri's shoulder. He shifted, covering Premala with his body. "Move," he commanded, shoving her back the way they had climbed.

The hiss of a mace arced through the air. Reeri twisted and landed a sizable fist in the ribs of a soldier. The man doubled over, stumbled, and slid through the debris. Gripping a piece of loose iron, Reeri tossed it at the last soldier, catching his sword and unbalancing him.

Reeri turned to Premala. "What do you believe now?"

Wringing her hands, she held his gaze. "Can't you call to her with your oath?"

"Unlike the Kattadiya, our connection is not a vise."

She bit her lip, blood bubbling betwixt her teeth. "Wessamony wants to rule the Heavens and destroy all we know?"

Reeri sighed. "Yes."

"But you don't."

It was not a question, and yet it was. "No."

She shook her head. "The reason doesn't matter, I suppose. We can't let anyone else get the relic. Not the Polonnaruwans, not Wessamony."

"No," he agreed again. Kattadiya were not to be trusted, he knew that well, yet there was something about this one. "We must save Anula first. She has the relic."

"We?" Premala squeaked. "What, like a truce, until Anula and the relic are safe?"

"Until my Yakkas are safe, too," he bargained.

"And then we…what?"

"Then together, we face Wessamony," Reeri said, seeing the shadow of the girl within, the one Anula must have seen. The one who was not dissimilar to either of them. "Together, we save the Heavens and the Earth."

Slowly, the girl nodded. "What do you need from me?"

47

THE COURTYARD SHARPENED INTO FOCUS AS THE TETHER suddenly soothed.

Smoke choked the courtiers' houses, flushing out any who tried to hide. Wood creaked and fire popped. War elephants trumpeted, a brass noise vibrating beneath Anula's feet.

But Reeri had found a new body.

Anula's pulse thundered, not because the soldiers pushed her and the Yakkas toward the pyre erected outside the administration building, but because she didn't know whether Reeri was safe or captured again. Was he the man fighting a soldier with only a cut of wood, or the man climbing the rubble of the gate to flee to the outer city?

No, Reeri wouldn't run away. He'd promised.

Minister, courtier, servant—she searched every soot-stained face. There were a hundred of them at any given time, at least another hundred family members. Auntie Nirma had made her memorize them all, yet Anula recognized none. She saw only cries for help, mirrored images of that terrible night. She swallowed the bile that crept up her throat and tripped as the soldiers shoved her against a pile of wood, spreading the Yakkas on either side.

It was only then that her attention shifted, grounding her to what was about to happen, with or without Reeri. The air in her lungs crushed out as the soldiers cinched thick rope tightly around her entire upper body, binding her to the wood at her back. Her stomach plummeted.

She blinked and a baby's bones cracked. *Anula!*

She blinked and Amma's face fractured in flame. *Anula!*

She blinked and she was fatherless, motherless, powerless. Anuradhapura would burn like Eppawala, with her standing watch, again.

"Anula!" Calu's voice snatched her from the nightmare. "Not to create a panic, but may I remind everyone that we will return to the aether if Anula dies?"

Thunder clouds roiled. The light beyond them was nearly gone; the equinox was only a few hours away. *Thrice-cursed blessings*. Even if Reeri was safe now, he wouldn't be soon. Not if she died here. Wessamony would come for the relic, and if she and the others were gone, if Reeri met him with empty hands—

"No," she asserted. She slammed the word into her spiraling thoughts, crumpled her fear in her fist, and threw it into the torch's fire. Anuradhapura wouldn't be the same as Eppawala. It wouldn't burn, and her Yakkas wouldn't be taken, because she was not the same as she had been before.

She strained a hand toward her pocket, where she'd hidden the Bone Blade, but the ropes were too tight. "Do something, Calu!"

"You do something!"

"And which of my cosmos-given powers should I use? The one that doesn't exist or the one that doesn't exist?"

"I will not break taboo twice." A shiver racked Calu. It spread across the rope, shuddering up Anula's spine.

If the Yakkas would not—could not act, and she couldn't reach the blade, then how did they get free?

"I won't let you die," Bithul growled, straining against the ropes. But not a hair split from the cords, and before he came up with another plan, the soldiers added another fifteen people to their group and brought the torches near. Anula's breath stalled.

If you do this right, songs will be sung about you.

And if I do it wrong?

A pyre will be built instead.

48

The deeper into the caves they traveled, the slicker Reeri's palms grew. Though a human bargain with the Kattadiya was not the best plan, it would have to do. For his family. For Anula.

"Why did you choose her?" Premala asked as she led him around yet another corner in the vast tunnel system. The narrow passage pressed against his wide shoulders, the abrasive ceiling on his head. Even the air felt thin and constrained.

"Anula?" He panted.

"You said you had a plan for a while, so how did she end up in it?"

Moisture leaked from the walls. Reeri dared not consider whether it was blood or what the Kattadiya truly did in the darkness… "She made an offering the Heavens could not resist."

A smile cracked the acolyte's face. "Of course she did."

Grateful for the distraction, he wiped his palms on his already-damp tunic and told their story, from his plans to hers, the bargain, and their shaky start. "I fell in love with her soul, as a bird falls in love with a song."

Premala was quiet, contemplative. Else she was terrified into silence at the notion of a human and a Blood Yakka having anything but a bargain betwixt them. On the next turn, light grew as they emerged into a wide connection point. The statue of the Divinity of Mercy peered down. Their bronze vase poured out a never-ending stream of clear water into a pool at their feet. The sight brought images of Anula's light streaming out of her body, the scent of her death, and the threat it brought to his heart.

His shadow writhed, but he clamped it down. Help was the only way he would save his family, and Premala was the only one willing. Mighty Heavens, it had to be enough.

"You found him," a voice said, thick with surprise. The guruthuma stepped out from behind the statue. Four others flanked her. "Exceptional work, acolyte. I admit I did not think you capable. Perhaps you have a place here after all."

Premala stilled, mouth half-open betwixt shock and fear.

"Restrain him!"

The Kattadiya pounced; one held a drum menacingly. Reeri tensed, yet the girl at his side launched herself before him. "Wait! I made a truce."

"I beg your pardon?" the guruthuma hissed. It shivered down Reeri's shadow.

"They aren't here to end us," Premala said, then explained it all, emphasizing his intention of ending Wessamony's scourge and crediting him with saving her from enemy hands.

"Lies," the guruthuma spat, eyes narrowed and frown fixed.

Reeri took a step back, ready to run. This Kattadiya would not see as Premala. Hatred clouded like a gathering storm.

"N—no they aren't." Premala wrung her hands. "Besides, Anula has the relic, and Polonnaruwa has her. She needs our help."

"Our duty is to the First Heavens, not to some consort and surely not to a Yakka." She pointed at Reeri. "Take him to the pit!"

Reeri spun—and tripped as a long drumbeat echoed out a meter. Three pairs of hands caught him.

"Wait!" Premala shouted.

They yanked at his arms, his shoulders, his waist, until they had fastened him tight with rope.

Memory-nightmares crept fast. "Premala," he called out.

"Wait, please!"

"We had a deal." His voice wavered as the Kattadiya dragged him deeper into the caves. Strong hands made stronger by faith.

The guruthuma's whisper chilled his bones. "Kattadiya do not make bargains."

Thrown inside the amphitheater, Reeri stumbled over loose rocks. The scent of iron and burnt cloth cloyed in his mouth as he took in the brown stains of dried blood smeared across the floor. His pulse beat swift as the beat of the drum ended and the revelation of his situation dawned.

"Premala," Reeri murmured again. It was one thing to be attacked with a tovil, his shadow ripped out of Darubhatika and sent spiraling for a new host. Time would have been wasted, but not compared to this.

If Wessamony had taught Reeri anything, it was that torture was never quick.

The acolyte wrung her hands for the hundredth time. It did not release Reeri from his bindings, nor liberate him from the hole, nor remove the terrifying masks that now adorned the three Kattadiya.

"I don't think this is necessary," Premala whispered. All confidence disappeared on stale air.

"That is why you are an acolyte and I am the guruthuma. Now hush." The woman lifted her chin as she circled the pit. "Yakka, I know of your powers and your bargain with the consort. Invoke your oath with Anula, bring her and the relic here."

"Our connection does not function that way. I do not control her. I doubt anything could."

The guruthuma raised a brow to the Kattadiya with the drum. "Begin, Sandani."

"Wait!" Premala stepped toward the other girl.

"Heed her, and join the Yakka in the pit," the guruthuma seethed. "Your banishment will reach the beaches of the island, to die alone on the sand."

Sandani hesitated, sharing a look with Premala. Then slowly, she sat, crossed her legs, and struck the first tone. The sound came before the sting. Reeri seized. The dark marking on his chest shivered and bit into his skin.

"This won't get us the relic," Premala blurted. "If—if we could get to the inner city—"

"Silence!" the guruthuma said. "Yakka, call Anula here with the relic!"

"I cannot." He would not, even if he could.

Boom.

Pain flared, sizzling up his markings and sending a bolt through his chest. His knees smashed into the rocks, adding fresh blood to the cave floor.

Boom.

It lashed at his shadow.

Boom.

As if it were Wessamony and his whip.

Boom.

Reeri landed on all fours.

"This is your fault," the guruthuma said.

A muscle twitched along Reeri's jaw. He glanced at the rocks beneath him.

The guruthuma scoffed. "Already seeking a way to kill us? I expect nothing less of you, Yakka. You are but pure evil. If you had not brought the Yakkas here, people would not be suffering. Anula would not have been cursed. You have destroyed all you touched."

The words slid down his spine, curled around his throat, and tightened like a noose.

Centuries ago this island had been blanketed in blood. It covered his hands. He had acted for personal gain, at the behest of humans, and even after centuries of guilt and shame, he had still returned only to cleave Anula's soul. But he had not. He had changed his mind. Because he saw which were his mistakes and which were not. And without the burden of blame, he could easily see where to draw the line. He was no monster, and he would not be convinced that he was. Not again.

"No," he grunted.

"Everything bad in this world can be traced back to you."

He laughed, dark and low. "You cannot break me, Guruthuma, or force me to abandon myself. Wessamony already did that, and Anula has put me back together."

She grinned, sharp and wild. "You forget the Kattadiya have the might of the First Heavens."

"I could never forget that."

Images flashed. First of Ratti flying through the air and Yakkas doubled over in suffering, snapping back to their shrines. Then of the call the Kattadiya made to cause the descent of the Lord—

"Bring. Her. Here." The guruthuma stood at the lip of the pit, eyes blazing. Reeri held her fury, accepted her challenge. She pointed at Sandani—

Boom. Boom. Boom.

The sound struck his shadow like lightning. The world shattered, and bile choked up his throat.

"Guruthuma Hashini, please! We're wasting time. He's not a

threat. He hasn't done anything to deserve this. He wants what we want: to get the relic and to keep everyone safe."

"I said silence!"

"But if he could do it without us, he'd never have come here."

The guruthuma whirled. "You believe his lies."

"I—I believe he didn't have to offer to work with us."

"You have been taken in by them."

"No."

The beat cut off. Heaving, Reeri craned his neck to see Premala tossing the drum across the room.

The guruthuma's anger flared. "Are you a Kattadiya or not?"

The girl flinched.

"Call her, now!" The guruthuma rounded on Reeri.

Yet he dared to not respond and kept his gaze on Premala instead. She was no monster either.

"Save them," he croaked. "Kill Wessamony."

"Do not speak to her! For Heavens' sake, Sandani, fetch the drum!"

Before Sandani could strike another chord and send him into oblivion, Reeri saw a figure wringing her hands.

And slipping out the cave door.

The drum beat, the women chanted, and time dragged on. Reeri's shadow twisted as it broke through skin a sixth, seventh, eighth—

The guruthuma cut the tovil off once again, right on the cusp of freeing him. Sweat slipped down his arms, and as his shadow snapped back inside Darubhatika. He retched.

"You are stubborn, Yakka," the guruthuma spat.

"You are no Heavenly gift yourself." His voice was grating and raw.

They had an audience now. The stairs filled with the faithful, dressed in beaded fabrics, ready at the call. Though their numbers had dwindled since he last saw them—a mere forty instead of hundreds—they stood staunchly still, condemning him once again.

The guruthuma scoffed. Reeri eyed her, the way she held her hand out to Sandani, purposeful and just, the way she circled, a smile of satisfaction curling wider with each strike of the drum. It reminded him of someone.

"Did the Divinities grant you this room?"

"I will hear no vitriol from your lips, Yakka. Call Anula."

"I cannot." He would not.

A hand swung, a tone echoed, and Reeri's shadow convulsed. Yet the anger in her eyes flashed anew. Not for Anula or the relic, but from his words.

"They do not know of this place, do they?" he rasped.

Only the chanting continued.

It drew his laugh. "I am right."

Feet shifted on stone. Unease filtered through the gathered Kattadiya at their guruthuma's lack of answer. Mayhap they had never questioned it. Mayhap they did so silently. He would bring it to life so that she would bring him to death. Shadow freed, he would find Anula.

"It reminds me of home." Reeri watched not the drum, but the women. "After banishment, the court of the Second Heavens became a torture chamber. Did your Divinities tell you? Yakkas' shadows are chained to the walls. Though Wessamony does not have the pleasure of a pit."

A chill spread down the stairs.

"This room might be a gift from the Second Heavens, not the First. After all, it was Wessamony's anger that banished us. The Kattadiya led him to discover our treason, did they not? He must have owed a great deal to you."

"Silence!" The guruthuma sneered. "You are a worm. A maggot that feasts on death. Your bargainers do not follow you out of faith but fear."

Reeri smirked. "A position you know well."

He looked to those gathered; so did the guruthuma. The air shifted, and not one of her Kattadiya dared meet her gaze. Caught betwixt fear and anger, she raised her hand to Sandani, and Reeri could nearly taste the release.

Pain, white and blinding, struck him.

Yet there had been no drumbeat. Still, strips of red flesh peeled from his body. He choked. The mehendhi was tearing itself free. But it did not fly toward Anula; it did not fly at all. It ripped from him and turned to ash.

Cursed blessings.

The tether was breaking. Anula's bargain was timing out. The moon must be rising, the Maha Equinox beginning.

His bargain with Lord Wessamony was coming due.

49

Beads of sweat burst down Anula's face as she fell against the rope binding her to the pyre. The tether quavered, shaking her worse than any fear of burning alive ever could. "Something's wrong."

"You feel Reeri," Kama inferred.

"He's in trouble." Anula grunted. Nausea rose and crashed on a wave of blinding pain, and suddenly the pyre disappeared. A cave flashed into view, with a pit full of red stones glistening menacingly and Reeri heaving as his shadow stretched and his markings flared. She blinked and it was gone. "Hashini. The Kattadiya have him!"

"Your connection has grown strong," Kama sang. "Can you speak to him? Soothe him?"

"What for?" Sohon hissed, craning his neck as the soldiers lit more torches. "Soon Anula will die, and we will all be back in the aether."

"No." Anula swallowed back bile. "They have a new tovil. It will tear a Yakka's soul apart. It will end your being."

"Mighty Heavens," Calu cursed. "They finally figured it out."

Anula couldn't let them perform it. Not now, not ever. The Yakkas were hers, their tether part of her; their dedication for Anuradhapura and all its people, hers; their love—

"So the Yakkas will be returned to the Heavens upon your death," Bithul clarified, "and the Blood Yakka will be no more?"

"Not if we save him." Anula surged against the rope. Its rough fibers pricked and scraped her arms, all the way down to her wrists. Her sweat-slicked fingers slipped off its edge. The Polonnaruwans knew how to keep their captives in place.

"Valiant effort, but I do not think that will work," Calu murmured.

"It's all I can do!" she snapped. "I'm not a Yakka!"

Calu flinched, but still he did nothing.

She turned on Sohon.

"What?" he growled. "Do you want me to eat our way out?"

"It would be memorable," Kama said. Sohon stuck out his tongue. But before Anula could yell at them again, point out that the soldiers with flaming torches were bending now to strike the pyre, that they were minutes away from death, Kama frowned falsely, a twinkle in her eye. "Who can think of love when they are consumed with death? Only a man burning for another, facing the darkness with the light of his own passionate flame. There is no line between beauty and pain." She smiled, sharp and bright. "I shall prove it to all."

Kama leaned close to the human on her left and cooed. "Pray to the Yakkas of Love."

The man, tearstained and shaking, scowled. "What? They can't help me now."

"Do it, and if they do not come to your rescue, I will kiss you as the flames engulf us. We shall end in our own ecstasy."

The wrinkle between his brows smoothed, his eyes lost

in Kama's, lost in the hope she gave and in the idea of feeling anything but the fire. "Great Yakkas of Love, hear my prayer, grant me strength against the Polonnaruwans to live. I offer my seed and love."

The soldiers tapped their torches to the ground, and flame roared up. Courtiers screamed, an echo of Amma ringing in Anula's ears, calling to that never-ending ache in her chest.

"What are you waiting for?" Anula shouted.

A spark caught on Kama's sari, devouring the beaded trim and eliciting her laughter. "Your prayer has been heard. I accept. Now free me!"

She blew the man a kiss, the air between them sparkling like the stars, until it landed on his lips. His eyes widened, darkened, deepened. And as the heat crept close, the man's muscles bulged like a usurper's and he ripped the rope clean in two. He reached across the thickening smoke and pulled the nearest soldier down into the flame, smothering them with their iron chest plate. The soldier wailed as he boiled inside his own armor.

The man's strength was unmatched, unchecked, and unbelievable. Anula blinked as the smoke and fear cleared, watching as Kama's devotee jumped from the pyre, grabbing soldier after soldier, smothering flame, leaving a path clear for the people to escape. And one by one, they did, whispering thanks.

Soldiers advanced to restrain him, yet as each hand clutched, the man grew. Another muscle, another inch taller, until he lorded over the soldiers, barreling through them like a child in a rice paddy field. He tore blades from their grips and turned them on their owners, drowning the remaining flame in blood.

Faith starts where strength ends, Anula. No one is above that law of the world. Not even you.

Anula hadn't known or dared to believe, but this...*faith* was more than she ever thought or imagined. She grasped that truth and the power behind it, and dove off the pyre, the Yakkas in tow. Kama kissed the man's cheek, and as they fled toward the Pleasure Gardens, he protected their backs, felling every soldier, strong enough to withstand the Polonnaruwans, just as he bargained.

"A world burning with love is good," Kama announced proudly.

Anula couldn't argue. She fisted her sari, picking it up to race the night. One hour was perhaps all they had now, all Reeri had, and from their placement in the inner city, it would take that long just to get to the Kattadiya pit. The image of him inside seized her chest. Not because of the tether, but because of the place he found in her heart.

But before they could reach the edge of the gardens, another cry rang out, followed by another, and another. This time not of soldiers, but women, children, husbands. The sound of their suffering became one, and Amma's cry echoed in their voice. Anula skidded to a halt and glanced back to see people still being caught, bound, killed. Their army was either dead or spread too thin across the courtyard, no one coming to their aid. Just as no one had come to Amma's, and no one to hers.

"Raejina Consort?" Bithul whispered. "We must move."

Digging nails into her palms, she bared her teeth up at the throne room's terrace, at another usurper standing watch as the people of Anuradhapura died.

"Mayhap I should do it again," Kama trilled in her ear. "Set a man on fire for love, take out those guards around him. You could claim your throne, without Reeri. Do you not long for it?"

"You cannot!" Calu hissed. "Look at the moon. Wessamony will descend soon."

Anula's nails broke flesh. Calu was right, Reeri needed her, *now*. But, *cursed blessings*, so did her people.

Every word, every promise, every direction Auntie Nirma had ever given scraped along Anula's arms. A mere four weeks ago, she would've taken the chance. She would have bitten back any fear, any doubt, would have gripped her necklace and charged. She would have placed the crown on her own head and sat on her new throne. But now…

The terror of her people pitched high, and Anula turned her back on the terrace. A spark flew from the courtyard to Anula, caught on the embers already glowing for Reeri, and flamed. "I won't leave them."

"O mighty Heavens," Calu spat. "We cannot save them and Reeri before Wessamony descends to kill us all."

"Yes, we can," she asserted. "If we think quickly."

Calu made a face at her, and an idea struck.

She grabbed his arm. "It's you. You have to use your power and unwind the soldiers' minds."

Calu shook her off. "Absolutely not. I will not break the taboo."

"If you do, we'll have a clear path to get everyone to safety and rescue Reeri before it's too late. I can't leave them here to die by a usurper's hand. Help me save them."

"No," he hissed. "Wessamony will punish me."

"He won't," she promised, sliding the Bone Blade from her sari. Its song sank into her bones, her heart, her soul. The rightness of her vow resonated deep. "I will protect you. No one will die by his hand again."

Saffron flickered in Calu's eyes, as if the song now sank into his shadow and lifted the fear from his soul. He glanced at the one remaining pyre and those fleeing for their lives. He sighed. "All right."

Anula squeezed his hand tight. "Thank you."

He rolled his shoulders and cracked his neck. "I can only unwind those whom I can see."

"That's all we need." Anula counted at least fifty men. Could he manage that many at once? Anula knocked the thought away, choosing to have faith in him instead.

"Be not afraid of your own power," Kama whispered.

Sohon added, "Ratti would be proud."

Calu's shoulders fell. The tension, too. With relief, he closed his eyes and deepened his breath. In and out, slow and steady. A breeze chilled the air, the soldiers took note and stilled, and for a moment, a hush fell over the courtyard.

Then the Polonnaruwan soldiers' eyes clouded over. Lips curled back, they turned on one another, feral as jungle cats. Sword met sword, spear met chest, teeth met flesh, and the courtiers were completely forgotten.

"Now!" Anula sprinted, the Yakkas and Bithul on her heels.

Soldiers fell around them. They swarmed out of houses and buildings and the concubine estate, only to be cut down by their own men. Anula plucked a bloodied sword from dead hands as she reached the final pyre, arced it back, and swung hard, cutting the rope. The Yakkas snuffed out the flames, creating a safe escape.

"Bless you," a woman cried, gripping Anula's hand as she helped her off the wood. "Bless you, my raejina consort."

"Where do we go?" a man asked. "Everything is destroyed."

"More soldiers will come!" Another panicked.

Bithul gathered what remained of his loyal guards, checking each of the ten to ensure they weren't fatally harmed. The last man, the one he'd trained with, was bloodied and beaten, but held out Bithul's cane, as if he'd fought solely for it. "Sir. What do we do?"

Taking it, Bithul clutched Shahan's hand. Then he lifted his gaze, and his men's eyes followed. "Anula?"

Thirty people faced her. Sweat-soaked and dirty, with none of her usual armor in place, Anula was exposed. No longer the raejina Auntie Nirma had cultivated, they saw her, the person she chose to be, with no crown and no title. What if they didn't want her?

She took a steadying breath. She was no usurper; they should have a choice. Stepping into the Pleasure Gardens, she said, "We save one more and find shelter, together."

Without waiting to see the choice everyone made, Anula walked into the Pleasure Gardens. The Yakkas flanked her, as the night darkened the grounds and the smoke from the pyres choked what little light the stars gave off. Her heart pounded. It was one thing to choose to follow a woman, a concubine, a wife; it was an entirely different thing to follow her into a dark unknown. They would have to trust her, believe in her, have faith in her. It wasn't until the turn for the cave entrance that she dared glance over her shoulder. Bithul and his guards, and thirty courtiers, were close behind.

She picked up her pace, gratefulness swelling, and without thinking, she whispered a prayer. One of thanks as much as hope.

She turned a corner—and slammed into a tree. "Ouch!"

"Anula?" a voice squeaked, and instead of the face of a tree, she saw Premala. The girl wrapped her in a tight hug. "Thank the Heavens."

"Premala, what are you doing?"

"Stay away from her!" Sohon stepped forward, wrenching them apart.

"W—wait!" Premala said. "The Yak—Reeri sent me."

"What? Where is he?" Anula demanded.

Premala wrung her hands. "In trouble. Do you have the relic?"

"Do you honestly believe I'd tell you if I did? Do I look like a—"

"Oh, shut your mouth for once!" Premala's voice rose above the smoke. It did not shake. "If you want to save Reeri, and the Heavens and Earth, and everyone else, bring the relic and come with me."

Anula snorted. "Are you telling me what to do, after nearly getting me killed?"

"Yes."

There was something different about her. The desperation was gone, as though she'd freed herself. Anula took note and raised a brow. "Where do we go?"

Premala glanced at the people behind her. "The tunnels. They'll be safest there while we fight." She spun on her heel. But before Anula could follow, she bent over in pain. A cry split her lips.

And Kama's.

And Sohon's.

And Calu's.

A piece of red mehendhi tore off each of their arms and shimmered into dust.

50

The netting and vines tore first.

Small heaps of powdered skin stacked at Reeri's feet, sizzling to nothing as blood drowned them. It was not until the elephant detached inch by inch that Reeri's heart began to stutter. When the last of his marking fell, their bargain would be null, making way for Wessamony to call upon his own: the one where the Yakkas met their final end and Reeri became their torturer.

And if Wessamony had the slightest hint that Anula carried the Bone Blade—if he heard it, if he saw—a crown would not be in her future. There would be no future at all.

Reeri lifted his head. "*Please.*"

Yet before the guruthuma or any of the Kattadiya could answer, the door to the amphitheater banged open.

Anula rushed in, soot-stained and a challenge forever set in her eyes. Without pause, she took the stairs two at a time, elbowing Kattadiya on her way. "Reeri!"

His name on her lips was a downpour in the midst of a drought.

She was alive. And she had come for him. Shadow and body

yearned to reach out of the pit, to brush her cheeks, to cup her face, to know that she was whole and hale and safe.

Yet she was not. Not while she was with him. "No," he murmured beneath broken flesh. "Go."

Anula ignored him, anger setting her jaw. "Cursed blessings, are you all right?"

"Restrain her!" the guruthuma commanded.

The Kattadiya did not move from the bottom tiers. More bodies had filled the amphitheater, men, women, and children, half-terrified and staring at the blood coating Reeri's body. Their own clothes were marred and torn, as if they had only just escaped torment. Yet three faces were missing from the crowd. Reeri swallowed. Mayhap they did not make it, or they were separated, or—

Kama flitted in first, Sohon right behind, and Calu brought up the rear. Relief drenched Reeri. Premala had listened. She believed. But as quickly as his heart had lifted, it sank. All whom he loved were in one room, easy targets for his Lord.

"Restrain her!" the guruthuma repeated, pointing to Anula a mere four stairs away. "She is dangerous!"

Not a muscle moved.

"What is she doing to him?" Bithul asked.

"Tearing apart his soul," Anula seethed.

"I am not the evil one here," the guruthuma snapped. "Kattadiya, restrain her! Get the Bone Blade! Do your duty!"

That whipped a few back in line. They reached for Anula—

"No!" a man shouted. "She saved us. She is no danger."

"It matters not what she has done now," the guruthuma growled. "She bargained with the Yakkas and brought them all back!"

The room caught its breath.

"Her rajas have been false. They have been mere masks worn

by the Blood Yakka, bent on watching Anuradhapura bleed to death. They let in the Polonnaruwa Kingdom—they let you be assaulted!"

"No!" Premala shouted.

But it was too late.

Betwixt the pit now soaked with the dying tether and the enemy kingdom's forces outside, the people of Anuradhapura saw only death. The stampede began. The guruthuma shouted for the relic, for Anula, but her voice was drowned by screaming.

Reeri's screaming.

The bindings on his hands caught fire and sizzled into ash.

Boom.

It was not a drum nor war cry that shook the earth and rattled loose the stones. It was Heavenly thunder.

"Reeri." A voice roared.

The elephant on Reeri's chest shivered, the last vestiges of the tether holding on tight. He lifted his gaze not into the face of the guruthuma, but into the face of his first tormentor.

His voice shook. "Yes, my Lord?"

51

A wind kicked up inside the amphitheater. It swept the skirts of the Kattadiya as they huddled closer together, bells and beads chiming. It whirled around the broken and bleeding, slamming closed the door to their only escape. The lock clicked in place.

The Maha Equinox had begun. Anula's heart skipped a beat.

Lord Wessamony was everything the stories of old described and more. Blue flames blazed up his twisted horns, sharp teeth were set in a snarl, and sharper nails dug into the hilt of the Great Sword—the one the stories said was pure gold, as long as three men stacked together, and blessed to do Wessamony's biding. It glowed, chasing shadows into tight corners.

The Lord of the Second Heavens snarled. Depthless eyes took in the people, the Kattadiya, and found them all lacking. The relic burned at Anula's hip. With a snap of his fingers, Reeri lifted out of the pit, flew into the air, and slammed against a wall. Kama, Calu, and Sohon followed, their two essence offerings falling from her grip to the ground, shattering the bowl. The Great Sword flashed out of Wessamony's hand and slid beneath the Yakkas' necks, trapping them against the stone wall. He stepped lightly toward them, a heart squelching apart beneath his feet. The Lord darkened. "Where be my Bone Blade?"

"My Lord," Reeri breathed. Anula didn't need to touch him to see the fear in his eyes or hear it shake his words. "We nearly—"

The sword pressed closer. Blood welled in a thin line along their throats. Anula flinched.

It was happening again. Her loved ones were being threatened. But the relic burned once more at her hip, a reminder that she was no longer that little girl. She swallowed the fear, imagining taking Reeri's, too, and stepped forward. "Murderer!"

"Anula," Reeri warned.

He should have known better. When had she ever heeded him before? She took another step toward the Lord of destruction. "Murderer."

Wessamony turned, flames flickering up his horns like the tail of an irritated jungle cat. "Ah, the one who offered a soul. Leave, child, else I take that offering to the grave."

His voice, at once booming and stern, also held the sounds of the cosmos, a tone that reverberated in her chest. It warned that he was not human, that he was not safe. Still, she clenched a fist and raised her chin. For Auntie Nirma. For Thaththa. For Amma.

For Anuradhapura.

"Why burn Eppawala? You had plenty of people willing to search for the relic before. You didn't have to kill the entire village," she accused.

"Anula, no," Reeri rasped, cutting his throat deeper on the blade.

Wessamony narrowed his eyes. "Who are you?"

"Did the cosmos deny you a heart and a memory?"

A whisper began behind her. Guruthuma Hashini quickly

prayed to her Divinities, one name after another spilling from her lips.

Wessamony frowned. Wind swept through the chamber like the wave of a monsoon, toppling the guruthuma over and scaring the Kattadiya into silence. "Why does the soul offering care for a village long ago destroyed?"

Trepidation chilled Anula's spine. Perhaps Reeri was right. Perhaps she shouldn't do this. She should throw him the relic and run. If she wasn't ready for a crown, she couldn't possibly be ready to set a Heavenly being to trial, force his confession, and mete out his punishment. She had no idea what the relic would do or whether Wessamony could fight back, let alone whether he would allow her to live long enough to hear his guilt.

But the sound of a door rattling, of her people desperately trying to escape another tyrant, pulled her from her doubts. She glanced at Bithul, forever at the ready behind her, and at Reeri, his promise to never leave her threatened.

The choice was simple. She had already made it, for the dead and for all those still living and yet to live. "I care because Eppawala and all her people were mine."

"You survived." A wicked smile spread, sharp teeth glinting in the Great Sword's light. "Yet you offer your soul. What a waste."

"Nothing is wasted when you seek your dreams, and I have long dreamed of this moment. Why kill all those innocents? You searched for the relic before, with only the seeker's death."

His horns burned blue. "Do not dare to think you know my ways."

"Then tell me."

"A bargain is a bargain. You know that full well. The seeker wanted to destroy the Polonnaruwans."

She narrowed her eyes. "The village didn't have to die to do that."

Wessamony laughed darkly. "Violence takes whomever it wishes. Have you not noticed how it waits beneath the surface of all men? A mere whisper of fear and they turn feral. Anuradhapura feared Polonnaruwa, how their lives would change if their laws and faiths and families were taken from them. Kill before killed, is it not the balance of nature? All I did was strike a bargain and utter a whisper. Men did the rest, as they always do."

Anula clenched a fist. Like Prophet Ayaan, he didn't lie, but he wasn't absolved either. Wessamony had been designed to destroy, yet he acted not out of balance, merely out of willful, sadistic, selfish choice.

"All that, and you still didn't find the relic," Anula pressed. "Was it worth it?"

A smirk grew. "Nothing is wasted when you seek your dreams." He towered over her. One sharp nail lifted the edge of her necklace. "Is that not right, Raejina of Poisons?"

Anula's chest rose and fell quickly. She didn't dare blink. Wouldn't give him the satisfaction.

"It is beautiful, is it not, man's undying hatred for one another? Their unquenchable thirst for dominance? They are the reason the Bone Blade is hidden so well."

The relic burned under Anula's sari. This was it, her moment of vengeance, justice for the cosmos. He was so near—she only had to take it out and slash it across his being. As Fate had done to Destiny. Her fingers wrapped around the hilt, and with a deep breath, she returned Wessamony's wicked smile. "I think you mean *was.*"

Thrusting it between them, heavensong erupted in the amphitheater, a multitude of voices in chorus. A collective gasp echoed on the stairs. It nearly caught Anula's breath.

"You found it," Wessamony hissed, horns glowing brightest blue.

"Let the Yakkas go."

"Hand me the blade," Wessamony said, reaching, "and your bargain shall be complete. You have done well, seeker."

"Let the Yakkas go," she repeated. "All of them."

"Anula," Reeri rasped another warning.

"He will not heed you," Kama said.

"Use it," Sohon quavered.

"What about the other Yakkas? Your essence—"

"Too late!"

Wessamony's flames flared. "Hand it to me now, soul offering, else all those in this room shall perish in a bloodshed more terrifying than your village's."

Anula shifted, placing herself between the murderous Lord and her people, including the Kattadiya.

"I am the Lord of the Second Heavens. You shall obey me!"

Anula raised her chin. "I am Anula of Anuradhapura. I obey no one."

Lips curling over long, sharp teeth, Wessamony growled, "Then you will be their demise."

A sharp-nailed finger pointed behind her.

Anula whirled to find Wessamony's target.

Hashini startled, twisted quickly, and wrenched a girl in front of her.

"Sandani!" Premala grabbed hold of her hand, flung her backward, and took her place. Right in front of the guruthuma.

The snap of fingers came first.

Then everything went white and silent and still. Only a deep anger stirred inside Anula. It burned, rising like heat in a room, until a hatred so red rumbled in her chest. She sneered at the face in front of her, disgusted with their vileness, their presence, their mere existence. They were not worthy of being there; they were not worthy of life. The kingdom shouldn't have to bear the burden that was *them*. Anula wouldn't allow it. She picked up a rock and swung, slamming it into their head, again, again, again—

A laugh boomed.

The world returned.

And beneath Anula's final blow, Premala's skull shattered.

"No." Anula's voice broke. Premala slumped into the pit.

Anula's stomach lurched. What had she done? What had happened? Acid burned up her throat. It was as though her thoughts had been poisoned against Premala and her will bent to a dark force… Anula dropped the stone, a chill racking her bones, vomit filling her mouth.

"You shall have one chance more." Wessamony smirked. "Hand over the relic, or kill all you care for."

She choked back bile—red sky, red hands, red—

"Anula!" Reeri's voice ripped her back. Cursed blessings, how were they to survive this?

Wessamony's fingers came together.

"No!" she shouted, fisted the relic, and ran away.

Wessamony laughed again. "You think you can escape me? Fine, let us play. Mayhap after your people have turned on you, you will no longer wish to save them." He pointed to a group of people on the stairs in front of her. "Bring me the Bone Blade."

Snap.

Kattadiya and refugees stiffened. Their eyes clouded over, white as cow's milk. Their heads cracked in her direction, and silently, they lunged. Hands latched on to the hem of Anula's sari and the clasp of her necklace; they hooked around her legs and thighs, twisted in her hair. They yanked and threw her backward. She slammed into a jagged rock, and the blade flew out of her grip.

It clattered onto Hashini's foot. She smiled, lifting it to the cave ceiling.

52

The Bone Blade bellowed its Heavenly melody.

"Great Divinity of Fate"—Hashini stretched her arm high, as if reaching into the First Heavens—"hear the call of your relic, return and claim what is rightfully yours, protect us from those who wish to use it."

Bright white light, purer than any Anula had seen, illuminated the amphitheater. Its warmth flashed across her skin. And as its song crescendoed, a fish as large and wide as an elephant burst through the air.

The Makara. The sea dragon.

Stories of old spoke of its existence, of how it lurked along the seashore, hungering for flesh and thirsting for fear. It was a tale told to children, to keep them far from the water's edge. It had worked on Anula. No one wished to be eaten by a fish. But if the Makara was real and lived so far away, how and why had Hashini summoned it?

Orange and pink scales glinted in the light of the Great Sword as it circled, as its blessed depiction had in the bathing pool—the first gift Anula had witnessed. Yet here there was no water, no shore to hunt upon. The Makara flicked its tail and funneled down, erupting in orange light before Wessamony. A Divine form emerged, neither male nor female, but both. Stars twinkled in their eyes.

A knowing skittered up Anula's arms. This was Fate.

"We meet again," they said to the Lord, voice melodic and skin sparkling, as if still made of scales.

Wessamony chuckled low. "The Heavens should have killed you when they had the chance."

"My thoughts precisely."

With a snap of Wessamony's fingers, stones surged from the pit and soared at Fate. They reached out a glistening hand and dissolved them to dust.

"Yes!" Hashini hissed, watching her precious Divinity.

Fate clapped their hands and ripped chunks out of the walls, crashing them against Wessamony. He snapped and they disintegrated. They fought on, as if only the two of them existed. Anula glanced at Hashini, the Bone Blade clutched in her fist, her eyes on Fate. There couldn't be a better distraction, for her or Wessamony.

A hand landed on Anula's shoulder and picked her up off the ground. She groaned, clutching her side. "Hurry. We must find a way out." Bithul angled her toward the stairs, aiming for the door where his guards worked at the edges, scraping off bits of stone and digging swords into crevices.

"No." She pushed away. "We have to kill Wessamony."

"I don't think you'll be able to get between them."

Another crash sounded, the floor shaking as the First and Second Heavens dueled. The amphitheater, which had once felt large enough to swallow half the palace courtyard, now felt tight, small, contained. A cage, for either her or Wessamony.

"We have to try. It's our only chance."

A crack whistled by them, and Bithul suddenly cried out. He stumbled, taking Anula down with him as the sound came near again.

Sharpened stones kissed Bithul's heels. Hashini growled, "You will not escape punishment for bringing back the Yakkas." She let loose another stone, and Anula jumped. "Nor for aiding and abetting the one who wishes to destroy us all."

The stone caught Bithul on the ankle and ripped across scarred skin. He howled. "Go! I'll hold her off."

Anula flinched and dodged again. In one hand Hashini picked stones from the edge of the pit; in the other, she held tight to the Bone Blade. "She has the relic."

"Do you know how to use it?"

"The sharp end goes into his chest?"

Another stone hit its mark. Bithul hissed. Hashini snarled and arched back again, as if her pile of rocks would only end when her target died. Bithul adjusted his stance. "I'll distract her. When I lunge, she'll have no choice but to drop either her weapon or the blade, and I have a feeling she'll not let herself be weaponless. Grab the blade and use it as quickly as you can."

Golden light flashed, stealing Anula's concentration. The Great Sword had shifted, reflecting the light thrown by Fate's scales as they spun around Wessamony. As the beam passed her eyes, she fell rigid. Blood was trickling down Reeri's throat, the cut deepening as the sword pressed closer.

Her heart skipped a beat. What if she was wrong? If the blade didn't kill Wessamony when she sank it into his chest, what would happen to Reeri? Would he find another body or be taken to Heavenly court, never to be seen again? Or worse, would he be forced to become the monster he feared, to torture his Yakkas for eternity?

No. That wouldn't happen. She had promised.

"I have to save Reeri first."

"What?" Bithul grunted, sweat beading on his forehead. "You can't stop a blessed sword."

Anula met his gaze. "I have to try."

"You know he cannot do this—only a human can. Is he what's most important right now?"

Another stone soared. He winced and rolled away. Anula ducked. The answer to Bithul's question sparked on her tongue. *Yes.*

Life was always most important. Even a Yakka's.

Especially Reeri's.

Because he cared.

And so did she.

Anula scrambled, leaping over broken stone and tearing to the other side of the pit. At the same time, Bithul's men cascaded around him, Shahan brandishing his sword at Hashini until she fled, hiding behind a wall of white-eyed people fighting one another.

"Save them," Bithul commanded. "They don't know what they're doing!"

Trading swords for fists and fabric torn from their clothes, Bithul and the guards separated and bound those under Wessamony's curse.

Anula pressed on, using the chance he bought her to finally close the distance to Reeri. His fear welled, not for himself but for her. An itch started at her fingertips. An urge that wasn't from the tether. It was stronger. With every step it grew, the yearning to touch him, hold his hand, cup his face, tear the sword from his neck, and kiss the wound better.

"Anula!" he shouted and winced.

A sharp pain nicked across Anula's back. She stumbled, turning. Eyes wide and full of anger, Guruthuma Hashini hefted a discarded sword.

"As I said"—she readied to strike again—"I care not who you are, Anula. You will not be the demise of us all."

She slashed, and Anula shifted, the tip of the blade barely missing her chest.

"Like you were the demise of Premala."

The words cut Anula's heart, sharp as any blade. "No. I—I didn't—"

"Am I mistaken, or is that her blood on your hand?" Hashini thrashed again and missed.

The blood burned on Anula's skin, evidence of her fault, but she hadn't meant to. Not Premala, the girl who'd made her desire friendship, not allyship. Her control had been stolen, her mind poisoned by—Anula stilled.

"Premala died because of *you*," she said, dodging another strike. "You threw Sandani in front of you. You were willing to sacrifice another to save yourself! Premala wasn't."

"I did no such thing," Hashini yelled, catching the edge of Anula's shoulder. "Faith has no place for selfish power."

"No," Anula said, grabbing a jagged stone, readying for the next blow. "But this was never about faith."

Seething, Hashini lunged. Anula let her, feinting to one side as she had seen Bithul do in training. She spun around Hashini, unclasped her necklace, and wrapped it about the guruthuma's neck. Pulling tight, gold bit flesh, and she slammed the stone into the sapphires.

Every vial shattered. Shards cut into Hashini's throat, tinctures and poisons seeping out fast. The remedies diluted one another. The poisons did not.

"I don't care who you are, Hashini," Anula said, for Uncle Manoj's journal always said these things were best served with something. Truth, perhaps, this time. "I will not allow your faith to poison any more of my people."

The woman fell, mouth wide in a gargled scream, the sword clattering to the floor. The whites of her eyes flared; the veins in her neck popped. Her skin turned purple, and redness burned the corners of her lips, consuming the puckered pink until they were ripped raw and festering with pustules. They spread and grew fast, covering mouth and nose and eyes. Until Hashini choked for air, blind and helpless, crumpling to the ground.

The relic clanged and rolled away, skittering into the midst of the fray.

53

REERI HELD HIS BREATH, DARED NOT TO SWALLOW AGAINST THE cold, sharp iron, lest the Great Sword took one more bite out of his neck, ended the life he possessed and sent him far from Anula.

At least she was safe, with the guruthuma disarmed and dying, yet the relic—

For the thousandth time, Wessamony snapped his fingers, blue flame scorching his twisted horns. A smile curled on his lips as he sensed his power, gathered it up, and poured it out on the remaining humans. Any who were not already safely bound stiffened, eyes clouding, lips pulling back, the violence of nature taking hold. All the while, the sound of sharpened iron skittered across stone.

They kicked the relic away as they raced toward Fate. The Divinity turned and lifted a hand, creating another pit betwixt them. Without hesitation, Wessamony's army fell inside. He snarled. Fate wasted no time, arcing their arm up and out. A bolt of lightning careened toward the dark Lord.

"Enough of this!" Wessamony boomed, baring his teeth and flicking his wrist.

The Golden Sword flew on the Lord's command. Reeri finally let out his breath, and the Yakkas crashed to the floor. Throat leaking, he watched as the sword rushed before Wessamony, the lightning striking the sharp gold and bouncing off, exploding instead into the wall. Rock rolled down, pulverizing the stairs and striking more than one person.

Reeri's heart skipped a beat. Was it *his* person? A plume of dust filled the room. He squinted and coughed, the dust stinging his wound, strangling his sight as he searched for Anula. Fate flicked their tail, breaking the cloud apart, and there, he caught her eyes.

Anula paused, and for a moment, it was just them. The cacophony of battle disappeared into a mere vibration. Only relief echoed at each other's safety, and desire sang. To touch, to hold, to run away. It caught in her lungs and stole his breath. O Heavens, if he could live in this moment for all eternity. If only—yet they both knew that if they wanted that chance, a future and a life, they must get the relic.

Anula's lips thinned, and she nodded before tearing her gaze away. She pivoted, scrambling to find the blade. The maelstrom crashed around Reeri, centering him back in the fight, his goal now refocused. He wanted that chance, and he would not let it slip by. A glint on the west wall caught his eye. Heavenslight. He moved before he thought.

Jostled in the fray, he fell, knocking loose a rock. It spun into the Bone Blade and sent it twirling over the edge of the new pit. Reeri reached out, the wound on his neck tearing—

And caught the relic as he tumbled into the hole with it. More crevasse than pit, jagged rocks cut as he crashed through, and his head bounced as he landed, his sight blackening. But he clutched the relic tight, heart beating swift. Not for fear of dying, but of dying now, leaving this body with the Bone Blade and having to find one within the cave not cursed by Wessamony's power. For if he did not act now, all would be forfeit. His brethren, his soul, Anula.

Sight clearing, he tried to stand and find purchase on the walls, but hands clawed at him, dragging him down and away, clamoring for the relic. Teeth snatched his elbows, tore at his neck, his arms, his face. They would end him, those cursed with Wessamony's power. He tried to fight them off, but they were too many. Panic rose like bile up his throat.

Until new hands grasped him tight, pulled him up instead of down, and heaved him out of the pit. Reeri gasped as Kama and Calu gently set him on the ground.

"Are you all right?" Calu asked, wiping at the blood masking Reeri's face.

"The blade." Kama's eyes widened. "You found it."

Reeri white-knuckled the ivory blade—the thing that would sever his binding to Wessamony—sever his brethren's, too. Mayhap it would be enough, offering a Lord's soul in exchange for every single Yakka. He had to at least try. He had to know he had done all he could to bring them back to life.

"Where is he?" Reeri growled.

"You cannot take him on now, not when he is at the height of his power," Calu said. "Even Fate has not stopped him."

"I have what Fate lacks." Reeri spat out blood, standing shakily. "A reason to kill him."

Kama clapped her hands. "Love. Is its fiery passion not beautiful?"

Before he could think to answer, Wessamony snapped again. Reeri jerked in his direction. The Great Sword dove after Fate. It nicked them twice before they swirled back into Makara form and flew up to the ceiling, momentarily leaving Wessamony alone.

Reeri's chance bloomed.

He gripped the Bone Blade tighter and rushed his tormentor without pause. "Anula! Now!"

Reeri did not need to look to know she would be there, for this was their plan, their fight, their freedom. She would not abandon her people, as surely as she had refused to abandon him.

But Reeri's movement caught Wessamony's eye. Twisted horns flamed bright. A sneer pulled his lips. "Was this your grand scheme all along, to be rid of me, like Destiny?"

"It was a good enough scheme to be yours for the First Heavens," Reeri accused.

Wessamony scoffed. "For the First Heavens, yes. Yet I am not a product of the First Heavens, and neither are you. Have you given any thought as to what may happen when I die? When Destiny met their end, I and the other Divinities lived, for I was not made by Destiny's hand nor connected to their existence. Yet all their blessings, all their gifts, all their creations ended. Would that not mean the same for the Second Heavens?" A wicked smile crept over his face. "Shall not my creations meet their end when I do, too? The cosmos has always demanded balance, Reeri."

Dread dripped down Reeri's spine and chilled his shadow. *No. It cannot be true.*

"Has your time in the aether taught you nothing? Obey me, or face final death."

Reeri glanced to his brethren, hard lipped and fuming. Fear etched on every tense muscle. It had become the thing that defined them. The thing that they had become.

Reeri would let it be no longer.

"My time on Earth has taught me one thing." He raised the Bone Blade. "You are not the Lord of the Second Heavens, but the Lord of Lies."

Wessamony boomed a laugh. "Then why hesitate, Blood Yakka? If I am lying, then you shall be free of me—free to live a life you always dreamed of: a human life."

Reeri paused. It was not that he desired to be human; he

desired communion. To be with his family. To be with the ones he loved. To be loved in return.

"You hesitate because you worry I speak true. You fear losing the chance to live. You fear never tasting your dream." Wessamony's voice grew cold. "As well you should. I lie not, Reeri. Yet hand me the relic and I shall allow you to atone. I shall give you one more chance to live again."

Reeri's heart beat swiftly. He glanced at his Yakkas and Anula closing the distance. He could not be the death of his brethren. And he could not leave her. There was so much he wanted her to know, so much to say.

Yet.

He could not allow Wessamony to destroy the cosmos or wreak havoc on any more lives.

"Do it," Calu shouted.

"We may all meet final death." Reeri said, the words thick and heavy.

"It is better than being tortured for eternity," Sohon said.

"We shall all be free," Kama sang. "Together, each and every one of us."

The words rippled through his shadow. All he desired, he had this entire time. And he always would.

They knew not what final death meant, whether it be nonexistence or transcendence outside of the Heavens. The cosmos had never said. But whatever it was, mayhap it was the same for humans and one day, when she passed, Anula would be there, too.

"Do you wish to take them all to their graves?" Wessamony growled. "This, too, shall be entirely your fault."

"My only fault," Reeri shouted, "was ever listening to you."

Reeri gripped the Bone Blade and lunged.

54

Final death.

The words rang in Anula's head, above the cacophony of the Kattadiya and the soldiers, of those under Wessamony's curse and those fleeing from them, above the swishing of the sword as it tried to catch the tail of what had once been a great Divinity. They bit at the mehendhi elephant on her palm and sank their teeth on the last remaining piece of her markings.

No. She skidded to a halt. Though she knew she'd chosen who she wanted to be, how she wanted to act, she hadn't realized she'd chosen something else, too. *Someone* else. And if he met final death…

Her heart squeezed.

"Anula." A voice blew past. Not Reeri's or Bithul's or any of the Yakkas'.

"Anula." It called again, loud and then soft. As if it were there and then far away. As if it were circling above. Anula looked up through the haze. The golden eyes of the Makara challenged her. "Act."

Her shoulders tensed. Reeri was still arguing with Wessamony, but if she closed the distance, if she placed her hand atop Reeri's and the dagger—he'd be gone.

The Makara flashed into Divine form and descended to the floor. The Great Sword dove. Fate lifted a boulder, and the sword rang out as it embedded, the rock a scabbard it couldn't escape. They tossed it aside. "I grant you permission to use my Bone Blade, Anula."

"I can't—I—" The words stuck.

"Do not let fear cloud your vision or sour your heart. Only you can fan the flames of the dream you hold inside."

The boulder erupted into shards as the Great Sword broke through. Fate fled, the ends of their long braid caught by its tip. The dust cleared as they swept away, and Anula saw him. Eyes full of longing and a question burning bright, Reeri stared at her. He pressed the Bone Blade, and his life, against the planes of Wessamony's chest. He paused there, for the same reason Anula's heart had skipped a beat.

Final death.

And as his brow tightened, she realized what Reeri was asking, what he was saying. This time, it wasn't only him who had a decision. This time, he wanted her to have a choice, too.

If Anula were any other girl, she might have told him to wait, to stay, but she wasn't. They had both dreamed of this; they had both chosen this. And in a perfect world, they would have chosen each other, too. The truth of it echoed in her heart, swelled bright in her soul, and mirrored in Reeri's eyes. She didn't need to touch him to see.

But the kingdom was far from perfect; only they could give it the chance to be perfect for others. Still. Reeri was giving them both a gift: the freedom of choice.

Heart heavy and threatening to rupture, she shouted, "Reeri!"

"Anula!" he called back.

Her name on his lips ached all the way down. Yet she mustered a smirk. "Do you want to talk about it?"

A sob broke Reeri's frame. The pinch between his brows faded. "I lov—"

Wessamony reached out, one clawed hand on Reeri's throat and the other on the blade.

Anula didn't think. She charged.

55

Sharp nails dug into Reeri's throat.

Two twisting horns glowed blue, as Wessamony's other hand tore past flesh and met bone.

Reeri gritted his teeth. His declaration lost on his lips as bloody sores pulsed up his back and along his arms. Pure destruction once more festering, taking hold, claiming the body that held him. Yet Reeri did not cry out, did not back down. This was freedom for all, chosen together. For as Kama had once said, he burned with a power mightier than any sword. He burned for love.

Taking a deep breath, Reeri gathered the might of Darubhatika and his shadow, then thrust his right hand through Wessamony's claws, ripping sinew and vein. A roar, feral as a lion and fierce as an elephant, rang out. Yet it was not his alone. A hand curled over his shattered skin. Anula gave him a nod, ferocity shining, and together they plunged Fate's Bone Blade into Wessamony's chest.

Fissures splintered across his form, heavenslight erupting from within. Heavensong crooned, reverberating in crescendo, shaking loose the walls, the stairs, the ceiling, until a seam ripped open the air and a dark hole swirled above them.

A cry broke Wessamony apart. His horns untwisted, his claws cracked in two, and as his grip fell loose, so too did Reeri's fetter. A weight lifted from his shoulders. A load liberated from his mind. An easy breath filled his lungs, and he heard his brethren sigh.

This was freedom.

Lovelier than they had dreamed.

Yet short-lived. For the tether yanked taut. It pulled and pushed and flayed apart, as if a rug undone, thread by thread. Reeri bent; a scream bubbled on his lips. Dread coiled around his throat as he saw Anula bend, too, retching. Red mehendhi ripped away and melted into the stone floor.

Mighty Heavens. She could not face final death, too. "Anula!"

Heavensong keening, Reeri stumbled.

Sohon fell, disappearing into a puddle of blood and bone.

Kama next.

Then Calu.

The world tilted and spun. Reeri collapsed to his knees, a name trapped on his lips and tangled in his heart. Skin slunk off, dripped and poured. Until four shadows wrenched into the air and followed their light-splintered Lord through the dark seam, careening into the cosmos.

The cosmos was rent asunder.

Stars flared and burst.

Aether stretched and shrank.

Red, yellow, green, blue light flashed and swirled.

There must always be balance.

Had that not been the one rule of the cosmos? The one

warning, the one constant? Had Reeri not been told what it meant?

True balance is an unending connection. A circle with no beginning and no end. All exists together, at the same time. For if one hole punctures a water tank, will not the entire thing drain?

Reeri had not merely punctured a hole. He had ripped a side off entirely.

The darkness swallowed Wessamony's screams. Spat them out and mimicked them. As they careened over stars and earth and court, things seen and things not, things that existed beyond, his body tore apart. Piece by piece. Until not even dust remained.

The cosmos spun and swirled and cast his soul into the sun, where it sizzled as if a leaf to fire. Yet still, the Yakkas flew on.

The Heavens lay split in two. A quake rumbled beneath them. A crack spread and quickly climbed the pearl-encrusted gates. Gilt stairs crumbled. The lake boiled, and waves crashed over domes and turrets, minarets and spires. For the cosmos was roaring, and out of its mouth spewed a fount, disintegrating all. Divinities dropped from their sphere, twisted and torn apart.

One. Two. Three hundred.

The gates fell and fragmented. The court collapsed and cratered.

The Yakkas flew out of nothingness. Shadows turned to fissures, leaking soul and stardust. The clan spun anew, into darkness so black that the stars were swallowed whole.

No. Reeri's heart ached as they twisted farther away, swirled and stretched, spun and snapped. *Stay.*

Ratti. Calu. Kama. Sohon.

Please.

A crack ruptured his chest.
Sank deep in his soul.
Silenced his heart.

There must always be balance.

56

Anula's heart stuttered.

Where the red mehendhi marking had once flowed intricately across her arms, where it had once flayed and torn and streamed with her blood, it now receded. Fading to brown and amber, it disappeared into open wounds.

No sting, no pain. As though it were mere ink.

Her lip trembled.

The Great Sword clattered to the floor and blinked out of existence. Wind blew out of the black seam that had swallowed the Yakkas and their lord, kicking up Anula's hair and sari, jangling her earrings and bangles. It drowned the cries of those waking from Wessamony's curse, stifled the sound of stone walls shaking apart, and swallowed the screams that opened the mouths of guards and ministers.

A thin finger of darkness curled out of the seam, slithering through the room like a snake in the brush, and plucked Bithul up by his heels. It tipped him over, stripped him of leathers and weapons, picked at the wounds Hashini had etched on his ankles, and flayed them open until only blood and bone whirled on the wind.

"Keep going." Fate's voice boomed as they landed before her.

Anula startled. The finger of darkness stretched around the room, unmaking victim after victim. But she had already acted. What more could she do?

A simple bone blade—Prophet Ayaan's voice surfaced—*imbued with Fate's power, able to cut off the Hand of Death.*

Cursed blessings.

The stories of old told of a time when the people of Anuradhapura had turned on one another. A time when they'd protected themselves instead of their village, when the idea of immortality had become tangible. Anula had witnessed a version of it in the first blessed painting she had experienced. How could she have forgotten? The relic hadn't been made to kill Heavenly beings. It had been forged for humanity. To cut the Hand of Death.

The Hand that held Bithul.

That had taken Reeri.

Kama. Calu. Sohon.

Anula gripped the relic tight and prayed, for the first time, with true faith. "Great Divinity of Fate, hear my prayer. Allow me to cut off the Hand of Death and save the lives stolen tonight!"

The blade warmed beneath her hand. Winds ceased. Sounds silenced. And the bodies left in the amphitheater paused, immobile.

Only Fate and Anula seemed able to move. Slowly stepping to Anula's side, the cosmos sparkling in their eyes, Fate said, "Let us begin."

The rocks stirred first, lifting into the air and fitting back into the walls and ceiling and stairs, like a peg to a hole. Dirt dissolved, the air cleared, and like stars winking alive in the falling night, they came—men, women, and children burst into the room the exact way they had left. Courtiers, Kattadiya, and, finally, Bithul.

Upside-down and motionless, flesh and blood knit themselves back together. Anula stared at the white specter standing at his side. A chill swept through her bones.

It was not a shadow, not the dark wisps of Reeri's banished form, nor was it bright and shining, a star or a sun. Its form pulsed to no drumbeat. Its color everything and nothing and one. A smile broke on one side, with no teeth or fangs gleaming. There was only a hole where a mouth should be, black as night, and from it emerged a pristine bone from which fingers, long and thin and innumerable, grew. They stretched until they touched Bithul's ankles.

"Is that…?" Anula couldn't find the words.

"Death." Fate found them instead. "Death and its Hand."

Anula's fingers flew to her throat, only to slip against bare skin. A shiver racked her spine.

"It will not linger long," Fate said, "afore it moves to the next."

It was a command, as much as a warning.

Tightening her hold on the Bone Blade, Anula stepped forward, only to find her feet never touched the ground. Her soles lilted on the air, her sari softly swirling, a hushed song catching the edge. Heavensong. It filled her, invigorated her, and the relic began to glow. Anula squared her shoulders. As she closed the distance between her and Death, its light grew tenfold.

A sizzle sounded. Smoke twirled on bone-white fingertips. Death's Hand flinched and drew away from her and the pure light she carried, away from the blessing.

"Now!" Fate urged.

Anula raised the blade high and brought it down quick.

The Bone Blade, made not of ivory but bones sacrificed willingly, cut through the Hand of Death like a knife through a mango. Swift and clean.

One by one, the fingers fell.

The mangled hand curled back.

Bithul flipped right side up, body unmarred and intact. He slowly blinked awake.

The white specter winked out, only to appear by another's side, new fingers finding their next victim.

"Go." Fate nodded.

Anula followed the specter. Cut once, twice. Every time Death moved, its Hand regrew and reached for another. But Anula moved, too, persistent in her purpose. Fingers fell, eroded, turned to dust and ash. People flickered slowly back to life. Minister, maid, concubine, Kattadiya. It didn't matter; Anula worked for them all.

When the last human was rescued, the seam grew darker, screeched along with the heavensong, and out it spat the Yakkas.

Kama. Calu. Sohon.

Reeri.

Anula's heart quivered.

The hole in Death's form widened into a lopsided grin. The Hand flew out and multiplied. Not its fingers, as it had before, but another hand grew from the first, another set of fingers reaching. And another. And another. Death aimed for all four Yakkas at once.

Anula's breath stalled. She couldn't cut them all at the same time. One bone stretched to Reeri's chest, lit the contours of his shadow, writhing as though locked in a cage of flame. Another cut across the room to catch Kama under her chin. Anula glanced at the relic and back at the specter, panic setting her hand and heart tremoring. Nothing in the stories of old spoke of this. She looked to Fate, but the Divinity was quiet.

Was she supposed to choose who to save? Would she be able to turn back time again, save another Yakka, over and over until they were all safe? If not, how was she to cut them all at once?

Then it dawned on her: She wasn't. She couldn't. Because she was *looking*, not *seeing*. If she shifted her perspective, there was more to the specter than fingers and hands. And therein lay the answer.

Anula spun, arced the blade and cut through not the Hand but the Wrist of Death.

One, two, three hundred fingers fell at once. The black hole receded into a small circle, a silent scream on Death's lips, rage strobing like a dying star.

Bang!

The seam imploded; darkness and light funneled fast, sucking the Yakkas back—Kama, Calu, Sohon.

"No!" Anula grasped Reeri's arm, but she slipped right through.

Tall and sharp and devastatingly handsome, Reeri's shadow blinked.

Saffron eyes caught her. Held her.

And disappeared into the cosmos.

"Wait!" Anula raced after, only for Fate to lock her in their arms. She struggled against them. "Let me go."

"You cannot follow."

"Watch me." She lunged out of their grasp, reaching for the swirling seam. Her hand disappeared into the darkness, scraping her skin.

Fate yanked her back. Anula's hand pulsed back into existence, throbbing as if she'd stuck it in fire. "If you follow, you shall not return. Blade or no."

Anula stilled. The knowing settled deep, and an emptiness echoed, where once there had been a tether. Cold air prickled her arms, where once there had been a marking. "Will they return?"

"All shall be revealed when time remains. Have you finished, or are there more to save?"

Anula glared. Had she saved the Yakkas or not? "I'm not saving Wessamony."

"I never said that you must."

"Then who?" Anula glanced at the Bone Blade, at the seam, at Fate. Hope sparked. "How far back can I go?"

Two Kattadiya had died, torn apart by each other's nails while under Wessamony's curse. Anula cut the Hand of Death for each of them.

Once the silent, unmoving battle between cursed and uncursed was finished, and every life brought back, Anula's gaze landed on Hashini, half dead. She didn't stop.

Instead, she made her way to the first pit, now the only pit, as the room had pieced itself back together. A slight young woman lifted out, her head stitching back together, beautiful tresses framing a delicate face. The specter of Death appeared, Hand outstretched. Anula lifted the Bone Blade and attacked. Premala's eyes flickered to life, and Anula pulled her into a tight embrace.

It was complete. The entire cave was restored.

Only the Yakkas were missing.

Sandani took her place, holding Premala as Anula flipped the blade over in her hand, the song's chorus unbroken. What she could do for the kingdom with this relic. Who she could save…

"Will it work only in here?"

Fate smiled, sad and knowing. "You cannot go back that far."

Anula ignored the pity. "I can't or the relic can't?"

"There is much the cosmos may do and much it may hold. We know not its limits." Fate turned to the seam's swirling mixture.

Anula bristled at another nonanswer but peered within, too. The colors circled faster, deepened and darkened, lightened and spread. The lines of a face emerged. Then a second. And a third.

Anula's breath caught.

Thaththa, Amma, and Auntie Nirma gazed back, backlit and sparkling with stardust.

"A gift," Fate said, "from the cosmos."

Anula's vision blurred. "Can I pull them out?"

"No." Fate gently took Anula's hands and placed them an inch from the seam's edge. "Though they be gone, their touch reaches far."

Her family stretched their hands across the dark expanse, broke through the lip of the seam, and wrapped around hers. It was like a kiss, spreading warmth from the soles of her feet to the tip of her head, and suddenly, she felt it. Good-night kisses and cold-morning cuddles, races along paddy fields, laughter at sunset and dancing under stars, bedtime stories and dreaming out loud… *Home* cracked her open.

Tears caught on her lashes. They streamed down her family's faces.

There was so much she wanted to say. How they were forever on her mind, how her heart stung when the sun rose and they were not there, how it ached when it set. How she woke in the night and cried until there was nothing left. How she would give anything for them to stay.

"I love you," she whispered.

Their tears glistened as they squeezed her tighter. A tingling welling from fingertip to toe. Thawing and melting her heart.

We love you, too. Anula didn't need to hear the words to feel them, to know them, for their peace to settle over her, a gentle hug that never let go.

And then they were gone.

The seam closed with a wink, and Fate gently pulled her back. "It is complete."

57

EVERYONE MOVED AT ONCE, BLINKING AS IF WAKING FROM A nightmare.

The amphitheater looked as if it were newly carved, the stone tiers sparkling in the torches' flames. Only the people were caked in dirt and sweat, smelling sharp as an onion.

"What happened?" a woman at the edge of the pit asked. Her eyes crossed in confusion, taking in the room, the people, and the three men beside her. Horror-struck, the woman who'd once held Kama checked on her son and husband, the adviser's family rousing from their deep sleep.

Bithul rushed to her side. "It's all right. You are safe now."

"No," said the last man Reeri had inhabited. He touched his bare chest. "Something is missing."

His proclamation echoed in the cavern of Anula's heart, reverberated off the empty space where once there had been a tether. She had no sense of how far away the Yakkas were or if they were in danger. She couldn't even tell if they were alive.

"Did I save them?" Anula asked Fate, pulse quickening. If

Reeri didn't make it, if cutting the Hand of Death hadn't worked... She grasped Fate's arm. "Why didn't the Divinities use the relic to revive Destiny?"

Fate eyed her with the vastness of a thousand stars.

A chill slid down her spine. "Does the relic not work that way on Heavenly beings?" It had been created by humans, intended to be used on humans. Perhaps—

"There is much unknown of the cosmos."

Anula bristled. "That's why I'm asking you."

"The cosmos is constantly changing," Fate said, looking out and far away, as though they could see it all unfolding. "It has changed again, made anew."

Anula fingered her empty collarbone and whispered, "Are they alive?"

Fate turned instead to Premala. "The change, too, is in you. It is in all of us."

Anula tracked Premala's steps, how she and Sandani held each other tight. Anula didn't need a tether to feel the promise made. Premala pulled the acolyte's chin close and pressed her kiss firmly.

It pinched at Anula. She knew she wasn't going to be given an answer but that she'd have to find it, somehow, someday. And she would. Reeri might have said it first, but she refused to leave him, too.

"I'm sorry," she said. "For killing you."

Premala laughed, as if she hadn't died and returned. "I'm sorry I nearly killed you, too."

"Please." A voice rasped. Anula's head snapped up. Coiled around herself in a corner, Hashini held on to the last shred of life. Poison ate at her lips, as it surely did at her heart. She reached out to her acolytes. "Help."

No one moved. Actions spoke louder than words and hers had sacrificed one of them. To her, they were replaceable, their lives meaningless and sisterhood a farce. She didn't deserve the Kattadiya.

Anula stepped between Hashini and Premala, but the young woman grabbed her arm. Hands entwined, she and Sandani strode forward.

"Please," Hashini murmured again.

"I'm sorry," Premala said, stern and steady, "but my guruthuma taught me that Kattadiya do not act for themselves, only for the protection of others."

What was left of Hashini's lips quivered, until she choked. Purple veins turned into a purple face as the poison stole her last breath. Premala turned away, her doe eyes meeting Anula's. Not wide with fear, but knowing. Seeing. "Thank you."

Anula raised a brow. "What are friends for?"

This time, she didn't squeak.

"What do we do now?" Bithul asked, eyeing the amphitheater's now-open door and darkness beyond.

Everyone else eyed Anula.

Even Fate. A smirk played on their lips, puckered like a fish, and Anula briefly wondered if the Makara had existed first or if Fate had, if one had always been both, or if banishment had melded them together.

"Yes," the fallen Divinity said. "Will you act again?"

"As my curves would suggest, I am not the raja," Anula said, tugging at her sari, brushing away the image of the last one's face. "I hold no power. Without a husband, I'm not even a consort. Besides, there's a foreign prince on the throne, and you said I couldn't go back any further."

"Action must not always initiate from the same place. You need not the Bone Blade. You have far greater powers at your disposal." Fate nodded to all gathered. "There is a hand of death hovering over your kingdom. Will you not stop the usurper and save your people? Is that not the path you chose long ago?"

Anula narrowed her eyes. "I would ask how you knew, but it seems you're not particularly fond of answers."

Fate's braid flicked like the tail of a fish. "Revelations are more useful than answers."

Anula snorted, but Bithul caught her eye. She knew his question without him asking.

Despite herself, Reeri's shadow face flashed in her mind. The ache echoed hollowly. A great chasm into which she could easily fall, as she had once before. Clenching a fist, she drew herself back. She wouldn't fall again, but she would survive again. Her path was not laid out before her, but chosen. The answer was as simple as it was difficult: she'd search for Reeri, for years if she must, but right now, it was the lives of those in her kingdom that were most important.

Less than a hundred were safely in the caves. They could flee, but to where, another kingdom? That still left the majority of her people behind. If she were the raejina, if Auntie Nirma's plan had unfolded without a hitch and she held the throne, she would fight back. End the Age of Usurpers and finish the war with Polonnaruwa once and for all.

But it hadn't. She didn't.

Besides… "We aren't a large enough army here to win against them."

"Anuradhapura has never had a large army." Bithul grunted. "Yet we have still prevailed."

"How?" Premala asked.

Again, Anula's fingers flashed to her throat. To the space where vials of tinctures and poisons had once hung. "Usurpers prize physical prowess, but we need only to be intelligent enough to use that against them."

"What do you have in mind?" Bithul asked.

Anula shook her head. "We would need a way back into the palace without being seen, which we don't have."

A collective sigh gripped the room.

"I do." Clearing his throat, Prophet Revantha emerged from the back, round-faced and unwrinkled, holding aloft his pendant of gold and rubies.

"The key," Fate lilted. "You have guarded it well these past centuries."

Prophet Revantha took the stairs. "Yes, my great Divinity. The order has kept their task well. It has been passed down to every prophet, as instructed."

"Mind sharing why with the rest of us?" Anula asked.

"Of course, my apologies. The pendant unlocks the doors inside the blessed paintings, the ones the Divinities closed after so many people lost their way in the cosmos when venturing to walk between them."

"The stories of old were true," Bithul breathed.

Half-true, Anula corrected silently.

"But if you unlock the doors for us to pass between paintings, what will stop us from being lost now?"

"He's the prophet," Premala said. "You can lead us through, can't you?"

Prophet Revantha rubbed his neck. "It is true that I see the cosmos when I meditate—it's what we are taught and why we're chosen as acolytes. Yet, despite years of trial, none have been able to map it. The cosmos is vast and ever-changing. Even the prophets are warned against walking."

Anula shut her eyes. Perhaps it was too dangerous for all of them to go through, but perhaps not for one. After all, it was she who knew where the ingredients were hidden in the raja's chamber, she who knew how to mix and serve. Perhaps only she must take the risk and act.

"I will lead you through," Fate said. Anula blanched.

"Then it's settled." Bithul clapped his hands. "We take back the throne, take back our kingdom."

Sandani tugged on Premala's arm. "The Kattadiya will be needed, to help those injured."

"But we have no guruthuma."

Sandani leveled a gaze.

Premala squeaked. "Me?"

"You saved me at the expense of yourself." Sandani turned to the others. "What more could we want from a guruthuma?"

"But..."

"Guruthuma Premala," one Kattadiya said. Then another, and another.

"Kattadiya do not act for themselves," Sandani quoted. "Only for the protection of others. You are a true Kattadiya. A true guruthuma."

Flushed, Premala's hands twitched, her lips slid between her teeth—but instead of the wringing and biting, she squared her shoulders and took a breath. "Thank you for choosing me, for always accepting me, even when I couldn't. I will always choose you, too, along with our people, the way Guruthuma Thilini taught." She turned to Anula. "We're with you, Raejina Consort."

Anula scoffed. "First of all, friends refer to each other by first names. Second, I am no longer a consort." She ignored the squeeze that brought to her heart.

"No," Premala agreed. "You're going to be the first raejina."

"No," Anula snapped. She rubbed her eyes, then softened her voice. "I don't want it."

"A wise leader knows when to share the brunt of a burden,"

Fate said. "I never said you must act alone, Anula. Share your vision and your dream."

"But you said only I can accomplish my dreams."

"Only you can spark the flame of your dreams, yet it takes a village to see them through."

The words settled warmly on Anula's arms, like a blanket on the coolest nights. And yet an itch bloomed. At her wrists first, then all the way up her neck. She was Anula of Anuradhapura. This was her kingdom. These were her people.

And that was important.

"I want to help," she said. "But I won't be another usurper. That Age ends now. A new Age begins."

"Then go as a soldier," Bithul said. "Fight for your kingdom, as I will."

The guards exchanged glances, moved to flank their trainer. In unison, they said, "As we will."

The Kattadiya picked up the anthem, Premala the loudest, and with all the people free from capture cantillating last, an army amassed. It lifted Anula, buoyed her soul, and she remembered who she wanted to be, who she wanted to be that person for, and what she could do.

An army needed weapons.

Her weapons.

Anula nodded, turning to Fate. "Let's begin."

58

The tunnels curved endlessly as Premala lead the patchwork army to the one and only blessed painting owned by the Kattadiya. She stopped in front of an old wooden door etched with stars. Why it was hidden away, Anula could only guess.

"So you're a thief after all," she said, thinking back to when she'd suspected the girl of sneaking into the concubine estate to pilfer.

"No!" Premala waved her off. "This painting was gifted to us, not the kingdom. We would never."

"It was only a jest."

"You're not as funny as you think."

"And you're not as timid."

Her entire body flushed. "Good. A guruthuma shouldn't be."

A throat cleared. Bithul looked pointedly at the door. "We haven't much time."

Premala nodded, placed a hand on the wood, and pushed. Flickering candlelight illuminated the tiny office, casting shadows on the pillows and one low table, where papers filled with drawings were spread—drawings of Hashini and other women, perhaps other past guruthumas. Hanging above it was a large canvas in which a young woman stood in the center of a dark cave, a lone fire revealing the absence of tunnels. Her eyes were closed, her chin tilted up to the Divinity of Luck touching her between the eyes, heavenslight sparking where finger and forehead met.

"Thilini," Anula breathed.

"Yes," Premala agreed, awestruck. Each of the Kattadiya touched their heads, in reverence or remembrance, before Premala bowed to Fate. "After you, Your Greatness."

Fate wasted no time with explanations. They strode forward, placed their hand on the canvas, and stepped through. The rest followed, one by one.

A soft breeze played with the tendrils of Anula's curls. The heat of the fire warmed her cheeks, and as she walked across the expanse toward the end of the canvas, she caught a glimmer in Thilini's eye. The first guruthuma's lips spread in a smile as she dipped her head in greeting. As though she knew, even then, that they would one day meet. Anula nodded back, and for once, the unknowing nature of the cosmos didn't feel unstable but pliable, filled with unending possibilities.

"We need a plan for when we arrive," Bithul said, pulling her back to the moment.

Anula refocused. If they did this right, she'd have her whole life to explore that thought. "Take your men to the inner city. Stop them as best you can. I'll try to work quickly."

"What about us?" Premala asked.

"Save the people. Put out the fires. Do whatever you can to disrupt Polonnaruwa's destruction."

"What work are you trying to do quickly?" Bithul asked, though the purse of his lips and crease in his brow told her that he knew exactly what she had planned. With or without a necklace.

"I have a bone to pick with the prince," Anula said, his image surfacing. Though no sky turned red, her vision shimmered with it, her eyes wide open.

"Perhaps I should accompany you."

A wave of tension crashed from behind them. Anula flicked a glance at the guards listening in, at their terse faces and the need in their gazes.

"A commander should be with his men, don't you think?" she asked.

Bithul turned. His men caught his eye and held him firm. Surprised, a flush sizzled up his neck. They didn't need to say the words. Bithul had always been their choice. He nodded curtly in acceptance, standing taller. It wasn't until Fate had led them outside of the fire's flickering flames and into the dark corners of the painting that Bithul spoke again.

"Are you all right, without knowing their…fate?" His voice was low, soft. It pinched at Anula.

"As all right as a pig being swallowed headfirst by a rock python, but I can't dwell on it. I did what I could, and now I'll do it again for others." The words rang true in her heart, echoed in the empty cavern of her soul. This was what she must do. After, she could search for him, as a seeker to a relic. If that's what she chose. Her path wasn't marked out by the Divinities or anyone else. She was free to decide, free to choose what was most important. The way the Yakkas had been in their last moments. The way Anuradhapura was about to be.

But she already knew that's exactly what she would do. She chose him.

"Fate was right." Bithul regarded her. "You are changed."

A smile lifted her lips. It didn't reach her eyes, but one day, perhaps it would. Only the cosmos knew.

"Pardon me, my raeji—my—um, commander." Shahan pushed

through, stumbled in front of them, and saluted. "I was thinking of our strategy. If we split off in more than one contingent, we widen our reach, but that lowers the number of fighters in each. I'm not sure such small groups can accomplish much of anything."

"The size doesn't always matter." Bithul shook his head.

Anula scoffed. "I know an estate full of concubines that will tell you differently."

"For prayer's sake!" Premala swatted at her. "We're in a blessed painting. Clearly you haven't changed that much."

Anula smirked as darkness suddenly consumed them, the black-and-gray veneer of the cave walls ending their walk. Fate nodded to Prophet Revantha. Hurriedly, the young man stepped forth, swiped a hand across the false wall, as if brushing away dust, yet instead of smearing the paint, the color completely vanished. A round silver lock appeared.

The prophet lifted the pendant from around his neck and pressed it into the lock's grooves. The rubies snicked into place. He turned it to the left until it clicked. He spun it quickly to the right and back to the left. A ticking sounded, and a network of iron rose up along the length of the painting, spindly round pieces twirling, connecting, and interlocking, until they disappeared into the blackened sky.

Light outlined a door. The prophet bowed to Fate and returned to his position. The banished Divinity regarded the small army. "Stay close, keep your hands to yourself, and follow only me."

They opened the door, and all stepped through.

The cosmos didn't feel like any surface she had treaded on. Not marble or stone or fur or grass.

Anula half expected to fall and catch, like entering a painting. But under her feet, the cosmos felt like the cool waves of a bathing pool if her soles never touched the floor.

As they glided through the everything and nothing, stars blinked, there and gone. Colors stretched in a rainbow swirled above and below, and it rolled in the far-off distance like the hills leading to the Mihintale and Ritigala Mountains.

A whistle sounded to the right. Every head craned to see, as if a Divinity might call down to them. But it was only a boy, waving enthusiastically.

"Come this way!" he called. "You can reach Galnewa." He pointed behind him, where the darkness of the cosmos was suddenly streaked green and blue and brown. The image of a paddy field coming into view.

"Galnewa?" a man behind Anula asked. "That's my home!" He glanced at her, at Fate, then stepped out of line. "I'm sorry, but I must know my family is safe."

"No," Fate said, but the man ran to the boy, and as their hands entwined, the painting winked out. And so did they.

A chill shivered down Anula's back. "Where'd he go?"

"Wherever the cosmos wants to take him," Fate said.

"How comforting."

"You don't know?" Premala asked, swiveling to her Kattadiya, counting silently.

"Why should I?" Fate countered. "Am I the cosmos?"

A terse silence passed down the line, each person tucking their hands at their sides.

"Are the lost ever found?" Bithul asked, as though Fate would answer.

"If the Heavens and Earth know not their location," they said, "yet the cosmos does, are they truly lost?"

"Do *they* know where they are?" Anula asked.

"Is the knowing so important, if it be good?"

"*Is* it good?" she pressed.

"Why would it not be? It created all." Fate turned, cutting off the conversation and continuing through the cosmos.

It was not only a boy whose form the cosmos took, calling out or speaking to them. Animals of every shape and size did, too. Cats rubbed against their legs. A school of fish followed them. Plants grew and died and grew again beneath their feet. A sense of awe and warning in every caress. A challenge to trust, to surrender. A promise to take them far away, to be good, in its own way.

Anula's fingers twitched. Perhaps a flower or a whale or a tree could take her to Reeri, or at least tell her of his end. The line paused, and she stared at the pink nelum growing around her ankle. Perhaps if she asked nicely, she could say goodbye to him, too. If the cosmos was truly good, it would want that for her, wouldn't it?

Bending her knees, Anula reached down, but a flash of color stopped her. It was a painting and the blurred edges of a wall. Though she couldn't see the entire room in which it was hung, it was clear enough to know that it was inside a stupa. Two more paintings appeared by its side, looking in on other rooms.

"Our walk ends." Fate regarded them once more. "Who goes first?"

Together they decided on Premala and her Kattadiya.

The women emerged into a half burning stupa, linking arms and escaping before it crumpled to dust and ash. Offerings became mere memories. They raced to the center of the city, the clank of the water tank beckoning them forth.

Next went Bithul and his men, out of a painting of war-seasoned commanders, only to land in the halls of the administration building with strangled ministers at their feet. They sneaked to the doors and burst into the inner city. Three contingents parsed off, Bithul's heading for the palace stairs.

Last, Anula stepped from the painting, fingers plugging her ears as the contents of the blessed gift climaxed.

Fate had smirked when she gave Anula the signal that it was her turn. Apparently, the portrait of Raja Mahakuli Mahatissa's harem was the only one available. She hadn't dared search the faces to find her own from last year. She wasn't that girl anymore.

Anula landed in a ransacked bedchamber—the raja's ransacked bedchamber. A voice broke around a song, not inside her head but within her bones. Anula shivered, stepping lightly over the glass and stone littering the floor. Vases and mirrors lay shattered, pillows and divans and paintings shredded.

Usurpers didn't tend to plunder their newly acquired palaces, unless they didn't intend to rule from there, or they planned to burn it and rebuild—or just burn it to send a message. Anula's skin crawled.

"Help!" A cry sounded.

Anula bolted toward it, thinking of maids and servants and guards who might have been caught in the middle of the chaos. She flung sheets in the air and found not a maid but a gift.

"Cursed blessings."

"Help!" the blessed gift raejina cried. The headboard was cracked in two. A chasm of air hung between the raejina's and raja's outstretched hands, unable to breach the edge of the wood.

The image sank in Anula's heart, filling the space of her soul. "Hold on."

She pushed the two pieces as closely together as she could. It would have to be enough for now. She was there for a different purpose. Anula swept a hand under the bed, grabbed the hidden treasure beneath, and flipped Uncle Manoj's journal to the final page. The one where he'd scrawled, *Skin-to-skin contact without self-poisoning?*

The recipe was quick and easy, the delivery merely a sultry

surprise. It didn't matter that she no longer had her necklace. There was no need for a remedy.

Dark clouds roiled over the palace, heat sticking Anula's sari to every curve of her body as she flew through the halls. Past room after room, doors unhinged, and gifts stolen or shattered. Flames flickered in the windows, her eyes latching to each as she passed, hope lodged in her throat.

The flood came first, soaking the ground with water from the irrigation reservoirs, the waves rising from soldiers' feet to ankles, and drowned out the flames. The banners of Polonnaruwa dropped next. Soldiers fell in great numbers, as a swell of guards and ministers and concubines and wives gathered in fight. Bithul was in the last window, climbing the palace stairs. His sword aimed for a man in a feathered helmet, like the one Commander Dilshan used to wear. But Bithul was not stealthy; the Polonnaruwan commander watched his advance, settled on the higher ground, and arced his own sword. Bithul ducked, rolled across the lower stair, and swiped at the commander's ankles.

With a scream, he plunged to his knees, then his hands. Bithul stood and swung once more, ending his command.

Pride swelled within Anula. They were doing it. They were ending the Age of Usurpers, taking back what was theirs, and declaring a new start, a new Age, a new beginning, together. She skidded to a halt in front of a set of carved wooden doors inset with silver and brass ornamentation. Now it was her turn.

For poison could stop many hearts.

But Anula yearned for just one.

59

Two carved lions faced her, mouths open in warning.

Do you dare? they seemed to ask.

Anula straightened her sari, realigned her bent gold head chain, her one bell-drop earring, what was left of her bangles.

Yes, she answered, then stepped inside the throne room.

Ten swords flew to her throat. The Polonnaruwan guards were tense and bloodthirsty, hunting dogs waiting for the signal to let loose.

"Down boys," Anula said. "I'm only a woman."

They took her in, shoulders relaxing, suspicion clearing. Indeed, she spoke the truth.

The prince rushed in from the terrace, fuming. "What is happening? Where did the water come from?"

"Perhaps the entire kingdom is cursed," Anula offered.

The prince's eyes snapped up. "*You*. Why are you still alive?"

A throat cleared unsteadily. The dogs were wary of their failed kill.

"My curse must have saved me."

"That's not how curses work."

"Are you sure?"

The prince spat. "Take her out."

"Before you command them to kill me again"—Anula raised a brow—"might I have a chance to be redeemed?"

A grimace lifted his lip. "Why would I allow that?"

Anula shifted, popping out a hip and pressing her shoulder blades tight. The prince watched her curves. "I was trained by the concubines. I could begin a new harem for you. A fresh set of Anuradhapura Jewels. You'd be the only one of your father's sons to own one."

He licked his lips, thirst rising as high as the irrigation tank tides. Anula ran a hand down her thigh. For although poison could be tasteless, it was always sweeter with seduction.

The prince waved his guards out the door. "One chance. Convince me that you aren't scraps fallen from the raja's tables, and we shall see if you deserve a future."

Anula lifted a hand, brushed her fingers through the prince's hair, and as the doors clicked closed, her other hand flashed up.

A knife glinted, right at the base of the prince's neck. He growled a laugh. "I heard the women here were bitc—"

"Careful," Anula warned. "I could kill you."

"No." He smiled. "You couldn't. I saw the knife in your hand all along."

"So why let your guards go?"

His smile curled, dark and dangerous. "My soldiers aren't the only ones having fun."

The prince snatched Anula's wrist, twisting it to the side. She let out a yelp, and the knife clattered to the floor. A hand clutched her neck, and the prince drove her back, slamming her into a wall. He leaned closed and breathed her in, nose tracing the length of her collarbone.

"You are no Jewel, but an imitation," he whispered, squeezing her throat tight. "One to be broken and discarded."

His other hand plummeted into her skirt.

"No," Anula choked.

"You have no choice." He smiled wider, crushing her throat tighter.

"I always," she croaked, "have a choice."

She grabbed each side of his face, pulled him close, and pressed a long kiss to his lips. He hardened against her and then—seized. He wrenched back, hands dropping from her neck and body, and clutched his chest before crumpling to the ground. Blood ran in rivulets from his eyes. Purple and blue veins popped. White crests frothed at his mouth, as if he were the ocean. Each wave a convulsion, the tide bringing his heart to racing and yanking back, stealing breath and pulse and life.

Anula wiped the coating off her lips.

There were so many ways to stop a heart.

This was, by far, Anula's favorite.

60

A HEAD FLEW OVER THE TERRACE RAILING.

It knocked down the last of the Polonnaruwan banners and landed with a splash at the base of the palace stairs, floating alongside its commander.

"Anuradhapura belongs to no man!" Anula shouted from the terrace.

Bithul and his guards took up the chant, as did the Kattadiya, and every man, woman, and child gathered in the palace courtyard.

A crack of thunder shook the ground. Not from the Heavens, but the sky. Roiling gray clouds raced across the city, and down poured the first Maha season monsoon.

61

THE SOFT PATTER OF RAIN CARRIED ON THE MONSOON WIND. IT drowned the fires and refilled the irrigation reservoirs. It breezed through the terrace doors, tousling Anula's curls. She hunched in the corner of the throne room, the place least destroyed, as survivors clustered inside. Eyes closed, she took a deep breath.

Anuradhapura was safe.

For once, no names marched through her mind. There was no longer a mantra, no longer a promise. She had fulfilled it. A new age had come, and her people were safe. They had done it together, Heavens and Earth. Her shoulders sagged with a long sigh. They had all answered Anuradhapura's cry for help—her cry—even when it had been silent.

A throat cleared, and Anula's eyes snapped open. Commander Bithul and Shahan met her in the corner. If she were a betting woman, she'd put all the raja's money on the younger one becoming first general. She was about to say so when Premala and Fate closed the small circle. It surprised Anula that no one else recognized the Divinity, that none from the Kattadiya caves mentioned they were here. Perhaps it was more difficult to see the Heavens on Earth than it was to imagine them far away.

Anula stood, a lightness to her shoulders despite the aching bones. "What will you do now?"

Fate raised their brows. "I shall return."

"To your place in the First Heavens?" Bithul asked, forever starry-eyed and faithful.

"Why should I do that?" Fate frowned. "I left for a reason."

"You mean you were cast out," Premala said, more question than statement.

Fate leveled a heavy gaze. "Do not listen to all you hear."

Anula cocked her head. "Does that mean Wessamony didn't convince you to use your power on Destiny?"

"I chose to leave, as I chose to hide the Bone Blade, so that none of the corrupted power spreading through the Heavens could touch me or you. So they could not destroy one another again."

The light in Bithul's eyes wavered. "But the stories of old—"

"Are only half-truths," Anula breathed, echoing Reeri's favored phrase. Bithul met her gaze.

"Anula." Fate called her to attention. "However you act next, know that a blood oath is owed."

"To you?" She glanced at her bare arms.

"To the Divinities," they corrected. "Now that your bargain with the Blood Yakka has ended, your oath belongs to them."

Anula's eyes flicked to Premala, the new guruthuma. Premala stretched out an arm and squeezed a promise into her hand. They turned to ask the Divinity more, yet Fate had vanished. Before she could react, Anula was shoved to the side. The crowd ruffled and squawked, growing loud. Two men suddenly threw fists.

"Stop!" Bithul commanded, his voice rising above the noise. Shahan rushed forward, splitting the men apart.

"Why is everyone squawking like bulbuls?" Anula snapped, walking into the center of the hall, the crush separating for her.

"Who's the raja?" the larger of the men spat, pulling from Shahan's grip.

"What?"

"We are without a ruler," the other man said. "We need a raja."

"Perhaps there is a son of one of the rajas past." A woman spoke out.

"Of course there are," an older one scoffed. "But they are bastards now. Their lineage stopped mattering when their fathers failed to keep the crown."

An argument lifted across the room. Villager and minister quarreled over bloodlines and feats of strength. The Age of Usurpers had always favored physical prowess, but that Age had ended, a new one begun. They couldn't act as they had before, or else nothing would change. It was time the people's lives mattered. It was time their voices were heard.

Anula stepped onto the dais. "We should choose. A man shouldn't be able to claim the throne because he won a battle. Didn't we just do that? Then we should choose our ruler. *All of us.* Together."

Surprise cleared the crowd's anger, dissolving the argument.

Anula grasped at her chance. "Each of us will have a voice. Consider who you'd want to rule—"

"I choose you." A voice boomed. The crowd turned. Bithul stood straight and unblinking, looking at Anula. "I choose you to take the throne."

"Me too!" Premala said.

Sandani smiled. "I stand behind Anula, too."

The crowd stilled. Wind blew through the room, kicking up sarongs and saris and the words of guards, villagers, Kattadiya, and ministers as they each raised their voice.

For her.

Anula shook her head. "I am no raja."

"No," Shahan agreed. He glanced at his commander, then back up to her. He stepped toward the dais and kneeled. "You are Anula of Anuradhapura. You bled *for* the kingdom, instead of bleeding it dry. We choose you."

The rustling of clothes came first; then knees bent and every head bowed.

Only Bithul stood, unwavering, forever faithful. "Do you accept, Raejina?"

62

THE COSMOS BURST INTO EXISTENCE.

Again.

The Heavens spread wide. Pearl-encrusted gates rose high from the center of glistening waters. Yet, where once there had been gilt stairs disappearing into another realm, where turrets and spires stretched to breach them, there lay two ivory structures. One on each end. One held the purveyors of unconditional blessing, the other of contractual obligation. For it was not balance if all favor came freely, nor if all aid came with a price.

And after centuries of tilted, soured, broken balance, the cosmos had righted itself once more.

Within the pearl gates stood a gilt door, unlocked and unbarred, through which the First and Second Heavens emerged. They pooled across the lake, Divinities to the right and Yakkas to the left. Not their shadows, but their true forms. Pure and hale and whole.

Reeri blinked, and there were his hands, long and slender. His heart fluttered.

His.

Fingers flew to his face, traced the square jaw, the rounded nose, and wide, full lips. They tracked the length of his neck, down his bare brown chest. No markings, no scars, no bulging muscles built for battle. It was all him. *He* was all *him*.

A snort broke free, and he could not tell if he was laughing or crying. Mayhap both. It did not matter. He closed his eyes, lashes brushing cheekbones for the first time in two centuries. He had missed the tickle. Yet not nearly as much as he had missed his brethren, his family. He paused. For so long, fear had kept him at bay, yet now…

Heart beating so swift he was sure he would fly across the lake, Reeri took a deep breath and faced the Yakkas. He lifted his lashes and took in their measure of him.

It was not filled with derision or blame. Nor hatred or shame.

Only one thing shone bright.

"Reeri." Ratti's voice cracked. She slammed him into a tight hug.

A sob broke him, flooded him, cleansed him.

Ratti laughed and wiped away his tears, as she had done for centuries, as he had dared not hope of her doing again. It was better than any dream.

"My little brothers," she cooed, pulling Calu to their side, wiping his tears as they fell like monsoon rain.

Reeri looked up, no longer in fear but expectation. Kama, Sohon, Baddracali, Anjenam Dewi, Wewulun, Bodrima, Gopolu, Bhooto Sanni, Morottoo, Bahirawa, the Riddhi, and a hundred more. As one, they rushed him.

Held him.

Loved him.

The pearl gates cleared again, the door yawning wide, allowing true communion in the Heavens for the first time. Yet not all had changed.

The Great Sword flew on the shimmering air, clean and sharp and gleaming in its own glory. It hung above the Yakkas, not in threat but in Heavenly patience, waiting.

"You have reset the cosmos to true balance," a Divinity said, starlight dancing in their depthless eyes. "Yet a Lord of the Second Heavens it still demands. There must always be balance."

The Yakkas stilled, staring up at the hovering sword. Not one reached out.

"We wanted only freedom," Reeri said.

"There must be one Lord," the Divinity said. "For though the foundations of the cosmos can only re-equilibrate, the rules in the Heavens may bend and reshape. Is a new Lord not then necessary, to choose such new decrees wisely?"

It was what Wessamony had wanted, for the cosmos to rise from its ashes, fresh clay for him to manipulate. Yet he had also wanted to be rid of his fetter.

"Do not fear. The cosmos has equalized communion between the two Heavens, so too with Earth."

"The new Lord can return to Earth?"

"For a *balanced* amount of time."

Reeri lost his breath. His eyes flashed to the sword dangling above him, a whisper of want in his ear.

"Do it," Kama cooed. "Take the Great Sword and be our Lord. Choose decrees that protect us and delight in our gifts. Go to Earth as you please and race the setting sun to the beach."

Reeri's hands twitched.

"She can run with you."

His mouth dried.

"Do it."

The memory of a whip in his hand surfaced. "No, I—"

"It is what *we* want," Ratti said. "Lead us into freedom."

"Take hold of your dream, Reeri," Kama cawed. "Together, we make it come true."

The whip fell away, melting on a fading memory. He was not Wessamony. And as long as he existed, there would be no violence in this court. Reeri lifted his hand and curled his fingers around the glorious Great Sword's hilt. Heavensong swam across the lake, sparking heavenslight and a loud cheer from all Heavenly beings.

"True balance has been long awaited," the Divinity said. "Do not sour it again."

"I will not," Reeri promised, voice booming and golden, hand vibrating with the power of the sword. The power of a Lord. "Life is too precious."

The Divinity smiled. "What shall be done first with the newfound freedom?"

Reeri turned to his brethren, his heart beating swift.

His.

Reeri nearly choked. "Live."

ANULA TOUCHED THE EMPTY PLACE AT HER THROAT AND glanced in the gilt mirror.

Tendrils of jasmine laced their way past the blood-and-grime-soaked sari discarded on the floor and wove into her long tresses. The scent of smoke leached out. The anxiety did not.

Breathing deep, she wrapped her robe tighter and hunched over a bowl of water, sinking a cloth inside. With the inner city half-burnt, there'd be no cleansing ceremony in the Kuttam Pokuna bathhouse with oils and prayers. Mercifully. It wasn't as though masking herself with perfumes would help her rule. She wrung out the water and began to scrub, her gaze fixed on her face in the mirror, not on the lack of mehendhi.

"You are going to take a layer of flesh off, if you continue like that," a voice said behind her.

"A new skin for a new Age," she scoffed, until the knowing spiked her senses. That voice—she'd heard it before. She dropped the cloth.

"I expected something less macabre for your first act as raejina."

Anula spun. Before her stood not a specter nor a ghost nor a shadow.

Sharp chin and sharp jaw. A long, rounded nose. Wide, full lips. Thick, luscious lashes and heavy brows curtaining—

Saffron eyes.

Her heart sped as she took him in. His midnight hair, his bronze skin.

His. His. His.

Shadow made flesh.

"How?" she whispered. "I thought you were dead."

"I was," Reeri said, saffron ablaze. "You saved us. The cosmos was reborn, the Heavens rebalanced. It is the same and yet new, all it was ever meant to be."

Anula's heart squeezed. "And your Yakkas?"

A smile lifted the side of his face. It was vibrant. "Free. Alive. The new Lord has granted them permission to descend when they are called to Earth through a bargain. No tethering necessary. No human possession required."

Hope flickered. "You can come whenever I call?"

"The Yakkas can, yet the Lord is bound by the balance of the cosmos."

She held her breath. "And who is the Lord?"

Reeri's smile slipped. "You may call me 'Lord Reeri, the Blood Yakka, of the Second Heavens.'"

Anula's hands numbed. "Then is this it?"

"No," he said quickly. "Unless you wish it be."

"No," Anula nearly shouted.

Light returned to his saffron eyes. "Then this is not the end." He shifted, suddenly nervous and awkward, clearing his throat and glancing at her through long lashes. "The Lord's fetter rebalanced as well. I may return once a year, during the Maha season."

Anula's heart skipped a beat. She stepped closer, the scent of cinnamon and rainwater wafting over her. "The whole season?"

He nodded.

"You can stay with me half the year?"

"If you wish."

The answer rose quickly, but she paused. This shouldn't be a choice all her own. She bit her lip. "And what do you wish?"

Reeri let out a heavy sigh, as though a dam finally breaking and the water released. "I wish to stay, Anula. I wish to stay by your side until your dying breath and every day into eternity."

The words crashed into her, set her heart free. She leaped into him. He caught her with strong arms and squeezed tight. Anula's fingers curled against his spine as she buried her face into his shoulder. His nose trailed up her neck, breathing her in. Every sense narrowed to his touch. She never wanted him to let go.

"I love you," she whispered into his ear.

"I loved you before I knew what love was," Reeri replied.

The words soaked through her and watered her soul. She kissed his neck and then his cheek, his jaw, his chin, his nose. And finally, she pressed her lips to Reeri's. Warm and soft and gentle.

"Everything a kiss was meant to be," he breathed against her.

"No," Anula purred. "It's so much more." She pressed harder into him, thirst swelling. They stumbled into the table, knocking the bowl and drenching her robe.

Reeri lifted her by her roundness, carried her across the chamber, and dropped her on the bed. She couldn't kiss him fast enough, hard enough, to keep up with the need roaring within her. He growled softly and tore the sash from her robe. It spilled open, baring her naked body. Reeri gazed upon her, hunger flashing in his saffron eyes.

A tremor rippled along his arms. "You are beautiful."

Heat grew at her core. He dipped his head, making a trail

of kisses on her neck, her collarbone, sending a sizzle across her breasts as he licked and nipped. She moaned as her nipples hardened beneath his tongue, groaned as he suckled. Warmth pooled between her legs.

He traced her curves and the arc of her hips. Gooseflesh prickled, her body trembling. His tongue flicked out, licking her from nipple to navel, tasting every inch. She dragged her hands through his silken hair. A groan quivered his lips. He breathed her name as he made his way down one thigh, lifting her leg onto his shoulder and spreading her wide. She trembled with anticipation, but he paused, his mouth finding hers again. Gentler this time.

Anula groaned, and he pressed a finger between her legs. She ground against him, begging him to go harder, faster, and when it still wasn't enough, she grabbed his hardness.

Reeri shuddered. "Are you sure?"

She pulled his hand from her legs and sucked his wet fingers. A growl vibrated his body. He spread her wide, and his head slipped below her hips. With deliberate slowness, he kissed her opening and blew a cool breath.

Anula whimpered. Once, twice, until she was pleading.

And then he gave her what she desired.

His tongue sent a shiver along her spine, igniting the heat at her core. He moved first in circles, tempting and teasing. The sensation tingled over her body, washing her with want and need and a kindling drenched in oil. He flicked and licked rhythmically, ripening her bud.

"Yes," she moaned.

The heat built within her, her toes curling with every circle, her hips grinding with the music he played on her folds. Faster he moved, stroking and nipping. Anula arched up, thrashing under his spell, until she was begging to be set on fire, praying to be taken completely, cursing at the stars watching from above, until finally, she broke like a monsoon cloud, pouring out.

"Cursed," she breathed when the deluge ended. "Yakkas."

"Yes?" Reeri reappeared, kissing the inside of her legs and then her torso, making his way to her lips, the scent of her on his mouth.

"Now is not the time for jests," she said, chest heaving.

He chuckled, a languid smile softening sharp features, entirely satisfied with himself. "What is it time for, then?"

Anula wrapped her legs around his waist and flipped over, straddling him. She bent forward and pressed a kiss to his neck, then his jaw, following it with her tongue.

"Wait," Reeri breathed. He brushed the spray of her hair to one side, cupped her seat, and slid her back to the bed. He wrapped her in his arms and whispered, "We have our entire lives to explore each other; mayhap we save something for tomorrow."

Anula pouted, her lips swollen, above and below. But he had a point. There was no rush, and she intended to explore every inch of him. She settled into his chest, memorizing its planes and the prickle of his hair, the way his arms made her feel safe, the way he smelled like home, and the way the fire within her burned steadily, satisfied and wanting simultaneously.

She would kiss him every hour of the day, touch him twice as often, just as she had dreamed.

They held each other for hours, or minutes, Anula didn't know which, nor did she care. Reeri ran his fingers through her hair, humming a tune in the language of the cosmos.

"You will be radiant in a crown," he said.

Anula's eyes flashed open. Her ease guttered.

Reeri paused, noticing the change. "I believe I promised you one, or do you not wish to complete our bargain?"

Anula swallowed, her gaze flashing to the raja—raejina's—crown. Spikes of moonstones and rows of rubies glimmered threateningly. "Fate said ours was gone. That I owe an oath to the Divinities now."

"Yes, that is true. Yet as long as I exist, I will keep my promises to you, Anula."

Fear twisted up her spine, quick as a viper and just as deadly.

"Do you want the crown?"

"No. Yes." Anula groaned and buried her face in a pillow.

A gentle hand rested on her back, rubbing soft circles across her shoulders and down her spine. She braced herself for the blessed gift to speak. Only to remember that it had been taken to mend.

"Do you want to talk about it?" Reeri asked softly.

One look and she was undone. Wrapping her arms around his waist, she buried her face into the curly hairs of his chest. "Yes, I do. What if I'm not any better than a usurper? I could make more mistakes, destroy the kingdom instead of rebuild it, and fail everyone."

"Those are good fears."

"How can fear be good?"

"It has come to my attention that when we fear letting others down, it actually shows our love. And if all we do comes from love, then have we not already begun in victory?"

"You sound so sure."

"I am, because we proved this. We loved and we won."

"But how am I supposed to do that again, and again and again, every single day of my reign?"

"Did we win alone? No, we won together, and with others. The cosmos created communion for this very purpose. We get to partner with others to do impossible tasks. The weight is not solely on you, Anula, because you are not alone. You must only look and see."

Faces flashed in Anula's mind. Kattadiya, courtier, soldier, citizen. Reeri. Who else would she add? Not that she was making lists. Though it was comforting to know who her allies were and who might become her friend.

"I believe in you, Anula," Reeri whispered. "In your heart and your soul."

Anula closed her eyes, listening to the sound of Reeri's heartbeat. To the breath level out in his lungs and the soft snores of his sleep. The tension leaked out of her to the rhythm of him, drifting her into placid dreams.

A hand swept down Anula's curves, softly waking her.

It squeezed her roundness, drawing a line over her hip, fingers curling around it, grabbing hard and pulling into the firm body of another. Reeri's hardness pressed between her legs. Anula moaned, running a hand down soft muscles, through thick chest hair, and into a bush.

"Anula," Reeri whispered.

She moaned again, finger circling his base, testing, teasing, delighting as it hardened.

"Anula."

Her eyes opened to their legs tangled. Reeri's hand held her backside, gripping it as though it might fall off. Her hand had found its way beneath his sarong and around his girth. She stilled, blinking up at him.

"Good morning, my Lord." She smirked.

He growled low, "Good morning, my raejina."

His grip tightened. He squeezed her roundness, leaned in and kissed her, biting at her lips. A thrill rocked down her spine.

"Thrice-cursed blessings," she breathed, then smashed her face against his. She ripped the blanket off and hitched her leg over him. He groaned as she straddled his hardness, rocking her hips. "I knew men prayed on their knees. Until last night, I didn't know Lords did, too."

Reeri quirked a brow.

"Your prayer has been heard, Blood Yakka, and here is my answer."

A shiver racked his body, and Anula slid down the rest of him. She tugged at his sarong, whipping it off, and memorized every naked inch of him. She trailed one finger across his collarbone, down the planes of his chest, over tightening muscles, to the dip at his hips. She smiled up at Reeri and sank.

Placing her hands on his knees, she slowly drove them up his thighs. She found his hardness, robust and ready, and took it in both hands. Her tongue flicked out to meet it. Reeri's knees wobbled and she tasted his want.

Up and down, she stroked, smiling as his head fell back, eyes closed and groaning. She licked him, kissed him, stroked him in a circle, his hips swaying to her rhythm. And then she swallowed him.

He buckled. Fisted her hair and moaned. "Anula."

She lost herself then, pumping faster.

"Anula," he gasped.

She sucked harder as he bucked and trembled, spurring her on.

"O Heavens," Reeri roared as he went over the edge. Warmth filled her mouth with heavenly sweetness and earthy salt.

"Are you pleased with my answer?"

A fire glinted in Reeri's eyes. "Pleased enough to pray again."

He grabbed her by the arms and pulled her back to straddling—

The door burst open.

They jerked to a stop, panic flooding them both. Was it Bithul or another guard? Had something gone wrong?

"Once you're crowned and it's official"—Premala's voice echoed through the chamber—"we need to clean up both the inner and outer city."

Reeri scrambled, wrapping Anula's robe around her and fumbling for the blanket on the floor.

"There's a significant number of injured and homeless. Bithul has sent scouts to see how far the Polonnaruwans reached into the villages. We need to tell the fisherman about the Makara. Fate can't actually be eating sailors and demanding sacrifices, right? I mean, I know they're a Divinity but—"

Premala paused, half-bent picking up a blanket off the floor. But it wasn't a blanket, it was a sarong. One that Reeri was also grabbing.

Premala shrieked, dropped the sarong, and spun around.

"No knock?" Anula shouted. Reeri hurriedly covered himself.

It took a moment for Premala to answer, and when she did, she giggled. "Friends don't have to knock."

"I must have missed that rule."

"Sorry, I didn't expect you to be...occupied. Nice to see you again, Reeri."

"Likewise," he mumbled.

Anula slipped off the bed, tightening the blue water lily robe around her and turned Premala around. "How did you know?"

"I've told you, the guruthuma can sense the Yakkas. It's hard to explain, but he has a vibration about him. I felt it enter the palace last night."

"I sense yours as well," Reeri said, now fully clothed. "A blessing not granted to many."

Premala blushed and smiled. More secrets of the cosmos Anula would never understand. Perhaps no one was supposed to and the cosmos was a mystery to be explored, instead of a question to be answered.

"Remind me why my friend is in my bedchamber so early in the morning."

"It's nearly noon." Premala blanched. "Your ceremony is about to start."

Cursed blessings. Anxiety flooded back, and a hand flew to the empty space at her throat—but Anula caught it before it landed.

"Are you ready for the servants to prepare you?" Guruthuma Premala asked.

Anula met her friend's gaze, then Reeri's. She took a steadying breath, remembering who she was, what she had gained, and that she was not alone. She'd never tell herself such a half-truth again.

"Yes," she asserted.

The walk through the palace to the throne room was nothing like it'd been before.

Anula passed door after ruined door, room after plundered room. Cushions and divans littered the floor in broken heaps, art either stolen or destroyed, as if their enemies had wanted to cut off their connection to the Heavens even if they couldn't carry everything away. Bronze statues and paintings were all gone, the whispers of destinies and songs of home silenced.

It should've dismayed Anula, and perhaps it dismayed everyone else, but Anula knew the palace wouldn't lie broken and plundered for long. Neither would Anuradhapura. They had freed themselves, and together, they would rise from the ashes.

Only one room remained untouched, whether by chance or blessing, Anula didn't know. Darker than all others, tendrils of smoke curled out like fingers, beckoning—the palace shrine. Auntie Nirma's final words swam in her mind. *Faith starts where strength ends, Anula.*

Perhaps she'd been right in that, too. Anula had found her own belief, and though it looked different than others' faith, it was no less strong. No less true.

The procession was short. The carved wooden doors, inset with silver and brass, swung wide. There was no opulence, no blooms around pillars or across tables, none that hung from the ceiling. Only the lamps remained, casting the room in a golden hue, glinting off the gilded throne. And where once she'd aimed for the seat in a jewel-encrusted hatte with fake sapphires at her neck, she now strode forward in her favorite red silk sari. Instead of wedding mehendhi, bangles rose from wrist to elbow, tinkling along with bell-drop earrings. No weight pressed against her; no frenzied thoughts spun in her mind.

Thunder rumbled outside. A cool Maha breeze whirled around all those gathered. Palace officials, central administrators, the board of ministers, all the wives and children of the inner city, the outer city, villagers, fishermen, and farmers. Anuradhapura was in attendance.

As she neared the dais, Prophet Revantha motioned to the guruthuma, who stood near the terrace doors and began a song. The sound of Anuradhapura swelled inside Anula's heart. Not only for Auntie Nirma's plan, nor for Amma and Thaththa and all those lost on the way. It swelled for those with her now and for those yet to come. The Age of Usurpers had ended. Now was the time of new beginnings. A time for the most important thing: life.

The song crescendoed, dovetailed to the end, and in a silence brimming with hope, Anula sat on the throne.

Prophet Revantha fitted the crown on her head. "Long live the Raejina!"

"Long live the Raejina!" the people chanted. "Long live the Raejina!"

Anula opened her mouth, her first declaration as raejina flowing from her lips. "Long live Anuradhapura!"

EPILOGUE

Anula hunched over the wide table, slipped the list out of the seam of her sari, and held it over the candle flame.

There was no hidden message, no last words from Auntie Nirma, yet Anula watched as their list burned, the edges curling in on themselves, darkening and dissolving, a weight along with it.

She dropped the ash in a small bowl, stirred the mortar and pestle next to it, and poured in the liquid she'd had delivered to her chambers—the raejina's chambers—after the coronation celebration. The midnight moon was hidden beneath the monsoon mist, and flame light flickered throughout the room, casting shadows on the remnants of the blessed gifts.

"What are you going to do with that?" a voice breathed.

Anula suffocated a sigh, regretting salvaging one blessed gift in particular.

"Are you going to use it on someone? Another enemy?" the blessed gift of Raejina Devi Dunni asked.

"No," Anula answered as politely as she could. The gift hadn't stopped speaking since Anula had her fixed and reunited her with her beloved raja. Luckily, one of the blessed gifts that had been recovered could mend all things, including the wood of a bed frame. The story of Anula's courageous victory spread fast through the palace, not on the lips of servants but of blessed gifts. So, too, did her crowning. And when the reassembled gift returned, Raejina Devi Dunni introduced herself and promptly decided to never close her mouth again.

"Then what are you making? You are the Raejina of Poisons, are you not?"

"A woman can be more than one thing, don't you think?" Anula responded, glancing at the journal's hiding spot. For the first time in hours, the gift quieted.

A bubble of liquid popped from the bowl, and a tendril of smoke rose like a viper striking. Anula slipped out the last thing she'd hidden in the seam of her sari for safekeeping. The ivory of the Bone Blade gleamed. There was no heavenslight, no heavensong, as if it were resting. As if it knew it had completed its purpose.

And it had. Just as the list had. Just as the bargain had.

A new age had begun, and with it, a new vision. Anula lifted the blade above the smoke and dropped it into the bowl. It hissed as it died, bones creaking and cracking, dissolving in the tincture one splinter at a time, until not even ash remained. Only peace.

"You are right," Raejina Devi Dunni whispered. "You are more than I think you are. But I believe you are more than you think you are, too. Do not worry my raejina, your loveliness and bravery will bring a husband's warmth to your bed."

"I don't need a husband for that."

"But you want one."

Anula growled. Perhaps it wasn't too late to break the frame again. Throw the pieces in the fire or the Kuttam Pokuna bathhouse—

Thump.

Anula jolted. A bound book landed unassumingly next to the bowl. The title, scrawled in gold script, read *Rise of the Raejina*.

"Sohon wanted you to have the first edition," Reeri said, smile reaching saffron eyes. "A coronation gift."

"You didn't disappear." She stood, taking him in again, as if she hadn't danced with him for hours at the celebration.

Reeri planted a kiss on her forehead. "Never."

His words, his touch, soaked into her. The rain's final arrival in a drought. "Aren't memory books written about the dead? Don't tell me you've come to warn me that I'm about to die. I'm not a fan of spoiled endings."

The Blood Yakka chuckled. "It is merely volume one. Your story has yet to finish."

"Among other things," Anula murmured, teasing the edge of his tunic, remembering how they'd started the day—or had tried to.

He touched her long earrings, fingers grazing her neck. A light kiss followed.

Anula shivered. "Are you here only to deliver my book?"

He met her gaze. "No."

She shifted, an invitation in her hips, a challenge in her eye. "Then are you here to pray?"

She slowly licked his lips.

"To watch me get on my knees?"

She nipped his ear.

"To hear me beg?"

Reeri trembled.

Anula grabbed his hardness. Saffron eyes flashed.

He growled low. "I am here because I love you."

"Why?"

His lips found hers, hand twisting into her hair. "You are beautiful, body and soul."

"Is that all?"

"No." He softened their kiss and deepened it.

The aching in her core flamed bright. A want, a need, a calling of something more blessed than a relic. Anula pushed into him, backing him into the bed and tipping him over the edge. She pulled off his sarong and tore off her sari, then crawled on top, wrapping over him like a gift. He stood at attention for her, and she lifted her hips, sinking down the length of him. Reeri rumbled from his depths, a thrum threading from his body to hers, a spark igniting the vastness within, twining around and through her very soul. His breath became her breath. His rhythm, hers. His heart, his soul, his love and want and need, hers. The moon, the stars, the sun flickered in and out, the entire cosmos colliding.

"That is why," he breathed. "You are my echo. The one with whom my soul communes."

Anula's soul fluttered, swelled...

"Mine," he rasped.

And she crescendoed.

Their forms moved in tandem. Slow at first, teasing the flames, kindling the fire faster and faster still. Anula's nails dug into Reeri's shoulders. His hand squeezed her seat. And she rode him hard.

"Reeri," she moaned, arching sharply, her breasts bared to the moonless night. His grip tightened as his hips jerked.

"Reeri," she begged.

His whole body hitched.

"Reeri!"

Anula ground against him, and the water tanks broke free. Their heads tipped back, veins popping, pleasure beating, their souls shivering as the wave crested and crashed—

"Reeri," Anula gasped, the fire drenched as the waves rippled upon her shore, and she collapsed.

A cheer rose up from the bed frame. "That's my girl," blessed Raejina Devi Dunni said. Anula chuckled. Perhaps she would keep the gift after all.

Saffron eyes snapped open as red tendrils swirled across Reeri's chest and twirled around her fingers, up her hands, and along her arms.

"Our marking," she breathed. "Did we just make a bargain?"

"No." Reeri blushed. "It is a marking from the cosmos. A sign of our connection, our communion. It is a gift."

He didn't need to say the last part. Anula ran a finger along the elephant face on her palm. The same one etched on his chest.

"Do you want me to take it away? I can, if you wish."

"No," she said quickly, feeling the warmth of the marking, and the meaning. "I want it."

Reeri cupped her face and brought her in for a deep kiss. "I love you."

Anula stared into saffron eyes, a handsome face, and a kind soul. "I love you, too," she whispered. "Do you want to talk about it?"

Reeri let out a laugh, bright and joyful as heavensong.

There were so many ways to stop a heart…

But only one that made Anula's soar.

AUTHOR'S NOTE

I've always been fascinated with little-known historical figures. So, when I came across Anula's story—how she was the first queen of Sri Lanka, but remembered only as a wicked woman who poisoned six husbands to get the throne, while her predecessor's atrocities weren't mentioned—I wondered, *What if she was saving the kingdom?* Five years of research and writing later, *Her Soul for a Crown* is finally in your hands. However, though this book has been inspired by historical people and mythology, it is not meant to be historically accurate. Creative liberties have been taken to reimagine certain figures and faiths, while paying homage to my heritage and giving Anula a chance at a better legacy than the one she was given. To get an authentic view, please seek nonfiction sources.

Anula's story began and ended in the first century BC, at a time of war and strife. Many accounts say that Chora Naga took the throne after Mahakuli Mahatissa died and reigned for twelve years before his consort gave him poisonous food. The "infamous

Anula" then fell in love and married a palace guard named Kuda Tissa, who may or may not have been a child. Either way, he was crowned and yet under her control, at least for three years, before he also found poison in his food. The next palace guard Anula fell for, Siva I, lasted for a year and two months. Seemingly tired of guards, she next married a carpenter named Vatuka, then a wood carrier named Darubhatika Tissa, then finally a palace priest named Niliya. The stories of old say that with each new husband, she gained political power and control, until after the sixth husband, Anula was able to reign herself—for a total of four months, before being usurped by a second son of Mahakuli Mahatissa who set her aflame on a funeral pyre. Anula is noted as the first queen in Sri Lankan history and possibly the first female head of state in Asia.

Reeri's story began and ended in ancient Buddhist and Hindu texts and in the oral recitation of Sinhalese mythology. The Yakkas are part of a larger system of gods and goddesses, magic and rituals. The stories are innumerable and the iterations wide, as religions, myth, and time change how deities and beings are viewed. But through them all, Reeri is forever depicted as the cruelest. Yakkas may be banned from killing humans, but they derive their pleasure from inflicting people with every form of disease possible. Blood is Reeri's penchant, in all eighteen of his apparitions. The stories of old say that the only way to be rid of him, or any Yakka, is through an exorcism-like ceremony, which includes masks and chants and dancing. The performer, known as a Kattadiya, is closer to a magician than a priest. And just as it's never noted why a god or goddess only bestows good gifts, it's not explained why Reeri is so cruel.

As you can see, I took many creative liberties, imagining Anula's life outside of marriages, as well as her desire for the throne. I also created my own faith, inspired by many very real religions, mythologies, and my own experiences in faith-centered communities. The Kingdom of Anuradhapura, which is now a UNESCO site that you can visit, has also been painted with a layer of fantastical imagination. As with any story, this book began with a question of what-if. What if Anula was not just power hungry? What if Yakkas weren't all evil? What if one person's villain was another's hero? What if two people, desiring the same goal, fell in love? What if love changed them? History can tell us so much, but it misses much more. I did not set out to retell or replicate Anula's world but to imagine what could have been. *Her Soul for a Crown* is a story, one that began in my head and ends in yours. Unless you, too, find yourself with questions. Thank you for reading.

GLOSSARY

aluwa *(å-lu-wah)*
a Sri Lankan sweet made from roasted rice flour with boiled treacle, cashews, and cardamon, served as a cookie

amma *(åm-mah)*
mom

bulbul *(bul-bul)*
a songbird

dolla *(doh-lah)*
offerings given in a tovil ceremony

guruthuma *(gu-ru-thu-mah)*
the formal reference of a teacher

hak gediya *(ha-k geh-di-yuh)*
type of conch shell that is used as a kind of trumpet in the traditional ritualistic music of Sri Lanka

hakuru *(ha-ku-ru)*
raw palm sugar

hatte *(hâtt-té)*
a blouse worn with a sari

hopper *(hop-per)*
fermented rice flour and coconut milk batter made into a bowl-shaped pancake with a crispy edge and a soft, spongy center

kahapana *(kah-hah-pah-nu)*
currency in early Sri Lankan kingdoms (third century BC)

Kattadiya *(kat-tah-di-yaah)*
a witch doctor, exorcist, or mediator between the worlds of humans and devils

kiribath *(ki-ri-buth)*
milk rice

maha *(mah-hah)*
bigger

Makara *(ma-kuh-ruh)*
a legendary sea creature

mandala *(man-duh-luh)*
various ritualistic geometric designs symbolic of the universe

mehendhi *(meh-he-n-dih)*
ancient art of decorating the skin using henna paste; a word of North Indian origin that has influenced the Sri Lankan culture over the years

pani walalu *(páni wål-luh-lu)*
a sweet made by deep-frying vigna mungo, or urad bean, flour batter in a circular flower shape, then soaking in sugar syrup

raejina *(rá-jih-na)*
queen

raban *(ra-baa-nuh)*
one-sided traditional drum

raja *(ra-juh)*
king

saaluwa *(saah-lu-wuh)*
a shawl-like scarf

sari *(sah-ri)*
fabric arranged over the body as a robe, with one end attached to the waist, while the other end rests over one shoulder, sometimes baring a part of the midriff

sari pota *(sååri-potuh)*
the loose end of a sari

sarong *(sá-rong)*
a large length of fabric wrapped around the waist and typically worn by men

seeni sambal *(see-ni sam-bhal)*
a caramelized onion chutney or relish, with flavors that are spicy, sweet, and aromatic

stupa *(stoo-puh)*
a dome-shaped structure containing relics that is used as a place of meditation

thaththa *(thah-th-thah)*
dad

tovil *(toe-vil)*
healing ritual

yak berayuh *(yak-be-ruh-yuh)*
cylindrical drum used to accompany dance sequences

Yakka *(yah-kah)*
demons of Sri Lankan folklore

yala *(yah-luh)*
lesser

PRONUNCIATION GUIDE

Anula Ramanayake
(å-nu-la råå-muh-nåå-yuh-kuh)

Anuradhapura
(ånu-råå-dhuh-pu-ruh)

Ayaan
(ah-yaan)

Bithul Perera
(bi-th-ul pe-re-rah)

Calu
(kah-lu)

Chora Naga
(choruh-naaguh)

Darubhatika
(dha-ru-bath-ik-uh)

Devi Dunni
(dev du-ni)

Dilshan
(dil-shah-n)

Don Upali
(don uh-paah-lee)

Eppawala
(ep-puh-wela)

Hashini
(ha-shi-ni)

Kama
(ka-ma)

Kekirawa
(ká-ki-raa-va)

Kuttam Pokuna
(kuttåm-pokunuh)

Mahakuli Mahatissa
(maha-ku-li maha-tis-suh)

Manoj
(mah-no-jh)

Naina Wijetunga
(nih-nah vijay-thunguh)

Nihal
(ni-haa-l)

Nimeka
(ni-meh-kah)

Nirma
(nir-mah)

Nuwan
(nu-wah-n)

Premala
(pre-muh-lah)

Polonnaruwa
(po-lon-na-ru-vuh)

Ratti
(rath-thi)

Reeri
(ree-ri)

Rehan
(ray-ha-n)

Revantha
(rè-vuhn-thuh)

Sandani
(san-duh-ni)

Shahan
(shah-hah-n)

Siva
(see-vah)

Tahan
(tah-hah-n)

Thilini
(thi-li-ni)

Vatuka
(vah-tu-kah)

Viran
(vi-rah-n)

Wessamony
(ves-suh-moh-ni)

ACKNOWLEDGMENTS

Writing a book is hard; becoming a career author is harder. It took nine books over thirteen years to see my dream come true, and in that time there were moments when I wanted to quit, when my faith in myself, my writing, and my purpose wavered, or flat out failed. I wouldn't be an author and *Her Soul for a Crown* wouldn't be in your hands today if not for the support and belief of so many people.

First, I'd like to thank God for giving me the passion for writing and the persistence to see things through. Thank you for your timing, co-creating, and never-ending delight in the stories we tell together.

To my agent, Samantha Fabien, thank you for seeing potential in my work—three books ago. You knew from that first phone call that Anula was meant to be shared with the world. I'm so grateful for all our phone calls, your strategy, keen eye, and encouragement. Thank you also, to the Root Literary team, for the collaboration and insight every author needs, at every stage of their career.

To my editor, Jocelyn Travis, thank you for seeing what this book could be, and for championing it so hard from the start. I will never forget how you went to bat for me and Anula. Thank you also for a wonderful debut experience.

To the Sourcebooks Casablanca team, thank you for helping bring this book to life. India Hunter, senior production editor; Heather Hall, managing editor; Manu Velasco, copyeditor; Emma Grant, manufacturing lead; Siena Koncsol, marketing lead; Maranda Seney, social media support. Thank you for such a beautiful cover: Diana Dworak, cover artist; Stephanie Gafron, art director; Stephanie Rocha, design lead; Tara Jaggers, internal design; Travis Hasenour, mapmaker; Victoria Layne, bonus art illustrator. To the sales, publicity, and social media teams, their fearless publisher, and all the rest who work behind the scenes.

To my critique partners, without whom I surely wouldn't be here today. God brings certain people into our lives and I'm forever grateful that each of you are in mine. Laura, Gaye, Christy: my A-Team. To the SCBWI crew, Ginny, and Danielle. Big thanks to my agent siblings who keep me sane and book writing retreats: De Elizabeth, Dana Choe-Murray Draper, Katie M. Wilson, Molly O'Sullivan, Camille Baker. Thanks also to the 2025 Debut Discord and guest AMA authors who gave valuable information and support. Major thanks to all the authors who blurbed this book. Special thanks to Scarlett St. Clair, for cheering me on for four years and helping Anula find her home. Extra thanks to L.L. Campbell, for being a wonderful writing buddy who checked in weekly and especially for your social media witchcraft. Thank you to all the readers, booksellers, librarians, reviewers, and bloggers who have supported me on this journey so far.

I would be remiss if I didn't thank the amazing team at my local independent bookstore, Best of Books. Thanks to Nan, Joe, and Elana for being the world's best bosses, and then for being some of my first fans. To Jenny, Shelby, and Dani for your excitement about this book from the very first draft, for your friendship, and for all the bookish fun.

To my friends who've been here since the beginning. Chelsea, for all the writing dates. Book Club, for widening my horizons. My mentors, Tim and Harold; my therapists and TP group. Special thanks to Thilini and Auntie Yasmin for their work on the glossary and pronunciation lists, and to Uncle Manoj and Auntie Nirma for answering all my Sri Lanka-related questions.

Last, but never least, to my family. Thank you for taking me to libraries as a kid and buying me bookstore gift cards for every birthday and Christmas, even when you wanted to buy something else. Thank you Mom and Dad, Grandma and Grandpa, Nanny and Poppy. I couldn't have made it here without you.

And to Jonny, thank you for always believing in me and for making my heart soar.

ABOUT THE AUTHOR

Alysha Rameera is a Sri Lankan and German American author who writes about little-known historical figures, romance, and magic—preferably all together. On non-writing days, you can find her baking at home or traveling the world with her husband.

Website: alysharameera.com
Instagram: @alyshasbooks